I0691518

THREE GENERATIONS OF STORMY PASSIONS.
. . . THREE WOMEN SWEPT UP IN THE
REVOLUTION THAT WOULD CHANGE THEIR
WORLD FOREVER. . . .

ANNA—Her secrets were hidden in a glorious past, a world of elegant amusements and imperial balls. As the shadows of revolution gathered over St. Petersburg, she watched her world crumble, watched her beautiful daughter make the same tragic mistakes. . . .

NADYA—Young, impetuous, dazzled by the court's opulence, bewitched by Count Alexei's passionate kisses, she was doomed to drink the bitter cup of bereavement and exile before she could find happiness at last. . . .

MARINA—Nadya's daughter had inherited her beauty, her fiery spirit, and survived the terrible ordeal at her mother's side. Now she would embark on her own bold adventure, determined to realize her dreams in America—land of endless promise.

WINDS OVER MANCHURIA

Alla Crone

Originally published by Dell

Copyright © 1983, 2001 by Alla Crone

ISBN: 978-1-5040-3027-4

Distributed in 2016 by Open Road Distribution
180 Maiden Lane
New York, NY 10038
www.openroadmedia.com

*To my two sons, Rick and Bill,
and to the memory of my mother*

ACKNOWLEDGMENTS

I wish to thank my editor, Coleen O'Shea, for her thoughtful suggestions, expert editing, and unfailing support during the progress of this work.

I also want to thank the staff of the Museum of Russian Culture in San Francisco for their generous and enthusiastic help in researching material for this book.

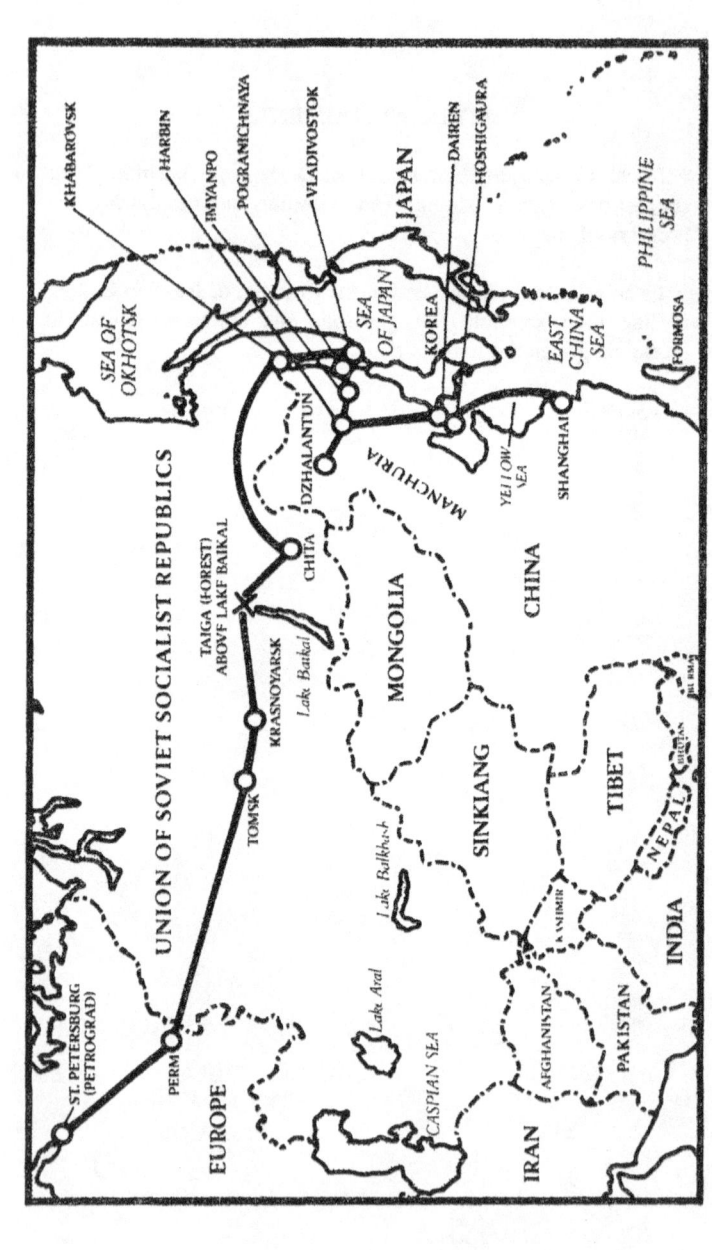

PART I

St. Petersburg, Russia

Chapter One

On the cold Sunday of January 9, 1905, the pallid sun hung over the rooftops of St. Petersburg trying to burn its way through a thin layer of clouds. By two o'clock in the afternoon the dull light had done little to warm the thousands of people milling in the streets. The gray snow that covered the ground muffled the noise, rendering a deceptive serenity to the city.

Out of the deep courtyards, across the canal bridges and through connecting streets, throngs of pedestrians were pouring into the broad Nevsky Prospekt and moving toward the Winter Palace. Rumors that a carnage had taken place earlier in the day on the other side of the Neva River circulated among the crowds, but no one took them seriously.

At the lower end of the boulevard, near the Admiralty Building by the Neva River, detachments of mounted Cossacks and Preobrazhensky Guards blocked the street, separating the crowd from the strollers in the Alexander Garden. The Cossacks, dressed in dark blue trousers with red side stripes, wide capes, and sheepskin hats decorated with tassels, held their restless horses in check and watched the crowds below them with guarded equanimity. Only the long leather whips each of them held indicated that something extraordinary was taking place.

A few blocks away, on a quiet, empty street, a tall, thin woman was running toward the Nevsky Prospekt. Although her skin was still smooth, the firm line of her set mouth and a look of anxiety made Anna Efimova look older than her forty-two years. Anna was cold. She had not taken time to dress properly before she dashed out of the house to search for her daughter, and now the fluffy angora shawl wrapped around her head did not keep the icy wind from chilling her. Anna counted the blocks: She was already on Morskaya Street and nearing Gorokhovaya. She would soon pass Kirpichny Pereulok, and from there it was only a short block to the Nevsky Prospekt.

Where could Nadya be? Mentally Anna retraced her steps and decided that she could not have missed her daughter if she had taken the shortest route between home and her friend's house. How foolish to have allowed a nine-year-old to walk this distance alone! But then how could Anna have known what was going to take place on this particular Sunday? Sergei should have warned her earlier. At nineteen, her son knew he wanted to be a doctor like his father, but he spent so much time at the university that he was not always aware of what was going on around him.

Anna sighed, and the sharp intake of air burned her throat. She stopped. Placing her muff between her legs to keep it from falling onto the dirty snow, she bent down and pulled her shawl over her mouth and nose. In a moment the pain eased, and she hurried on.

Maneuvering through the crowd that had collected on the Nevsky Prospekt, Anna hurried toward the Alexander Garden. There she carefully skirted the double row of guards on her right and stopped on the sidewalk, looking for her daughter. A boy and a girl about Nadya's age were playing with snowballs. Behind the children a large crowd of men and women was moving up the broad path toward them, and as she scanned the crowd, Anna saw her daughter. Bundled in her sturdy broadcloth coat, its rabbit collar tightly buttoned on the side and held securely with her mother's thick angora scarf, Nadya stood clasping her satchel's leather strap tightly in her mittened hands and stomping her feet to keep warm.

Suddenly, out of the corner of her eye, Anna saw a sweeping movement across the street. She turned. The front rank of the guards had dropped to their knees and was taking aim directly at the garden. The children dropped their snowballs and scampered up a nearby tree, while Nadya raised her satchel and, clutching it to her chest, dashed across the street toward the Nevsky. A few more steps, and she would have reached the corner and been out of sight of the guns, but at that moment a volley of shots rang out. Nadya stopped, as if frozen to the ground. Blood pounded in Anna's ears as she pushed toward her daughter, maddeningly hampered by the crowd.

The children were no longer in the tree. The guards shot into the air, and the snow-covered girl, blood pouring from the right side of her chest, had fallen onto a bench, screaming and flailing her small arms wildly. The boy was sprawled near her on the ground, facedown, motionless. Others were scrambling for cover as Nadya, propelled by panic, ran.

Oh, God! Nothing mattered but to reach Nadya. Ducking through the frantic crowd, Anna managed to catch her by the sleeve. "Nadya! Nadya!"

At the sight of her mother Nadya's face crumpled. "Mama, oh, Mama!"

Clinging to Anna's chest, Nadya trembled, her teeth chattering so hard she could hardly get the words out. "Oh, Mamochka! They are shooting the children! The little boy . . . the little girl . . . they're shot! In the garden! . . . Mama, I'm frightened!"

Anna pulled her toward Morskaya Street. "Run! We mustn't get caught in this mob!"

Forcing their way through the throngs of people who seemed to be pushing in different directions, mother and daughter were halfway across the Nevsky when more gunshots pierced the air. Nadya rushed into the fold of her mother's arms and buried her face against her mother's shoulder. Anna looked over Nadya's head and saw the backs of pedestrians skittering down the side streets.

Stunned for only a few moments, Anna grabbed Nadya by the arm and ran to the other side of the Nevsky. Still a block away from the Politseisky Bridge and the Moika Canal, they shoved their way toward them. When the screams and the shots started again, Nadya's legs buckled, and she stumbled behind her mother.

"Mama! I'm scared," Nadya said, sobbing. "I can't run anymore!" All of a sudden a stocky woman ran wildly past Nadya and knocked the child off-balance into the slick snow. Nadya's satchel skidded a few feet toward the center of the road, and letting go of Anna's hand, the child went after it.

"Nadya! Come back!"

But Nadya moved in the opposite direction. She reached down to grab the satchel by the straps and then froze. A glistening red streak was crawling toward her, and through the running throngs she glimpsed the huddled shape of a woman on the ground, a pool of blood spreading around her head. Anna pulled Nadya up.

"Over here! This way, Nadya!"

As people around them jostled and ran, stumbling over one another, Anna dragged Nadya around the corner. Here the shouts and screams were muffled by rows of buildings that separated them from the Alexander Garden. The frosty air bit into Anna's face, and in the sudden silence, she could hear her heart pounding fiercely. She glanced down and saw her daughter's face streaked with tears. The little girl stopped and hugged herself.

"Mama, there was a woman down there! I saw blood! On the ground, Mama!" Nadya began to whimper. "Mama, she'll be trampled to death!"

"Nadyenka, I know! I know! What can we do?"

Near the door to their house Nadya paused, but Anna pulled her inside the courtyard. There she stopped and hugged Nadya. "We're safe here, thank God!"

"Mama, why did the guards shoot the children?"

"Nadyenka, my child, it was a terrible mistake!" Anna said. "Seryozha ran home from his classes to tell me that the Putilov factory workers marched this morning to see the tsar. All they wanted was to ask for better living conditions! They were still on the other side of the Neva when the Cossacks ordered them to disperse. The marchers ignored the order; they said they were petitioning the tsar peaceably!" Anna stopped, her voice shaking.

In a moment she went on, still hugging Nadya. "The troops shot at the marchers before they reached the Troitsky Bridge!"

"But why the children, Mama?" Nadya persisted.

"Nadyenka, I'm sure the guards got nervous when they saw a large crowd converging on them. They must have meant to shoot over their heads, but you see, the children climbed the tree! It was a dreadful mistake!"

Nadya fell silent. The enormity of what she had just witnessed showed plainly on her ashen face as Anna led her into the vestibule of their flat with its familiar medicinal smells. She helped her out of her coat, which Nadya hung in the wardrobe with trembling hands, carefully smoothing the folds to keep them from wrinkling. Anna watched, aching for her daughter. The children: Nadya had seen them skating, laughing, playing with snowballs, and then sprawled in puddles of blood.

Nadya broke into Anna's thoughts. "Mamochka, my stomach is upset . . . I'm going to be sick!"

Quickly Anna took Nadya into the bedroom and made her lie down. The little girl shivered until the down comforter warmed her, and she soon dozed off. Anna sat down in an armchair by her daughter's bed. She needed a few minutes to regain her composure before joining her family. Her head swam. How many people were out there, being trampled to death at that very moment? The children. Surely, it had been a terrible mistake at the Alexander Garden; those angry men! What a shock for her sweet, obedient daughter and what a horrible memory to have for the rest of her life!

Anna shuddered. Out there, on the streets . . . those innocent people, simple and trusting, asking for nothing more than an extra loaf of bread and a little more space in their wretched living quarters. Ah, if only Alexander II had not been assassinated that March Sunday twenty-four years ago! How tragic, how ironic that it had happened on the very day he was to sign the papers approving the plan for a constitutional monarchy. Perhaps then this terrible massacre today would not have taken place.

With each year, unrest among the poor seemed to grow steadily, and the Putilov factory workers incited by their leader, the radical priest, Father Gapon, had decided to march that morning to the Winter Palace. It was to be a peaceful march, Sergei had told her earlier: workers carrying icons and singing hymns. Peaceful, indeed! A bloodbath it had turned out to be, and her sympathy for the trusting victims intensified.

What a relief to be away from the violence outside, to feel secure in the sanctuary of her own flat, with its crowded rooms, homey smells, and warmth! She smiled wryly, remembering. Maybe her modest middle-class home was bourgeois and small by the standards of the Count Persiantsev and Prince Poltavin palaces, but here she was the mistress, enjoying the love and loyalty of an affectionate husband and a dutiful son and daughter. What more could a woman of her station want? Of course, living in those two palaces had been pleasant—in all honesty, she could not say that she had been unhappy either at the Persiantsevs' or, earlier, at the Poltavin estate of Pavlikino—but there she had been neither servant nor mistress.

Chapter Two

It had been Anna's destiny to be born to the overseer of the Poltavin estate and to lose her mother at birth. In truth, she was always grateful to Prince Poltavin, who had taken her into his household and reared her as his ward. Her father died after a fall from a horse when she was five, and she grew up with Poltavin's daughter, Princess Aline.

At Pavlikino or in the city, the girls did not go to school, and Anna was treated as an aristocrat whom it was customary to tutor at home. Studying with Aline, she was taught to play the piano and to speak French and English. Invited to the same parties, they went everywhere together and later attended the same balls. Yet always there was the subtle distinction between them: Princess Aline Poltavina, a delicate, fragile beauty, an aristocrat's daughter groomed for a brilliant marriage to someone at the tsar's court, and Anna, a shy brown-eyed ward, whose best hope was to make a decent match with someone from a well-to-do middle-class family. So, when at the age of seventeen, she met Anton Efimov, the son of local gentry, she was flattered by his obvious interest in her as an individual in her own right, not as a path to the more beautiful Princess Aline.

Anton confided his dream of opening private practice in the capital after his studies in medicine had been completed and dedicating as much of his time as possible to the care of the poor. He had been left a small legacy after his parents died, and with the stipend he would be getting from the military medical school in St. Petersburg, he should have enough to achieve his dream.

Anna admired his stalwart pursuit of his goals, and that warm, languid summer of 1880, when she turned eighteen, she fell in love with the gentle, serious Anton. Bathed in moonlight, they strolled together through the arbored lanes of the Poltavin park, while Anton disclosed his carefully laid plans for the future.

Some of his ideas, however, were disturbing. Too radical, Anna thought, a bit more liberal than even their beloved tsar, the Liberator, would have approved, and she told him so. Anton shrugged.

"Nothing can be gained if we don't push beyond the established rules, Anna. I can assure you, I'm not a radical, but I do believe in social reform without violence. It has been almost twenty years since the tsar emancipated the serfs, and there is talk of a constitutional monarchy." Anton paused, broke off a jasmine branch from the latticed arch, and, after smelling it absentmindedly, handed it to Anna.

"The tsar should not delay too long," he went on. "Already there have been several attempts on his life, unsuccessful, granted, but attempts nevertheless, and I think it's because the emancipation created its own set of complications. What we need, Anna, is a government consisting of enlightened, progressive leaders, not the reactionary bureaucrats we have now who jealously guard the autocracy of the tsar."

"But what can *we* do, Anton?" Anna asked, not at all sure she wanted to be involved in his dangerous ideas.

Anton took her hands in his. "If we are ever asked, we can help the needy. But right now we can think of other matters." He pulled her closer to him and smiled. "Don't look so frightened, Anichka. I have a penchant for rhetoric, I know. As for ourselves, we can get married and bring up a few good, liberal Efimovs. Will you wait for me?"

For the first time in her life, Anna felt a sense of complete happiness overcome her. She had captured a good man's love and was grateful for her good fortune. How could she have known then that her heart had a will of its own and would betray her later? But on that silvery, shimmering night, she accepted Anton's shy proposal with gladness. It did not bother her in the least that her happy moment was shadowed by the announcement of Princess Aline's engagement to Count Pyotr, the older son of Count Persiantsev, an old and distinguished servant of the tsar's. No, Anna did not mind at all. She was glad to keep her happiness private, and when Aline, bubbling, ecstatic, finally noticed a certain sparkle in Anna's eyes and asked about it, Anna was reluctant to tell her.

Aline stopped her giddy chatter long enough to take in Anna's news and then, summoning her good manners, commented lamely, "Oh, *c'est merveilleux*! We can have a double wedding!"

Anna shook her head. "No, Aline, Anton and I cannot marry right away. You see, we have to wait five years until Anton finishes medical school."

Clapping her hands, Aline cried, "Splendid! Then you'll come to the Persiantsev Palace with me to live!"

"It may be longer than that," Anna said. "After Anton finishes school, we can marry, but then it will take him four years and seven months to pay back the stipend he will owe. If he does not get assigned to St. Petersburg but is sent away to a rural area, I'll have to stay here and wait."

Aline patted Anna on the shoulder. "I'm sure Count Pyotr will be able to arrange for him to be assigned here."

After Aline's wedding Anna moved to the Persiantsev mansion in St. Petersburg. The imposing aquamarine building on the Neva Embankment was built by the count's ancestor who had come from Persia early in the eighteenth century. Secure in the knowledge that her future was assured—that a hardworking, loyal man was studying to achieve a worthy profession and eventually they would marry—Anna was content to wait. She saw him infrequently because his studies demanded most of his time, and when they did meet, it was for tea or dinner at the Persiantsevs.

"I feel bad not spending more time with you," Anton told her on one occasion. "Yet you haven't complained, and I want you to know I appreciate it. I'm a lucky man!"

They were sitting in the Persiantsevs' blue parlor, where Anton's drab gray suit looked out of place against the furniture's silk upholstery and Empire daintiness.

"I know how hard you're studying, Anton, and it would never occur to me to complain."

He walked over to the marble fireplace, studying the crackling flames for a few moments. His sparse bony frame was silhouetted against the moving light, and the large Venetian glass mirror above the mantel reflected his pensive face.

"I love you, Anna. You must never doubt that." His voice was strained. "I sometimes worry about all the wealth that surrounds you." He waved his hand toward the embroidered silk-paneled walls. "I won't be able to give you such luxury. Those glittering balls you attend and the elegant clothes you wear—it will not be so grand when we marry."

Abruptly she rose and walked over to stand beside him. "I've been brought up in these surroundings, Anton, and they don't impress me. As for these clothes"—she looked down at the lace flounces on her skirt and shrugged—"I accept them from Aline because I feel I earned them. You see, most of my time is devoted to her needs." Anna hesitated for a second before going on. "She complains a lot about her health, and I'm beginning to wonder if she is becoming a neurotic."

An impish grin spread on Anton's face, illuminating his whole countenance. "I shall be glad to treat her imaginary ills in the future, and you—you have become my joy. My studies, my long hours seem lighter when I think of you."

He pulled her to him, then checked himself. Slowly he raised her hands to his lips and kissed each separately with a lingering caress.

A warm, tender glow spread through Anna. She loved this quiet, studious man, so unlike the frivolous officers in glittering uniforms she met at the Winter Palace. A whirlwind existence it was, capable of spoiling a young girl, but it was also shallow and transient, and she kept reminding herself how lucky she was to have Anton.

While she waited, her life at the Persiantsev Palace was carefree and predictable. Anna found it all glamorous, elegant, yet frankly tiresome. The only highlight in her life had been the day she was presented at court—that awesome establishment of glamorous grand dukes and gracious grand duchesses, and above all, the brilliant, handsome Alexander II himself.

Yet, it was the tsar's second wife, the beautiful Princess Ekaterina Dolgorukaya, renamed Princess Yurievskaya, who appealed to Anna the most. In the days before her marriage the princess befriended Aline and Anna and invited them frequently to have tea with her in her apartments. The imperial family resented the tsar's wife because she was not of royal blood and because she had been his mistress while his first wife, Empress Marie, was still alive. The royal children's refusal to accept her undermined her position at court. Perhaps the empathy Anna felt toward the princess was the result of her own position in the Persiantsev household. Although she was treated kindly, she nonetheless knew her proper place was in the background. A privileged friend but not an equal, she looked forward to the day when she and Anton would be married and she had a home she could call her own.

Until then she bided her time and looked forward to the next big event of the social season, the Palm Tree Ball at the Winter Palace on the night of March 12, 1881.

Chapter Three

Anna always looked forward to the *bals des palmiers* that the emperor gave at the Winter Palace, for they were relatively informal parties with the ballroom transformed into a garden paradise. Scores of palm trees specially nurtured at Tsarskoye Selo were brought to the capital in crates and placed in the ballroom. Around each tree, an intimate supper table for about fifteen people was set with Sèvres china, its vivid cobalt blue offset by shining silver and crystal goblets. The thrill of the evening came when the tsar made his rounds of the tables to sip a glass of champagne or taste a piece of pastry and chat with his guests.

On this particular night a festive mood pervaded the Persiantsev Palace because Count Pyotr's younger brother, Count Yevgeni, had arrived that day from Paris, where he was serving as military attaché at the Russian Embassy. Several days before his home-coming visit, which was to last a week, servants were readying his rooms in the west wing and whispering.

"It's a shame the younger brother is not as serious as Count Pyotr."

"I overheard talk about a hushed-up scandal in Paris."

"He should marry and settle down."

Anna spent all day helping Aline prepare for the ball. Then, after hurriedly dressing herself in a white gown of moiré silk and lace, she caught her hair in a net of gold at the back of her head and tied a pink velvet ribbon around her neck to highlight the dress.

Back in Aline's bedchamber, Anna watched the countess ready herself for her appearance before the court. Aline chose to wear her official court dress of crimson velvet embroidered in gold, with velvet cutaway sleeves reaching almost to the ground. On her head she wore a matching crimson *kokoshnik*—a diadem embroidered with pearls and rubies. As many times as Anna had seen Aline dressed in her court gown, she still caught her breath at the magnificence of the young countess's attire.

Although she looked pale next to Aline, Anna was perfectly comfortable in her own dainty gown until they descended the marble staircase into the main vestibule and she was introduced to Count Yevgeni Persiantsev.

In his blue uniform tunic frogged with gold braid, elkskin breeches, and gleaming topboots, the handsome Count Yevgeni stood taller than his older brother. Arrogance shone from his dark and sparkling eyes as he gazed at Anna with a curious, daring look that frightened her.

She was happy to escape the scrutiny of the young count and enter the flurry of activity in the ballroom. Baskets of orchids and long rows of laurels and rhododendrons stood against the walls, and camellias and pink roses decorated the emperor's horseshoe table in profusion. The tsar graced the room with his august presence, and Anna had never seen him look so elegant. Dressed in a long white tunic with the high collar, sleeves, and hem trimmed in blue fox, pale blue breeches, and black boots, he moved among the tables unhurriedly. Although his courtliness charmed his guests, it was obvious to Anna that his eyes were only for Princess Yurievskaya, dark-haired and delicate beside him.

When the tsar paused at the Persiantsev table and everyone rose to greet him, his brilliant blue eyes settled on Anna.

"Princess Yurievskaya tells me you are affianced, mademoiselle," he said kindly. "My best wishes to you." His French was flawless, and Anna, curtsying deeply, murmured, *"Merci, votre majesté."* Unbidden came Anton's words about the aristocrats dining in French and the peasants starving in Russian, and she flushed uncomfortably.

Princess Yurievskaya laughed and, reaching over the table, patted Anna on the arm. "Color becomes you, *ma chère*."

As the imperial couple moved on, Count Yevgeni raised his brow and bent over Anna's hand in mock deference. "This calls for a celebration, Anna! May I have the honor of this mazurka and a glass of champagne afterward?"

Her gloved hand felt icy as she placed it on his proffered arm. Throughout the evening he monopolized her time and whispered pleasantries in her ear that she could not remember later. Nothing like this had ever happened to her before, and when Aline was suddenly overcome with a headache and wanted to leave early, Count Peter said to Anna, "I see you're having a good time, so why don't you stay and let my brother bring you home?"

Common sense whispered to Anna to decline, to go home right now, but the glamorous onslaught of the dashing officer dazzled and won. She felt giddy. Hers was perhaps the most modest of all dresses in the ballroom, without ribbons of diamonds catching the ruffles in her skirt or ropes of pearls cascading down her neck, yet this handsome aristocrat was paying court to her!

Count Yevgeni waltzed her into the adjoining hall, where supper was being served, and led her to the buffet table, which held an immense silver bowl of lemonade, along with champagne, tea, ices, and tortes. As though sensing her thirst, he handed her a pear-shaped pink ice, and she savored its soothing coolness.

He was attentive and entertaining; but his powerful personality crowded her, and she felt uneasy with him. She longed for Anton, his sweetness, his unaffected simplicity.

When it was time to leave, she welcomed the sobering frosty air outside. In the sleigh she felt the count's leg press against hers under a fur throw, and she did not know whether the warmth that suddenly coursed through her veins came from the fur or from this man, whom she suddenly wished she had never met. He reached for her hand and squeezed it, and by the time they entered the Persiantsev Palace Anna knew he had gone too far.

At the door to her room Anna gave him her hand, and as he tried to pull her toward him, she resisted.

"I enjoyed your company, Count Yevgeni," she said formally, "and I want my fiancé to meet you. I'm sure you will find him interesting."

A hint of a smile touched Yevgeni's lips. "A subtle rebuke, mademoiselle?"

Anna stiffened, trying to control the shaking of her hand still imprisoned in his.

"I'm sure I don't understand, Count Yevgeni. Living here as I do, I hope we shall be friends, and it is natural that I would like you to know my fiancé."

She had scored a victory. It felt good. But that night in bed she couldn't stop thinking about him. He intrigued her. The shame of it! She would have to avoid him during the coming week while he was in St. Petersburg. She should be dreaming about Anton, about their life together, the comfort and the emotional stability she always felt in his presence.

Yet all night Count Yevgeni continued to haunt her with his whimsical smile.

The following day tragedy struck, and the painful edges of grief lingered long after the week had gone by. Over the rooftops, across the frozen canals and the hushed streets, through the large double windowpanes of the Winter Palace, the sound of explosion reverberated.

In the elegant rooms of Princess Yurievskaya it rattled the delicate porcelain vases that graced her inlaid wood desk and knocked the emperor's photograph to the floor, breaking the glass.

Princess Yurievskaya, still in her pink negligee in spite of the afternoon hour, was having tea with Aline and Anna, whom she had invited the night before. For an hour Anna had been sitting quietly, listening to the two women chat. She paid little attention to their conversation, studying the beautiful princess instead.

When the explosion came, Princess Yurievskaya jumped up and ran to the window. "Oh, my God, what was that?"

Aline put her arm around her waist. "Don't worry, Your Highness; it could be a number of things."

The princess was shaking. "There have been so many attempts on his life; I'm always so frightened for him."

It was true that several attempts on the tsar's life had been made since the time in the Winter Garden when a hatter's apprentice saw the assassin's gun and deflected the shot. Then there was the attempt on the quai when the tsar was taking a walk. The schoolmaster who fired four times was such a bad shot he missed every time. On another occasion the imperial train was delayed in a Moscow station because of a faulty engine, and the tsar was spared when the assassins sabotaged the wrong train. Finally, there was the bomb explosion in the Winter Palace dining room when a tardy dinner guest saved the tsar's life by delaying the meal. The tsar was charmed, Anna thought; nothing could destroy him.

As she dwelt on that thought, another, more violent explosion shook the windows. Princess Yurievskaya let out a piteous cry and clutched at Aline's arms. "Oh, dear Lord, he should be leaving Grand Duchess Catherine's palace now. He visits her every Sunday after the trooping of the colors at the Mikhailovsky Palace. I begged him not to go today! Prime Minister Loris-Melikov told him that the police had picked up a terrorist leader, someone by the name of Zhelyabov." She looked anxiously at Aline. "Have you heard of him?" When Aline shook her head, the princess hurried on. "Loris-Melikov warned the tsar that there were others still at large, but my Sasha would not listen. Especially today because the grand duke Dmitri, who is taking part in the parade for the first time, is his favorite nephew. What if . . ." She frowned, bit her lip, and let the sentence trail unfinished.

Anna walked over to the princess and, gently touching her arm, handed her the half-empty cup of tea. "Your Highness, your tea is getting cold."

The princess looked at the cup, then turned and ran to the window. Silence filled the room, heavy and chilling, and in it, the ormolu clock's dainty pendulum took over, ticking off the seconds, striking the hushed air with mechanical precision.

Anna could not remember afterward how long they had waited, until a weeping servant girl burst into the room and dropped to her knees, wringing her hands.

"Your Highness! *Bozhe Milostivy*, merciful God, how terrible! Oh, Your Highness!"

Princess Yurievskaya pushed the wailing girl aside and disappeared into the hall. Hurrying after her, Aline and Anna saw the princess, her lacy negligee flowing in the air, run toward the tsar's study. Large splashes of dark blood led the way up the staircase, along the corridor, and into the study.

Without a word, Aline ran back to the parlor, picked up her reticule with shaking hands, and turned to Anna. "We had better leave. We shouldn't intrude on the imperial family at a time like this."

They should see if they could be of any help to the princess, Anna thought, but Aline was pulling her by the sleeve. As they started down the steps, carefully avoiding the bloodied area, the door to the study flew open, and several men carried out Princess Yurievskaya's inert body. The front of her pink negligee was soaked with blood.

Outside, the Preobrazhensky Guards stood with bayonets fixed in belated vigil. Thousands of people, kneeling bareheaded on the snow in prayer, had already surrounded the palace grounds, and the two women had difficulty finding their sleigh. The motionless crowd was silent, and this terrible quiet enveloped Anna with a sense of impending doom.

They were about to enter the sleigh when Anna heard the announcement "Long Live Tsar Alexander the Third."

A soft collective moan rippled through the kneeling crowd, and Anna stopped. "Aline, we should go back. Princess Yurievskaya may need us now!"

But Aline shook her head and averted her eyes. "I have one of those terrible headaches coming on, Anna, and I couldn't be of any help right now. Why don't you go back and I'll send the sleigh after you later?"

Without a word Anna ran back to the palace. She found Princess Yurievskaya still in a faint and two shaking maids, their eyes glazed with terror, opening drawers and looking for smelling salts. Anna ordered them to remove the bloodied negligee from the princess instead, and after that had been done, she gently began to slap her face. A few moments later the princess opened her eyes and focused on Anna, then let out a sharp, clawing scream. Then came the sobs and, finally, the words.

"Anna, his leg . . . it's gone. . . . Gone! . . . He was torn apart, my Sasha! . . . Good Sasha . . . Oh, God! . . . He's dead . . . dead!"

Anna put her arms around the distraught woman, who beat her fists against her until the hysteria was spent and the weeping princess fell back on the pillows. Silently Anna sat by her, knowing it was a time when words, no matter how well meaning, could do no good.

She did not know how long they stayed like this. The winter light faded into darkness, and the dusk lengthened its shadows across the floor. Anna dared not leave. Somewhere in another part of the palace the imperial family must be grieving together, but no one came to see Princess Yurievskaya. Quietly the maids turned on the lamps and withdrew.

Suddenly the princess gasped. Pulling herself away from Anna, she grasped her by the shoulders and cried, "My God! His final wish . . . Anna, help me! I've got to do this for him!"

"I'm at your service, Your Highness. What do you wish me to do?"

"The manifesto! The paper he was going to sign today to

prepare the way for constitutional monarchy! . . . I must take it. I must give it to Loris-Melikov, before the new tsar finds it! He did not agree with his father's proposed reforms."

"Where is it?"

"In his desk. I have the key . . . come with me . . . hurry!"

Anna ached for the princess. It was unseemly to invade the privacy of the dead tsar, but when the country's future was at stake, surely no one could blame her.

The two women slipped out of the princess's boudoir and ran toward the tsar's apartments. Anna supported the trembling princess through the long corridors. When they entered the tsar's rooms and neared his desk, the princess again dissolved into tears.

"Anna, I can't . . . he . . . he's dead. . . . Oh, my God, he's dead! My Sasha! . . . I can't do it!"

"You must, Your Highness. You said so yourself. In his memory; for the country. Please!"

"No! I can't touch anything of his. . . . You do it, Anna. . . . Here! Take the key . . . it should be in that drawer over there . . . take it, quickly!"

Anna opened the drawer and pulled the proposed manifesto out, but before she could close the drawer, a hand clamped around her wrist and the papers were pulled from her fingers. Behind her the princess gasped, and Anna wheeled around to face the new tsar's brother, Grand Duke Vladimir. How had he entered the room so quietly? How much had he overheard?

Unhurriedly the grand duke pulled the key out of the drawer and, without a word, stalked out of the room. He was not as large a man as his august brother, but his self-assurance, his regal bearing, his unmistakable authority intimidated Anna.

Not a word, not a single word did he deign to say to her or to Princess Yurievskaya! For years afterward Anna shuddered at the memory of his touch, of the firm, large palm encircling her wrist and the paralyzing fear that powerful contact engendered.

Back in the princess's rooms the widow sobbed. "Oh, Anna, how horrible . . . how shameful! . . . He acted in his brother's interests to be sure . . . but the callousness . . . to do this while his father's body is still warm. . . ."

There was nothing Anna could say to comfort the princess, so she stayed by her side until the grieving woman fell into an exhausted sleep. Then she slipped out quietly and left the palace.

At home, in the privacy of her room, Anna wept. She could not find any reason for killing this gentle, liberal tsar, who had emancipated the serfs and abolished corporal punishment. Tears stung her eyes, and she longed to see Anton, to have him explain this utter injustice. The tsar strove to improve the lot of the oppressed, and the very ones benefiting from his reforms killed him! How could this be?

For days afterward Anna grieved: for the dead tsar; for Princess Yurievskaya, who, she was sure, would now be further alienated from the imperial family.

And the city! The city grieved, too. The pastels of St. Petersburg were draped in black at every window, every balcony, and every door. Foreboding pervaded the Persiantsev Palace, hung in the air, followed Anna from room to room. She waited for Anton. He did not come for three days, and when he did, he held her without speaking. Anna clung to him.

"Why, Anton, why? Is this how our people reward the tsar for his liberal reforms? Shame on us. Shame!"

Anton pushed her away slowly and clasped her hands in his. "Anna, listen to me! Please listen. The tsar's assassination will set us back a hundred years. The poor did not kill him!"

"Then who did?"

"The *narodniki*—People's Will, they call themselves. They are an offshoot of the Social Revolutionary party, and their purpose is to engage in acts of terrorism and to wipe out the monarchy."

"But Alexander the Second was a liberal, and his son is an avowed autocrat! They defeated their own purpose!"

"I'm not so sure, Anna."

Dry-eyed and frightened, Anna listened to what Anton had learned. The liberal zemstvo, the assembly of the city of Tver, had praised Loris-Melikov for working toward a better relationship between the people and the government. The terrorists realized that such a democratic foresight on the part of the prime minister would make their work toward a revolution impossible. With the liberal tsar removed, his autocratic successor would surely implement reactionary measures, thus causing the dissatisfied masses to support the terrorists.

"Have the assassins been caught?" Anna asked.

"The bomb that killed the tsar also killed the terrorists." Anton began to pace the floor. "But their leader, Sofia Perovskaya, is still at large."

They sat down on a silk-covered love seat, and Anna poured tea with shaking hands. The smell of birchwood burning in the large porcelain stove brought back childhood memories of warmth and security, and for the first time in three days Anna relaxed. She leaned over and kissed Anton timidly on the cheek. His day-old stubble scratched her lips, and when he responded instantly by drawing her to him in a firm embrace, she was embarrassed by her overt gesture and pulled away. He released her immediately and picked up his glass of tea in a silver and gold holder. Turning it around, he studied it and then said, "It's a shame to use such finery. It belongs in a museum."

He put the glass down and turned to look at her. "Anna, we love each other, and it is not wrong for us to kiss when we are alone. This is the first time your lips have touched me of your own accord. Do you have any idea how happy it makes me?"

A warm glow spread over Anna, flushed her face, tingled her fingers. She put her head against his shoulder. "Anton, I do love you!"

Without a word he drew her to him and kissed her on the lips. Anna inhaled deeply, fully, and held the breath full of the homey smells of him, the musky, seasoned odor—a secret mixture of this man. *Her* man.

Before he left, Anna took him to see Aline. But when they entered the parlor, Count Yevgeni rose from the chair. Anna could not hear her voice as she made the introductions. The peace she had felt only moments before in Anton's arms had disappeared.

"Congratulations to you on your engagement," the count was saying, and Anton was nodding and smiling.

"Thank you, Count, I am a lucky man."

What was the matter with her? She disliked the count; of that she was sure. He was not gentle like Anton. Arrogant. That was it! His arrogance bothered her. She had to say something, start a conversation.

"What grief our country is suffering now!" she heard herself say.

Yevgeni nodded. "Yes, the tsar's death is tragic."

"Do you know what happened to the manifesto?" Anna blurted out without thinking.

"What manifesto?" Anton asked anxiously.

Yevgeni threw Anna a curious glance, then looked at Anton. "The manifesto that would have been the first step toward parliamentary government," he said. "It was to be an announcement that members of the zemstvos would be invited to participate in the Council of State." Yevgeni pursed his lips and raised an eyebrow. "I think the tsar pushed this system of elected local assemblies too fast. They replaced the authority of the nobles without proper training to deal with the complexities of provincial laws."

He is haughty, Anna thought. *Haughty and proud. I wonder what he would say if he knew what role I played in trying to save that manifesto?*

"Any change takes time and adjustment," Anton said quietly. "A constitutional monarchy would put an end to the revolutionary elements in our country."

Count Yevgeni looked at him sharply. "Our peasants are ignorant and understand the present system better. Too much leniency would foment terrorism, not abort it. In any case, it's academic at this point. A new era has begun with the reign of Alexander the Third."

"I hope for the better," Anton added.

Yevgeni's mouth curved in a slow smile. "Our new tsar is a staunch autocrat. His Majesty has decided to destroy his father's manifesto. Mark my words, the new reign will crush the liberals. I, for one, am all for it."

For a few moments Count Yevgeni studied the two people shocked into silence before him, as though he had suddenly realized to whom he was speaking. Then a broad smile brightened his face. "But I'm forgetting my manners. Forgive me! May I offer you a glass of brandy or a cup of tea?"

The chameleon change of the count's countenance was remarkable. Anna stiffened and heard the forceful, plangent drumming of her heart. That extraordinary man! Imperious one moment, disarming the next. It was this duplicity that caused her heart to hammer so painfully.

Wasn't it?

Chapter Four

Count Yevgeni's prediction came true. Tsar Alexander III vigorously pursued an autocratic policy. To Anna he appeared to be a man determined to avenge his father's death by crushing mercilessly any liberal thought that dared surface. Princess Yurievskaya, who had retired from the Winter Palace to her private mansion, wrung her hands and bared her soul to Anna.

"The tsar cannot resurrect his father by vengeance! He must be blind not to see that the autocracy is doomed and that his only hope to save the monarchy is through a parliamentary rule."

Anna listened and pitied this beautiful, tragic woman whose protector was gone and who reminded her now of a blooming flower that had been snapped and left to wilt in neglect. Surely she could not add to her anguish by telling her that she agreed with her.

As the months slipped into years, Anna developed a fear of Count Yevgeni's visits to St. Petersburg. An uneasy friendship had grown between them. He no longer made overt gestures toward her, but now he sought her out to talk, to argue over the latest in literature. Anna found that he was not as shallow as she had first imagined, and when he told her that she was the first young woman he had known with whom he could talk intelligently, she was flattered.

Yet it had become a feverish existence, one of dread and anxiety, which carried her into an impossible conflict. Yes, she knew that the only way to resolve it was to avoid seeing him. But that was not easy to do, for every time he returned, he spent entirely too much time with her, hunting out her innermost thoughts and teasing her about her loyalty to Anton. "You're a perennial bride without a groom," he once said laughing, and Anna fretted.

It had been almost four years since that night in March 1881 when she first met him. It was February now, and she must think of the approaching Shrovetide week, with its troika sleigh rides, masquerade balls, and festive food. The events of this gala week were her favorite. She loved those feasts so much! Stacks and stacks of blini, the pancakes served with mounds of black and red caviar, and smoked salmon and cured sturgeon, and heaps of sour cream and melted butter.

She must remember to send a note to Anton, reminding him of the Shrove Sunday blini dinner he had been invited to attend at the Persiantsev Palace. He must not forget that! He had become so absentminded of late, what with his increased load of studies toward the end of his training and the constant battle to make ends meet. Poor Anton! He worked so hard, seemed thinner and more quiet than before. She would have to hire a good cook to fatten him up after they were married. A chilling thought crossed her mind. Would they have enough money to hire a cook, or would she have to do the cooking herself? She wouldn't mind.

She could hardly wait to get away from the Persiantsev Palace and start her own life! She and Aline had nothing left in common. The countess was preoccupied with clothes, the latest gossip, and her ailments. More and more she blamed her ill health for her inability to conceive a child, a disappointment that caused friction between Count Pyotr and Aline. Tense, acerbic dialogues had encroached upon their marital relationship and made Anna avoid their company as much as she could.

On Shrove Sunday the dining room table was set with courtly

elegance. After checking the setting at Aline's request, Anna hovered near the door of the grand salon, increasingly embarrassed by Anton's tardiness. When dinner was announced and Anton still had not arrived, she began to worry. It was not like him at all to be late for an appointment, especially for such a festive occasion. He was already an hour overdue.

Aline touched her arm. "I'm sorry, Anna, but we shall have to proceed with dinner without Anton. It will be less embarrassing for him if he slips in unobtrusively later than if we keep the rest of our guests waiting."

Trying to cover her confusion, Anna nodded without looking up. She couldn't imagine what was keeping Anton.

The dinner seemed to go on forever. She hardly ate the blini when they were passed to her, crisp and steaming in the folds of a starched linen napkin. She did not drink the wine and barely touched the *plombir,* the ice, creamy white and colorful with candied fruits.

Bits of conversation floated over Anna, lingered, drifted away. She listened politely, grateful that Yevgeni was seated at the other end of the table so she did not have to cope with his nearness. Her ears began to hum with a repeated refrain: Anton was not there . . . something must have happened to him . . . and her imagination ran wild.

Dinner was over, the guests had eventually gone home, and Anna was alone in her room. Anton had not come, and there was no note.

She spent a fretful night. The possibility that she might one day lose Anton had never occurred to her. A long, long life without him would stretch into obscurity. She would exist, not live. But in the morning, while she was still in bed, the servant Fenya brought her Anton's note, and she was so relieved she wanted to cry. Impatiently she tore it open and then, incredulous, read it twice. Hurriedly scribbled, it said that he had been detained at a meeting and been unable to leave in time, and that he would come see her in the evening. That was all.

With each passing hour, Anna's annoyance grew, compounded by embarrassment for her fiancé who had shown poor breeding

—an unforgivable sin among the aristocrats. She could hardly face the family throughout the day. Thank God Count Yevgeni was nowhere to be seen, and Anna kept to her room most of the afternoon.

By the time Anton arrived in the evening she could barely contain her irritation. His apologies were weak, and Anna's anger turned to hurt. "Why couldn't you have left the lecture hall in time, Anton? What was so important that you couldn't send a note to me or to the Persiantsevs?"

"It was not a medical lecture, Anna. I didn't want to write about it in a note for reasons I shall explain." Anton took her hands in his. "I'm sorry to have upset you, my dear. Believe me, if I could have sent a note, I would have; but the meeting was called unexpectedly in a private flat, and there was absolutely no way for me to notify you."

"What meeting? Whose flat?"

Anton was silent for a moment, then said softly, "One of our medical students belongs to a group of nihilists, and I attended their meeting out of curiosity."

Anna backed away. "You mean you attended some silly meeting, endangered both of us, and embarrassed me by not showing up for dinner, all for the sake of curiosity?"

"First of all, I didn't endanger you, Anna. You didn't even know about this meeting, so how can you say that you were involved?"

"You know very well how paranoid the police and the tsar's Okhrana can be; they investigate everything, and you can end up in Siberia."

"What is it that bothers you more—the possible danger I placed myself in or the embarrassment I caused you before the Persiantsevs?"

Stung, Anna took a deep breath. "And what's wrong with having good manners?" she retorted. "I was mortified for you and for myself last night."

"I can't believe that you're a slave to conventions. I admit it wasn't polite not to notify my hosts, but under the circumstances it was physically impossible for me to do so. Is one so governed

by protocol in your milieu that an omission like this is unpardona-
ble?"

"You had time to go to the meeting, yet you had no time to send
a note to me."

"I didn't come here to quarrel, Anna. I'm sure that when you
have time to think it over, you'll see how unimportant this incident
is."

"Aren't you going to apologize for your faux pas?"

"I plan to do just that. Contrary to what you may think, I *was*
brought up to mind my manners."

"There's no need to be sarcastic, Anton."

"I'm not sarcastic. You're the one who is overreacting."

"What's happened to you, Anton? I don't recognize you!"

"Perhaps we should part for a while, Anna. You need time to
calm yourself."

With a short nod Anton walked out of the room.

Anna stood shaking. He had reversed the argument and put *her*
on the defensive. Her gentle, kind Anton had turned out to have a
stubborn streak. The years ahead no longer promised to be as
idyllic as she had imagined.

For the next hour Anna stayed in her room. She didn't want to
witness his apology to Aline and Count Pyotr, imagining their
exquisite tact, which would minimize his blunder and make him
undoubtedly feel less guilty than he should be. She was angry, so
angry!

She had to get out of her bedchamber, find an empty room
—there were so many elegant parlors in the palace—and sit quietly
in some deep chair. Her flying thoughts were crowding her, and
she needed to control them.

Cautiously she opened the door and listened. With luck, she
wouldn't run into Aline or her husband, not right now. It was quiet
in the corridor. Anna walked softly on the Persian hall runner
toward the far end of the hallway. Having turned a corner past the
blue damask parlor, she had reached Yevgeni's apartments and
was passing his gilded doors when they suddenly swung open and
the count walked out.

"Anna! What a pleasant surprise! I haven't seen you all day. Where have you been hiding?" And then: "How lovely you look!"

In his scarlet brocade smoking jacket tied with a tasseled sash, he looked young, his features vibrant, finely etched in his handsome face.

"Thank you, Yevgeni," Anna murmured, and tried to pass, but Yevgeni peered at her closer and barred her way.

"You're agitated, Anna. What happened, my dear?" He took her elbow. "Please let me help. Won't you come in?"

His tone was light but kind, and his voice had a caressing quality, the exact combination needed to soothe. His touch had felt like velvet. *Why isn't Anton like this? Yevgeni always says the right words; I need them now. Need them!*

A door closed around the corner. She turned, and her dress rustled. The light from his room spread a golden carpet at her feet.

"Come in, Anna. A glass of cognac is just what you need."

She shouldn't be afraid of him. How foolish to be afraid of everything. Surely there was no harm in accepting comfort from another human being.

She had never drunk cognac before. Something burned inside her, started a fire, spread to her hands, her legs, her lips. It flamed in other parts of her tightly laced body, thrashing to get out, enveloping, hurting. She had never dreamed she could feel this much, burn so much. She—serious, quiet Anna. And then his fingertips were upon her, driving her wild. His lips consumed her. Madness. She went mad in Yevgeni's arms. Frenzied. It wasn't she in that canopied bed tearing at her laces, writhing against Yevgeni. A demon possessed her and swept her up to a mountain peak, then triggered a strange and brief eruption. It was such a relief she cried out. Actually cried out! For shame of it. And afterward she could not bring herself to look at him. In the darkness, stealthily, she picked up her clothes and ran away.

Did one glass of cognac do this? Oh no. She, Anna, had let it be. Her body, her weak, flaming body, had betrayed her. How had this happened to her—a properly brought-up young woman who had only a few hours earlier chastised her fiancé for a minor transgression? (What righteous indignation!) She was now a fallen woman. Ruined for life, and by a man whom she had always feared and did not love.

She stayed in her room for two days, pretending illness, and sent a note to Anton that she could not see him for a while. Worse, she could not bear to see Yevgeni again. He was to leave the following day, and she could not face him. She didn't love him, and she was ashamed. She had lost control, and she was sure her thoughts were so loud everyone would hear them and know what she had done.

Anton would know. He would read it in her face and be shattered. It would destroy his love, she was sure of that. What could she do? She couldn't marry Anton now. She had been honest all her life, and she had to be honest or she couldn't live with herself. *Live with herself*. Oh, God! She would have to live her life out as one of those pitiful crones, the fawning sycophants shadowing the palace rooms.

No! She couldn't face that. Her secret had to stay hidden. A lifetime of payment for one night of folly. She loved Anton. She did not want to hurt him. Paying for her mistake, she would be a better wife. Of course! The marriage would take place, and he would never know.

The alternative was worse.

The nausea started violently, without warning. At first Anna thought she had eaten too much of the fish *pirog* the night before. The piecrust had been yeasty and must have lain heavily in her stomach, she told herself. But the next morning it was the same. And the next. Then she ran out of excuses. Terror crawled like vermin up her arms, skittered over her body, bit into it. Aline was tolerant, sent camomile tea with Fenya. Anna didn't know where to turn, knew she couldn't confide in anyone. That was the worst of it, for confession rose to her lips, choked in her throat, went down again. Certainly she couldn't tell Aline. Disgrace, banishment from the palace would follow, and she didn't know where she could go. Panic swept over her. Only one small hope remained: confess her shame to Anton and plead, debase herself, beg him to marry her now. She would accept any condition he might impose.

But where would she find the courage to face Anton, to watch his face crumble in pain or, worse, in disgust? But she had only two choices: swallow her pride and let Anton be the only one to know, or avoid Anton and let the whole world witness her disgrace. That was unthinkable.

Tonight she would tell Anton. She couldn't wait any longer. They would have to be married at once. He was almost finished with his studies, and his diploma was in sight. She didn't know how she was going to tell him or what excuse she could give him, for it would be dishonest to put the blame on him and say that she had been hurt and sought solace with Count Yevgeni.

But Anton did not probe. She did not have to tell him who it was. He knew. He asked only if Count Yevgeni had left for Paris. Anna did not think she would ever cry again, her eyes had been drained of tears. With a supreme effort to keep calm, she explained that it had been a single blind mistake and that she would do anything he asked. She swore she could not remember the details of that night. *But she did remember. The heat of her desire. Her unrestrained, shameless surrender. The ecstasy.*

"Anton," she said, "I'm not asking you to forgive me. I know it's too much to expect, and I can't make you believe the truth, that I have waited faithfully for you this whole time. I ask you only not to punish me with a lifetime of doubt for one mistake."

Anton looked at her. Two large tears spilled over, made glistening tracks down his cheeks. A squeezing, pressing pain spread in her chest. "Anton, I'd give anything to have spared you this pain! I love you. Only you! I always have and always will."

When Anton did not respond, she moved toward him and timidly reached out to touch his arm, but he shrank away and clasped his hands, pressing his elbows against his body.

"Please! Don't touch me! I need to think."

He raised his hand to fend her off and left the room.

They were married quietly without fanfare, and Countess Aline was disappointed. "What's the matter with you, Anna? Don't you want a wedding dress with a veil and bridesmaids and the choir welcoming you into the church?" And when Anna told her that she wanted complete privacy for her happy day, Aline looked hurt. "Suit yourself," she said, pouting. Anton never mentioned the secret between them, and when Anna tried to discuss it, he became stern and peremptory. He forbade her to bring up the subject ever again, and she obeyed.

In the privacy of her thoughts, she vowed to become his loyal wife and a reflection of himself. When the little boy was born, she named him Sergei and watched with trepidation Anton's reaction when he first saw the child. Anton behaved like a proud father, and her fears of his rejection were calmed.

It took more than ten years to bring Anton closer to her again with the arrival of their own child: a plump pink and white little girl. Anton named her Nadezhda, and Anna read a meaning into his decision because *nadezhda* meant hope. She called the baby Nadya, her joy and her blessing.

During those ten years Anton not only had paid back his years of military service but had established medical practice with an office in their flat on the Moika Canal. Count Pyotr had indeed used his influence to have Anton assigned to the capital during his payback time and had retained him as his private family physician. When Anna objected because she wanted to get as far from any association with the Persiantsevs as she could, Anton pointed out that extra income would always be welcome and that the count's family demanded little of his time.

After the birth of a long-awaited son, Count Alexei, in August 1889, Aline was less preoccupied with her health. Anna could think of no reason to give Anton for her objection without arousing his suspicion that she was still disturbed by Count Yevgeni, who on his rare visits to St. Petersburg was now accompanied by a French wife with whom he established a permanent residence in Paris.

In May 1896, four months after Nadya's birth, the Efimovs found themselves in Moscow accompanying the Persiantsevs, who had traveled to attend the coronation of Nicholas II, whose father, Alexander III, had died unexpectedly of dropsy in 1894.

Anna, who was nursing her baby daughter, took her children with her. The ten-year-old Sergei was bored with the pomp of the coronation processions down Tverskaya Street and waited impatiently to be taken to Khodynka Field, on the outskirts of Moscow, where, his mother had told him, there would be lots of entertainment for the children.

So it was that four days after the coronation, on May 18, Anna planned to leave baby Nadya with the nurse at the Metropol and take Sergei to Khodynka Field. But the night before, on her way to the Bolshoi Theater to attend a performance of Glinka's *A Life for the Tsar*, Aline, resplendent in diamonds and rubies, said to Anna, "I can't understand you, Anna. Why do you want to take Seryozha to Khodynka Field tomorrow? Our coachman rode out there this afternoon and reported to Pyotr that the field is already mobbed with hundreds of thousands of peasants sitting around bonfires and sleeping on the ground, crowding near the booths and pavilions to get as close to tomorrow's free beer as they can. That's hardly the place to take a young child. Why don't you let him play with Alexei, and you and I go tomorrow to do some shopping? It's always fun to see how Moscow competes with us in elegance!"

Anna hesitated. She rarely made a promise to Sergei, but when she did, she made a point of keeping it. "I don't know, Aline," she said uncertainly. "I told Seryozha about the free *pryaniki* that would be given out. He loves those cookies. Besides, he's looking forward to seeing the trained bears and the clown's performance. I can't disappoint him."

Aline shrugged. "Suit yourself, but I don't see why Anton doesn't take him instead."

Anna couldn't argue with the obvious, but she could not tell Aline that whenever she could, she avoided asking Anton to do things for Sergei.

But Anton walked into the room and overheard Aline. Surprised, he turned to Anna. "Of course you'll go with Aline. I had no idea you were planning to take Seryozha to Khodynka. I'll be glad to take him."

Anna would long remember Sergei's pale and tear-streaked face when he returned with Anton from Khodynka Field. His lower lip trembled as he spurted out what he had seen: a mob of people fighting to get to the counters and trampling one another to death. "There was screaming and blood, Mama," he said in conclusion, bursting into tears.

Anton stroked the child's disheveled hair and said to Anna, "Evidently someone started the rumor that there wouldn't be enough iron mugs to give out as souvenirs and that the free beer would quickly run out. This caused a stampede, and we ran for our lives. There must be thousands out there crushed to death!"

After Sergei had calmed down and had time to think, he asked his mother, "Mama, why are people so poor that they have to kill one another over a mug?"

Anna had never forgotten her son's simplistic question which mirrored the growing ills of the country.

Now, nine years later, as Anna sat in her daughter's bedroom in the Moika Canal flat—the shots in the Nevsky Prospekt still ringing in her ears—she was dismayed that it was Nadya's turn to see people killed on the street. Little Nadya, whose taut and frightened face had finally relaxed in sleep. How dreadful, Anna thought. How unspeakable that both her children—Sergei on Khodynka Field in Moscow and Nadya here in St. Petersburg —should be innocent witnesses to violence and carnage.

Chapter Five

Nadya remembered her childhood in clear but disjointed vignettes. Her family lived a few blocks off the Nevsky Prospekt, in a rented flat set in a deep archway connecting the street with the inner courtyard. The large rooms with tall ceilings and hardwood floors were filled with leather divans and slipcovered armchairs. The smell of seasoned rawhide and musty books permeated the family study, where the wall behind the divan was covered with broad panels of needlepoint embroidered by Nadya's mother while she listened to her children recite their nightly lessons.

Nadya's memory of her mother was of a woman whose life was filled with household chores, the daily problems of her friends, and concerns over her husband's patients. She constantly worried if her credit would stretch with the local merchants throughout the month and if there would be enough money to pay the rent.

As long as her mother was alive, Nadya thought she would never need to look at the calendar, for toward the latter part of each month Anna's shoulders stooped lower and the furrow in her forehead deepened.

In one corner of the flat Nadya's father, Anton Stepanovich, had his office. It smelled of iodine, camphor, and carbolic soap (he insisted the floors and baseboards be routinely scrubbed by the charwoman), and he cared for the sick in that room with single-minded tenderness. Nadya remembered him—skeletal and fidgety—forever darting from the examining table to the medicine cabinet with its row of apothecary jars to his desk.

His waiting room was always crowded with patients, many of whom had no money to pay him. "I cannot be selective with my patients," he retorted to Anna's frequent objections. "All who need help are welcome here. As long as we can make ends meet, I'll care for them, and if they cannot pay, I get rewarded in other ways."

He did not elaborate on what kinds of rewards they were, but Anna persisted. "We're the poorest doctor's family I know," she said. Anton Stepanovich just shrugged and did not respond, and Nadya knew that the chasm between her family and the privileged class was vast.

For several years after that fateful Bloody Sunday Nadya had recurrent nightmares. They always centered on the bleeding woman she had seen on the ground. Nadya would wake up whimpering, her pillow wet with tears.

Her brother, Sergei, whose room was next to hers, would wipe her cheeks and rock her to sleep in his arms. Cozy against his warm chest, Nadya was comforted. Although she did not resemble her brother, whose kind gray eyes and sandy hair were so different from her brown ones, she felt closer to him than to her parents, and it was to him she carried an injured finger or a broken doll, sure of his attention. Anna believed that complimenting a child would spoil her and encouraged Nadya to be self-reliant at an early age. That walk on the Bloody Sunday had been the first step of her independence. "Family relationships are based on mutual trust and respect, Nadya, and it's your responsibility to see that the trust we have in your judgment is not betrayed."

Nadya worked hard to maintain that trust and glowed with happiness at her mother's infrequent praise. Stern and reserved, Anna was often preoccupied, so Nadya turned to her brother for advice and support. Because Sergei always seemed to have time for his sister, when he left for the famous medical school in the city of Kazan, Nadya was desolate. In a rare display of affection, Anna took Nadya in her arms and said, "Nadya, if Seryozha had stayed in St. Petersburg, he would have had to attend a military medical school, and that means payback time in the military service. Your father and I would have been separated for more than four years if Count Persiantsev had not used his influence to keep him in the city after he finished school."

"Why doesn't Papa ask Count Persiantsev to arrange for Seryozha to stay here, too?" Nadya asked with a child's deductive logic.

Anna abruptly released Nadya, moved to the other end of the room, and said quietly, "No, Nadyenka. We won't do that."

There was sadness in her mother's voice, and instinctively Nadya knew the subject was closed.

When she was twelve, Sergei came home for Christmas, and Nadya, who had missed sledding on the ice hill on Admiralty Square because her mother had forbidden her to go there alone, could hardly wait for him to take her. Earlier in the autumn, when the Neva froze, she had stood at the square, watching the yearly procedure of erecting the scaffold for the sled run. Close to its base, she had tilted her head up to look at the top. It was as high as a three-story building, and it made her dizzy. She watched as the workmen drilled holes in the frozen earth, placed the poles inside, and poured water around the bases. Within minutes the water froze, cementing the posts. Then large blocks of ice were laid on the steep slope, and water was poured over it to smooth the run.

The morning after Sergei's arrival he took her up the steps of the scaffold, dragging the sled on the track alongside. Once at the top Nadya turned to him. "Seryozha, I'd like to go down alone. You can watch me from the top."

But Sergei was adamant. "Absolutely not! I don't want to see you breaking your neck. Have you lost your mind? It's dangerous!"

"I'm not a little girl anymore, Seryozha," Nadya said firmly, embarrassed by the smiles of eavesdropping adults.

"She's right, you know!"

The voice came from behind, and Nadya wheeled to see a robust, smiling young man slap her brother on the shoulder. Sergei beamed. "Vadka! Where did you come from? Good to see you!"

The two shook hands and clasped each other's arms. Then Sergei turned to Nadya. "Meet my friend from the university, Vadim Razumov. He's studying to be a lawyer. Vadka, this is my *sestryonka*, Nadya."

After solemnly shaking Nadya's mittened hand, Vadim turned to Sergei. "How about it, Seryozhka? Your sister looks old enough to go down by herself."

Sergei hesitated. "Nadya, why didn't you tell me earlier that you wanted to try it alone? I would have brought my own sled and gone behind you. Just in case."

"If that will make you feel better, I have my sled here," Vadim volunteered, "and I'll be glad to go down behind her. Better yet, why don't we both go down together?"

Without waiting for Sergei's reply, Nadya sat down on her sled, but Vadim stopped her. "When you ride down alone, it's a lot more fun to lie down on your stomach. Safer, too; if someone runs into you, you won't have that far to fall!"

Nadya lay down on the sled without a word and, in the next instant, was pushed down the slope. For a second she closed her eyes—it was so steep and fast! About midway down the hill the slope curved more gently, and at the bottom it straightened out into a long, flat run. Delighted with her success, Nadya lifted herself and turned to look back. That was a mistake. Her sled had not yet come to a stop, and her body's movement toppled her to the side. She was so angry with herself she nearly burst into tears. Sergei's friend would think her a silly child.

"Are you hurt, Nadya?"

Sergei's anxious face was bending over her. Determined not to let them see her tears of frustration, she swallowed hard and shook her head.

"Wasn't much of a fall here, but up there"— Vadim pointed to the steep part of the slope—"it would have been another story." He smiled at Nadya. "You managed expertly in the difficult part. The sled tilted when you turned around, that's all."

He didn't laugh at her. Nadya looked at Vadim gratefully. His hazel eyes twinkled, and she forgot her humiliation. What a nice, kind man!

She did not see him again for many years, but the warm glow of gratitude lingered.

In school Nadya was a good student not by virtue of her natural intelligence, but through diligence and perseverance. She was a dreamer, spending her free time over books of poetry, trying her own hand at composing romantic stanzas. She made no lasting friendships, avoiding the shifting loyalties of her classmates in favor of her brother's stability. She could tell him things she would never confide in her mother.

Anna was secretive, and it never occurred to Nadya to question her mother about her youth. She knew that Anna had been reared with Countess Aline and lived in the Persiantsev Palace until she married her father, but it did not seem strange to Nadya that her mother rarely visited the countess and never went to palace balls. She simply could not visualize her tired, aging mother dancing. Impossible! So Nadya had never met Countess Aline or been inside the Persiantsev Palace.

Thus, when she turned sixteen, a memorable event in her life took place on the night of January 25, 1912. Her father, responding to a call from Count Persiantsev, for the first time took her to the palace with him.

It was the night of St. Tatiana's Day, a popular name day when festivities took place all over the country in honor of every Tatiana in Russia. When the call came from the palace, there was no one home except Anton Stepanovich and Nadya. Anna was visiting a neighbor, and Sergei was at a students' ball.

Picking up his medical bag, Anton Stepanovich looked at his daughter curled up on the sofa with a book. *She has grown shapely and so pretty with those dreamy eyes*, he thought affectionately, and suddenly halted in the foyer.

"Come with me, Nadyenka," he said, smiling indulgently. "You've asked often enough to see the Persiantsev Palace."

Nadya pushed her rich brown hair off her face and looked up at her father, her eyes alert and shining. "I'd love to see it, Papa!"

"Good. It's a clear night, and I'll enjoy your company on my walk. Come on, child, your books will wait. Bundle up well. I'll wait."

Outside, it was very cold. The moon shone bleakly from the dark sky, but even on a winter night Nadya loved her city, this Venice of the North, with its 101 islands, its network of canals and bridges connecting the broad Neva with its tributaries, Moika and Fontanka. Her romantic image of St. Petersburg was one of the few points on which she disagreed with her brother, for Sergei tended to view it with a practical eye. "What's so glamorous about the Moika?" he once asked her. "Nowadays, instead of Moika, they call it *pomoika*—the garbage heap."

But Nadya did not share her brother's irreverence, especially not on a festive evening like tonight. Ahead of her the golden dome of St. Isaac's Cathedral reflected a silver sheen from the pale moon. Four hundred kilos of gold, it was said, had gone into the construction of the cathedral. Nadya looked at the ghostly edifice rising above the rooftops and remembered her brother had told her sixty men had perished in agony from mercury-vapor poisoning while fire-gilding the dome, and she acknowledged the vast chasm between the laboring poor and the rich.

Deep in thought, Nadya did not see the troika until Anton Stepanovich grabbed her by the arm. "Look out, Nadya!"

Trotting horses pulled a shiny painted sleigh down the street in front of them. As they waited for it to pass, Nadya caught a glimpse of an officer in the green and red uniform of His Majesty's Preobrazhensky Guards and next to him a woman wrapped in sable and wearing a sparkling tiara haloed by a gauzy shawl.

"Why so pensive, child? Watch your step, you almost stumbled right into the snowbank. What's on your mind?"

"Papa, does the tsar know of the workers' conditions? I wonder if he ever sees the real hovels. Do you suppose they still put false facades on villages along his travel route the way Potemkin did for Catherine the Great?"

For a few moments Anton Stepanovich was silent. Then he shook his head. "It's my fault for leading you and Sergei into this line of thinking. We must be moderate in our views. Remember, major reforms in our government have to be carefully planned."

"What are the ministers doing then, Papa?"

"I'm sure they're doing their best, and we, the middlemen, do our share to help those who suffer. There's hidden power in this approach. It's like collecting kopecks: Little by little you get a ruble. Think about it!"

Nadya wasn't satisfied. "Papa," she said pensively, "if something isn't done soon, we're going to have a revolution. Seryozha said so the other day."

"Watch what you say, Nadya! The moon is hazy tonight, and it would be hard to see the policeman's black uniform in such a light. I wouldn't want him to overhear you."

They were at the foot of a few broad steps that led to the grand entrance to the Persiantsev Palace. Count Pyotr, Nadya knew, was an important official in the tsar's Ministry of Education and had been a prominent reactionary in the cabinet of Alexander III. His only child, Count Alexei, now twenty-three, was a hussar in the Imperial Guards, the apple of his father's eye and doted on by his mother, the Countess Aline.

Dr. Efimov was frequently summoned to the palace by the hypochondriac countess. He rarely spoke of his aristocratic patients, and when he did, it was to shake his head and mutter that between the mother's pampering and the father's rigid support of the autocracy of the tsar, he wondered what kind of character the parents were molding in the young count.

Now, as they stood in front of the palace, the windows were ablaze with lights. A solemn liveried footman in a red coat and white breeches, white stockings, and buckled shoes swung the doors for the uniformed guests and their glittering ladies swathed in ermine and sable. Timidly Nadya started up the steps, but her father pulled her to the side.

"There's another door for us, Nadyenka. Over here!"

Nadya followed her father to the side of the mansion, where she saw a less imposing entrance.

"Is this the black entrance?"

"Not necessarily. To us the black entrance is for servants only, but in a large establishment, like this one, there are many doors."

"I see. We're not good enough to enter through the main door because you don't have gold-braided epaulets on your shoulders and I'm not wearing silk or satin. That's the truth, isn't it, Papa?

Yet you are a doctor, and they need you to cure their ills. It makes me sick. I won't go in. You go alone!"

"Don't be foolish, child. You can't stay out in this cold while I'm inside."

The door opened, and Anton Stepanovich pulled his reluctant daughter forward. An old nanny wearing a huge white apron met them at the door. Clasping her hands, she wailed, "Thank the Holy Virgin, you've come quickly, Anton Stepanovich! Her Excellency, bless her tender heart, gave me strict orders before she left for the reception rooms that I'm to keep my charge in his room, but the young falcon refuses to stay and is determined to join the ball. What am I going to do with him?"

"Don't worry, Agrafena Yegorovna, let's see first what's wrong with him," Anton Stepanovich said soothingly, following the old woman through a series of darkened rooms. When they reached a closed door, Anton Stepanovich turned to Nadya. "Wait here, child, until I come back to fetch you."

Nadya nodded, and her father and the nanny disappeared into the adjoining room. The door shut firmly behind them, but not before Nadya caught a glimpse of a crackling fire in the hearth and, in the mirror above it, a shadowy reflection of a tall man.

She turned and walked around the study. The light hardwood floor was inlaid with darker woods, and although thick Persian rugs covered most of them, Nadya could discern delicate floral designs in uncovered areas. On the mantel above the marble fireplace an elaborate bronze clock stood on a malachite base. A few leather armchairs were grouped around the fireplace, but what attracted Nadya the most was an ornate ormolu desk with intricate patterns of multicolored inlaid woods. She had never seen one so beautiful.

Bending over the desk, she ran her finger over a sleekly polished surface. The top was strewn with papers and several leather-bound books. Nadya bent closer to read the titles. *Fathers and Sons* lay on top. She had heard from Sergei all about Turgenev's major novel, which had caused such controversy the author was forced to leave his country. Next to it was Voltaire's *For and Against*, which Nadya had read in spite of her mother's objections.

Dostoyevsky's *Notes from the Underground* was beneath the other two books. Whoever read these was surely aware of the lot of the poor and possessed a curious mind.

The door opened, and Nadya swung around. Silhouetted against the mobile light of the fireplace, the same tall figure she had glimpsed in the mirror stood on the threshold. Dressed in the red and white hussar uniform of the Imperial Guards, the handsome young man stepped into the room and walked over to her.

"You must be Nadya, Anton Stepanovich's daughter?"

The man's dark hair shone with a bluish tinge in the dim light. Arched brows crowned surprisingly light blue-gray eyes that were slightly tilted at the corners and seemed out of place in an olive-skinned face. Right now they studied her with a mischievous twinkle.

Totally stupefied by this gorgeous man straight out of a romantic novel, Nadya gaped at the hussar.

"Allow me to introduce myself: Count Alexei Persiantsev. Your father is collecting his instruments and will be here presently. As you see, I'm only slightly wounded, and he mended me in short order."

Count Alexei stretched out his left hand and showed her a bandage over his wrist. "A stupid carelessness; I'll be good as new in a few days."

Nadya continued to stare. A glimmer of amusement appeared in his eyes. "Have we swallowed our tongue today?" His Russian was colloquial, and Nadya gulped in astonishment. She thought all aristocrats considered speaking Russian gauche and used French instead. Suddenly she found her voice.

"I have not swallowed my tongue. I was simply surprised that you speak Russian so well."

"Oho! You have spirit! I gather you take a dim view of the spoken French? Does it pique your Russian pride?"

Irritated by her reaction to the count, which she could not understand, she raised her head defiantly. "I confess I have trouble understanding why it is fashionable to avoid speaking our native tongue. We shouldn't be ashamed of being Russian."

Anton Stepanovich entered the room, carrying his large medical bag of faded leather. "I see you've already met my daughter, Count."

He smiled broadly and, it seemed to Nadya, a little obsequiously. Strange that she had never noticed before how worn her father's bag was. She had never seen him in the role of a subordinate, and it irked her.

Count Alexei chuckled. "Yes indeed, Anton Stepanovich. Your daughter has spirit. I'd watch her closely!"

"My daughter was brought up to speak her mind honestly." Anton Stepanovich's voice was cautious.

Count Alexei nodded. "That's a commendable quality. I like spirited women." He clicked the spurred heels of his high boots and kissed Nadya's hand. "I hope to see you again, mademoiselle."

Nadya flushed. Only married women got their hands kissed; why was the count doing it to her when he knew that she was not married?

Anton Stepanovich thrust a quick, searching look at the young count and then, taking Nadya by the arm, propelled her toward the exit.

"Good night, Count. Keep your wound clean, and I shall check it in a couple of days."

Outside, Nadya fumed. "He mocked me, Papa. He made fun of me! And you! You were so different inside that palace, not like my papa at all! I don't understand it."

"Nadya! Who gave you the right to speak this way to me? Did you get this from your brother? I won't tolerate disrespect from my children."

"I'm sorry, Papa. I didn't mean to be rude. It's just that I don't understand why you must use the side entrance. You're not their servant. You're their doctor, and they are the ones who should be treating you with great respect."

"What makes you think they don't, Nadya? Has Sergei filled your head with prejudice against all nobility? I must talk to him about this. When I was young, I, too, thought that equality in our country could be brought about easily. I soon realized that nothing can be achieved quickly without bloodshed. As for the Persiantsevs, they are my patients, and I give them no more deference than any others who come to see me. Let's not quarrel. The count had grazed his wrist in a fencing match, and his mother nearly fainted at the sight of blood. I've patched him up, and we need not dwell on him anymore."

But her father's conciliatory words were lost on Nadya. The vision of the exquisitely groomed nobleman hovered before her eyes, and the opulence of the palace interior made her feel inadequate and awkward for the first time in her life. She did not like the feeling, yet could not shake the memory of the elegance she had just witnessed. It haunted her. As for the young count Alexei, she hoped she would get another chance to stand up and show him that she was not the naïve little bourgeois he must have thought her to be.

Chapter Six

In spite of the conflict within her, Nadya enjoyed her father's company that night. She rarely saw him during the day except at the dining room table, where she listened to his dismayed accounts of being caught in the quagmire of bureaucracy. Although he never openly criticized his government, the entire family was aware of the grave injustices in their country's class system. Although serfdom had been abolished by Tsar Alexander II in 1861, the rich still controlled vast lands. The peasants' freedom seemed to make little difference to them, for they toiled endlessly for a few kopecks and were virtual slaves to the landowners. Bewildered by the responsibilities of their newly gained independence, the emancipated serfs knew only that with few exceptions their poverty had worsened.

But then, city workers fared little better. Perhaps that was why the students, themselves impoverished, began to incite rebellion among the peasants and factory workers, calling for reforms in the government.

Away from the dining table, Nadya listened raptly to her brother, ten years her senior and a man of the world at twenty-six. Bony and angular with a square jaw and light gray eyes, his sandy hair unruly, he often quoted Marx and Engels and attended mysterious meetings he called *besedy*, promising to take her along when she was older.

There were several groups of activists in the country, Sergei explained. One was the Social Revolutionaries, or the SRs, who worked with the peasants. They were behind most of the murders in the early part of the century, and they frightened Nadya.

Then there were the Social Democrats, or the SDs, followers of Marxist ideology who believed the revolution must start with the urban working classes. The SDs had split into two groups: the Bolsheviks, led by Lenin, and the Mensheviks, with someone called Plekhanov as their leader. Lenin, she understood, wanted a revolution, while the Mensheviks favored milder measures in changing from autocracy to democracy before introducing social-ism into the country.

It was all very confusing to Nadya. She yearned to attend the university on Vasilyevsky Island and be among the students with whom Sergei kept in contact even after getting his medical degree and joining his father's practice, but in 1912 she still had two years of gymnasium, or secondary school, to finish.

Highly principled, idealistic, she analyzed everything Sergei told her. When she heard that Lenin's real name was Vladimir Ulyanov, she immediately questioned his motives. "Why is this Lenin ashamed of his parentage?" she asked.

Sergei shrugged. "It seems the popular thing to do. There's a new socialist newsletter in circulation this year, called *Pravda*. It was started by a Georgian who calls himself Stalin. His real name is Joseph Dzhugashvili, and I guess he wants the world to know he's a man of steel, hence the name—Stalin. Who knows why Lenin changed his?"

Nadya listened, unconvinced, to her brother, who had slipped into the parental role. Sergei helped Nadya with her homework, expounding on the censored history books and, aware of Nadya's talent in poetry, extolled the radical element among contemporary poets whose lyricism was tinged with strong political overtones.

Recently Nadya had begun to curl up on the divan in the study, her back propped up by embroidered pillows, and listen to Sergei debate heatedly with one of his university friends.

"Sooner or later all the nobility, merchants, and peasants will have to meld," Sergei said one evening shortly after Nadya's first visit to the Persiantsev Palace. He was sitting in an oak swivel chair in the study, leaning on a rolltop desk and facing Yakov Oblevich, a chemistry student he was coaching for his exams. Nadya, her legs tucked under her, sat in the corner of the divan at the far end of the room and listened intently.

"Yes, and about time," Yakov agreed. He was a wiry young man with black curly hair and myopic eyes, and Nadya was never sure if he ever saw her clearly at all. Now he took off his pince-nez, breathed on the lenses, and wiped them with a large handkerchief. Then, after clipping the glasses gingerly on the bridge of his nose, he squinted at Sergei. "It's archaic to think we could have continued to have class distinction as sharply delineated as in the past."

Sergei nodded and threw a sidelong glance in Nadya's direction. His frown softened, and he smiled. "Are you sure, Nadyenka, we're not boring you with our discussion?" When Nadya shook her head, he hesitated a moment as if deciding whether to continue and then went on.

"I really don't care who does the work, the SRs or the Bolsheviks, as long as the ultimate result is achieved. A great step forward was the assassination of Stolypin last September. He was a real obstacle in our path."

Nadya sat up. "Aren't there any peaceful means to bring about reforms in our government?" she asked.

Yakov squinted at her. "Violence is necessary in any revolution, Nadya. I assure you, his removal was necessary."

"How can you use such an academic term as 'removal'?" Nadya cried. "Murder would be a better word! Papa said that Stolypin was a good president of the Duma and that he was a great statesman who could have averted the revolution."

"That's just it. He was a threat to our work."

"And what exactly is your work?" Nadya wanted to know, shaken by the casual reference to Stolypin's assassination.

The two young men exchanged quick glances. Sergei turned to face his sister, then walked over to her. Sitting down beside her, he took her hand and patted it gently. "Nadya, I'm not sure you're ready to hear all this. I'll tell you, but you must keep it secret. You see, our goal is to abolish the monarchy and establish a democracy in which common people would have a voice."

"Why do you have to do that? We could have a constitutional monarchy like the one in England. It works for them. Why couldn't it work for us?"

Sergei shook his head vigorously. "It's too late for us." He paused, a distant look clouding his gray eyes, then went on, his mouth twisted in a crooked smile. "They don't tell us in our school history books what a weakling our present tsar is or admit that his German wife is influenced by Rasputin. Some holy man he turned out to be! There are reports of his licentiousness and meddling in government affairs. He's leading the tsarina by the nose simply because he seems to be able to cure the heir to the throne whenever he is ill."

Sergei rose and walked back to the desk. "So you see, Nadya, we can't depend on our tsars to obey any constitutional government. Our Duma is a classic example of that type of governing body. It's impotent!"

Nadya was appalled. She thought of the peaceful demonstration on January 9, 1905, Bloody Sunday. She remembered the incident vividly and continued to have nightmares about it, though now she felt silly telling Sergei about them.

Suddenly uncomfortable with her conflicting emotions, Nadya shifted on the divan. A certain amount of violence was evidently necessary to bring about a democratic government. A tooth for a tooth and an eye for an eye. Was there truly no other way, she wondered, and weren't there always two sides to every story?

A few days after that evening Nadya was walking home from school when Count Alexei pulled up alongside her and leaned out of his highly polished ebony sleigh. "Jump in, Nadya, I'll give you a ride home."

Her first impulse was to decline, but the temptation was strong, and after hesitating for only a moment, she took his proffered hand and climbed into the sleigh.

This time he was charming and insisted on taking her for a ride to point out his favorite landmarks, his enthusiasm apparently genuine and contagious and she was more mesmerized by his voice than by his words. She had never been in a private sleigh before, and her slight feeling of guilt at having accepted the ride was almost completely obliterated by the thrill of being ogled by passersby who smiled and stopped to watch the handsome couple. Her cheeks were burning from excitement and frost, and although in her padded cloth coat she felt out of place next to the dashing officer, she was glad that at least her inelegant felt boots were hidden beneath a rabbit fur throw that covered their knees. Suddenly she felt Count Alexei's warm breath on her face as he leaned toward her. His attention had shifted to her, and he asked about her studies, her interests. He was a superb, disciplined listener who had the rare ability to focus on a speaker with total concentration, as if nothing interested him more than what he was hearing. He knew when to ask a question, when to probe deeper, and she was enchanted.

A block from her house he ordered the coachman to stop. "I'm not sure what your father would think about my kidnapping you today. Rather than get you into trouble, I'll let you walk the rest of the way." He smiled. "You see I haven't eaten you alive, and I apologize for my flippant manner the other night at the palace. I was irritated by the fuss made over my slight mishap, and I guess I took it out on you. Not very chivalrous of me, I admit. Am I forgiven?"

Nadya smiled shyly. "Forgiven."

He took her hand but did not kiss it this time.

Dazed, she walked home slowly along the winter-hushed street with no sound to disrupt her elation but the snow crunching under her *valenki*. Later that evening, when Sergei squinted at her intently as if he were reading something unusual in her face, she decided to savor her secret herself.

In the weeks that followed, Count Alexei several times picked her up on her way home and took her for a ride in his sleigh. No one at home noticed that she was occasionally late from school. But one day Anna wiped her hands on the towel after clearing the dinner dishes and quietly motioned Nadya to follow her into her bedroom.

She sat down in a soft armchair and studied Nadya in silence for a long time. A slow flush rose to Nadya's face under her mother's scrutiny. Then Anna sighed.

"Your face is glowing, and there's a sparkle in your eye, child. Who is it?" Anna smiled a rare warm smile, and it transformed her face wondrously. Nadya felt her blush deepen, and suddenly her hands were busy with the folds of her skirt.

When she remained silent, Anna probed. "Is it a boy in your class or someone in a senior class?"

Nadya shook her head. Anna raised her brows. "Then who?"

Some strange, mysterious instinct sealed her lips, and Nadya refused to answer. Anna leaned forward. "Are you ashamed of him?"

"No!" The denial burst out before she could think. "Of course not! It's nothing, Mama, nothing! A few rides home in a sleigh with an officer of the guards I met through a friend, that's all!"

The lie came out forced, and words tumbled over one another. Anna relaxed in her chair and squinted at her daughter. "Then why are you so defensive about it? It's natural for me to be interested, you know. I'm your mother! I was young once, too. . . ." Anna paused, as if some images of the past were surfacing before her. Nadya waited, seeing a side to her mother she had never suspected existed. At length Anna sighed.

"Have it your own way, Nadya, but whatever you do, be careful. Pray to our Lord for guidance. Pray hard. One reckless deed, and you may regret it the rest of your life."

Nadya went to her room confused about why she had been reluctant to tell her mother the truth. She had never heard Anna say anything derogatory about the Persiantsev family, yet somewhere in the back of her mind a small voice insisted she say nothing about seeing Count Alexei.

Chapter Seven

───────────────────

Winter slipped into a muddy spring, and in the advent of blooming lilacs and perfumed jasmine Nadya fell in love. The sleigh ride had been replaced by a victoria, Alexei explaining that he preferred the carriage to the new and cumbersome family automobiles. Now Alexei used the coach only to bring them to the nearest park or garden, and the two walked for a while before he took her home.

Frequently they went to the Summer Garden, where mythological statuary created by eighteenth-century Venetian sculptors evoked a world of fantasy. Their paths were flanked by tall lindens and unpruned elms, lilac bushes and green lawns.

Nadya and Alexei were strolling through these pristine lanes when one day he offered her his arm. The snugness of his gentle pressure sent unbidden electricity coursing through her veins. Although only one arm was a willing prisoner, she knew at that moment what it would feel like to have her body encircled in his arms and pressed against his chest. She caught her breath and held it, eyes momentarily closed, delicious dizziness floating through her, and making it difficult to concentrate on what he was saying about a book he had read.

"I see you enjoy a variety of literature judging from the books on your desk," she finally commented.

"What books?"

Nadya named the three she had seen. Alexei shrugged. "Oh those! I like to study great writers. They have always been the voice of our conscience, but I'm afraid our people are used to suffering and wouldn't be content unless they were miserable. There's a certain comfort in the expected. Take it away, give the poor self-reliance, and they'll panic."

Nadya was disappointed. "Are you saying that nothing should be done for the oppressed of our country?"

"Not at all. Something is being done for them all the time. All I'm saying is that to listen to the radicals is to court disaster. Total equality and liberty do not exist in our world."

Taking her arm, Alexei led her along a narrow path. Jolted anew by the touch of his arm, Nadya moved on. In the romantic novels she read there was talk of a beating heart and a love that blossomed and grew, but never of the things that were happening inside her body, strange and pleasant things that made breathing difficult and her hands tremble.

Alexei gently steered her forward. "It always frustrates me to have to see you for so short a time. I wish . . ." He let the sentence drift unfinished.

"You wish for what?" Nadya prodded.

"I wish I could sneak you into the Arcadia nightclub. We could dine there and spend the whole evening together in total privacy."

Shocked, Nadya stopped and faced him. "Alexei! I could never go there! Isn't it a gathering place of the demimonde where the Gypsies sing? I overheard my brother telling his friend about it. Proper unmarried women are never seen there."

"Well, it isn't exactly a palace ballroom, but it's the only place I know of where we can be sure of being undisturbed. No one will ever look for you there."

The temptation was great, but Nadya demurred.

"It'll be the first time since we've known each other that I'll have you all to myself," he coaxed persistently, "and you needn't worry about being seen; I'll reserve a private dining room."

A sweet longing spread over Nadya at the thought of being alone with Alexei. Surely she could trust this lovely man who had seen her often for the past five months and had never behaved improperly. The pressure of his arm, the frequent holding of her hands were gentle signals that he liked her. Besides, there was so much she wanted to tell him and never enough time to put her innermost feelings into words.

Yet the notorious name of the nightclub was shocking. How could she bring herself to go there? What excuse could she give at home for being out late at night? Her instinct whispered warnings —a nagging voice that wouldn't go away.

"I'd like very much to spend more time with you, Alexei, but I can't take the chance of being seen going into that place. It wouldn't be proper."

They were rounding a corner, heading toward the intricate wrought-iron palisade of the Summer Garden when they nearly collided with Sergei. All three stopped. For the longest moment of her life a silent tableau etched on Nadya's memory: the tall dark aristocrat in immaculate uniform beside her, calm, self-assured, smiling politely at her brother; Sergei, shorter, leaner, his gray suit limp, studying Alexei with suspicion; and herself, frozen with fear and embarrassment at having been caught red-handed, watching the two men with divided loyalty. Finally, she found her voice.

"Count Persiantsev, may I present my brother, Sergei."

"I'm delighted to meet your brother again, Nadya. We met once, years ago."

Alexei's courtly bow and warm smile were received with open hostility by Sergei, who bowed stiffly and shook hands with obvious reluctance. Then he turned to his sister. "Does Mama know you'll be late?"

"She has never scolded me before, and I'm sure she won't miss me today."

The moment she said it, she knew she had betrayed her trysts. Sergei looked at her sharply, then took her arm and gave Alexei a curt nod.

"I'll take my sister home, Count. It's getting late, and she should be back."

"I have my victoria waiting outside. I'll be glad to give you both a ride."

Sergei's cheek began to twitch. "Thank you, but we're perfectly capable of walking. Our house is only a short distance away, as I'm sure you already know."

Alexei bowed and turned to Nadya. She held her breath. *Oh, please, please, don't say anything to compromise me further*, she thought wildly, but Alexei, with exquisite tact, shook her hand and said, "It was nice seeing you today, Nadya. Give your father my warm regards."

Instead of going home, Sergei pulled Nadya to a secluded spot in the garden. He berated her for betraying her family trust and the principles for which they all stood. The more he talked, the angrier he became. As Nadya listened, it occurred to her that she hadn't really done anything so terrible to cause such a vehement reaction in her brother.

"I see nothing wrong in meeting the count in broad daylight, Sergei, and as far as his title is concerned, you can't fault him with the accident of his birth. I don't understand why you are so angry with me. I don't feel that I've betrayed my family trust. After all, Papa is private physician to the count's family, and as far as Count Alexei is concerned, I find him quite liberal in his views."

"Don't be naïve, Nadya. How can an aristocrat who enjoys the privileges of his position be a liberal? And if you think there's nothing wrong in your seeing the count, why have you kept it a secret from the family?"

Questioned on behavior that she herself could not explain, Nadya raised her head defiantly. "Because I wanted to avoid this sort of accusation, that's why! As for Count Alexei, you're wrong about him. Why, only today he offered to take me to a gathering of liberal poets here in St. Petersburg."

"Bah!" scoffed Sergei. "I know all about those intellectuals. They live in a world of utopia, writing poetry that leads nowhere, nothing but escape from reality."

"Why are you so bitter, Sergei? What have *you* done for the world to talk so authoritatively about a group of people you hardly know?"

"Oh, I know them all right. They are idealistic fools! I'm involved in a much more productive work." Sergei stopped suddenly, flustered at having revealed his own secrets.

"Like what, for instance?" Nadya asked, her curiosity aroused.

"Like helping write and print leaflets for the masses, introducing the workers to Marxism, attending secret rallies and recruiting individuals for our work. I belong to a group of doers, not dreamers," he finished defiantly.

Nadya moved away from Sergei, her own discovery forgotten, and looked at him searchingly. "I hope Papa doesn't know about this. You know how conservative he has become lately. But *I* am interested, Seryozha. I do hope, though, you're careful in what you do. You can be arrested if the authorities find out about it."

"Don't worry. Our network of agents is excellent. I'm well protected. We have to be. Soon—very soon—the socialists will win, and then we'll see how your dandified Count Alexei is going to behave."

He grabbed her by the arm. "Why do you think he's seeing you? If you're afraid to let your family know about these clandestine meetings, why doesn't he take you to his palace to meet his parents? Do you honestly think he has serious intentions toward you—a mere bourgeois?"

Many years later Nadya understood that this was when Sergei had made his mistake. How could he have known that he had touched on unspoken, suppressed doubts she herself harbored and that by voicing them, he had challenged her to dispel them?

Tossing in her bed that night, Nadya thought about Alexei's invitation to the nightclub. If she had had any reservations, she was now determined to accept it for the sole purpose of proving not only to Sergei but, above all, to herself that her brother was wrong.

The very next day she scribbled a note to Alexei telling him she had reconsidered and would be glad to spend an evening with him at the Arcadia.

Through the turbulent years that followed, that impetuous night remained with her as a beacon of singular, untainted happiness.

Years later she shook her head in wonder, remembering how easy it had been to leave her house undetected. Strange, how vivid in her memory were certain details of that night, while others, no matter how hard she tried to recollect them, stubbornly eluded her.

It was difficult for her to recall the evening meal with her parents. Her mother seemed pale and leaner than ever, and she remembered her father's preoccupied grunts in response to her casual remarks. She had chosen a night when she knew Sergei would be late coming home from the Institute of Research, where he was spending more and more of his time. She only picked at her food, saving herself for the sumptuous meal she knew would be offered in the nightclub.

Once in her room, she waited until her parents had resumed their nightly routine of mending and reading and then slipped out, unobserved. Her only regret was that she had not dared wear her most becoming Sunday frock—a white batiste dress with a wide cummerbund that flattered her lithe figure. Honest as she was, it would have been difficult for her to explain her appearance in a festive outfit if she had been seen leaving the house.

Instead, she wore her green cotton dress, its ruffled collar the only ornament that framed her face and luxurious hair that was twisted into a knot at the back of her neck. She was pleased with the result, for she had succeeded in transforming the image of a schoolgirl with bow-tied tresses into a fetching young woman.

Her rendezvous with Count Alexei was at the iron grille gate of the Summer Garden, and rounding the corner toward it, she discovered she was not alone on this clear white night. Couples strolled unhurriedly along the promenade, their soft voices wafting toward her. She paused at the corner, hugging the fence, afraid to chance recognition by a friend.

The gentle air of the summer evening began to work its magic on Nadya, and moments later she was inside the victoria with Alexei and racing toward the nightclub.

Her capricious memory blocked out the next several minutes. Perhaps she wanted to obliterate her sense of awkwardness in walking into a nightclub where she felt conspicuous and inappropriately dressed for the evening, anxious to get through the crowded place and to the private dining room he had promised to reserve.

Once inside the spacious salon, Nadya stood wide-eyed. Bathed in the glow of soft lights, the red velvet furniture harmonized with gold brocaded draperies, tasseled and ribboned around the lace-curtained windows. It was more than a dining room. Cushioned divans and deep armchairs were cozily arranged in one corner against burgundy velvet drapery that covered the middle of the wall. Alexei, however, steered her to the opposite end of the room, where a linen-covered table was set with gleaming china and silver for two.

She remembered the food served at that epicurean dinner so clearly she could taste it years later, but the dialogue between them evaporated into the magic night as surely as the passing of the night itself.

They nibbled on beluga caviar spread over tiny slices of thin white bread, its flavor enhanced by champagne, which they sipped from heavy crystal goblets, the sharply cut stem cold in her trembling fingers. She had always loved the delicate flavor of the red salmon caviar she had at home over hefty chunks of buttered rye bread, but eating these tiny gray-green pearls immersed in the bubbly sweetness of the wine was an intoxicating experience. The pungent smoked goose and the iced fruit bombe that followed were delicacies she had only read about.

When the meal was over, Alexei unbuttoned the collar of his dolman and leaned back in his chair. His exposed neck made him appear unexpectedly vulnerable, and Nadya fought a powerful urge to touch his skin and kiss the hollow of his neck with tenderness and devotion. A tingling warmth trickled through her veins. The room took on a silken atmosphere, and somewhere beyond the thick walls the Gypsy violins began to sing.

As she listened to the music, she dared not look at Alexei. She could hardly believe this was really happening to her. Alexei was introducing her to a world which otherwise she would never have known, a world of elegance and charm that touched the senses and thrust the mind into a different dimension, where bourgeois conventions were out of place.

When the strains of a Viennese waltz replaced the Gypsy song, she was pulled to her feet, encircled in Alexei's firm embrace, and whirled around the room. Although of medium height, she fitted perfectly against his tall body.

"You're a beautiful dancer, Nadya," Alexei marveled. "You follow my lead with such ease. I wonder who taught you."

Pleased with the compliment, Nadya smiled. "Sergei taught me. I've danced only with him."

"You mean you've never danced with anyone else?"

There was genuine surprise in Alexei's voice, and Nadya flushed, reluctant to remind him of her youth or to confess that she had not yet attended a ball.

"Sergei is the best dancer I know," she said, then added hastily, "until I met you, that is!"

Alexei's eyes narrowed, and he tightened his grip around her waist. "You talk about him so much I'm glad he is your brother. Otherwise, I might be jealous!"

He whirled her faster and faster until dizzy and unsteady on her feet, she slumped against his shoulder with an embarrassed laugh. "I've never danced this fast before," she said breathlessly. His warm lips touched her neck, and it was then that she felt her breath cut off by a fire surging through her body.

The night became a fusion of rhythms and lyrics, a poem of senses, a thrill in the velvet of touch. Details melted away: the fleeting hesitation, the embarrassment in moving toward the heavy curtain at the end of the room which she originally had mistaken for a draped window and which turned out to be a hidden niche with a cushioned sofa behind, the discarded clothes, the darkened room, the feathery eiderdown. All this had blurred, receded, and she was consumed by delicious pleasure from his gentle, unhurried coaxing.

His tenderness and restraint, almost reluctance, to show his passion lulled her fears and inflamed her. Time ceased to move. It was a dream, yet not a dream, a gradual union of senses that flowed, stopped, and held suspended for an exquisite instant, then plunged abruptly into a current which gathered momentum and grew to become a centripetal force that no power on earth, no power at all, could have controlled at that moment.

So potent was the force suddenly straining to escape, so

excruciating in its urgency, that the pain, when it finally came, was transformed into a welcome release from this unbearable, subliminal experience.

So Nadya, removed from her daily humdrum life and enveloped in luxury, showered with attention and treated with respect and sensitivity, floated to the heights of a fantasy world where love and submission excluded all doubts and common sense.

Having crossed her Rubicon without reservations, she could not but marvel at her good fortune for having been chosen by such a perfect man. She would not have wanted it to be otherwise, for in spite of what happened in years to come, she never regretted that first night.

Nadya viewed the world around her through half-closed eyes during the ride home through the deserted streets. Encircled in Alexei's arms, filled with languor in the afterglow of satisfied intimacy, she did not speak, afraid their voices might destroy the fragile world around them.

This time Alexei let her off only a few doors from her house. "I dare not come any closer. Will you be all right, *golubka*, my dove?" he whispered, kissing both her hands.

She nodded and smiled, and he squeezed her hands. "When shall I see you again?"

"As soon as I can get away."

Her room was filled with the balmy air of the summer night, and Nadya, stretching luxuriously under a light eyelet coverlet, closed her eyes and smiled. She felt wondrously buoyant. Alexei had behaved like the gentleman that he was, and it had been her own passionate nature that seduced him. It was intoxicating to discover the power she held over this aristocrat, this refined and handsome man. He loved her, and they were pledged to each other for life.

In the subsequent days and weeks she stole the hours from evening study, grateful that she was able to get passing grades with a minimum of work. She led a double life now, and the bliss began to spill into her domestic existence. She knew that no plans could be made until after she had finished school, and in the meantime, a life of duplicity added spice to her days and made the hours spent without Alexei bearable. She began to write impassioned poems, which she hid in her drawer, and studiously avoided her mother's probing looks.

Then, within a few months, she discovered that her mother was dying.

Chapter Eight

An early autumn replaced the summer months, and when winter came, it cleansed the city with a layer of fresh snow. In the quiet of its muffled sounds, whispers of violence in the world drifted to the Russian capital, but Nadya ignored them. Her affair with Alexei had taken on a pattern. When her evening absences from home had become difficult to explain, their trysts at the nightclub were replaced by afternoon rendezvous. It was easier for her to tell her parents that she'd be late from school on certain days than have to endure Sergei's brooding, suspicious eyes or Anna's sighs and searching looks. Only one more time did her mother try to question her. "I don't want you to regret anything later, Nadyenka," she told her with such sadness that Nadya vehemently denied seeing anyone at all. It was her own affair, and she resolved to keep it that way. Nothing at all must intrude into her private happiness.

Alexei had arranged a quiet time in his apartments at the family mansion, where they would be left undisturbed. By now she had overcome the embarrassment of having to slip in the side door of the palace, where the servants were discreetly absent and where she hurried along the corridor to his suite.

She had come to know his rooms in minute detail. Rare volumes of first editions in moroccan leather filled his study. Some lined the glassed-in cabinets; others lay stacked on side tables or were left open on his desk. A heavy crystal decanter of brandy, half full of the ruby liquid stood on a silver gallery tray with two snifters by its side.

In the adjoining bedroom his four-poster bed was effectively screened by its loosened brocaded baldachin, and the rest of the room was cluttered with family photographs, soft armchairs, a Karelian birch armoire, and matching nightstands.

Whenever she crossed the threshold of his study, she never failed to feel the magic of its surroundings. The door would close silently, and she would fancy herself a countess who belonged to the Persiantsev family.

Her doubts about their continuing relationship always evaporated in his presence, only to reappear when the sobering drabness of her family life greeted her at home. What were Alexei's intentions? She realized that she was still in school, but she could see no reason why they couldn't dream together about their future . . . unless he had no plans for them at all. No, she could not allow such disloyal thoughts about the man who told her over and over how much he needed her! He had become an intense and vocal lover, telling her repeatedly in an infinite variety of Russian endearments how much he adored her.

This afternoon Nadya saw Alexei's victoria waiting for her in the usual place behind the Summer Garden. The coachman greeted her with deference, and she suddenly enjoyed the clandestine nature of her affair, believing herself to be more experienced and mature than any of the aristocratic girls who lived within palace walls and were jealously guarded by their families.

Whatever pangs of guilt she might have had in the beginning about losing her innocence had been rationalized away by the self-image of an avant-garde woman who was planning to become a dedicated champion of the poor, once she was out of school. She had not stopped to consider how she was going to reconcile the two extremes of her goals—to become a socialist, on the one hand, and to marry a member of an aristocratic family favored at the imperial court, on the other. With the optimism of ingenuous youth she trusted the future to take care of itself.

On this day Alexei had been waiting for her in the bedroom, and when he emerged from it with the eagerness of an ardent lover, she forgot her doubts. He was wearing a satin-sashed smoking jacket of pale gold with quilted lapels, dark blue trousers, and a white silk ascot neatly wrapped around his neck. His eyes glowed with affection.

"Nadyenka!"

He scooped her into his arms and buried his face in her hair, tugging at her bow and loosening her braid.

"Let me look at you!" He pushed her back slightly and searched her face. "How lovely, how fresh you look, my *golubka*! Your large, tender eyes, the soft curve of your face—you're beautiful, and I've missed you more than you can imagine!" He kissed the hollow of her neck, sending rippling shivers down Nadya's spine. Suddenly weak, she felt dizzy as he lifted her in his arms and carried her to the canopied bed.

"Alexei, Alexei, I love you!" she heard herself cry, floating on the crest of rising desire, eager to blot out all thought of herself as Nadya Efimova, a schoolgirl from a bourgeois family. Instead, she was a countess—yes, Countess Persiantseva, Alexei's wife—and she had a right to his bed with its lace-bordered sheets and satin comforter and to the luxury of the silk-paneled walls of this palace. She was determined to resolve her conflict, but right now the intensity of his passion thrilled her. She enjoyed the heady power she held over him when, in the fusion of their bodies, he trembled and begged for her caresses with the fiery words of masculine impatience.

In the aftermath of their lovemaking she lay cradled in his arms, clinging to his muscular chest, tasting its salty beads of moisture on her tongue, and breathing in the musky fragrance of his skin.

Oh, she did not want to give up the fragile idyll of this afternoon! But the clock ticked on the mantel, the delicate bronze hands moving on, and time slid quietly to the moment of parting. It hurt. It always hurt, but before she was out of the palace, she was already planning their next meeting.

On this particular day her mother greeted her at the door. Of late Anna had shown unsteadiness of gait, stumbling over thresholds, as if raising her feet were too much of an effort, and bumping into furniture, bringing purple bruises to her arms and legs. Nadya had dismissed her mother's clumsiness to her middle age.

"Today I needed you, Nadya, to help me knead the dough. You know it's Matrona's day off. It seems you're always late on the days I need you."

It was not like her mother to be peevish, and Nadya looked at her closely. Purple rings circled her eyes, and blue vessels pulsated visibly through the shiny skin on her temples. Impulsively Nadya put her arms around Anna. "Oh, Mamochka, I'm so sorry to be late. If I had only known that you would be doing the dough, I'd have come home sooner."

Anna patted Nadya on the back and sighed. "I seem to be always tired lately. Perhaps when the spring mellows, I should go into the country for a few days of rest." She took Nadya's face between the palms of her hands and looked at her intently. Nadya felt the roughness of her mother's skin, the cold of her fingers, and found it difficult to endure the probing look in her faded eyes.

"Come, Nadyenka, our world is here in this house. How sad it is that dreams of youth do not survive. Come!"

Nadya held her breath, but Anna said no more.

A week later, when Nadya came home, she found her mother lying on the leather divan in the study, shivering uncontrollably. She threw her books on the desk and knelt by her side.

"Mama! What's the matter? Are you sick? Where's Papa? Why didn't you have Matrona bring you a blanket and some hot tea? Have you caught a chill?"

Nadya's questions poured out uninterrupted. Anna's eyes were half-closed, and her whispered words whistled in her throat. "Matrona has gone to the butcher shop. . . . Papa was called by the countess . . . Nadyenka, I need him home . . . as soon as possible . . . run to the palace and fetch him!"

"Yes, Mama, I'll go immediately!"

After throwing a blanket over her mother, Nadya ran out of the house. A thrill at the unexpected chance of seeing Alexei fought its way through her alarm. The joy that surfaced, however, brought with it a sense of guilt and she was thoroughly ashamed. Anna would never have dared disturb her husband on an important call, especially to the Persiantsev Palace, if she were not gravely ill indeed.

Chapter Nine

———————————————

Nadya pounded on the side entrance to the palace—the door that had become so familiar to her during the past few months. Alexei's *nyanya* opened the door and peered at Nadya over her metal-rimmed spectacles. "The good doctor's girl, aren't you? What brings you here?"

Her scratchy voice made Nadya shiver, but before she could answer, Alexei appeared behind the old woman. If he was surprised by her unexpected appearance, he didn't reveal it.

"Come in, mademoiselle." His smile was courteous and formal. "Nyanya, it's damp outside, let's not forget our manners!"

Oh, how nice it would have been if he had shown some small sign of pleasure at seeing her—a momentary lowering of his guard or perhaps some spontaneous gesture. She needed that warmth, but then, part of good breeding was to hide one's feelings in public, wasn't it?

With a quick glance at him—she dared not linger on his face —Nadya took a deep breath. "My mother is very ill, and I came to fetch my father. Is he here?"

Alexei shook his head. "Anton Stepanovich left about an hour ago. I'm sorry your mother is ill. Is there anything we can do for you?"

The old *nyanya* grabbed Nadya by the arms and turned her around with surprising agility. "He told me he was going to the Nevsky Prospekt to buy candy and then to the Alexander Nevsky Monastery to walk in the cemetery, to cleanse his spirit, he said. Hurry, girl, he may still be in the shop on the Nevsky."

"Wait!"

Alexei pushed past the old woman and steered Nadya outside. "My victoria is at the front entrance. Get in, I'll tell the coachman to drive you." He lowered his voice. "I'd go with you, but I'm afraid the tongues would wag, and there'd be some explaining to do at home. Good luck, *golubka!*"

With a few words to the coachman Alexei stepped back and bowed to her formally.

In the victoria Nadya held on to the armrest, her head spinning. The coachman, modestly dressed whenever he picked her up, was now resplendent in a red caped coat and matching three-cornered hat trimmed with gold braid and fur. She felt out of place in such an elegant coach. If only Alexei could have come along! Some explaining to do at home, he had said. She did not understand. There was nothing wrong in helping their doctor's daughter find her father in an emergency. She felt alone and frightened.

On the Nevsky Prospekt she ran into several candy stores and even went to Aux Gourmets, the most elegant confectionary in the city, although she doubted she would see her father there. At the large Gostiny Dvor department store she asked the coachman to stop and then searched the ground floor.

She realized she was wasting time. Getting back into the victoria, she told the coachman to race to the cemetery at the end of the Nevsky Prospekt. Once there, she was sure she'd find her father quickly. His favorite composers, Tchaikovsky and Rimsky-Korsakov, were buried near each other, and he often walked there in order to get away, he said, from the rush of the living. Beyond the gate she hurried along the wide road. The wind whispered and tugged at Nadya's heart the way a timid child pulls at the sleeve to ask questions. The restless wind fretted. It darted and whined and hid in the crevices of old cracked tombstones, and she imagined that it had huge, hollow eyes with deep pools, which concealed the souls of all the dead buried in the cemetery. She did not like this part of the graveyard and wished Sergei were by her side right now, helping her find their father.

She sensed her father's presence before she actually saw him. Stooped, his arms resting on his thighs, he was sitting with his head bowed, studying something on the ground between his feet. His overcoat of gray broadcloth hung loosely about him. He was hatless.

"Papa!"

He raised his head and looked at Nadya without surprise, as if he had half expected to see her.

"Papa, I've been looking all over for you! Mama is sick—very sick. Something must be terribly wrong with her, for she sent me to the Persiantsevs' to get you. They told me you might be here. Count Alexei insisted I take the victoria, and it's waiting for us outside."

She had always known her parents to be loving and solicitous of each other, yet now her father moved with deliberate inertia, as if he were loath to give up these moments of solitude. Surely if he knew how sick mama looked . . .

"Papa, let's hurry. Mama is alone in the house, and I've already been gone too long." She threw an exasperated look at him. "Papa, please!"

Finally awakened from his strange trance, Anton Stepanovich patted her on the shoulder and hurried after her. When the victoria pulled into their street, Nadya realized that her father had not been surprised at the news of her mother's illness. She looked at him.

"Papa, did you know Mama was ill? What's wrong with her?"

Nodding lightly in rapid succession as if in answer to his private thoughts, Anton Stepanovich looked away. Nadya could barely hear him.

"Yes, I knew. But what I hadn't expected was that it would go this fast. Nadyenka, my child, your mother has leukemia. It's an acute form, and there's nothing medical science can do to cure her." He blew his nose, busily wiping it with a large handkerchief.

Nadya flinched. What was he trying to tell her? Could it be —Nadya was afraid to finish her thought.

When they entered the flat, a frightened Matrona met them at the door. She was a peasant girl who helped with the housework and ran errands, always cheerful and smiling, and the terrified look in her eyes unnerved Nadya. Pushing her aside, she ran to the study.

Anna seemed asleep, breathing shallowly, irregularly. Anton Stepanovich knelt beside her, opened his medical bag, and ordered Nadya to leave the room. In a few minutes he came out, tears streaming down his cheeks. Nadya had never seen her father weep, and the sight of his grieving face shocked her.

"Nadyenka, go to your mother, child. She wants to see you."

Nadya rushed in. Anna turned her head slowly. "Come closer, Nadya, my strength is ebbing . . . it is hard to talk."

Nadya knelt and slipped her arm around her mother's shoulders. "Mamochka, you'll feel better soon, I know. Papa will help you."

Anna shook her head. "No, Nadyenka. Your father has done all he could. My time has come. I don't know how long it will be, but don't grieve for me. I go in peace . . . without regret. . . . You are a grown woman now and can take my place in caring for your father. He's a good man—an upright man . . . protect him if you can from too much sadness. And now there's something I want to say to you before Seryozha comes home."

Anna moved restlessly on the divan as if grasping at her draining energy. A few moments later she went on, her voice gaining strength from her words.

"Nadyenka, dear girl, I know your secret. You cannot fool a mother's heart. I don't know who it is you love . . . but I suspect. I can't condemn you, but if the wedding does not come, then marry someone else. A married woman is forgiven many sins, and if the pull is too strong for you, keep your former love discreetly in your heart. Do I shock you? We women must adapt ourselves to life's arrangement the best way we can in order to keep our sanity, even if it means resorting to a lie for the sake of expediency. . . . I did a foolish thing once . . . long ago . . . and for the rest of my life I refused to admit the existence of a strong emotion within me. I regret it now, Nadya. It probably would have made no difference in my life, but at least I would have been honest with myself and maybe . . ."

Anna left the sentence unfinished and stroked Nadya's hair. "You're strong, and I'm not afraid for you."

How thin and transparent her arms are, Nadya thought irrelevantly, half listening to her mother's words and watching Anna's hands grasp the blanket and pull it up to her neck.

"I know Sergei has filled your head with his idealistic thoughts about freedom," Anna went on, "but you listen to me, Nadyenka. We are decades away from that kind of freedom. It includes love, even if he doesn't realize it himself. A fallen woman is not admired in our society, and above all, you want to keep your self-respect. . . ."

Anna's voice trailed off into a whisper. "Keep your standards high, but not too high. . . . Then the disappointments will not be so shattering. I go soon, child . . . bury me at the Alexander Nevsky . . . under the lindens somewhere."

Choked up, Nadya ran out of the room and called for her father. Anton Stepanovich hurried into the study and closed the door behind him.

In her room Nadya sat on her bed, stunned. Her mother was dying, and her incredible words were sinking in slowly. Mama knew of her affair with Alexei. She had known and did not condemn her. On the contrary, she had told her that for the sake of respectability she should marry someone else. Her mother, too, had doubts about a marriage between Nadya and Alexei. But then Anna didn't know Alexei as Nadya did. Yet the doubt was revived. What exactly had her mother been trying to tell her?

Nadya was confused. She couldn't marry someone without love, not after having experienced intimacy with the man she adored. Ecstasy would turn into indignity. Maybe it was possible to love two men at the same time with a different kind of love. Perhaps another woman could, but not she, Nadya. Her love was intense, pure, uncompromising. She had room for only one man in her heart. Besides, it was only a matter of time before Alexei and she would be married. It couldn't be otherwise.

Anna lingered for two more days. She asked for her daughter, but when Nadya came in, she could no longer talk. Struggling to raise her head, she held Nadya's glance with a desperate urgency to convey a message. Slowly, shakily, she lifted a white, shriveled hand and pointed to the top shelf of her bookcase. The effort was too much for her, and she dropped back on the pillow, her fluttering eyelids closed. Uncertain of what her mother was trying to tell her, Nadya pulled a taboret to the bookcase and, standing on it, reached with her hand to the top shelf. Feeling her way among the dusty volumes and stacked magazines, she picked up a soft leather volume lying hidden behind a row of books. It was fastened with a leather flap and a locked brass fitting. She ran her hand over the shelf again but could not find the key.

Nadya took the book to her room, and that evening she held it for a long time. Her mother's diary. Surely, that was what it was. She had seen many such diaries in the stationery stores. And now her dying mother wanted her to read it. But it was locked, and Nadya could not bring herself to cut the leather strap. Something within her rebelled against mutilating the old leather-bound volume. She turned the diary over and over in her hands. Why not be honest with herself? What was really upsetting her was the responsibility of burrowing in her mother's soul. Perhaps some descendant of hers who would not know Anna could read the diary objectively in the future, but she, her daughter, could not. After all, she shouldn't presume that her mother wanted her to read it. Much more likely she wanted her daughter to safeguard it from other curious eyes. Of course! She would hide it and guard it.

And that is what she did.

The next day Anton Stepanovich emerged from the bedroom.

Gaunt and stooped, dark rings circling his eyes, he called to his daughter, "Nadyenka, go next door and fetch Olga Ivanovna to come help with preparing your mother—" He did not finish the sentence, waved his hand weakly, and went to his study. Nadya tiptoed to the door of the bedroom and peered inside. Her mother was lying peacefully on her back, her hands crossed on her chest, eyes closed. *She's asleep, that's all. She's only asleep*, Nadya kept thinking. She couldn't make herself go in and kiss her mother's cold forehead as she knew she should. Instead, she turned away and went to the next-door neighbor for help.

When Sergei came home and found his mother dead, he shut himself in his room without a word and stayed there for a long time. When he emerged, his eyes were red from crying, and when Nadya tried to talk to him, he yelled at her to keep out of his way.

After the neighbors had bathed and dressed and combed her mother, they laid her out on the dining room table and lit the vigil light beneath the icon of the Virgin Mary. Against her mother's hands they leaned a small icon of St. Nicholas, the miracle worker, and then withdrew, leaving the grieving family to mourn in privacy. The next day a nun was summoned to intone prayers while Sergei went out to get a coffin.

Nadya sat in the room, shivering from imaginary cold. She did not sleep that night. She kept hearing her mother's voice, encouraging, chiding, sighing, and all her simple daily words reverberated softly and distantly in the silence. In the morning Nadya heard the level pitch of the prayers but did not listen to the words. She sat and looked at the lifeless form that had been her mother. A pale glow of the morning sun filtered through the curtains, touching Anna's bloodless hands. That couldn't be her mother! Nadya wanted to leave the room and found no energy to move. To spend the day with this eternal stillness was perhaps the worst of all—to feel the air of death in all the rooms, the dreadful permanency of her mother's silence. Nadya pressed her elbows against her ribs to stop the shivers. Dust particles floated and swirled in the shaft of light enveloping the room in a gossamer shroud. She focused on the tiny specks and never moved until Sergei came home.

After they had lowered Anna into the deep cavity at the cemetery, Anton Stepanovich picked up a handful of sandy earth and threw it into the open grave. It made a hollow sound as it hit the lid of the coffin, and Nadya felt a spasm in the pit of her stomach. She vowed to avoid funerals from that day on, to cling to the memory of the living.

How could she have known then that her mother had been one of the lucky ones to have died a year before the Great War and four years before her country went mad with fratricide?

Chapter Ten

When Nadya turned eighteen, she was graduated from the gymnasium. In anticipation of Alexei's proposal she was counting the days since he had left on a trip to Paris. It was his fourth absence in a year, and upon his return he would describe the fabulous city in detail.

But Alexei did not come home.

June ended with the assassination of the Austrian heir to the throne, Archduke Franz Ferdinand, and his wife, in Sarajevo, and one month later Europe was at war. On August 2, 1914, Sergei said to Nadya, "I'm going to the Palace Square."

"What for?"

Sergei's mouth twisted. "To witness history in the making. Look out the window. Everyone is hurrying in that direction. If you were outside, you'd feel the pulse of the excitement."

"Don't go, Seryozha! There may be bloodshed again. This time you may not get off so easily."

"Silly girl. There isn't going to be any bloodshed today. We're going to hear what the tsar has to say."

"Father Gapon, too, went to see the tsar in 1905, and it became Bloody Sunday. I'm not going to let you leave the house alone. I'll go with you."

Sergei seemed to waver, then relented. "I'm leaving right away, so hurry!"

At the Palace Square there must have been five thousand people waiting for a glimpse of the tsar. Nadya and Sergei pushed their way in and listened to the whispers around them. "Germany has declared war on Mother Russia! That *nyemka*—the German woman in the palace—is responsible for this!"

A woman was wringing her hands. *"Oi*, our sons, our brothers will perish, but we'll hold our land against the invaders!"

When the tsar appeared on the palace balcony—a slight and dolorous figure in uniform—the throng knelt and a chorus of "God Save the Tsar" rose above the square. Sergei, his lips suddenly tight, pulled Nadya by the sleeve. "Come on, Sestryonka, I've changed my mind . . . we have nothing to do here."

They threaded their way out of the crowd and headed home across St. Isaac's Square. There Sergei paused before the German Embassy and pointed to the bronze horses on its roof. "The mob's mood is ugly. Mark my words, they'll ransack the embassy. The anti-German sentiment is strong, and the tsar hopes it will deflect the workers' anger away from him. I can assure you it won't. Whatever unity our people feel right now will quickly dissipate in combat, and the war will speed up the revolution." He laughed a cold, mirthless laugh. "The tsar is playing right into our hands, Sister!"

His voice sent ripples of fear through Nadya. "Why are you so full of hate, Sergei? What has the tsar done to you personally?"

"It's not only the tsar. It's his whole entourage, the select few who think they're better than the rest of us. Well, we'll show them, and soon!" Sergei shook his fist toward the Winter Palace.

"And who is 'we'?"

"The Bolsheviks, Nadya, the Bolsheviks! Lenin alone knows the psychology of the masses and how to use it."

"I don't know what he can do while he's hiding abroad."

"He's waiting for the moment to return, and when that happens, watch out!"

At night Nadya tossed in bed, confused and torn by her conflicting loyalties. She loved her brother and wanted to be involved in his activities, but Sergei's impassioned words frightened her. She suspected that what went on at the *besedy* he attended would shock her, and that's why he had not yet taken her with him. In spite of her beliefs that democracy was long overdue in Russia, deep in her heart she could not agree with the radical measures advocated by the Bolsheviks.

Invariably her thoughts turned to Alexei. She loved him with a deep, uncompromising love, and although he was an aristocrat, she was sure that his deep feelings for her would surmount their differences and that she would bring him about to her way of thinking.

A week later the mood at the family dinner table was somber. Anton Stepanovich looked particularly tired as he poked at his cabbage soup without appetite. Nadya placed a worried hand on his arm.

"Papa, why aren't you eating? You work so hard you need to eat."

Her father smiled. "You're my little mother, aren't you? I'm too tired today. All this excitement about the war and then the hysteria at the Persiantsev Palace over young Count Alexei. The countess is acting up again, this time over her son's orders to the front."

Sergei looked up sullenly at his father. "I don't know why she should worry. I'm sure the old count will find a way to keep his precious offspring from going to battle."

"You misjudge him, Sergei. He's very proud that his son is going to war and is encouraging him to leave right away. That's why I was summoned there today. The countess has the vapors because Count Alexei is due to leave in three days."

"I thought he was in Paris?"

"He was. But he came home two days ago."

Nadya rose and collected the dirty dishes. Her hands shook so badly that she had to clutch the plates, afraid to drop them. The way to the kitchen was through a narrow pantry. *One step after the next. Don't trip over the leg of the chair, and watch the floor planks that rise and fall with each beat of the heart. Two more steps, maybe three, then out of the dining room, through the pantry swinging doors, and into the kitchen. Matrona has already gone for the day, thank God. Place the dishes on the kitchen table. Carefully. Quickly, over to the sink and relieve the tightened stomach of its dinner* burden.

Home two days and hadn't called her. How could this be? Maybe she had missed his call, and the victoria had waited for her yesterday in the usual place. She'd go there. Tonight. There was so little time left. He must be frantic trying to reach her. Of course. She'd leave after the dishes were done and run to where the victoria would be waiting.

War. The cursed war. The tsar and the tsarina and their holy Rasputin were safe, but Alexei had to go. She'd see him tonight. She'd talk to him, beg him to be careful, and she'd love him with a passion of complete abandon.

But the street behind the Summer Garden was empty. She stood in the shadows, and, in spite of the humid air, drew her muslin shawl around her shoulders. Victorias rolled by, but none stopped to fetch her. Why hadn't he been in touch with her? She lingered, conjuring up foolish excuses for his not leaving the palace, and at last, disappointed, went home.

The next day she waited in the same place for a whole hour past the usual time without seeing the victoria. In the evening she slipped out again. This time she went directly to the Persiantsev Palace, where she watched the side entrance from across the street. Afraid to attract attention of a policeman by standing in one spot, she walked slowly up and down the sidewalk, but never too far in either direction. She counted the steps—twenty paces up the street and twenty back, then twenty in the opposite direction and back again—all the time keeping her eyes and head turned slightly toward the palace. For the first time in her life she resented the white night where there was no cloak of winter darkness to hide her from onlookers.

One more day and one more night. In the end she ran out of excuses.

The day after her father had mentioned that the young count had left for the front, she went to the post office. She knew that when Alexei wrote her, he'd address his letters to general delivery.

There should be a letter for her. There *had* to be. She nearly tore the letter out of the postman's hand as he handed it to her and then ran outside to read it.

> My Nadyenka, my *golubka*,
> You must know from your father what has happened in the last few days. What frustration not to be left alone long enough to see you! I'm on my way to the front now and cannot write everything that is in my heart. So much to tell you—to share with you. I shall miss you terribly. I love you —love you madly. I don't know when I shall be able to write again, but keep watching for my letters. Let's hope this war will not last long and I shall come home to you soon.
> Your adoring Alexei

Nadya walked home on air. ". . . so much to tell you . . . to share with you . . . cannot write everything that is in my heart . . ." What a thoughtful man he was to take precautions in his letter in case it fell into wrong hands and embarrassed her. How romantic not to have mentioned marriage on paper. Those special words he surely wished to save for the day when they would be in each other's arms again.

Oh, how she loved him. . . . She would pray for his safety, and she would not complain. How could she? She was safe at home while he was endangering his life at the front. She must not think about that. Her thoughts must not attract disaster.

Once she knew that he was gone, it became easier to resign herself to the idea that she might not see him for months. In the meantime, she had duties at home, and there were opportunities for her to get involved in the war effort. Surely she could do something to assuage the hardships of the poor and the dispossessed. There was no question of her going to the university—she was needed by her family. Her father's practice and Sergei's additional earnings from tutoring students helped make ends meet.

Determined to live one day at a time, she kept to herself and watched the developing events with alarm.

In the spirit of patriotism, St. Petersburg was renamed Petrograd, German suffix *burg* being replaced by the ancient Russian word *grad*; Sergei thought it childish and argued the point for hours with his friend Yakov Oblevich. The German Embassy was attacked, just as he had predicted, and the bronze horses on top of the building were thrown into the Moika. The country's mounting hatred centered on the German tsarina. The people blamed her for the failures of Russian campaigns and even criticized the imperial women for donning white uniforms and nursing wounded soldiers. Although Nadya thought it a noble gesture on the part of the tsarina and the grand duchesses to do menial and at times difficult work at the hospital, she realized that it did little to curb the grumbling, unfair and tinged with fear as it was.

Nadya began to write impassioned patriotic poetry, some of which was published. Before long Sergei seemed to sense a change in her, a subtle withdrawal from the outside world, and as in years past, he started to spend more time with her. They talked of the war and of their daily problems, avoiding the deeper substance of their lives, as if each feared to discover dark corners neither was willing to probe.

Then, one day, Sergei burst into the house, shouting something about his friend Vadim Razumov's dying mother and calling for his father and sister to come with him.

Nadya was filled with sudden warmth, remembering Vadim's kindness to her at the sled run when she was twelve.

It took them less than twenty minutes to reach the other end of the Nevsky Prospekt and turn into a familiar side street where Nadya had spent many hours browsing in a bookstore.

She pulled her brother by the sleeve. "Seryozha, where does she live?"

Sergei nodded toward the bookstore. "She rents a room next door to where she works."

The bookstore. Nadya closed her eyes remembering. Many times she'd been in the two-room bookshop lined with ceiling-to-floor shelves, stacked with rare, hard-to-find classics at prices Nadya could not afford. Yet she loved the smell of aged leather-bound volumes. She would sit on a wooden taboret, glossy from constant use, and busy herself with leafing through the dusty books, pretending she was making up her mind which ones she would buy. All the while she sensed that the elderly lady behind the counter was aware of her hunger for literature and tolerated her presence. The kind lady of sparse words who went along with Nadya and played the rehearsed scene of "Didn't find anything today, my dear? Well, maybe next time," was Razumov's mother!

Now she wanted in some way to repay Vadim's mother for her kindness.

It was like stepping into the night. The autumn sun and the fresh air vanished, and they walked into a blackness weighted with the pungency of a stagnant sewer. Like a cat with honed night vision, Sergei bolted up the steps, leaving Anton Stepanovich and Nadya holding on to the railing behind him, their feet cautiously sliding over each step.

By the time they reached the third floor Sergei had already opened the door. A dim light filtered into the hall, shadowing the walls and the narrow steps.

Framed in the doorway, a solidly built man of medium height blocked the entrance to the room beyond. A mane of brown hair hung in unruly thickness over his forehead and ears, and thick brows arched over large hazel eyes that looked at Sergei with a mixture of warmth and pain. As he moved his face out of the narrow shaft of light, Nadya caught the sharp angle of his jaw, the muscular neck, the frayed edge of the shirt's open collar. Memory of that Christmas six years before, when she had gone sledding and met him at the ice hill, came flooding back.

"Too late, Seryozhka. It's all over. *Spasibo droog*. Thank you, my friend." His voice was deep and resounding in the empty corridor.

Sergei put his hand on his friend's shoulder. "Vadka, I brought my father and Nadya with me. I thought we could help." He shook his head and let his hand drop.

Vadim turned toward Anton Stepanovich, his face in the shadow now, the leonine head silhouetted against the light. "Thank you for coming; I'm sorry to be meeting you under these circumstances. Please, let me lead you downstairs through this dungeon."

Before any of them could protest, he slipped past them and started down the stairs. The door remained ajar, and there was just enough light to see the outlines of the steps.

Out on the sidewalk Nadya shook hands with Razumov warmly. Vadim smiled. "I see that Sergei's *sestryonka* has grown up. You're a kind girl to come along today. Thank you."

Impressed by the power and the warmth of his personality, Nadya decided it would be superfluous to say any words of condolence to this man, who looked to be in complete control of himself in spite of the sadness in his eyes.

Anton Stepanovich touched Vadim's arm. "Don't you want me to give you a death certificate?"

"Thank you, Dr. Efimov, but I'd best get in touch with the clinic where Mother received care and let it follow through on this."

"It isn't necessary, you know. I could save you that chore while you took care of other details."

"I don't want to appear ungrateful, but the truth is I'm used to taking care of things myself. I appreciate your willingness to be of help, but doing necessary tasks will keep my mind on other things." Vadim's voice was friendly but firm.

His grief is private; he doesn't want to share it with us, Nadya thought, studying him surreptitiously. There was an aura of confidence about him, a feeling that he knew exactly what he wanted and was at ease with himself.

On the way home Nadya asked her brother why he had never brought Vadim to their house. Sergei thought for a moment, then said, "I guess I never thought about it. We meet and talk at meetings."

"He's a strong man of definite opinions," Anton Stepanovich commented, then added hastily, "in a courteous, quiet sort of way. I like men like that."

Sergei nodded. "You're right, Papa. I remember Mother saying to us whenever we argued, 'Children, lower your voices; tone makes the music.'"

Several days later Vadim came to call and stayed beyond the customary twenty minutes a formal visit prescribed.

They sat in the study, in the cozy atmosphere of the family

room, rather than in the more formal front parlor, which doubled during the day as the patients' waiting room and was always permeated with medicinal smells. Vadim fitted easily into the crowded study, very much at ease next to Nadya on the leather divan. After exchanging a few words with their guest, Anton Stepanovich excused himself and went back to his office. Sergei rose, opened the glass doors of the book cabinet, and, reaching into the back, pulled out a small bottle of brandy.

"I hide this for special occasions. How about a sip to warm your blood, Vadka?"

"Thanks, Seryozha, but none for me. I've just come from the workers' meeting at Vyborg, and I'd feel guilty sipping this luxury after what I've seen and heard there."

"What happened in Vyborg, Vadim?" Nadya asked, leaning forward. Ordinarily reserved and shy in the presence of new acquaintances, she felt no such reticence with Vadim. *He fits in with us so well,* she thought, *as if we'd known him all our lives.* Familiar, friendly. A nice man. A sincere man with an unaffected manner. She liked him.

Vadim looked at her for a moment before answering. "What did I see in Vyborg, you ask? Nothing but misery. Whole families live and work in one room, renting a curtained-off corner to a stranger, their beds nothing but a row of planks. While we conducted the meeting, everyone smoked, yet a few steps away a baby slept in a makeshift cradle fashioned out of burlap sacks and suspended by ropes from a hook in the ceiling."

Nadya was horrified. "That's dreadful!" she cried. "I've never heard of anything so sad."

"Not surprising, Nadya," Vadim said. "After all, you're still a child yourself."

"I'm not a child. I am eighteen years old."

Vadim patted her hand. "Well then, Nadya, after eighteen years, welcome to Russia."

He said it with irony rather than sarcasm, and Nadya, filled with pity for the unknown infant, turned to her brother. "You've never told me about such squalor."

"I saw no need to give you graphic descriptions of something that has existed for centuries. I felt you'd learn about it soon enough."

"Is that all the workers can afford?"

"As it is, their pay is only twenty-two rubles a month," Vadim said quietly. "You see, Nadya, unless you can do something about it, why bother to examine a shocking situation? I'm sure your friends don't know about such things either, so you needn't feel that you're the only one uninformed."

Nadya flushed, realizing that Vadim unwittingly had put her on the defensive. She looked at Sergei. "Why don't you let me come to one of your meetings? I want to learn and help." She paused for a moment, then added, "Although I wonder if we shouldn't wait until the war is over."

"You may have a point there——" Vadim began, but Sergei interrupted.

"On the contrary, Nadya, this is the best time to bring about a change. When people are suffering privations, when hunger knocks at each door of the *izba* in the country, that's when they will pay attention to our words."

"But who will guide them now?"

"We will. The intelligentsia and the students in particular have to incite the workers and make them demand better treatment and greater reforms. For who is leading our country now? The tsar is constantly changing premiers, and now our country's destiny is dictated by that madman Rasputin. Do you wonder why we want a new government?"

Nadya touched Vadim's sleeve. "I'd like to go to one of your meetings. Will you take me with you?"

Vadim hesitated, then looked at Sergei. "What do you say, Seryozha?"

Sergei shook his head. "If the government hadn't outlawed public meetings, I wouldn't hesitate, but our secret *besedy* are dangerous. You know yourself, Vadim, that we're vulnerable to a police raid at any time. I don't fear for myself, but I'd hate to endanger Nadya."

"How about bringing her with you to our favorite *traktir* near the Liteiny Prospekt? With so many transients coming and going in the pub, we've been able to talk unnoticed, and I think we're still relatively safe there."

"I guess it would do no harm to let her come along," Sergei conceded reluctantly.

"When can I go with you?"

Nadya's excitement was mounting, and she hoped it wasn't too obvious. Her brother was overprotective of her; he had trouble getting used to the idea that she was already eighteen and no longer a child. How lucky she was to have met Vadim again! Thanks to him, she would come to know the people of her country first hand.

Vadim's eyes twinkled. "Well, Nadya, we'll meet at the *traktir* next time. I'll teach you how to drink vodka!"

Chapter Eleven

"Well, well, what do I see? Sergei's little sister has come to join us! Miracles do happen, don't they?"

The voice belonged to Yakov Oblevich, who was sitting in the *traktir* with two men and a petite dark-haired girl. Nadya had just walked in with Sergei and Vadim, and it took her a few seconds to adjust to the poorly lit room and see through the haze of smoke.

She shook her shoulders to get rid of the gooseflesh the creaking of the heavy front door had made crawl over her arms. All the tables were taken, and people milled around, drinking and talking. Once-white tablecloths, yellowed with time, were spotted with dark stains and littered with bottles of beer and glasses of tea.

On the left, along the length of the room, a wooden counter displayed bottles, glasses, and plates of food, mostly sausages and sliced ham. Waiters in white aprons filled orders at the counter and skittered deftly among the tables.

As they approached their friend's table, Nadya saw that Yakov's hand cupped a small shot glass of vodka. The young man squinted through his metal-rimmed pince-nez and leaned back with a wide sweep of his arm. "Take a chair. Join us, comrades!"

Sergei pulled out a bentwood chair for Nadya, and she noticed that no one at the table rose to greet them.

Yakov looked at Sergei and nodded in the direction of the girl sitting beside him. "You haven't met Esther Fisher yet, Sergei. She's our new member, fresh from the country. Esther, this is Sergei Efimov, his sister, Nadezhda, and Vadim Razumov."

The dark-haired girl nodded slowly without smiling. After they had sat down, Sergei introduced the other two men to Nadya as his classmates, Ivan and Fyodor Shlyapin. Their haggard, anxious faces gave them prematurely aged appearances, and Nadya was surprised to learn that they were Sergei's contemporaries. She looked at Esther, who hadn't said a word. Long, thick eyelashes concealed nearly black and what seemed like fiery eyes of the young woman, and although her hair was tightly pulled back, a few curly wisps framed her face in defiant disarray.

Yakov's mouth spread into a thin line as he surveyed Nadya with narrowed eyes. "How come we're honored by your sister's presence, Sergei?"

Sergei pointed at the small glass in Yakov's hand. "A few swigs of that, and your mouth gets in the way, Yashka. A foggy brain and a loose tongue are a dangerous combination in our line of work."

"Your behavior is strange, Yakov," Nadya said quietly. "In our house you act quite differently."

The moment she said it, she regretted it. Yakov continued to smirk. "Well said, Nadya, but not all of us have had the privilege of good breeding. Esther here and I came from a village so dilapidated and poor that our Jewish families had to think of where our next piece of meat was coming from or how long it would be before a crooked pole collapsed the roof in our shed." Yakov raised his glass to Nadya in a mock toast, then went on. "Parlor niceties were low on our priorities."

Nadya met Esther's eyes for an instant. The young Jewess frowned and pulled the glass of vodka out of Yakov's hand. "You've had enough," she said quietly, her voice melodious and firm. "Nothing is to be gained by your sarcasm. Besides, poverty does not preclude good manners, so hold your tongue."

"A fine introduction for our young friend here," Vadim said, and turned to a passing waiter. "Bring us hot tea, my good man, and some black bread." He smiled at Nayda. "I'm in an expansive mood tonight."

Kind Vadim, Nadya thought. *He wants to welcome me into their group with the traditional bread and salt. Leave it to him to break the tension!* Yakov was drunk and had to be excused. And Esther by his side: a young intense girl . . . yes, intense, that's what she was, tuned like the strings of a violin—taut and sensitive. Nadya looked at Sergei. Her brother was staring at Esther with eyes wide and shining, a luminescence in them she had never seen before. She concealed a smile. Dear Seryozha, at last someone had caught his eye. But before she could dwell on this observation, a musician with an uncombed beard and a tattered shirt, his eyes milky and unseeing, felt his way to their table and lowered himself onto a stool next to Vadim. Tremulous, the sounds from his concertina ventured forth, silencing the crowd with a plaintive tune of old Russia. The melancholy ballad soared up into the smoke, reaching out to the young people around the blind man.

"We might as well talk under cover of music," Yakov, who had returned, said. "Fyodor, what news do you have for us today?"

One of the brothers glanced at the blind musician, hesitated for only a second, then pulled a stack of papers from a briefcase. "These are some of the pamphlets we've been able to print for distribution." He handed them to Yakov, and as he did, Nadya caught the heading "Proletariat of all nations, unite." Fyodor pulled another few pages out and this time, without looking at Yakov, handed them to Sergei. Nadya glanced over his shoulder. "Kill the Yids, save Russia!" it said.

Yakov grabbed the sheets out of Sergei's hands. His face turned red, and he hit the table with his fist. "Bastards! That's the proof that our ranks are infiltrated by the police. They've started a counterrevolutionary campaign against us."

"We don't know who originated these slogans," Vadim said, "and it really doesn't matter, so long as we make sure the workers know it doesn't come from us."

In the discussion that followed, they argued over who was going to write the next pamphlet for the factory workers, and after

Yakov had extolled Esther's skill, all agreed to let her be the writer for the group.

"A kopeck in the name of Christ!"

A querulous voice from behind startled Nadya. She turned to see a thin, stooped monk in a cone-shaped black cap, icicles dripping from his spindly whiskers and beard, bow to her obsequiously. "A kopeck for building the Lord's house in my village, kind people!" he intoned, turning and bowing again, this time to Vadim.

"We ourselves have little, and we don't believe in your God, *strannik*. But we have bread on the table; here, have a chunk!" Vadim's deep voice dominated the table as he broke off a piece of black bread, salted it, and handed it to the monk, who took it with a shaking hand and bowed deeply.

Through the mixture of smells Nadya suddenly inhaled the familiar aroma of fried cabbage.

"Pirozhki!"

A peddler's voice rose above the din at the door. "Anyone for *pirozhki?*"

On an impulse Nadya waved to the peddler and bought two cabbage *pirozhki*. She broke one in half and handed it to the monk.

Vadim's eyes met hers and held; he smiled. "True charity is not selective, is it?"

"I've never thought about it in those terms," Nayda said. "I'm sure hunger doesn't seek out its favorites."

Just then Esther leaned toward Ivan Shlyapin. "Ivan, I need paper for the pamphlets. I can write out the text on graph paper, but we need a fresh stack for printing."

"I can't get you any more," Ivan said. "My source is no longer available. The owner has become suspicious, and I don't dare try again."

"Well, then I'll have to do my own lifting. It shouldn't be too difficult."

"You mean you get the paper through illegal means?" Nadya asked.

Esther looked her straight in the eye. "You're too polite, Nadya.

What we mean exactly is that whenever the money runs out and we can't buy another supply, we steal."

"But you run the risk of being caught and thrown into prison as a common thief!"

"I won't get caught." Esther's voice was calm and assured. "I've had plenty of experience. I see it shocks you. Well, let me tell you something. My mother and father were scrupulously honest and taught me to be the same. I won't tell you what happened to them or to me. Honesty will neither save nor feed you. So you accommodate to survive."

Nadya studied her carefully. She realized that something dreadful must have happened to the young woman to have made her so bitter and cynical about life. There was a strange fire in her eyes that glowed, ready to explode, and seemed to fascinate Sergei. Nadya looked at her brother with tenderness. His sandy hair was neatly combed, and a new haircut exposed the mole near his right ear. A few bristly hairs stuck out of it rebelliously, no matter how often Sergei tried to cut them. Nadya suppressed a desire to put her arms around her brother and hug him. His face was turned toward Esther, listening, studying her intently as if nothing else mattered at that moment.

When it was time to leave, Yakov was so drunk that he leaned morosely over his cradled glass of vodka and refused to rise. The Shlyapin brothers pulled him up and half carried him toward the door. Sergei was quick—too quick—Nadya thought, to volunteer to take Esther home. Vadim caught Nadya's eye, smiled, and nodded. "Let's go, Nadya, I'll walk you home."

Outside, the damp mist of the November night shrouded the snow with a thin veil. A bluish carpet crunched under their boots, and for a while neither spoke. They shook their shoulders inside their coats, bracing their bodies for the change in temperature.

"Why isn't one of the Shlyapin brothers conscripted into the army?" Nadya asked.

"Ivan has leukemia, and doctors do not give him long to live. This makes Fyodor an only able son in the family and thus exempts him from serving."

"I wonder who this Esther Fisher is," Nadya said more to

herself than to Vadim. "There's such an air of tragedy about her —it seems to have hardened her. Such a beautiful, intense girl. She and her family must have been victims of a pogrom or something equally terrible."

"I don't know, Nadya, but from the way she talked, there is surely a story to tell. But then, considering the times we live in, which one of us can say there hasn't been some tragedy in our backgrounds?"

There was a quiet sadness in Vadim's voice, and Nadya threw him a sidelong glance.

"You're right; there are so many who have suffered some kind of loss in their lives. And what about you? You must be still grieving over your mother's death."

"Yes, I am. We were close. You see, Mother and I came to Petrograd after my father died of tuberculosis. He was a schoolteacher in Novgorod, where I was born. When we came here, Mother found work in the bookshop, and I tutored students in English while going to law school."

"English? Why English and not French?"

"French is a parlor language—useless except in the salons of our nobility."

For the first time Nadya detected a touch of bitterness in his voice. "Did you learn English in defiance of current trends, or was there another reason?" she asked without looking at him.

He was quick to answer. "I had nothing to gain by defying conventions. My choice was for practical reasons. My father, with great foresight, predicted that English, not French, will be the universal language in the future, and for a lawyer I deemed it more useful to learn English."

"Well, then I'd like to learn it, too."

Vadim slipped his arm through hers. "I'd be delighted to teach you. It'd give me an excuse to see you more often."

His candid words disarmed Nadya completely.

"How about giving me my first lesson right now?" she said teasingly.

"In the middle of the wintry night, cold enough to freeze our voices, you ask for a lesson? Very well, you will get it. But don't complain, for I won't let you go home until you say your first words correctly."

"Can't be all that hard," Nadya said. "I had no trouble with French."

Vadim stopped and swung her to face him. Their steaming breaths mingled, and Nadya's face warmed. Under a dim glow of the streetlamp Vadim's eyes twinkled. "Beware, Nadya, I'm a hard taskmaster."

"I'm not afraid. Give me a phrase."

"Ready? Repeat after me, 'Thank you.' "

Nadya looked at him suspiciously. "First tell me what it means."

"Oho! Cautious young lady! I like that. Be relieved, for I'm only teaching you to say thank you. Now say it! 'Thank you.' "

Nadya watched his lips and repeated, " 'Sank you.' "

Vadim burst out laughing. "I knew it! I knew it!" His laughter was so infectious that Nadya joined him without knowing what was so funny.

"Let me in on the joke, will you?"

"I'm sorry, I'm not laughing at you. English grammar is remarkably easy for us to learn; imagine, the nouns have no feminine or masculine endings, and there are no suffixes in declensions. But—and here is the catch—the spelling and pronunciation are something else! The sound *th* is particularly difficult for us, so I anticipated your saying 'sank' instead of 'thank.' A dirty trick on my part, but you didn't disappoint me."

It was impossible to take offense at Vadim, and Nadya struggled with the *th* sound, trying to please him. It suddenly became very important to her to please him, and before they reached her house, she succeeded.

"Good girl. You'll have no trouble learning it quickly."

As time went on, Sergei absented himself from the house more frequently, and because he was secretive about it, Nadya suspected he was seeing Esther. *As if I would mind, silly,* she thought good-humoredly. She had more time to spend with Vadim, who filled the void she felt in Alexei's absence and gave her a respite from the nagging worry for her lover's safety.

In spite of Vadim's warmth and humor, in spite of her responsibility for running the household, which gave her little time for leisure, a vague restlessness had taken hold of Nadya. The familiar coziness of their study, her favorite books, the evening talks with Vadim over the endless cups of tea no longer sufficed, and she found more and more excuses to pass the Persiantsev Palace and fantasize about its interior. She missed its elegance, its beauty, and in the face of her sympathies with the poor, she was ashamed of her yearning for material luxury. She should be fighting this unworthy trait in her character, but then, perhaps it wasn't that unworthy, only human. Besides, she must not forget the opportunities that the future promised. Married to Alexei, she would be able to do much for the cause of the underprivileged, not only by helping them financially but by establishing a line of communication between the privileged few and the suffering majority. She did not know yet how she was going to go about achieving all this, but she knew the first step would be to secure Alexei's support. It would take tact and perseverance, but she was eager to try.

November slipped into December, Christmas went by, and then, one day in February, Alexei wrote that he was coming home on leave and could hardly wait to see her.

Chapter Twelve

On a cold and cloudy February afternoon Nadya slipped into St. Isaac's Cathedral. Although she was not religious and in the past had questioned her mother's faith, she was nevertheless drawn to this church. It was not to pray, but to enjoy the opulence, the kind she had enjoyed in the Persiantsev Palace and had missed acutely since Alexei's departure for the front. After going with Sergei and Vadim to the dark, stuffy *traktir* and then moving about their own flat, which was drab with fading colors and permeated with disinfectant smells, her spirit cried out for beauty.

There were no afternoon services in the cathedral, and it was all but empty. Amazing, how light it was inside—all warm pinks and whites and pearl grays of the marble. She was sure that no one had seen her slip in. It wouldn't do—would it?—to have to explain her need to Sergei or Vadim; neither would understand.

She knelt by the railing in front of the altar and, bending low, pressed her forehead against the marble top. Its coolness soothed her. People said marble wasn't cold, it breathed, it was alive, and she believed it. She ran her finger along the edges of the square inlays of lapis lazuli. How smooth and silken they felt, and so did the longer strips of malachite. The vivid blues and greens—a treasure to enjoy. And the mosaic icons that lined the first two rows of the iconostasis—what a legacy they represented! Such beauty here—surely it wasn't wrong to love it!

How wonderful to let the mind float to heaven, to smell the scent of incense drifting from behind the gates of the iconostasis. If only Alexei were kneeling beside her now, how perfect it would be. She wondered where he was at that moment. Was he safe, or was he fighting somewhere in the trenches? His last letter, brief, hurriedly scribbled, told her little except that he was moving from one staff headquarters to another and was coming home on leave this month. She hoped it was really true and he was not trying to keep her from worrying. She realized that she knew nothing about his personal life, and she wondered how much he was protecting her. He hadn't learned yet—had he?—that she was resilient and strong, that she would be a true partner to him in marriage.

Then "Nadya!" Half whisper, half shout, her name was said harshly. Dear Lord, how was it that she had not heard her brother's footsteps? What should she do? What could she say?

He took her arm and pulled, but Nadya resisted. As long as she stayed where she was, he wouldn't dare raise his voice. He knelt on one knee beside her.

"Since when have you become religious? What kind of hypocrite are you? You come to the *traktir* with me, subscribe to our cause, and then I catch you praying. You've heard us say over and over that religion is the opiate of the people—and we didn't coin that phrase ourselves!"

Nadya listened to his tirade, surprised at the intensity of his anger. "If you keep quiet for a minute, I'll tell you why I'm here. You needn't accuse me of being a hypocrite. I don't come here to pray. I wouldn't know how."

"Then why?"

"Because this is the only place that gives me seclusion and time to think."

"What do you need seclusion for? You can have it at home in your own room. This is nothing but a marble morgue!"

"It's all in the point of view, Seryozha. Look around you." She raised her hand to silence him when he tried to interrupt her.

"Look at all this beauty and magnificence. How can you possibly call it a morgue?"

"Did it ever occur to you how much bread all this marble, gold, and lapis could have bought to feed the hungry?"

There he goes again, preaching, Nadya thought suddenly, *and I don't like it*.

"I don't want to talk about it anymore, Seryozha; this is hardly the place to have an argument."

"Then follow me outside."

"No. I want to stay here awhile; when I come home, we can discuss it then. Frankly I don't see what else there is to discuss, and I don't understand why you're objecting so vehemently to my being here. Please leave me alone."

Without a word Sergei rose and stalked out of the church.

He stopped on the sidewalk and took deep gulps of raw air into his lungs. He was choking. Not only had Nadya openly defied him for the first time ever, but she was obviously lying to him. All that monologue about the beauty of the church; what nonsense. She went there to pray. Even from a distance, when he had seen her go in, he could tell she was behaving furtively. He guessed for whom she was praying: Count Alexei. Ever since he had seen them together in the Summer Garden, he suspected that she was seeing him secretly. He had no definite proof, but there were so many little signs that added up to a whole.

The sharp air cut at his lungs. Sergei welcomed the pain. It took the edge off his anger, the anger that made him ashamed, for it always went back to its source. After all these years (how long had it been, twenty years?) it still rankled him to think about it, and he thought about it in flashes of colored scenes that flickered on and off like an electric light: vivid scenes, hateful.

He had been only nine at the time. His father had taken him to the Persiantsev Palace one afternoon when the countess had another attack of vapors and Dr. Efimov was summoned to attend her. His mother checked his gray serge suit to make sure it was pressed, brushed it with a small brush, and sent him off with his father.

At the palace the *nyanya* took his hand and led him to the nursery while Dr. Efimov ministered to the countess.

It was an airy, bright room with tall windows and a clutter of toys and blue and gold wallpaper; he remembered that wallpaper for some reason: big peacocks and bluebells. In the middle of the room stood a little boy a few years younger than he. Sergei had never seen a real live boy dressed in velvet before and stared at him with an open mouth, and as he stared, the boy's face colored.

"Close your mouth, *malchik*! Don't you know it is not polite to stare?" he said.

The *nyanya* led Sergei closer to the boy. "This is Sergei Efimov, the doctor's son. He is here to wait while the doctor is with your mother." Then, turning to Sergei, she said, "This is young Count Alexei, Seryozha. He will play with you."

Count Alexei led him reluctantly to his toy soldiers lined up on the parquet floor, and as the boys knelt beside the colorful little army in green and red, blue and white uniforms, Alexei began to name various regiments. Fascinated by the dazzling array of toys, Sergei picked up one of the soldiers, but Alexei wrenched the toy figure out of his fingers. Surprised by the sudden hostility, Sergei shoved Alexei away with his elbow and grabbed another soldier. A fistfight ensued, and as the *nyanya* tried to separate them, the double doors flew open, and Count Persiantsev walked in with Sergei's father.

Over subsequent years Sergei had wiped out the memory of the hurtful words his father said, but the injustice of being scolded in front of the haughty boy and, above all, the humiliation of being called an ill-mannered child by Count Persiantsev, were entrenched deep in his subconscious. As Dr. Efimov led his son out of the room, the count's parting words followed them: "I don't want your son's behavior to interfere with your medical duties, Dr. Efimov. You'd better leave him home next time." His father's quick acquiescence—"Yes, of course, Count, rest assured this will never happen again. I'll see to it!"—hurt Sergei to this day, and he could never understand his father's sudden outburst against him. He had not done it before or since. Sergei's smoldering resentment of the Persiantsev family grew and the personal hurt he felt expanded to encompass all the aristocrats in Russia, along with his sympathies toward the underprivileged.

Today had been a particularly trying day. The printing press had broken down, and Esther had telephoned him to see if he could find someone to repair it. One of the Shlyapin brothers was a mechanic, but Sergei could not reach him until that night, so he went, instead, to the post office where Esther worked as a typist. He took her to the nearby *pelmennaya*, where steaming *pelmeni* in bouillon would be a special treat on a frosty day.

As they ate the delicious meat dumplings at the tiny dinner table, enjoying the heat permeating their stomachs, Sergei watched the dark girl across from him and wondered if she realized that he knew her tragic background. Yakov had told him that her parents had been killed in a particularly vicious pogrom when she was sixteen, and although she ran into the fields, she had been caught and raped. The local rabbi and his wife had been kind and, taking her with them to live in another village, helped her face life again. When her schooling was over, she had run away from the memories and come to the city, where Yakov recruited her for their secret work.

Sergei, both fascinated and perturbed by her, could not sort out his conflicting feelings. She must have felt his stare and, looking up from her plate, stopped eating.

"You are staring at me. I do not like that. Speak. What is on your mind?"

Her remarks were uncomfortably succinct, leaving Sergei no room to clothe his words in subtleties. An extraordinary girl. He had never met anyone like her. What could he say without revealing his real thoughts?

"I was wondering if you ever take time to relax, to seek diversion," he finally asked.

Esther put her spoon down. "Whatever made you ask that? My life is now dedicated to a worthy cause. It takes organization and careful planning to achieve what we have set out to accomplish."

Sergei studied her curiously. "And what is your purpose exactly?"

"The same as yours. To bring about the revolution as quickly as possible."

"But you cannot do it alone. You need people around you; you need to communicate with them, make them understand your ideals."

"It can best be served through the printed page. Speeches are often impassioned, and passion is fleeting. It burns itself out and is quickly forgotten."

"You propose to work behind the scenes, is that it?"

Esther shrugged. "I follow my instincts. I never believed in empty rhetoric."

"What makes you think all rhetoric is empty? Sometimes it is necessary to pound new ideas repeatedly into the minds of simple people."

"Perhaps. But my pursuit is narrow and concise. I aim to destroy the decadence that is spreading like a miasma at the highest level. Once that is done, I plan to join my aunt in America."

"America! Why work for a cause and then abandon it at the moment of triumph?"

"There is no triumph for me in this work, only vengeance."

"You are intrepid. I fear for you."

"I am quite independent and self-sufficient."

"Don't you know that independence carries the burden of responsibility?"

"And you don't think I can be responsible for myself?" She lit a cigarette and squinted at him through the exhaled smoke. "I don't need to be preached to, Sergei. You're attracted to me"—she smiled at his obvious discomfiture—"and I don't reject your interest. But don't probe into me too deeply. I'm a private person."

Sergei gulped a spoonful of the soup to cover his embarrassment. "I meant no offense. Since we're working together for the common cause, I want us to be friends."

"Then let's be friends on the basis of what we see, without scraping at each other's soul." A corner of Esther's mouth went up in a half smile. "Don't you know that if you disturb the layers of dust, they may choke you?"

She paused for a moment, then said, "Now, tell me about yourself. You're a doctor, yet in the middle of the day you're spending time with me. What about your patients? Shouldn't you be with them?"

Sergei smiled. "You're very perceptive. I have no patients of my own. I only help lighten my father's load. You see, my primary interest is in research, and I spend most of my time at the institute."

"And your particular interest is?"

"New drugs to combat infectious diseases. And now, aren't you the one who is disturbing the layers of dust?"

Esther's smile was fleeting, and Sergei briefly enjoyed its warmth. "Touché! I stand corrected. And now that we know a little about each other, we can return to our common interest. Let me know when you reach Shlyapin. My hands are tied until that press has been repaired." She stubbed out her cigarette and rose. "I'd better get back to my work before I'm fired."

Outside, it had been blustery. After taking Esther back to the post office, Sergei had started for home. He raised the collar of his coat and, hiding his mouth in his muffler, dug his hands deep in his pockets. He was dazed. What a difference between this girl and his sister! Nadya always listened to him, and even when she argued, it was with deference and respect. Esther showed no such deference to his masculinity, no sign of awareness that she was anything less than his equal. In short, she behaved like a man, yet she was conscious of her femininity, her special brand of allure.

He was irritated by her, fascinated, piqued. And as he thought about her, he was suddenly aroused. The cold wind stung his face, his eyes teared, but the heat within him quickened his breath. It was then that he had seen Nadya slip into the cathedral.

He had vented his bottled-up emotions on his sister and was ashamed of it. He didn't need to be reminded of Count Alexei at that particular moment or to have Nadya defy him openly in the church. What was happening to him all of a sudden?

Standing outside the cathedral, his lungs and his body aflame, Sergei fought for control.

Nadya remained in the church. She had lost count of the hours, but she knew the longer she delayed going home, the better were the chances of Sergei's temper cooling off, and she wanted to avoid this discussion at all costs. The deep and abiding need for Alexei was her private secret, and she wasn't about to confide it to anyone, least of all her brother. She was carrying Alexei's last letter in her muff, and she held on to the thought of their reunion, the dreamlike, all-important rendezvous for which she had waited impatiently this long time with trust and hope. Her name, after all, was Nadezhda, and it meant "hope." Soon her dream was going to come true.

At the door she hesitated. On an impulse she bought a candle and went back behind the tall pillars to a white marble side altar, where she lit the taper before the icon of St. Nadezhda. Then, slipping her hands into her muff, she went outside.

It had begun to snow. Large flakes settled on her coat, clung to her eyelashes, powdered the sidewalk. She crossed the square, hurrying around the equestrian statue of Tsar Nicholas I, and turned into a side street. She did not want to go home. Not yet. It was a long walk to the Summer Garden, but she was drawn to it in spite of the cold. Walking in the back of the garden, she ran her mittened hand along the black grille, scooping the fluffy layer of snow.

A horse snorted ahead, and as she looked up, her heart stopped, leaped, then beat wildly. An ebony victoria was parked ahead, and Alexei's coachman was waiting by its side. As she approached him, he bowed and handed her a note.

She unfolded the note with fumbling hands. On the Persiantsev stationery with the family crest engraved in gold, was Alexei's broad handwriting. The words danced before her: "I shall be waiting for you tomorrow night, my love."

Chapter Thirteen

She was barely through the door of his study when she found herself in Alexei's arms.

He was crushing her. His body trembled, pressed against her, his arms sliding up and down her back; she could hardly breathe and felt his heart close to hers. It seemed to her that he needed to make sure she was real and that she was folded willingly into his arms.

And then the words came, a stream of them. More like a torrent they were; no sense in them at all, and all the sense in the world! Their own language, the music of love, silly and deep, meaningless and profound, and so tender.

Oh, she loved him so! She was with him in the familiar room she knew so well and had dreamed about these long months. She caught a glimpse of the burning fire, a reflecting sparkle in the crystal glasses set on the table, the iced champagne bucket with the white linen towel over its edge. No time for that now. Did he carry her to the bedroom, or did she walk, leaning against his shoulder? It didn't matter. She hugged him. Nothing could take him away from her now. The agony of passion was so acute, so pressing that his gentle touch would have been unbearable. He surely knew it, for his strong, forceful hands made the exquisite balance to the tumult inside her. Their hunger for each other consumed them. It was madness, delirium, frenzy. She thrust herself against him in mindless abandon, the urgency for joining so powerful, so uncompromising that it swept her into a vertigo of semiconsciousness.

Thought was shunned, chased by the force of their fusion. Sustaining this pitch was impossible, and her sweep upward was violent and swift. Her mind reeled, tumbled, rose and tumbled again. She could not let him go. She needed to touch his skin, to move her lips across him and savor him again. He was alive, he was with her, and he was hers. . . .

Slowly, as she lay in his arms, the silence began to speak. The fire crackled in the hearth; the starched bed linens rustled; Alexei's breathing whispered in her hair.

The fury had been spent, but sleep had not yet followed. His hand was now tracing the outline of her face, the contact feathery, unhurried, the same hand that had been strong and demanding a few minutes before. This time, however, she welcomed the gentle journey of his fingers, her skin responding with a shiver. The slow caress, the silken touch—was it designed to soothe or to arouse anew? Delicious . . .

She raised her head and looked into his blue-gray and clouding eyes. Where hands had been, his mouth began to follow, its warmth and moisture softer than his touch. She felt his gentle kisses in the hollow of her waist. His lips traversed her waiting belly, his mouth insistent, its purpose single-minded, relentless, and rousing her from semislumber to wake her, hold her breath, alert, incredulous, bewitched.

Thoughts darted through her mind like startled birds. He couldn't—oh, God, he could! He loved her totally; there was no need for further proof, and nothing else could have surpassed this bliss. The room had faded; the world had stopped.

She soared weightless, suspended in her senses, unable to translate her rapture into words. There surely were no words to tell him what she felt. Some things were tainted by the sound of words —inadequate, mundane, and better left unsaid—and that is how it was with her in this, her sacred, private world.

He must have felt the same. The way he loved her was the way he said to her that she was now his wife. It couldn't be otherwise.

Deep in reverie, she watched him put on his smoking jacket, tie his sash, and then lean over her with a smile.

"Nadyenka, my sweetest love, I had such lovely things planned for tonight: champagne, the warmth of the fire. . . ." He paused and, after walking over to the fireplace, threw in another birch log. Then he came back to the bed and gently pulled the coverlet back. "Please, *golubka*, get up and join me by the fire. The champagne may taste even better for us now; we can savor it and celebrate our reunion."

Slowly she dressed and walked over to the fireplace. Sitting next to him on a love seat by the fireplace, sipping the bubbly champagne from a heavy crystal goblet, Nadya watched the restless tongues of flame lick the bricks and compared them to her flying thoughts. How soon—the question drummed happily against her heart—how soon would she be sitting thus again with a wedding band on the ring finger of her right hand?

The ormolu clock on the mantel sounded eleven times. She loved that clock, the meticulous craftsmanship of the bronze horseman on top, the dial's roman numerals on the white face, the melodious chimes. She looked around the room and sighed. She loved everything in it; it was furnished with elegant taste; there was no way she could improve it. It held such private memories for her that she did not want to change a thing. Suddenly a disturbing thought surfaced. If Alexei's mother decided to furnish a new, larger bedchamber for the newlyweds, she, Nadya, would have to insist on keeping this one. She turned to Alexei and leaned her head against his chest.

"Beloved, I hope your mother will not want to give us a new bedchamber; this one holds so many wonderful memories for us."

She felt him stiffen, but no answer came. She pulled away and looked at him. "Alexei, did I say something wrong?"

There was pain in his face, and her heart turned over. She couldn't imagine what she had said to have hurt him so. She searched his face and saw something else: a look of total, shocked surprise. Why should he be surprised? Then slowly, sickeningly, suspicion rose and grew. And as it did, she shook her head in mute denial of the dreadful thought. Her throat was closing, and it was difficult to breathe; she had been warm by the fire, yet now her fingertips went icy. She slid away from him far into the corner of the narrow love seat and continued to shake her head, breathing deeply, her mouth tight, afraid to speak.

Alexei leaned forward and grasped both her hands in his. She tried to pull away, but he held them.

"Nadyenka, my love, how tragic this is! Oh, God, how could I have let this happen? I thought surely you understood that it could never be. You seemed so—so sophisticated, and I thought you knew that ours was a beautiful relationship without marriage."

Piteously Nadya whispered, "You mean you don't want to marry me?"

Impulsively Alexei pulled her into his arms. "That's not what I mean at all. I only wish I could! Darling, we're bound by the mores of society in which we live. I'm expected to marry and produce heirs to the Persiantsev name, but I can't marry the one I love."

"Why not?"

It wasn't her voice. A stranger had said that. And what he was saying to her did not make sense. Only his face reached her—the pained, agonized face, as if he, not she, were the injured one. This couldn't be happening. He had loved her so completely only minutes before; her nerves still vibrated with the ecstasy that lingered in every fiber of her body—a pleasure that refused to relinquish its hold even now. But he was still talking, and she must listen.

"Nadyenka, my love, dearest love, I thought you knew the obstacles and accepted the situation."

"You mean our clandestine rendezvous, the way you kept me from meeting your parents?"

When he did not answer but tried to embrace her, she pulled back and went on. "Oh, yes, I couldn't help noticing!" Her voice shook. "I thought it was because I was still in school and you wanted to wait until I had finished."

Alexei winced. "I should have known. You're so idealistic that I misled you!"

"No. Not idealistic, but naïve and blind. Even now I still can't understand why you won't marry me."

"Darling, I'm trying to explain! I'm expected to marry a daughter of some titled grandee, someone whose family is highly placed."

Nadya held back her tears. "I'm not some uneducated chambermaid or an illiterate peasant of whom you would be ashamed. I can hold my own before anyone."

"Nadyenka, you don't understand. It has to be someone received at court, someone among the nobility."

The room darkened before her eyes. She must not faint. She was strong, always had been. She rose and gripped the back of a chair to steady herself.

"I see. I wasn't born into the right family; that's what you mean. And just what would happen if you did marry me?"

"It would be a *mésalliance* that would ruin my career, and my family would disown me."

Slowly, deliberately, Nadya gathered her belongings. "In that case, there is no point in my staying here any longer. I must be on my way, Your Excellency."

Alexei barred her exit. "Please listen to me! I was going to tell you of my plans tonight, before"—he flushed as his eyes traveled fleetingly toward the canopied bed—"before I lost my head. *Golubka*, I was going to tell you how much you mean to me, how much I want our love to be permanent. I found a lovely house not far from here, where we could see each other freely and which we could furnish together to your liking. I wanted to be sure you understood that our relationship would be permanent."

The temptation to slap him, to hurt him physically, was overwhelming. He had toppled from his pedestal, and she was looking at a different man. She couldn't believe it. She was to become a member of that demimonde where a woman lived on the periphery of her lover's life—in essence, a kind of reflection of that life, not a part of it. There was a name for women like that, and it was only in the degree of their lovers' affluence that the name took on a cloak of shady respectability.

"What you really mean," she said, struggling to keep her voice from trembling, "is that while you marry someone else, I'm to be a kept woman." She swallowed her tears and went on. "You misjudged me badly, Count Alexei."

She did not belong to his inner circle of court habitués, and he wanted her to accept that. Now she wanted to weep and beg him to marry her, but somewhere deep inside, some hidden force helped her keep a semblance of dignity in this undignified exchange.

"How could you?" she managed to whisper.

"My *golubka*, my dove, don't punish me. To insult you was the farthest thing from my mind. I would never do it deliberately, you must know that. I love you. Do you hear me? I love you, and I need you. Our life can be so beautiful, so carefree and happy. We don't need the court. As soon as this accursed war is over, I'll take you to Paris, to London, to Rome!"

"I really didn't know you, did I? Or you me. You think you can buy me with promises like that? I never cared about being presented at court. All I ever wanted . . ." She choked on her tears, coughed, then said, "All I wanted was to love you and be your wife."

The blood pounded in her temples, and a ringing started in her ears. She no longer heard what Alexei was saying, but she could see. And what she saw appalled her. The proud, handsome aristocrat knelt at her feet. Watching him, she could not bear to have him touch her. She began to back out of the room, and when she felt the door handle beneath her hand, she paused.

"Alexei, you lack the courage either to defy society or to give me up. I'll do it for you."

Alexei raised his arms toward her. "I beg you, don't leave!"

Anguished, Nadya cried, "You can't have it both ways!" and ran from the room, the palace, and out into the cold. Slipping by the bundled, waiting coachman, she vanished into the dark night.

For days afterward Nadya fought to hide her humiliation. The inability to pour out her anguish to anyone was agony. At first she stayed in her room for long hours, weeping freely, the four walls and the icon of Our Lady in the corner the only witnesses to her shame. When the tears were spent, she breathed hot breath on the terry-cloth towel and applied it to her swollen eyes to soothe the eyelids. But in the silence of the room Alexei's last words—"I beg you, don't leave!"—began to echo and pursue her in rising crescendo, a taunting sound, unbearable, and she fled the house. Once outside, she walked, seeking the crowds and trying to forget.

Pedestrians scurried along the streets cutting through the frosty air with single-minded speed, pushing past, unaware of her existence. She began to run aimlessly until she reached the crowded square before St. Isaac's Cathedral. There she turned her back on its golden dome. It had now become a part of Alexei, and she would never enter it again.

How foolish to look for solace in the crowds; instead, she felt a greater sense of loss. Even nature had conspired against her, for the usually overcast February day had suddenly turned clear, and brilliant. Today she would have welcomed the clouds and their oppressive gloom that would have matched her mood with needed empathy. She was crowded by a multitude of emotions. Which one was the stronger: humiliation or the pain of rejection by the man she loved? She could not tell.

Indeed, anger was the worst: the futile anger at herself. She had refused to see the obvious—she, who deemed herself mature. How defeating not to have been true to herself, to have closed her eyes to reason and deluded herself with convincing lies. And that was the most painful feeling of all: this impotent rage, this wasted energy in self-recrimination.

At home the most trying time was at the dining table when she had to endure her father's discussion of the latest gossip at the Persiantsev Palace or feign interest in Sergei's political diatribes. Then, one day during a meal, she heard her father say that Count Alexei had returned to the front. Funny how this news gave her a sense of relief. While Alexei was in the city, she felt his presence in the air she breathed and in the food she ate, felt the pressure of his pursuit, saw his victoria waiting patiently for her at the usual place, knew his letters were piling up at general delivery. Now she could summon courage to collect them and read them without the danger of giving in to their persuasive plea. And then perhaps someday she would be strong enough to face him again without weakening.

She had gathered the soup plates and returned with the meat, her hands, well trained in the household chores, performing automatically, while her mind was a distance away. Now she looked at her father as he poked his fork absentmindedly through the mound of beef Stroganoff.

"The crusty old count," he said, "has been sheltered from the seamier side of life and remained ignorant of it, but the war has changed that."

Sergei threw his knife down on the table, and it clattered against his plate. "Papa, you surprise me! How can you say that? All he had to do was to take a ride through the villages on his estates or, better yet, visit the Vyborg quarter right here in the city."

"The count is now aware of the plight of the poor, and he's doing something about it. He has begun to open his palace to the poor several times a year to feed them. What's more, he does this privately, without fanfare. He doesn't seek praise and does it strictly for charity."

Nadya's lips tightened. Poor Papa, what had happened to him? The aging process had mellowed him so much that he was seeing only what he desperately wished to see. The count did his charity privately, he said. Of course. But not for the altruistic reasons Anton Stepanovich naïvely believed. Young Alexei did things privately, too, Nadya thought bitterly. Oh, yes, so privately. Heaven forbid that their peers find out about their respective weaknesses: the father with his self-serving conscience to feed the poor and the son—well, she wouldn't voice her opinion.

The letters she collected at the post office testified to that. Painful. That's what they were—painful. Begging her to return to him; appealing to her sense of duty to a fighting soldier whose life could be forfeit at the whim of fate; asking for her sacrifice without offering any of his own. She felt insulted. He must have thought her gullible enough to fall for his lofty clichés.

She did not destroy his letters. In reading and rereading them, she mouthed his words, and it gave her satisfaction to see that she was the stronger of the two. Never would she agree to see him again. Oh, God, she needed strength to survive such a decision. Perhaps her love for him had been tinted with the glamour of his surroundings and reinforced by his suave, worldly courtship. She had to believe that. *Had* to.

Slowly she began to see her home in a different light. Whereas before she had rebelled against its smells, its bourgeois trappings, which glared at her from every corner, now she found a comforting warmth in the familiar sense of belonging. She took a renewed interest in Sergei's underground work, even helped Esther edit her pamphlets on occasion. She missed seeing Vadim, and when she asked her brother about his friend, Sergei shrugged and said, "I see him often, but come to think of it, he hasn't been to the house recently, has he?" Then, looking at her suspiciously, he asked, "Have you had a quarrel?"

Unaccountably Nadya felt a flush rise to her face. "Why should I quarrel with him? He's a good friend."

Once or twice, she thought she saw him in the street; but he vanished when she tried to look for him, and she ascribed it to her befuddled imagination.

Her trips to the post office became a kind of ritual. Although the letters were less frequent now, they continued to be passionate, almost desperate in his pleas to tell him that she still loved him. But she refused to give him that satisfaction. Then, one day, the postman at window 43 told her that there was nothing for her. She should have been relieved that he had finally given up; instead, she was disappointed and somehow piqued. As she emerged from the covered courtyard onto Pochtamskaya Street, Vadim greeted her on the sidewalk.

"Good afternoon, Nadya. May I walk you home?"

As casual as that. After weeks of absence, without a word of explanation, he picked up the threads easily and simply. Nadya smiled. It was impossible to look at him and not return his infectious smile. All at once she no longer felt alone. Vadim's presence warmed the air, and for the first time in many weeks she once again was part of the world.

"We've missed you at the house. Where have you been?"

He gave her a shy look. "I've kept my distance, but I've been watching you for quite some time."

It was hard to be angry with him, yet Nadya felt a vague stirring of panic, wondering how long he had been doing this and what he had seen. How much did he know? Outwardly she maintained her calm. "I didn't know you were a detective in addition to your other talents," she quipped.

Vadim shook his head. "Not at all, Nadya. I sensed from your frequent and aimless, I might add, wanderings through the city that you had a problem. I also guessed that you needed to be left alone for a while."

She looked at him sharply. "And now you feel I need company?"

He nodded. "That's right. Tell me if I'm wrong, and I shall disappear again. But let me first add this before you answer: There comes a time in one's private struggles when a friend's presence has"—he paused, searching for the right words—"a supportive influence on the state of mind. I want you to consider this."

He knew. For the shame of it, he knew! Somehow he had found out. Nadya's thoughts whirled, sending hot spurts of embarrassment into her cheeks. Vadim did not seem to notice and, taking her arm, gently steered her across St. Isaac's Square toward the entrance of the elegant Astoria Hotel at the corner.

"Have you ever been inside?" he asked, and although his question implied her place in society, she did not take offense.

She answered readily enough, "No, but I'd like to see it."

How nice that with Vadim she did not have to strain or pretend a worldliness she did not feel. A rush of relief filled her to be able to be herself!

They entered a spacious foyer. A restaurant was to their left—a large, imposing room with high ceilings, crystal chandeliers, and spotless linens. Waiters floated noiselessly among tables, and the conversation was hushed. Vadim stood at the door, letting her take it all in, then led her to the opposite side of the lobby, where comfortable chairs were grouped in a wide, circular space with writing tables conveniently placed by the windows. The silk upholstery was in pastel greens and blues, giving the room an airy atmosphere, but when Vadim asked her if she would like to sit down and talk for a while, she refused. No more pretending at something she was not. No more would she reach beyond the familiar world she knew.

Back on the street, they walked silently. Then Vadim said, "Nadya, I'd never presume to pry into your private life, but I want to say something that is easier to hear from a friend than from a member of your family. Nothing that happens to us is wasted. Life is a long and strenuous lesson, and the devil of it is that in the final analysis you stand alone. So I am not going to offer any comfort or advice to you. All I want you to know is that a loyal friend, the kind of friend who is always on your side, can be of tremendous help. And we *are* friends, aren't we?" He leaned over and looked at her with a grin.

"It's a rare friend who offers his friendship without asking any questions," Nadya said quietly. "Thank you, Vadim."

"I prefer it this way," Vadim said cheerfully. "It leaves us free of the burden of confidences."

Gradually her embarrassment disappeared, and for the first time in weeks she believed the hazy sun above was shining directly upon her.

Chapter Fourteen

A year had passed since Nadya's breakup with Alexei, and it was now March 1916. Over a period of several months she had been drawn into the *besedy*, where she and Sergei met frequently with Vadim and Esther. The foursome worked closely together, but this time it was more out of friendship than devotion to the revolutionary cause that Nadya had joined them. Her enthusiasm waned after she had felt a feverish atmosphere at the meetings, an almost palpable hatred in the air directed against everyone who stood for affluence and high position in society. She watched with alarm the near fanaticism that guided Esther and Sergei in their work. Heads together, faces intent, they pored over the pamphlets spread on the table before them, weighing each inflammatory word as if their lives depended on it. Nadya sensed that Vadim, too, was halfhearted in the effort and attended the *besedy* for the same reason as she.

When the leaflets were ready, Nadya and Vadim took them to the homes of students and workers who carried them to specified centers for distribution. It was on these long walks through the streets of Petrograd that Nadya and Vadim grew closer together. Her dependence on Sergei lessened, and it was Vadim to whom she now turned for companionship, enjoying his warmth, his quiet wisdom, his obvious affection for her. She felt secure with him, and gradually her respect for the young lawyer grew to encompass a deeper emotion, one she vaguely identified as a love between friends.

She grew as a poet, and her name was becoming recognized in the publishing world as a promising writer. Vadim praised her talent and encouraged her.

"I don't know about you," he told her one day as they were making their rounds delivering pamphlets, "but I'm not at all sure we're going in the right direction with all this subversive work. You'd do better to devote full time to writing poetry. With the war on, we need unity, not disruption, in the country. It's one thing to encourage liberal thought and quite another to propagate overthrowing the monarchy. Esther, in particular, is vulnerable with her pamphlets. She frequents factories to solicit followers, and sooner or later the police will catch her red-handed."

Nadya shuddered. "I can't understand my brother. I'd think he would try to influence her."

"Sergei is infatuated with her, and it's difficult for him to be objective. I tried to talk some sense into him the other night, but he minimizes the danger. What he doesn't realize is that the past has an uncanny way of surfacing at the least propitious moment, and Esther can be labeled a subversive even if she abandons her work."

Immersed in her activities, dividing her days between keeping house for her family and spending her evenings with her friends, Nadya nevertheless could not keep from dwelling on her past. By now she had to admit that she would always love Alexei and that the best she could hope for would be to reduce the pain which followed her everywhere. Common sense told her that she should avoid certain areas of the city, but some mischievous gremlin within her taunted and pushed her to stroll along *their* paths.

One late afternoon the air shimmered, carrying clusters of words, whispers of memories, To her left, in the shade of an elm, a bench stood empty, and she sat down, caught in nature's music. Tiny whiffs of a gentle breeze wrapped around her neck, played with a loose curl, whispered in her ear, "Nadyenka!"

His voice. A hot wave of pain washed over her, and she caught her breath. It was so sudden. The bitterness, the hurt had had time to hide and shrink into a sleeping ache, but what of love itself? Suddenly the languid afternoon air was filled with sounds and words and even the fragrance of the man she still loved.

"Aaah!" Nadya cried. She pressed in her stomach and bent over to rid herself of this unwelcome pain that had surfaced with such unexpected force. She thought: *I must carry the burden of this love throughout my life.* She clutched her arms fiercely. But what if they met again, could she resist him still? A shiver raced through her body. A small voice prompted: *Get away from the garden, Nadya; the memories are too fresh for you. . . .*

Suddenly a cacophony of sparrows and blackbirds burst forth from a tree behind her, and Nadya, her heart racing, jumped up and started toward the exit. She hadn't walked far before she nearly collided with Vadim, Sergei, and Esther.

"I knew I'd find you here, Sestryonka," Sergei said, "your favorite place. I'm glad we caught you. Looks as if you were on your way out."

"I was," Nadya said, calmer now, then, noticing Vadim's arm barring her way, smiled. "But I see you have other plans for me."

"Not exactly," Esther replied, glancing curiously at Vadim.

Sergei took Nadya's arm. "Let's find a secluded place."

They found a couple of benches among tall lilac bushes. Vadim sat down beside Nadya and, covering her hand with his, looked at Esther. "Now tell us, what's all the secrecy about?"

"Nothing but good news. The tsar is playing right into our hands." Esther's eyes sparkled, and Nadya worried. It wasn't safe to be so one-sided. Sergei must be made to see the danger.

"News is pouring in from the countryside," Esther hurried on. "There's decay everywhere. You know that Rasputin and his orgies are the talk of Petrograd, yet nothing is done to improve transportation and bring food to the cities. The workers and peasants are passing word that they will rise against the tsar and the leaders of our government."

She looks like a black swan, Nadya thought, studying Esther's tightly curled shiny hair, her glowing eyes. Even her black coat with grosgrain ribbon trim was somber.

"There's something else," Esther was saying. "We must make room for the incoming deputies from the provincial zemstvos. They will be our new leaders, men who know what ails the country and how to cure it. I wonder if some of them could be lodged in your flat, Sergei."

Sergei hesitated. "I'd like to help, of course, but because my father is private physician to the house of Persiantsev, it would be a mistake to bring him to the attention of the revolutionaries."

"I thought your father's sympathies were on our side." Esther's disappointment was obvious.

"He's a conservative," Sergei replied, glancing at Vadim, who only nodded and squeezed Nadya's hand tighter.

Nadya gave Vadim a sidelong glance. He must be worried about Sergei and Esther. How good it was to know that he thought along the same lines as she. Suddenly she felt warm and breathless.

"Anyway," Sergei said, "with Father's medical practice there are too many patients going in and out every day, and it would be impossible to keep our activities secret." He took Esther's arm. "Come on, Esther, I'll help you get the pamphlets for distribution."

Nadya watched them walk down the lane. There was no doubt in her mind that Sergei was in love with Esther. It pleased her, for in spite of her worry about Esther's radical fervor, she was captivated by the girl's ardor and determination.

"Come, Nadya," Vadim said, "let's sit here for a while now that they're gone. I came here specifically to talk to you. In private."

Nadya sat down, folded her hands in her lap, and looked at Vadim with mild curiosity, wondering what he was going to say. He had a soothing influence upon her, was kind and understanding; but at times he was secretive, and it bothered her. He never told her how much he knew or what he suspected. He was always in control of himself, ready with a whimsy; only now there was something else in his face she hadn't seen before. She took a closer look, and as their eyes met, Nadya caught her breath. The friendly, familiar mask had dropped, and in his hazel eyes there shone a new light: not a friend's affection, but a man's love for a woman.

"I love you, Nadya," he began quietly. "I have loved you for a long time. I think you've known it all along. I've never been eloquent with words; they get in my way and never seem to say exactly what I intend." Abruptly he clasped her hands. "Marry me, Nadya. We're so much alike. We're both lonely, even if for different reasons." He smiled mischievously. "We've gone along with Sergei and Esther because we like them, not because we believe in their cause. Admit it!"

He squeezed her hands and shook them gently. "Marry me, Nadya!"

She felt a thousand different ways: surprised (she should have been less blind), distressed, and . . . pleased. She could not understand that feeling of warm pleasure because she knew what she had to tell him.

"I've never had a friend whom I loved more than you, Vadim," she began, desperately trying to find the easiest words. "You're my best friend, and I love you dearly; but I cannot give you romantic love—affection, tenderness, but not romantic love. You see—"

Vadim raised his hand quickly to stop her. "Don't say any more, Nadya. Words are so permanent. You can't erase them. I know a lot, and what I don't know, I can guess. Don't worry," he added, seeing her distress, "I keep my own counsel."

Vadim rose, stuffed his hands in his pockets, and kicked a small stone with the toe of his shoe. He watched it bounce along the path, then turned to Nadya. "Romantic love. What is it? A fleeting dream! That kind of love is porous, Nadya. It will not last. Life's pressures will come in, contaminate it, or coexist in an uneasy truce."

Nadya regained her composure. "I had no idea you were such a philosopher."

"Not at all. Just practical. A warm affection, a love based on companionship and mutual understanding, is the true foundation for a marriage. No illusions. What do you say?"

So it was that she agreed, for it seemed the right thing, the only thing to do, and then went with gladness into his arms. His embrace was warm and pleasant, and she put her arms around his neck and kissed him back. His sinuous, firm body pressed tighter, touching her with controlled tremor. A lock of his tousled hair brushed her forehead, and somewhere deep within her a chord responded. She hadn't felt this good for many months. She *could* marry Vadim, for she loved him. That other love would remain hidden, and although its fire was still unquenched, it would not tarnish her loyalty to Vadim. In that her mother had been right. It *was* possible to love two men. But just now she must concentrate on this new happiness. Seryozha and Papa will be so pleased. She closed her eyes and smiled, nestling in Vadim's arms.

At the iron gates Sergei looked back once more, but Nadya and Vadim were nowhere to be seen. He was pleased to see his good friend court Nadya, and selfishly he was delighted to have time with Esther. On the rare occasions they were alone a feverish excitement overcame him. This strange, unorthodox woman! It rankled and shocked him whenever she implied, quite casually at that, her approval of free love.

Her fanatical fervor, her single-minded vengeance against the autocracy that had murdered her parents and violated her had infected Sergei with its virulence, but in her desire to defy everything that stood for the established mores of society, he felt she had gone too far. Sergei could not reconcile this casual approach to the most intimate of human relationships with the sanctity of marital love. The more he thought about it, the more he desired Esther, but he didn't know how to approach her. He was such a novice at such things! He couldn't bring himself to tell her that he, a man who had reached the age of thirty, a physician, had never had a woman.

A physician! Sometimes he wondered if he had the patience to be in private practice. It wasn't enough to prescribe laudanum, a bromide, or suction cups for bronchitis or to listen to the chests of his consumptive patients; he had to hear their woes as well. And so he fled to the Institute of Research at every opportunity. For hours he pored over colonies of microbes, some deadly, some not, but all waiting to be conquered. This was his greatest love, and he dreamed of devoting full time to research. He wondered now if he disliked contact with his patients because he felt his loyalties were on a collision course. In medicine he was committed to cure the human ills through healing, but for the cause of revolution, violence and death were unavoidable.

Deep in thought, he waited outside the printer's until Esther came out and handed him the pamphlets. They walked in silence until she tugged at his sleeve. "Sergei, you're miles away! We're almost at my flat. Don't drop those leaflets."

Near the archway to her courtyard they were greeted by her *dvornik*, who stopped sweeping the sidewalk in front of the entrance and, leaning on his broom, studied them curiously.

"He knows everyone who lives in my courtyard, not only the tenants but those who come to see them," Esther said, and then added with one of her rare chuckles, "You're a marked man, beware!"

Sergei was not amused. "I think our tradition of having *dvorniki* is a nuisance. Instead of cleaning up, they spread the dirt from place to place and pass on the gossip. It can be dangerous."

Esther shrugged. "They're far more harmless than the police."

They had entered the hallway at the far end of the inner courtyard. It was dark, and the steps were slippery. At the top of the first flight of stairs Esther placed her package of pamphlets over those Sergei was holding and then opened the door to the communal flats. It took a few moments for his eyes to adjust to the darkened hall. All he could see were four doors with brass locks and an open doorway into a spacious kitchen with four well-scrubbed tables and one stove. Instinctively he looked around again and counted: four apartment doors in the hall, four work-tables in the kitchen, yet only one stove. He looked at Esther. She was watching him with an amused look, then turned and put the key into her lock.

"There are four burners on the stove, aren't there? One burner per family, that's—" The sound of running water drowned the rest of her sentence, and as Sergei turned, he caught a glimpse of a young man scrubbing the tub in a large bathroom at the opposite end of the hall. Again Esther noticed his furtive glance.

"Yes, rules are strict. Our communal bathroom has to be left clean every time we use it. And that goes for the toilet, too!"

Sergei winced. Evidently there was nothing sacred in her vocabulary, he thought. This was the first time Esther had invited him to her place, and Sergei looked around curiously. It was a large room with a high ceiling, but because it was cluttered with furniture, it seemed small. A huge oak wardrobe stood in the middle of the room. A rope, strung between a knob at the top and a nail in the wall, supported a plaid blanket, behind which, Sergei was sure, was her bed. He placed the pamphlets on the large table in the center of the room, pushing aside its only ornament, a menorah, and then sat down on a threadbare brown plush sofa. In front of him were two small tables piled high with papers and books. Not a picture anywhere, not even a snapshot.

After Esther had brought hot water from the kitchen and made tea, they settled at the table.

"Do you have any photographs of your parents?" Sergei asked.

"Everything was lost in the pogrom. Of all our possessions this is the only thing I was able to bring out," Esther said, waving toward the menorah, "and that only because the rabbi thought I must have it. A devout Jewish girl, he said, shouldn't be without one."

The sarcasm in her voice was unmistakable, and Sergei reached out to touch her hand. "You're driven by hate and revenge. I can see that. Leave some room for love in your heart, will you?"

Esther did not pull her hand away. "Death of the soul is indifference, not hate. As long as I'm capable of hating, I can also love."

They finished their tea, talking about the war and the rising prices, and then began to sort the pamphlets into separate stacks to be distributed later at the factories.

After all the leaflets had been stacked, Sergei sat down again. "Have you thought of what direction your life is going to take when you avenge your parents"—he was careful not to mention her rape—"and the government you so hate is brought to its knees?"

"It's not in my nature to gloat. I want to see justice done.

Beyond that I haven't thought much about myself. I told you before that my only dream is to go to America."

"How about personal happiness? Don't you ever yearn for a man to love you for yourself, not as an object of lust?" That was as close as he dared approach a painful and sensitive subject.

Slowly Esther raised her eyes to him. For the first time the deep brown pools swirled with tenderness, embraced him, drew him into their depths. He inhaled sharply, in an effort to slow down his racing heart.

"Everyone wants to be loved," Esther said quietly. "When love overshadows lust, then it becomes something precious and terrible."

"I don't understand. Why terrible?"

"Because it involves a risk. If you accept a gift of someone's love and give one in return, then you become vulnerable."

"You speak from experience?"

"Not in the past. In the present." Esther rose abruptly and walked over to the opposite side of the room. Looking out the window with her back to Sergei, she said quietly, "I haven't been with another man since I met you, Sergei. Are you aware of that?"

The room whirled, catapulted, righted itself. He moved toward her. She turned and went into his arms willingly, fiercely. He had never dreamed he could feel such unbearable passion for this woman, driving him mad with desire. And what if he had thought her a virgin, would his lust be as great, as impossible to control as now? Her eyes, clouded with passion, were looking at him from below, and her body moved against him with a sensuality that made him ache and want to crush her in his arms. He wanted her. Nothing mattered but to possess this lithe dark girl with her silken olive skin who writhed beneath him. Suddenly, they were on the bed, and hastily taking off their clothes.

Those glowing eyes, the parted ruby lips that glistened, and the tongue that darted out to drive him crazy . . . he couldn't wait any longer. She was ready for him—he felt it—and he plunged himself into the final, culminating union. This first, this moist and soft, soft haven that enclosed him, this cradle of his passion belonged to him! His woman. All his past fantasies paled before this wonderful, this perfect sensation.

Then, cruelly, a nasty thought shot through his brain: Who else had touched this softness? Who else had been enveloped in its warmth, had moved and thrilled inside this bliss? Another man. A stranger.

To his horror, a cramp spread in his groin, and cold beads of shame moistened his brow. Abruptly, painfully, he collapsed. He withdrew from her clumsily and rolled onto his back, mortified by the emasculating fiasco.

For a few moments Esther lay quietly beside him. Then, after slipping out of bed, she threw a flannel robe over herself, picked up a cigarette from a nearby table, lighted it, and inhaled.

"Your first time?" she asked bluntly, squinting at Sergei through the smoke. Instinctively he pulled the blanket over his muscular chest. He couldn't answer. She had no right to ask. Some things were sacred and private with a man. She should know that.

Esther did not pursue her question. She took a couple of puffs on the cigarette, stubbed it out, and resolutely walked over to the bed. There she stood looking down at him and then said, "I take the blame. It was my fault."

Suddenly, with a swift movement, as though she were afraid she might change her mind, she threw off her robe and let it drop to the floor. "I have not known what it means to love, and I have never loved a man. Until now."

She was so beautiful, standing there before him, that he lost his breath. Tears welled in his eyes, making her naked body shimmer. He had never seen such perfection, and he watched mesmerized as she stretched herself beside him. Minutes before, she had been an eager recipient of his passion, but now a tender, sensitive woman was coaxing him to love with a flowing cadence of her hands —tender, unhurried, and, oh, so finely attuned to pleasing him!

Esther, Esther, my angel, what are you doing to me?

She took her time caressing him, and this time there was more to her touch than passion. Perhaps it was the gentle loving sweep across his cheek and neck, or maybe the sweet and playful rumpling of his hair had worked the miracle; but when at last she placed his fingers on the trembling points of her body and pulled his hand across her soft and pliant belly, he was ready for her.

The war, the revolution, their cause and work must wait. He loved her!

Chapter Fifteen

Glistening icicles clung to the mouths of wide, rusty drainpipes of the building at which Nadya stood in line for sugar. All around her were sounds of early-morning life. The store that sold sugar would not be opened until nine o'clock, and there was more than an hour to wait. People, mostly women, had been lined up since three that morning, and at five o'clock Esther had taken a place three blocks away from the store. Nadya had replaced her at seven, so that Esther could leave for work at the office of *Severnye Zapiski* magazine. Although Nadya had been in line only a little more than an hour, her legs were already tired. She was in the eighth month of pregnancy, and the added weight made standing particularly difficult, yet she insisted on taking her turn in line even if no more than for an hour. "I need the exercise and the fresh air," she told Vadim, who gave in. He should be there in a few minutes, but in the meantime, her attention was drawn to a tea vendor moving slowly along the street with a large teakettle steaming in one hand. A dirty white apron partially covered his sheepskin coat and came down to the tops of his *valenki*. A circular wooden container firmly attached to his waist held six or seven glasses, and when Nadya gave him three kopecks, he filled it with tea, and handed it to her.

As she sipped the hot liquid, her mind wandered. She had

learned to tune herself out of the incessant chattering she heard on the streets. Never one to indulge in or listen to gossip, she discouraged any fraternizing with the women around her. Of late the lines were so frequent and so long that waiting there had become a respite from home chores and a socializing time for the waiting women.

The past year had been full of momentous events in Nadya's life, giving her little time to dwell on the past. When she told Sergei that she and Vadim were going to be married, her brother had gone to Esther and asked her to marry him. He said to Nadya later that he had been prepared to argue about the benefits of marriage versus an alternate relationship, but to his unimaginable pleasure Esther had agreed at once.

"You're my ready-made family," she had said simply to Nadya, confessing her fears that Anton Stepanovich might reject her because she was Jewish. But Nadya's father had accepted her with open arms.

"How could I object to Esther and be honest with my liberal views?" he said to Nadya. "I may not approve of the radical trend the revolution is taking, but I am equally appalled by the pogroms and the persecution of Jews."

So the flat was filled with the two newly married couples living under the same roof with Anton Stepanovich, who beamed with happiness at his enlarged family. The two women had become good friends. Esther did not enjoy housekeeping and willingly left the household chores in Nadya's hands, helping only with the dishes. Their maid, Matrona, had left them to join in the peasant uprising, Nadya suspected, and the arrangement at home was much to her liking. She was still the mistress of the house, yet she had in the family another woman whose friendship she enjoyed.

Now, with only about one month left before her delivery, Nadya was touched by Esther's concern over her well-being. It was also heartwarming to see the tenderness between her brother and his wife. Sergei was no longer intense and withdrawn, and he glowed with happiness. How wondrous it was to watch her Seryozha's face when he sat with Esther in the parlor, going over the day's events! Nadya understood and excused Esther her commitment to the revolution, for she sensed that Esther's love for Sergei was as fiercely uncompromising as her dedication to avenging herself and her parents.

What a time to have a revolution, when the country was still at war with Germany and needed unity to protect Russia from the enemy! Order and discipline were crumbling all around.

When the revolution struck last February, the police and the Cossacks, who were supposed to maintain order, had joined the rebellious crowds. In March people on the streets sang the "Marseillaise" and hugged one another, celebrating the tsar's abdication.

It seemed to Nadya that everything the tsar's government had previously done was an afterthought—too late to pacify the growing discontent among the masses. Even Rasputin's murder in December 1916 by members of the royal family had failed to stem the revolution's onrush. It did not help to learn that one of the assassins, Prince Yussoupov, was married to the tsar's niece. Three months later the tsar abdicated in favor of his brother, Michael, who, in turn, refused the throne, and the monarchy finally collapsed. After a three-hundred-year-old reign the House of Romanov was no more; the white, blue, and red standard was replaced by a blood red flag.

Then, one day, Esther ran home from her office to tell them that Alexander Kerensky, a member of the Duma and an SR sympathizer, had taken over the Provisional Government. Nadya was relieved and hoped that some semblance of order would now be established.

That night at home, Esther said triumphantly, "The Putilov factory workers were largely responsible for this."

"Those Putilov workers are forever striking, aren't they?" Anton Stepanovich said warily, putting his papers away.

Esther bristled. "They're no longer asking for more bread or better living conditions, Papa. This time they are striking for the long-overdue overthrow of the monarchy."

Anton Stepanovich sighed. "I wish there were less violent ways to change from autocracy to democracy."

"It's the tsar's own fault, Papa. He paid so much attention to war that he ignored our internal problems. All those *ukazy* he issued—one more hysterical than the other. Childish to issue an order to fine a citizen three thousand rubles for speaking German!"

Nadya agreed with Esther. Ludicrous! Who had three thousand rubles to spare when the price for a few potatoes had risen in a short time from fifteen kopecks to one ruble twenty? Butter was nearly impossible to find, and when you did, who could pay one ruble fifty a pound? Clothing was no better, and she had to patch her *valenki* because new boots had tripled in price.

Insidious fear nibbled at Nadya's insides, for in spite of the fall of the monarchy, there still was an air of impending disaster of unknown dimensions when she heard cries of "Bread! Br-e-a-ad!" and watched angry women shake their fists and storm shops the vacant windows of which displayed signs of No Bread, No Meat, No Kerosene.

Thank God that at home, with the door closed to the growing storm, peace and unity reigned. Nadya marveled at her newly found happiness, different, to be sure, from the one she had dreamed about, but happiness nonetheless. Strong yet gentle Vadim was her rock, and he belonged completely to her. A tender and considerate lover was her Vadim, and she loved him.

Yet that other love, that other yearning had never left her, had become an unnerving presence that pursued and shadowed her contentment. And always, oh, yes, always there was the proximity of the Persiantsev name, the constant reminder of that family's existence when her father brought every detail of their lives to the dinner table.

After the tsar's abdication Count Pyotr had had difficulty adjusting to the Provisional Government and had retired. Countess Aline's ailments had increased with the worsening of the political climate, and her longing for her son, who no longer was able to come home on leave, contributed to her ill health. The family had decided to close the palace and move to their country estate in the Crimea. Anton Stepanovich seemed to age overnight.

"I've grown to know the family so well," he said to his children, "I feel as if I'm losing a limb with their departure. It's been so long, so many years that I've taken care of them. It will also affect us financially. Since I won't be their family physician any longer, we'll have to depend on my practice entirely."

Nadya did not trust herself to comment on the Persiantsev family, afraid to betray her secret feelings. She loved Vadim with a quiet warmth, and his love for her was undemanding of the limitless, consuming passion that she had once experienced with another man and surely was incapable of giving to her husband. But she made up for it with tenderness and deep affection and loyalty and the special understanding that comes from kindred minds. Whether he suspected that she still loved Alexei or hoped that time had dulled the passion, Nadya never knew.

She did not regret having known the ultimate in love. She often caught herself studying her tired father and wondering about his relationship with her mother. It was impossible to think that Anna had been capable of arousing or living through that kind of passion with Anton Stepanovich. When she had told her daughter on her deathbed to take from life what she could and not miss an opportunity for love, it could well have been because she herself had never experienced it.

Nadya still kept her mother's diary hidden. Someday perhaps she would overcome her reluctance and read it, but not yet. Nadya continued to write poetry but was dissatisfied with her work. Her love poems she hid from Vadim, and the patriotic ones that she thought were her best the censors now judged to be seditious and refused to publish. Uncertain of the direction she should take, Nadya no longer submitted them.

"Come on, *bourzhuika*, move! This is no place for dreaming!"

The woman's rough voice brought Nadya out of her reverie. She had become inured to the nickname of *bourzhuika*, separating her from the common folk with that curious distinction of better and sturdier clothes. The waiting line had not moved, for it was not yet nine o'clock; but as Nadya looked around her, she noticed that several people had dropped out ahead, and she had not closed the gap. She moved forward quickly. Vadim would be here soon. Perhaps there would be sugar today. She needed it for nourishment, for the baby she was carrying.

She was not sure whether having a child right now was such a good idea, but she had had no say in that and looked forward to pouring her love out on her baby. Vadim's baby. She wondered if the child would have his looks, his whimsical smile, and grew up to have his sense of humor. She hoped so. But that was yet another month ahead, and now she had to inch her way toward the sugar.

Two women behind her were gossiping and giggling over some private joke. Mildly curious, Nadya listened.

"—heard this morning. Too bad Kerensky escaped. He deserves to be strung up like the lot of them. Now the revolution is ours. We, the people, have won!"

"All I care for is food and fuel."

"You'll get it now. Our Lenin will see to it right away."

Nadya worried. The tsar and his family were under arrest and confined to the city of Tobolsk in Siberia, but at least they were under the humane protection of Kerensky's Provisional Government. Lenin and the Bolsheviks were something else. Since Kerensky did not end the war, the people grumbled and listened to Lenin, whose impassioned speeches at his headquarters in the Smolny Institute drew huge crowds. Although the Menshevik and the Social Revolutionary parties outnumbered the Bolsheviks five to one, Nadya knew that as soon as Lenin made good on his promise to end the war and sign a separate peace treaty with Germany, he would rally the army behind him and the Bolsheviks would be in power.

"Food and fuel," the woman in line behind her had said. Nadya could not argue the obvious. This morning she and Esther had already stood a total of three hours.

Loud, derisive laughter brought her attention back to the street and her cold, tired feet. The women's voices droned on behind her.

"—my Vasily brought me this golden brooch from the palace they sacked on the Fontanka yesterday. The riches they got from just one family! Imagine! All that, while we starved."

"That's a nice trinket you have there. Wish I could have one like it."

"Don't you worry. You'll get one, too. Vasily said they're planning to sack the Blue Palace on the Neva Embankment today."

Nadya's heart jumped. For a long time the Persiantsev mansion had been known as the Blue Palace. Thank God the family had decided to move to the Crimea. The palace would be sacked —there was nothing she could do about that—but at least the Persiantsevs were safely out of the capital.

Sadness spread through her. Memories stirred: the canopied bed in his bedchamber; the crackling fire in the marble fireplace in his study; the love seat; the ruby decanter; his special fragrance . . . his love. Oh, Nadya, chase them away, shut the memories out! But they wouldn't go away, and she had to stand there, pretending the sugar was the most important thing of the day, when the Persiantsev family mansion and possibly the servants who had been left behind to care for the palace were in danger.

There was something indecent in defacing beauty; it was sinful to pilfer, to destroy wantonly for the sake of destroying. There was a popular saying: "Let the pig sit at the table, and it will place its feet on the table." And so it was with the unbridled freedom of the ignorant mob. She did not want to listen anymore. The less she knew, the better for her. Perhaps if she shut her mind to what she was hearing, the ugly rumor would go away.

"Nadya! Here I am! Go home, my dear, it's so cold. I'll get back as soon as I can."

Vadim. What a welcome sight he was: kind, thoughtful, smiling. Nadya leaned her head briefly against his shoulder, his chin frosty against her forehead. Then she smiled at him and hurried home.

Pregnancy was a burden. Her legs felt heavy, swollen from standing, and when she reached home, she was glad to stretch out on her bed. Everything was quiet in the house. Esther was gone, Anton Stepanovich was still asleep, and she could hear Sergei beginning to straighten the waiting room at the other end of the flat.

She would sleep a little and then fix breakfast. No rush to tell her father about the intended sacking of the Persiantsev Palace. He would be sad, upset. And maybe the woman was wrong. Maybe they would pick another palace. Maybe—at once she was ashamed of her thoughts. She wanted some other palace to be sacked, not the one she knew. A selfish wish. Her father was right: Your own shirt was closest to your body.

She drifted into sleep, and when she woke, it was late morning. She had overslept. Her father was out, and only Sergei was home. Nadya went to the kitchen to fix herself tea with milk. Where had her father gone? Maybe to the hospital to see a patient. He was spending a lot of time lately at the military hospital across the Neva. Vadim, she supposed, was still waiting for sugar. Well, she would keep the water hot for him; he would want a cup when he came home. The October air was raw, especially in the morning hours. Even tea was hard to get nowadays, and she would keep the tea leaves brewing in the small pot; no use wasting them.

She sat down at the kitchen table with her cup. The hot liquid felt good in her stomach. The child moved inside her, kicked. She smiled and patted her swollen abdomen. She could hardly wait to hold the warm infant in her arms, to feel it snuggle against her breast, making contented grunts while suckling. Soon, soon . . .

The door opened, and Sergei walked in. "Is there any hot water left for your old brother?" he asked, smiling at her clumsy figure. "Getting impatient?"

Nadya smiled back and nodded. "Sit down, Seryozha. I'll see if there's enough for you and Papa."

"You'll have to boil some water for Papa later. He was called early this morning to the Persiantsev Palace. Seems the countess had an attack of her migraine and they had to delay their departure. Papa went to see if he could talk her out of staying in Petrograd. He suspects she'd try anything not to leave the capital."

Nadya rose and pressed her hands against her chest. Her heart hammered painfully. So painfully! It hurt to breathe. She had not heard him rightly. *Please tell me I did not hear you rightly, Seryozha! The Persiantsevs left the city; they must have! They were supposed to days ago! And Papa . . . oh, God, surely Papa did not go there!*

Sergei was by her side now, concern on his face. "Nadya, what's the matter? You're so pale! Have your pains started? Answer me!"

Nadya shook her head. She was gasping for breath. "Papa . . .

at the Persiantsev Palace. Seryozha, they're sacking the Blue Palace today! I heard the women talking . . ."

In an instant Sergei was at the telephone on the wall, placing a call to the palace. He waited for a few agonizing moments, then hung the receiver back on the hook. "There's no answer. I'm going over there!"

"Seryozha, don't go alone! Go fetch Vadim; he's still in line for sugar. You know the place—near the Filippovs'. Hurry!"

She stood in the middle of the room, watching Sergei grab his overcoat and run out of the flat. The door slammed behind him, and the house fell silent.

She was alone. The baby stirred. An elbow or a knee pressed sharply against her. She placed her hands across her abdomen and stood there helplessly. She was glad she was alone, that the first patient wasn't due for many hours yet, for she couldn't bear to smile and chat right now. If only Esther were home! A vibrant strength emanated from her sister-in-law, and Nadya guessed that they all fed on it in varying degrees. Yes, she wished she had Esther by her side. Silly to worry so; Papa was not a Persiantsev. Surely everyone could see that. Sergei and Vadim would bring him home, with luck, before the mob got there.

God, let it be so! But even if they didn't get there on time, they'd have no trouble explaining who they were. After all, they were on the side of the revolutionaries; they were friends!

Better get down to the chores of the day. Tea-stained cups were still on the table, and she could finish straightening the waiting room, which Sergei had begun to tidy. Her stomach fluttered, and the palms of her hands prickled with perspiration. It was too much. Heavily she lowered herself onto the kitchen taboret and, taking a cube of sugar in her mouth, sipped her tea. Then, hugging herself to stop the twitching in her arms, she stared at the wall. She concentrated on a familiar object, a staple of every Russian home: a loose-leaf daily calendar, each page listing the saints whose name day it was, on the reverse side of which there was always a wise quotation or a piece of useful information or sometimes a line of humor. She thought it would be a good idea to tear off today's sheet and read what it said, but to do so required an enormous effort. She could not move. She just sat and stared at it. The round clock at her elbow ticked loudly.

She waited.

Chapter Sixteen

———————————

At the corner of the Nevsky Prospekt and Moika Canal Sergei collided with Vadim.

"Look out, dear *shurin*! You almost made me drop this treasure!" Vadim shook the kilo sack of sugar in the air.

Sergei ignored the remark and grabbed Vadim by the arm. "They're going to sack the Blue Palace today. Papa's there!"

Vadim wheeled. "Run!"

The two young men crossed the Nevsky and covered the distance to the Neva Embankment in a few minutes, running through less crowded Gogol Street, skirting the Horse Guards Riding School and the Senate, and finally turning onto the English Quay. The atmosphere around them was strangely charged: an uneasy marriage of menace and festive mood. Workmen loitered on street corners, carrying pickaxes and sticks; soldiers with rifles patrolled the streets; and men and women in work clothes, arms linked, strolled along the wide boulevards singing the "Internationale."

The English Quay, where handsome dandies and beautiful women used to promenade in the afternoon, was mobbed by crowds brandishing inflammatory slogans. It was filled with seemingly aimless people, more hushed than those farther in the city. Sergei and Vadim soon discovered the reason for such behavior. They did not have to see the Blue Palace to know they had arrived too late. From the distance the sound of broken glass was light and tinkling—an incongruous sound, Sergei thought, for an ignominious act. Scores of men and women armed with clubs and stones were swarming at the main entrance. The doors were wide open, and from across the street Sergei saw workmen and soldiers with rifles and bayonets sliding across the parquet floor and running up the grand staircase.

"We haven't got a chance going through this entrance," Sergei said. "Let's try the side door."

If that one were locked, he reasoned, they could break the window and climb in, unobserved, while the mob was occupied elsewhere. The door was open, the narrow servants' corridor empty. Sergei followed his instincts, leading Vadim through the maze of gilded and brocaded rooms. How many years had it been since his disastrous visit to Count Alexei's nursery? Twenty-two? Twenty-three? He could barely remember the grand salon of red velvet and the parlor of blue silk, but he did remember the quiet serenity of the palace rooms, their thick walls shutting out the cacophony of street vendors vocalizing their wares and the *izvozchiki's* rolling wheels. Now there were screams and shouts and coarse voices, along with pounding feet and sickening sounds of destruction. They'd have to talk fast to the attackers, vicious in their rage—the soldiers, the workers, their women. The most important thing was to hold their attention long enough to explain that Anton Stepanovich was not a member of the Persiantsev family.

The assault seemed to be taking place in the front part of the palace. "I hope they stay here long enough for us to get Papa out," Sergei said, running along an upstairs hallway.

They stopped at an open door to what might have been a woman's boudoir. The pinks and mauves of the silk walls swam before Sergei's eyes as he and Vadim took in the scene before them: turned-over chairs, torn lace curtains on the floor, pictures askew on the wall, spider web cracks on the mirror over the mantel. Countess Aline was lying on the chaise longue in a lavender silk peignoir. One arm dangled over the side; her other hand lay across the side of her face, as if shielding it from a blow. She might have been asleep were it not for the look of terror and a thin ribbon of blood running from her temple down her jawbone and soaking the ostrich feathers, now crimson, at her neckline.

At the foot of the chaise, arms stretched toward the countess's feet, lay Count Pyotr, his head bludgeoned and twisted at a grotesque angle. Mesmerized, Sergei stared at the couple, reluctant to check them for vital signs, his professional instinct dormant. With an effort he pulled his gaze away from the bodies and saw his father's medical bag on the other side of the chaise longue. Where was Papa? Sergei had never known him to forget his bag.

"Seryozha, over here!"

At the sound of Vadim's voice Sergei wheeled. At the far end of the room was another door, and against it, half-sitting, half-slumped, was Anton Stepanovich. In one leap Sergei was beside his father, feeling for his pulse, raising his half-closed eyelids.

Vadim's hand pressed on his shoulder. "Seryozha, it must have been instantaneous. I'm sure he had no time to feel anything."

There was a hole in his father's forehead: small, neat, and lethal. Hot rage pulsed through Sergei. A woman's shrieks somewhere in a nearby parlor faded behind the thudding sounds of his heart. The scum!

Boots scratched on the parquet floor, and a coarse, derisive voice boomed in the room: "Aha! Another couple of pigeons! *Bei bourzhuev!* Kill the bourgeoisie!"

Two soldiers with rifles and bayonets swaggered into the room, their faces gloating, one of them buttoning his pants.

Sergei rose to his feet, fists clenched, his body jerking out of control, jaw muscles locked in a cramp. Out of the distance came Vadim's conciliatory voice: "We're with you, *tovarishchi!* We're members of Comrade Lenin's Council of Deputies. There's been a terrible mistake. My comrade's father has been shot. We came to get his body."

One of the soldiers backed off and barred the door with his bayonet. "No one takes any bodies out. And you! You don't look like one of us. Do you take us for fools?"

The other soldier took a step forward, his rifle lowered at Vadim's chest.

Vadim shook his head. "My comrade is a doctor, and so was his father."

"Aha! I thought so. Pandering to the aristocrats. Lackeys! We'll show you what we think of the likes of you!"

With a swift, vicious kick of his heavy boot, the soldier hit Vadim just below the knee. Taken by surprise, Vadim doubled over, swinging forward the sack of sugar he was still holding. It caught on the tip of the other soldier's bayonet, and the white granules poured out onto the polished floor. The sight of the hard-gotten sugar going to waste was the last straw for Sergei. Galvanized into action, he lunged at the soldier, but the man saw him and leveled his rifle. In the same instant Vadim jumped between them, his arm out to deflect the shot. His foot slipped on the sugar crystals, and the bullet spun him around. Enraged, the soldier fired several more shots, and Vadim crumpled. Sergei grabbed him but lost his own footing and fell beneath him.

For a moment Sergei was stunned and didn't move. One of the soldiers swore. "*Bolvan*, you damn fool, Fyedka! What if they really were with us?"

"Never!" grumbled Fyedka. "Look at their clothes!" He kicked at the two prone bodies, hitting Sergei painfully in the thigh.

"Just the same, let's get out of here. There must be gold for us in other rooms."

Fyedka leered. "The plump maid you just saddled wasn't enough, eh?"

The other man shoved him toward the door. "I meant another kind of gold. Maybe earrings for my woman."

The men shuffled out of the room and slammed the gilded doors behind them. When their footsteps receded, Sergei stirred, moving slowly from under Vadim, careful not to hurt his wounded friend. Warm blood had been running over Sergei's neck, soaking his collar and shirt. Vadim was bleeding heavily and had to be taken to the hospital at once. Suddenly Sergei remembered his father's medical bag. It would have bandages, and he could perhaps stem the hemorrhage before he tried to carry Vadim out. He didn't stop to think just how he was going to carry his friend out of the palace unobserved. First things first.

He freed himself from Vadim's unconscious body, its inert weight settling on the floor behind him with a gentle thud. He reached for the medical bag and took out the bandages. Then he turned to examine Vadim for the first time.

Sergei the doctor knew at once that his friend was dead—the glazed eyes, the bullet-riddled body, the blood-soaked clothes —but Sergei the friend refused to accept the obvious. He dropped to his knees, felt for Vadim's pulse, slapped his face, shook him. Then slowly he slumped over and wept. *Vadim . . . my friend . . . my brother* . . . Sobs tore at his guts, churned bile in his throat. A nightmare. It was only a nightmare! He raised himself and looked at Vadim once more, his hands flat on the floor, the coarse sugar cutting his palms beneath his weight.

Sugar. In shock, his brain switched focus. Sugar! Nadya. Esther. He was the only man left in the family to look after them. He had to get out of the palace.

He rose, took a few steps toward the center of the room, listened. The sounds of splintering furniture and shouting still went on at the far end of the palace. The women's screams had ceased. How many servants had been killed along with their masters? It was quiet here in the death room. His gaze wandered to the Persiantsevs lying against each other on the chaise longue. The bastards. They had even died comfortably; they looked so tidy and clean, not messy like Vadim or awkward like Papa. The bastards! Leeches on the poor. Curse them! Damn them to hell!

Deranged by grief and fury, Sergei grabbed a cloisonné vase from the table and hurled it against the window. Shards of glass splintered, sparkled for a second in a prism of light, and fell. He ran to the fireplace and in one violent movement swept the clock, a porcelain figurine, and a silver candlestick that had somehow survived the looting off the mantel. A small chair with a petit point seat stood in front of an escritoire. After grabbing it with both hands, Sergei raised it over his head and smashed it against the dainty desk.

He threw his head back and roared with demented laughter. The sound filled the room and echoed in his ears. It broke his rage. Fool, fool! The soldiers would find him alive and finish him off! He had to get out, to save himself for his women. But he couldn't take the bodies out. Too risky. He could carry away only the medical bag. He couldn't tolerate the thought of filthy hands rummaging through the bag, pilfering his father's stethoscope, touching his surgical instruments. Hurriedly he snapped the bag shut and picked it up. Then he looked at his father for the last time.

Good-bye, Papa. The words that should have been said would now be said, the tenderness shown that needed to be shown. Oh, Papa, I did love you! Sergei put down the medical bag and gently pulled his father down onto the floor; he crossed his hands on his chest and closed his eyes. He then looked at Vadim and noticed that his friend was still clutching the remaining sugar. He pulled the sack out of his hand and picked up the medical bag. He shouldn't have touched the bodies. The soldiers would realize that he had survived. But then he was safe, for they didn't know who he was. He must be losing his mind. Whether he touched the bodies or not, the soldiers would know he survived because they would find him gone.

Hurrying now, he closed the door behind him and slipped out of the palace through the empty back corridor. In spite of continuing shouting at the other end of the palace, he saw no one. His sight and hearing were blocked by shock, and his body responded to physical impulses by instinct.

Sometime later he found himself inside St. Isaac's Cathedral, kneeling at the railing of the side altar, well hidden by massive pillars from the center of the church. He could not remember how he'd got there, but he knew why he had been drawn to it: not to pray to God, but to curse Him, to give in to his grief in the only place where he could allow his tears and sobs to be heard without attracting curious glances. He was a physician, wasn't he? And he knew why he needed this catharsis before he went home and faced Nadya. She would need him to be strong; he was her only support now.

Nadya, his little sister. How was he going to tell her, eight months pregnant, that her husband and her father both had been killed that morning? Killed? No! Senselessly murdered because they happened to be there at the wrong time. It was one thing for the mob to kill their oppressors out of vengeance, but quite another to murder indiscriminately the very ones who championed their cause. And he and Esther had surely championed them!

But the most difficult thing of all was having to tell Nadya that Vadim had been killed trying to protect him, her brother. He did not want to think about that right then.

He was indebted to Vadim for life. His friend's unborn child would become Sergei's child. He wept. These could be his last tears for a long time. Thank God for Esther. His own, his loving and adored Esther!

When Nadya saw Sergei's blood-stained shirt, she cried, "Seryozha! You're hurt!"

Esther, who had returned home earlier and was in the other room, rushed in, but Sergei raised his arms and shook his head to reassure them.

"Where's Papa?" Wildly Nadya grabbed Sergei's arms. "Papa? Where is he?"

"Nadyenka, dear one, Papa is dead!" Sergei put his arms around Nadya and held her tight. "He didn't suffer at all. Remember that. He did not suffer!"

Nadya wrestled out of Sergei's embrace and backed away. "Dead? . . . No! . . . Oh, merciful God, no!"

Esther came from behind, put her arm around Nadya's shoulders. In a small voice Nadya asked, "How? . . . Did you—did you see it happen?"

Sergei shook his head. "No, we were too late. Vadim and I ran all the way, but we were too late."

"Where's Vadim? Where did he go? Not after the sugar again!"

Sergei led Nadya to the chair and pushed her down. Then he turned to Esther. "Get me a glass of water." He waited until Esther had poured a glass from a pitcher on the kitchen table. Then he turned to Nadya, who was shaking visibly.

"Nadyenka, get yourself in hand. Papa is not the only one. Vadim is gone, too."

"Gone? What do you mean . . . gone?"

"He was shot, trying to save me. The soldier leveled his rifle at me, and Vadim tried to deflect it. We fell, and they thought we both were killed. I had to leave. I couldn't take the bodies out."

Bodies. Is that what they were now? The walls closed in. The air was siphoned out of the room, and Nadya could no longer breathe. "No . . . no . . ." she mouthed, her voice gone, her head and hands shaking in mute denial. Papa. Vadim. Not both at once. No! God, no! It was too much. Too much! Dead . . . killed . . . My father. My husband. Dead.

The ceiling, the walls crushed her. She was being dragged down, down, into a dark pit, and then, mercifully, her mind blacked out.

When she came to, she was lying on her bed, Esther's and Sergei's faces floating in and out of focus. She tried to get up, but Sergei held her. "Stay down awhile, Nadya. Here, drink these valerian drops, they'll help."

She didn't want to lie down. It felt far worse lying down. She pushed the medicine away and raised herself.

"Tell me how it happened."

"Why torture yourself, Nadyenka?" Esther said, gently stroking her hair. "It won't bring them back."

"I want to know how it happened!" Nadya cried. "Don't you understand? I've got to know! If you don't tell me, I'll imagine things! I'll torture myself! . . . Tell me, do you hear?" Hysteria was rising in her voice, and she couldn't control it.

Esther placed her hand on Sergei's arm. "Maybe you'd better tell her. She needs to know." When Sergei hesitated, she insisted, "Don't you understand? She *has* to know."

Haltingly Sergei told her how they had found Anton Stepanovich and the Persiantsevs dead in one room and how Vadim had died. Nadya listened, face hidden in her hands, both feet firmly planted on the floor. Papa had died quickly, painlessly from one shot. And Vadim had died quickly, too, but not so painlessly, riddled by bullets, carrying sugar to her, his pregnant wife. Kingdom in heaven, dear ones. She crossed herself more from habit than intent. *Rest in peace. My God, they're lying there on the floor, in a heap, maybe dragged away roughly . . . their arms and legs limp, their heads lolling . . . Oh God, no . . . no!*

"Seryozha, we have to—we must get the—" She couldn't bring herself to say "bodies." "We must take Papa and Vadim out of there, give them a proper resting place beside Mama."

Sergei did not move, and Nadya cried, "Do you hear? Go ask Yakov Oblevich to help you; the soldiers, the workers would know him! Hire a *tyelega*." At the thought of hiring a cart and having the coffins rattle on it, Nadya began to cry. "Seryozha, I can't bear the thought of their being left unattended like—like—" She shook her head and dissolved into tears.

Sergei knelt beside her. "Nadyenka, listen! We can't go in there. There are soldiers posted to guard the palace now. We risk being killed ourselves if we try."

"Don't you understand? My father, my husband, lying there, neglected . . ."

Sergei rose to his feet. A muscle twitched in his jaw. "Nadya, be reasonable. Don't you see, if anything happens to me, not only you and Esther but your baby as well will be left without a man to protect you."

Nadya stopped crying. Slowly she raised her head and looked at Sergei. Vadim had died so that Sergei could live. And if it had been the other way around, would she have preferred that? No! She shut her eyes tight to hold back the stinging tears. She would never see Vadim's dear face again; but her brother was still alive, and she shouldn't jeopardize his life. Still, to leave Vadim and Papa unattended, unwashed was unthinkable. Her papa. She was twenty-one and almost a mother herself, but right now she felt like an orphaned little girl.

Orphaned. The Persiantsevs were dead, too. Another link in a chain that tied her to Alexei: They had lost their loved ones at the same time, in the same place, in the same way. She should count her blessings. Sergei, her dear brother, was alive; so was Esther. Her family, her dear ones. And the baby soon to come, a part of Vadim to love forever.

And what about Alexei? He had no one left. He was an only child. There was an uncle, Count Yevgeni, somewhere in Paris;

but he never came to Russia anymore, and she had never heard Alexei talk about him. Maybe she should write Alexei, tell him that there *was* someone who was grieving with him. She would have to think about that. Right now, though, she wanted Vadim and Papa brought home.

"Seryozha, if you won't go, then ask Yakov Oblevich to do you a favor. He and the Shlyapin brothers can talk the soldiers into letting them take Papa and Vadim out. Please! Hurry! Before they take them away."

"Nadya, anyone asking for the bodies would be immediately suspect and in danger. I can't ask someone else to risk his life in our stead."

Esther stepped between brother and sister, tears streaming down her face. "Sergei, I understand how Nadya feels. The same thing happened to me, you know. I wasn't allowed to go back and bury my parents. I've never forgotten it." She bowed her head. "I never found out what they did with Papa and Mama."

"Do you think I have no feelings myself?" Sergei shouted, his voice shaking. "I was there! I saw them . . ." His voice broke. He coughed, then went on. "I'm as outraged as you, but common sense must prevail. There's nothing more we can do for them except remember their sacrifice for us." He hit the table with his fist. "We can't bring them back to life, damn it, and we must think of the living!" Angrily he pointed to Nadya's abdomen. "Think of the new life!"

Nadya rose slowly and wrapped her arms around Sergei's neck. The blood on his neck had caked, turned brown. She leaned her head against his cheek. He was right, of course, her brother. The mind agreed, but the heart wept. And then, suddenly—so suddenly that she gasped and wailed thinly—came a stabbing pain in her low back, its force so powerful, so unexpected it took all her strength not to slump to the floor.

She grabbed her back with her hand, and in that instant a violent cramp contracted her lower abdomen. She held her belly with her other hand and stared at her brother with terrified, shocked eyes.

"My God! It can't be! I'm not due for another month. . . ."

But it could be, and she knew it. She had heard of shock-induced labor, of premature birth.

Sergei leaned over her, his strong arm around her waist now. "Nadyenka, don't panic. It's not all that early. I'm glad you're home. Come with me. We'll get you comfortable, and then I'll call a colleague to come and deliver you. He lives nearby."

He led her to the examining room and helped her gently onto the table. Nadya gasped and moaned between spasms, the fury of pain blocking out her grief. Sergei was gone out of the room only a short while, and when he returned, she heard him give Esther curt, quick instructions. He leaned over Nadya. "My colleague is not at home, and I don't dare take time to look for anyone else. I'll have to deliver you myself." Then he turned to Esther.

"Get more towels, and bring that tray of instruments over here!"

She was sure someone was tearing her spine apart, twisting her abdomen, pulling her insides. Where were the spaced contractions she had heard about? Her body was being pounded and broken all at once.

"Push, Nadya, push!"

Sergei's voice was far away; she had drunk the laudanum he gave her, and now all that mattered was to get rid of the pain. She pushed and screamed and held on to Esther's hand. How long did this last? How many hours? She thought that time had stopped and the pain would never go away. Then, abruptly, the crushing agony was gone. The relief was so great she fell back on the pillows, her muscles loose, her body limp, and there came the most glorious, the most beautiful sound she had ever heard—the lusty yelp of a baby. *Her* baby.

"A chubby girl, Nadya! Oh, thank the Lord, a healthy little Katya!"

Nadya wept. Oh, God, her own little baby to love and to cherish. Vadim must have told Sergei that the girl was to be called Katya. Vadim! He'll never see his little girl! Tears poured forth: copious, healing, comforting tears. Esther stood over her silently, wiping them off with a towel, stroking Nadya's moist hair, pushing it off her forehead. Nadya turned and clasped her hand.

"Esther, I can't believe it! Vadim . . . Papa . . . gone forever, and I won't see them ever again!"

"Sh-sh-sh, Nadya! I know . . . oh, how I know!" Esther bent over and, cradling Nadya's shoulders in her arms, rocked her. Then, as Nadya's sobs subsided, Esther turned to Sergei and helped him bathe the baby.

After Nadya had been moved to her own bed and fallen asleep, Esther slipped out to their neighbor Olga Ivanovna and asked her to come in and sit with Nadya. Then she returned to the parlor and stood before Sergei, who was sitting in a chair with his eyes closed. He looked pale, drawn. Poor Seryozha. So much grief in one day. She never dreamed she could love so deeply, could allow her heart to open to a family again. But she had, and was glad. Now it was her turn to do something for Nadya and Sergei.

"Seryozha," she said, "I've worked with some of the Bolshevik organizers; I've been to Vyborg, spoken to the workingmen. They know me. Let me go to the palace and get Papa and Vadim out." She raised her hand to silence him. "No, wait! I won't be foolish and go alone. I'll find Yakov Oblevich and maybe take the Shlyapins with me. I'll do better than you could, for your face is not as well known as mine, and they will surely remember me."

"Absolutely not! They may connect you to the Persiantsevs, think you were a monarchist working as an undercover agent for the police. I can't take a chance on having anything happen to you. You have to understand that!"

Esther averted her gaze. "Seryozha, I know exactly how Nadya feels. I want to do this not only for her sake and yours but for my own as well. It's"—she shrugged, searching for the right words —"it's like failing to do what you know is your duty not once, but twice! I've got to try."

"No!"

The shout was loud and frantic. Suddenly Esther understood that Sergei had taken all he could that day, and it would be cruel to continue the argument.

"Very well," she said quietly, "I won't add to your anguish, Seryozha. I have to return to work now, so don't wait up for me tonight; the next issue of our magazine is overdue, and we'll be working late. Olga Ivanovna is coming over to sit with Nadya and the baby, while you see your patients."

Impulsively Sergei took Esther in his arms and held her tightly against him. "Forgive me, Esther! I guess I'm still in shock. I simply can't take on another worry right now." His voice cracked. "I love you so!"

Esther clung to his chest. She could hear his heart pounding. She raised her head and kissed him on the mouth slowly and tenderly.

"My Seryozha!"

He crushed her against him, his hands on her head, fingers threading through her tangled curls. "My darling, you are my life, my sustenance; you fill the very air I breathe!" He kissed her hard on the mouth; his lips slipped to the side of her face, her neck, then back up to her eyes and cheek in light, frantic kisses.

Esther pulled back, took his face in her hands, and smiled at him. "My own Seryozha, what happiness you've given me!"

Then, turning away quickly, she picked up her coat. "Now don't you worry about me if I don't come home until late. Don't wait up for me," she repeated. "You need your rest, and remember, Nadya and the baby need you more than I do right now."

Outside, Esther walked briskly toward the office of *Severnye Zapiski*. If Sergei became suspicious, she did not want him to catch up with her and extract a promise that she would not try to retrieve the bodies from the Blue Palace, for that was exactly what she was determined to do. She would ask Yakov Oblevich and the Shlyapins to help her. She was not foolish. If more than one familiar face showed up at the palace, the better their chances of success would be. Besides, it would take several of them to carry the bodies out. Even though she was free that day, she had invented the late working hour to keep Sergei from becoming suspicious and going to the palace at night.

She, too, was in shock from the day's tragedy. Although she mourned Anton Stepanovich and Vadim, her grief was not as intense as either Sergei's or Nadya's, but the killings had exhumed carefully buried memories of her rape and her parents' deaths. She had lived with the grief of those memories and was determined to spare Nadya a similar burden.

Over the months since her marriage to Sergei, whom she loved with an intensity she never dreamed possible, she had also come to love Nadya like her own sister, had acquired a loving and close family, and now she was going to do her utmost to bring Anton Stepanovich and Vadim home. She was not afraid of the workers or the soldiers who would be guarding the palace tonight. She had been seen at the Smolny, where she listened to Lenin's speeches ever since his triumphant return to Petrograd the previous April. She had been at the Finland Station, milling with the excited workers who had come to welcome home Lenin and his wife, Krupskaya. She had nursed sick wives in their hovels and was called the guardian angel of the Vyborg quarter. She—a guardian angel! She did not deserve the nickname; nevertheless, she hoped it would be useful tonight. To fear that she could be linked to the Persiantsev family and be dubbed a monarchist spy was ridiculous!

Sporadic shots in the distant Liteiny Prospekt area sounded several times, but Esther was used to them. A red glow illuminated the sky over that region, and she stopped for a moment to look. How sad it was! This long-suppressed hatred that had erupted after centuries of silence and subservience now threatened to envelop the whole country. She could hardly blame the mob. Given the chance, she might have done the same thing to the killers who had taken part in the pogrom in her village five years ago.

When Esther reached Yakov's rented room, she knocked, but there was no answer. A neighbor poked his head out of his door. "He hasn't been back since this morning," the man volunteered, looking Esther over curiously. "Any message?"

"Yes. Please tell him Esther and Sergei want to see him as soon as possible."

Disappointed, she headed for the Shlyapin brothers' flat. After she had explained what she wanted, the brothers exchanged glances. "We would need a *tyelega* and coffins. Where would we get them tonight? It's already six o'clock!"

"What can we do?" Esther asked. "I've got to get Anton

Stepanovich and Vadim out of the palace tonight, before they are taken away. As it is, we may already be late."

"We can hire a couple of droshkies and have them wait on the side street to attract less attention."

Esther shuddered. The image of Anton Stepanovich and Vadim on the seat of a droshky was grotesque. But there was no alternative, and she knew it.

"Please, let's hurry!"

At the front entrance to the Blue Palace a couple of soldiers barred their way. "Where to, comrades? What's your business here?"

"We've come to take out two relatives of mine who were shot accidentally here this morning," Esther said, hoping her voice sounded calm and authoritative.

With the torch raised high above his head, the soldier peered at Esther closely. "Relatives? Any relatives of those inside this *khoromy*"—the soldier thrust his chin toward the palace—"is an enemy of the state."

The Shlyapins slapped the man on the back and guffawed. "Come on, comrade, we are all members of the Bolshevik party. Here are our identification cards; take a look for yourself."

The soldier shoved the papers aside. "I don't need your identification. I have my orders."

Why, Esther thought with rising panic, *he doesn't know how to read! What are we going to do? Bluff him! Speak with authority!*

"How can we prove that we have a right to go in? All we want is to remove two bodies."

Obviously uncertain of what to do next, the soldier became agitated. He hawked to gain time, wiped his mouth with his sleeve, and then grabbed Esther by the arm.

"Come with me. I'll take you inside to the commissar on duty. Let him decide what to do with you."

When the Shlyapins moved to follow, the soldier poked them with his rifle. "Not you! The *grazhdanka* here said the bodies were of *her* relatives. You wait outside."

Esther was led into a small room near the main entry hall of the palace, where she faced a commissar behind a desk. After the soldier had reported what Esther wanted, the man behind the desk studied her through a narrow ribbon of smoke.

"Haven't we met before?"

"Perhaps, tovarich commissar," Esther said, straining to keep her voice even. "I've attended many meetings and have distributed our revolutionary pamphlets at various factories and barracks."

"Then what's the connection between the relatives you want to take out and the aristocrats who lived here?"

Esther was trapped. She had never been a good liar and knew that telling the truth would be her only hope of success.

"One was the family physician, and the other came to—"

"Family physician? How are you related to him?"

"Father-in-law."

Leaning on the desk with both hands, the man rose slowly from his chair. *Large as the paws of a bear*, thought Esther, and a fine tremor shook her body as the man walked unhurriedly around the desk and stood beside her.

"Father-in-law, eh? Well, well!" he said, towering above her. "Let's see your papers, *grazhdanka*."

There it was again, that new term *grazhdanka*—citizen, used by the Bolsheviks as a means of address to do away with class distinction. Esther pulled her identification card from inside her coat and handed it to him.

"You work for *Severnye Zapiski*, I see. A journalist!"

Esther nodded, not sure what he was leading up to. The man squinted. "A revolutionary with relatives inside the Blue Palace. Which side are you working on, Citizen Efimova?"

"You can check with the leaders of my cell, comrade commissar. They'll vouch for me!"

"I don't have time to check on everyone who comes in here. You're under arrest, *grazhdanka*. Anyone connected or related to the Persiantsev family is to be detained and interrogated. You'll be taken to the Kresty Prison, and if you are found innocent, you shall be released."

Outside, she could see the Shlyapin brothers on the corner by the droshky. She hesitated as long as she could before climbing into the waiting truck, making sure the Shlyapins could see what was happening. It was a cold night. There had been no fresh snowfall for several days, and the streets were covered with packed dirty snow. The night was blending into a sinister nightmare.

Somehow she must convince the prison warden of her innocence.

Chapter Seventeen

Sergei spent a fretful night. Too tired to stay awake and wait for Esther, he thrashed around in bed and fought his nightmares.

The weight of grief was crushing him, compounded by the thoughts of his duties as the last Efimov man. Slowly he raised his eyelids to the milky light of an October morning creeping through the window curtains onto the wooden floor beside his bed. He had to fight the impulse to bolt out of bed and run to see his sister and her baby. Everything was quiet in the house, and they must be asleep; he should move carefully, so as not to awaken Esther. Gently he turned over to see if she was still asleep or, as often happened in the past, lying quietly with one arm under her head, eyes watching his movements with amusement. But this grim morning Esther was not there. In spite of his disturbed sleep, he had not heard her slip out of bed.

Having dressed quickly, he went to Nadya's room. At the door he heard the tiny grunts of his newborn niece suckling at her mother's breast. His niece! A warm glow spread through him. He approached his sister's bed and gazed down at the baby. Nadya covered herself and looked up at Sergei.

"Isn't she beautiful, Seryozha?" she whispered, and began to cry.

Sergei nodded, staring down at the tiny girl, her round unfocused blue eyes wide open, a minuscule wet mouth formed into a perfect O, a glistening baby tongue flipping in and out, surprised at the abrupt withdrawal of nourishment.

"Did you hear Esther leave this morning?" Sergei asked, tucking the the blanket around the baby.

"No, I didn't. I thought she might be still asleep."

"Would you like some tea or hot milk, Nadya?"

"No, thank you. I'm not hungry. I keep thinking about Papa and Vadim . . . I can't believe they're dead. . . . Oh, Seryozha, what are we going to do? How can we abandon them to a common unmarked grave?"

"Don't dwell on it, Sestryonka. Remember, we have to think of the living. Concentrate on little Katya."

Sergei hurried out of the room, afraid Nadya would see his own anguish. He should fix himself and Nadya some breakfast this morning, nourish their bodies while their souls grieved. But he went back to his bedroom instead of the kitchen. He approached the side of the bed where Esther usually slept, pulled the covers back, and ran his hand gently over the pillow. The down had not been depressed, and the sheet beneath the cover was unrumpled.

Sergei straightened up. It was apparent she hadn't slept in their bed at all last night. She hadn't come home from the office. Late hours, she had said. But all night? Heavily he moved into the kitchen, picked up the receiver, and called the office of *Severnye Zapiski*. "No, Dr. Efimov," the woman answered, "your wife is not here," and, "No, she wasn't here yesterday. You see, the office was closed all afternoon," and "No, she did not call to leave a message."

Sergei hung up the receiver and stood by the phone, a fine tremor spreading through his limbs. She had not gone to the office yesterday because it was closed. She had misled him deliberately, and he knew why. The loyal, determined Esther had deceived him and gone to the Blue Palace. Sergei's stomach tightened, and his head throbbed. He couldn't go to the Blue Palace, and there was no point in telephoning the Shlyapins or Yakov Oblevich—they would be away from their rooms by now. Yet staying home and doing nothing were intolerable.

He must not tell Nadya yet. She had enough to cope with right now. Olga Ivanovna was due any minute to check on her, and he would ask her to stay while he slipped out.

Against his better judgment, Sergei headed toward the Blue Palace. He did not stop to reason out what he would accomplish by going there, well aware that he could not approach the guards at the door. Several soldiers stood at the main entrance, guarding a couple of trucks parked on the street. He dared not jeopardize his own safety by asking any of them about Esther. It was a new and distasteful feeling to be forced to hide from danger, to guard his person for the sake of his family. His anxiety for Esther had to take second place in his priorities.

It was very cold, even for the end of October. The damp chill crawled through his coat, discouraging any idling along the Neva Embankment. He could not permit himself to linger without arousing suspicion of the Red Guards. All around him life pulsated. The Bolsheviks had taken over the telephone exchange, the Winter Palace, and the main government buildings, and Sergei dared not go to the police. He had heard rumors that Kerensky had fled Petrograd, but no one seemed to know where he was. Perhaps he would bring troops back with him and reestablish order. In the meantime, Lenin had issued a proclamation that the Provisional Government had been deposed and the power was in the hands of the Petrograd Soviet of workers and soldier deputies. Although the transfer of power appeared easy, an element of terror lurked beneath a surface calm.

As Sergei had anticipated, both the Shlyapin brothers and Yakov Oblevich were not at home, and the *dvornik*, who was sweeping the yard, knew nothing of their whereabouts. "Give me your name, and I'll tell them you were here," he said, sweeping the dirt off the sidewalk with his broom of birch twigs. Unaccountably the sound annoyed Sergei. He shook his head and walked briskly out of the courtyard. *I'm a fugitive in my own city,* he thought in amazement. *A fugitive from an invisible pursuer. How long is this going to last?* Esther was languishing somewhere. Where? Sergei's fingertips were icy with dread. He *had* to find her, and when he had found her, he would scold his wife and hold her close and love her. *Oh, Esther, why did you do such a foolish, trusting thing?*

When darkness fell, he would return to Yakov's room. Yakov would know something; he would help him find her. But when night came, he did not have to go in search of Yakov because Yakov came to see him and gave him the Shlyapins' message.

"They were afraid to come to your house," Yakov said. "They saw Esther being pushed into a truck in front of the Blue Palace and heard the guard yell to the soldier to drive to the Kresty Prison. The Shlyapins are afraid to come to see you themselves. They're worried about being seen entering your flat and being linked to the Persiantsevs."

All Sergei could think of was that Esther was alive. He felt laughter rise in him. All that mattered right now was that he would see her again, and the thought that she had been arrested seemed of lesser importance.

"Thanks, Yashka! Oh, thanks! What a relief to know where she is! I'll go there immediately and explain that she was arrested through error."

Yakov did not answer right away. He took off his pince-nez and wiped it in an obvious gesture to gain time. After glancing at Sergei, he busied himself with replacing his glasses on the bridge of his nose.

"I tell you, Sergei, the situation is such that if I were you, I'd get ready to leave Petrograd."

"Yashka, you must be out of your mind! Esther is at the Kresty Prison, Nadya has just had a baby, and you're telling me to leave Petrograd?"

Yakov nodded. "Yes, I am. The Red Guards are unpredictable; they follow the whim of the moment. They're out to kill as you have seen for yourself. Death has lost its meaning!" Yakov shook his head and twisted his mouth in a crooked smile. "It's hardly the kind of revolution we bargained for, is it, my friend?"

Sergei hit his fist into the palm of his hand. "Our people have gone berserk, haven't they?"

"When there's even the remotest connection with the aristocrats, they go wild. You see, it was enough for them to learn that your father was Persiantsev's personal physician. Now your whole family is suspect."

"But I have no connection to the Persiantsevs personally! I haven't set foot inside the Blue Palace since I was nine years old!"

"They won't stop to weigh your guilt or innocence. Besides, didn't young Count Persiantsev court your sister at one time?"

Sergei nearly blacked out with rage. "That's nasty, Yakov. Who told you about that?"

Yakov put up his hands in mock self-defense. "Take it easy, Sergei! What's wrong with that? I happened to see them walking in the Summer Garden once or twice."

Sergei controlled himself with difficulty. "Who would know about an innocent courtship that was over a long time ago?"

"Who knows how innocent it was, Sergei? Surely not the Bolsheviks. And the servants talk, you know. Like it or not, your name is tainted by the Persiantsev House. Also, sooner or later your sister's published work will draw the Bolsheviks' attention. They'll find something subversive in it. I'm only giving you fair warning to be prepared to leave on a moment's notice. I'll make every effort to warn you in time, but I can't make any promises."

With one hand on Yakov's shoulder, Sergei offered him his other hand. "I know you mean well, Yashka. Thanks for the warning. But I can't leave without trying to get Esther out of prison."

Yakov pursed his lips and nodded several times. "I understand. But remember, sometimes it takes more courage to act a coward then to face danger against great odds. Above all, your going to the Kresty Prison is risky. If Esther is being questioned, you may only damage her chances of release by going there and identifying yourself."

Yakov shook his head, started to leave, and paused at the door. "Get out of Petrograd, Sergei, while you can!"

Sergei stayed awake most of the night, agonizing over what Yakov had told him. He had known, of course, of the lawlessness on the streets, but he had refused to see its burgeoning proportions, had been convinced that his sympathies and work on the side of the revolutionary cause had earned him immunity from danger. It had never occurred to him that his father's connection to the Persiantsevs would be held against his family. Still, he was sure that Esther's record as a dedicated activist would get her out of prison. Yakov was exaggerating.

Restless, impatient for the morning to come, Sergei planned his strategy, weighing every word he would say to the prison warden.

In the morning Nadya dissolved in tears. "I'm sorry, Seryozha, I know it must be agony for you, but I can't bear the thought that something dreadful has happened to Esther, too. My God, where could she be? It's been two nights and a day. No message, nothing! What are we going to do? Have you tried the *Severnye Zapiski*?"

Watching his sister's anguish, Sergei knew he could no longer hide the truth. Taking her hands in his, he said, "Nadyenka, you were asleep last night when Yakov came and told me that Esther has been taken to the Kresty Prison for questioning." He hesitated, then told her why.

Nadya gasped and hid her face in her hands.

Sergei went on. "Yakov insists we do nothing for fear of linking her to the Persiantsevs. He says we should get ready to leave Petrograd because we ourselves are in danger. The Red Guards are out for blood, and anyone connected with the aristocrats, even remotely, is on their wanted list."

Nadya lifted her head and stared at him. "Leave Petrograd? He must be joking! Where would we go? Anyway, it's out of the question right now. After Esther has been released, we can think about it."

Nadya leaned across the table where they were sitting and placed her hand on Sergei's arm. "What can we do to help Esther? We should talk to Yakov again. Maybe he knows someone close to the prison officials. It should be a simple matter of clearing up the misunderstanding."

Sergei stood up. "Nadyenka, Yakov took a risk coming to our house last night. The Shlyapin brothers are afraid to be seen here. So, you see, Sestryonka, we've become pariahs overnight. I'm going to the prison. I must try to get Esther released myself. We can't leave Petrograd without her, but in the meantime, Yakov is right. We should be ready to leave on a moment's notice."

"But where would we go?" Nadya cried.

Sergei threw his arms up. "I don't know, Nadya! We have to think about it. One thing I know: We can't break through to the west. It's too late. But there are the Urals and, beyond them, Siberia. We can lose ourselves in its vastness and with luck, wait out the madness somewhere in its bowels."

"Oh, Seryozha, what has happened to us? It's too much all at once . . . too much!"

"I know, I know, but we must be strong. We *have* to be strong."

"Be careful at the Kresty Prison, Seryozha! Remember, a clever calf can suckle two mothers. You may get farther with those people if you hold your temper and swallow your pride."

"I won't do anything foolish; there's too much at stake."

"Wait! Don't go yet, Seryozha! In the afternoon, when it starts to get dark, you'll have a better chance of getting away from them if you have to."

Sergei hugged his sister. After the initial outburst of grief she was trying hard to pull herself together, and her valiant effort did not escape him. Perhaps she was using her attention to detail as a shield to block out the enormity of the tragedy that had engulfed them at a time when, he knew, she had to keep her strength for baby Katya.

Yes, the least he could do for her was be careful. Thank God the days were already short, and he would not have to wait too long before the afternoon light would dim and he could leave their flat.

The Kresty Prison was a dreary building, somber and foreboding. At the entrance he asked to see the warden but was shown instead to a small office where a rachitic functionary was poring over papers at the desk.

At the sound of the footsteps he raised his head and in a nervous, reedy voice said, "Yes? What is it?"

"Comrade Rosen, Citizen Efimov is asking to see you," said the soldier who brought Sergei in.

"Rosen" flashed through Sergei's mind. A Jew. He might be

more sympathetic toward a Jewish girl once he was convinced of her innocence.

"Well? What do you want? I haven't got all day!"

The man's eyes, shifty and dark, were skittering all over the room and never once settled on Sergei. Undaunted, Sergei explained the purpose of his visit.

". . . and so you see, Comrade Rosen," he concluded, trying to speak with assurance, "my wife, who suffered a pogrom in her village during the tsar's reign, is the least likely person to be involved with an aristocratic family, much less deserves to be brought here."

"That's assuming that she *is* here at all. Leave your name and telephone number, and I shall look into the matter."

"I'm sure her name is on your list. Esther Efimova. *Esther—*" Sergei repeated, emphasizing her Jewish name, but the man interrupted.

"Yes, yes! As I said, leave your name, and you'll be notified."

Sergei's patience snapped. "Comrade Rosen, my wife disappeared two days ago without a trace, and witnesses reported that she was taken to this prison. It seems to me that it is unjust to hold prisoner an activist who has been working—"

"Whom are you accusing of being unjust?" the man screamed at Sergei. "What is your connection to the Persiantsev family anyway?"

Swallowing his anger, Sergei lowered his voice and spoke slowly. "I already mentioned that my father was their physician and my wife went to the palace to remove his body after he was accidentally shot."

A crafty glimmer appeared in the man's eyes. "Why did your wife go to do a man's job? Where were you?"

Suddenly Sergei felt as if he were treading on weakened planks of a bridge, each step threatening to plunge him into an abyss below. "I was delivering my sister of a child at the time."

"And your wife couldn't wait a few hours until you had gone there yourself?"

"We were afraid my father's body would be removed from the palace and we would not be able to find it later."

"What is your specialty, Dr. Efimov?"

The voice took on the businesslike, detached quality of a petty, disinterested clerk. Something in its casual tone, inappropriate to the exchange of a few moments ago, alerted Sergei to danger.

"I'm a general practitioner, but I spend as much time as I can at the Institute of Research."

"How long have you known the Persiantsevs?"

Sergei's muscles went rigid at the mention of the hated name. "I've never set foot inside their house," he lied.

"You haven't answered my question. Answer directly: How long have you known them?"

"My father treated them for their illnesses ever since I was born."

The voice rose a pitch. "I'm not interested in your father—he's dead! I'm asking you once more: How long have you known the Persiantsev family?"

Sergei's hand tightened into a fist, and unobtrusively he moved it behind his back. The Persiantsev name stuck to him like a leech, and like the parasite, he could not seem to free himself of it.

"I met the Persiantsevs only once, when I was nine years old," he heard himself say, "and have never seen them since."

"And you expect me to believe that in all the years your father served them, you've never been to the palace?"

The questioning was turning into an interrogation. He was now suspect and, as such, a liability to Esther. Yakov was right when he said that an act of cowardice sometimes required more courage than foolish bravery. Sacrificing himself would serve no purpose except jeopardize the lives of those whom he loved.

"My father was never their friend, and there was no reason for me to have gone to the palace. But I see that I have already taken up too much of your time, Comrade Rosen. I'd appreciate it very much if you would look into the matter. With your permission I will come back for the results at the time you specify."

A smirk spread on the man's face. Sergei hated himself for the obsequious speech, yet he felt a strange sense of triumph in having succeeded in placating the irascible little man behind the desk.

With a grunt the man started to sort his papers, dismissing Sergei with a casual "Check in two or three days."

All attempts at finding Esther failed. Day after day Sergei haunted the Smolny, the Kresty Prison, pleaded with bureaucrats, stolid Bolsheviks, and silent clerks. All to no avail. Everywhere he went, he encountered confusion and derision and, at times, threats that forced him to grovel before stubborn men and women inflated with their own importance. Esther had vanished without a trace.

He walked the familiar streets, passed the old buildings he had seen and lived with all his life; but now suddenly they looked forbidding, and he felt alienated, a stranger in his own city. He was dazed. The hours, the efforts he and Esther had devoted to overthrowing the monarchy had recoiled upon them with vicious force. They wanted justice and equal rights for all, yet he who had championed the revolution was now its innocent victim. His wife was in prison, and he was unable to secure her release. Shock and rage choked him, and around every corner his suspicious mind saw lurking workers waiting to kill him.

After two weeks Sergei, gaunt and anguished, finally faced the truth. Esther was not going to be released soon. The accusation that she was somehow connected to the Persiantsevs must have outweighted her reputation as an activist. She was being used as a scapegoat in the mass vengeance against the nobility and the former ruling classes. The thought that she might not be alive stabbed him and left a pain to gnaw deep inside.

The enormity of his loss overwhelmed him, and at night, alone in his room, he vented his frustration by pounding his fists against the brass railings of the bed, glad for the distraction of physical pain. Amazing how acute his hearing had become. It bothered him to hear little Katya's screams for food, the screams that came every four hours with clocklike precision. He thought: *I must provide for them; they need me—Nadya and Katya. My sister is not capable of making a living in this world turned upside down. What can she do? I must pull myself together.*

He no longer went to the research institute but stayed home and carried the full load of his father's practice. Patients came and went. He listened to their hearts and chests, prescribed medicines, droned instructions, and avoided their curious glances.

He thought he'd go outdoors and lose himself in the streets for a while. But there was too much space outside, and it oppressed him.

The short days of November ended in midafternoon, the darkness shielding the faces from recognition, granting anonymity to the bands of young hoodlums prowling the streets, lurking in courtyards sacking and looting. Red Guards with rifles in hand seemed to be everywhere, not only surrounding banks and other official buildings, but inside cafés and theaters, trigger-happy and drunk with power.

The extraordinary commission that Lenin had created early in December to struggle against sabotage was fast becoming the notorious Cheka. Night after night their commandos swept through the city, and the Red Terror had begun. No place was safe.

Sergei went home.

Nadya had recovered from childbirth, grieved with Sergei over their mutual loss, and withdrawn into her private sorrow. She did her chores of mothering in silence and did not ask for news. Quietly she went about collecting clothes and packing trunks, spending hours over minor decisions.

She rummaged through the wardrobe, picking out warm clothing, substantial and sturdy items for survival, not the dainty, pretty ones. Two things she could not leave behind: her mother's diary and her poetry. The first was duty; the second . . . well, it was a living part of her. Nadya picked up the diary. She had never broken the seal, and sooner or later she would be honor-bound to read it. It had been her mother's deathbed wish, she realized now. Perhaps this was the time.

Resolutely Nadya cut the flap and opened the diary at random.

. . . My happiness is over before it has begun, and the future haunts me as a specter shrouded in shame. I know without a doubt that my life shall be—must be—a Calvary of penance from now on. . . .

Nadya began to tremble and quickly shut the diary. She had had no idea that something so terrible had happened to her mother. Quiet, serious Anna, carrying a secret burden all her life! Suddenly Nadya yearned for her mother to be there, to hug and say that she loved her and to ask her to share her burden as woman to woman. But reading the cold pages of the diary alone—she was not ready for that. Somehow she couldn't bring herself to go on. It would have to wait until sometime in the future.

A few days later Yakov came to the flat. It was the first time that he had come during the day, and Nadya's stomach knotted with dread.

"Nowadays," he began, wiping his boots on the door mat, "you can't trust the telephone; who knows who might be listening? So I came as soon as I could." He turned and looked at Nadya. "I'm sorry to tell you this, but I have heard that they have finally come upon your published work. They've set it aside for discussion. This means only one thing: You're now under suspicion, too. You can't wait to see what their decision will be. I want to impress upon you both that with two things against you now—the Persiantsev connection and your poetry—you must—I repeat —you *must* leave the city at once!"

Neither Sergei nor Nadya said a word. After Yakov had left, Nadya nursed Katya, put her back in her crib, tidied the room, and tried to keep her mind busy. But her mouth was dry, and her hands were moist with panic.

The Persiantsev link. Her poetry. So much of it was her fault. Her innocence, her trust, her impetuous heart. They could not run to save themselves and leave Esther behind. It was unthinkable. She picked up the satchel with the manuscripts and hid it carefully behind the stacked trunks at the side of her wardrobe. When Esther was released, they would pick them out and flee.

She stayed in her room, listening for the homey sounds in the flat. Everything was quiet, except for her brother's nervous footsteps: three steps between his bed and the door; slight pause; turn around and three steps back.

Then Sergei walked into her room. She looked up into his pale face. He was shaking and looked feverish.

"Nadya, we shall leave tomorrow. There's no sense in taking any more risks."

"How can we leave without Esther, Seryozha?" Nadya asked helplessly.

Sergei ran his hand through his sandy hair, lowered himself heavily into an armchair.

"We have to. We must." His voice was hoarse, barely above a whisper. "Lord forgive me! There is no other way."

"I know why you're doing this. Because of me. I couldn't live with my guilt, Seryozha. You forget, I love Esther, too."

"Don't make it any harder, Nadya. Do you think it's easy for me to say that we must go?"

"But leaving Petrograd would mean betrayal! How can you even think of leaving?"

"What are you saying to me? What are you saying?" Sergei suddenly screamed. Clenching his fists, he shook them in the air. "I'm the one who had to make this agonizing choice. To be torn between two loyalties . . . like this . . . God, oh, God, help me!"

Nadya held her breath. He looked old, so old! Pity welled within her. He was her brother, and she was making it more difficult for him.

They stood looking at each other, the immensity of what they were about to do, what they had to do, hanging heavily between them.

Katya woke up and began to whimper. Brother and sister turned to look in the crib. Little arms flailed the air; tiny hands, unable to grasp anything, waved aimlessly; pink legs had worked themselves from beneath the blanket and were drawing up and kicking frantically at the tangled covers. Her mouth opened, and out came a lusty cry.

Sergei put his hand on Nadya's shoulder and pointed at the baby. "There's our reason for leaving, Sestryonka, a single, uncompromising reason. You see, my Esther is a survivor; we must believe that. I've appealed to everyone I know to get her released; but it's been two months since her arrest, and now the time has come for us to leave. We'll manage to keep in touch with Yakov somehow. Eventually we'll find her after she has been released." His voice wavered, and he put his arms around Nadya. She buried her face in his neck.

"Oh, God, how are we going to live with our guilt?"

"We just have to, Nadya. Vadim died protecting me, remember? Would you have me stay and risk his child's life? Which is the greater wrong then?"

Nadya pulled away and looked at her brother. His eyes were dry, but the anguish in them was terrible to see. Tenderly she pulled his head down to hers, brushed her lips over his forehead. "Forgive me, Seryozha," she whispered.

She had to go out and get some food. She hoped there would be lots of sausages left since she would buy as many as possible to take along on their journey. Journey! Sergei talked earlier about going across the Urals, hiding somewhere in Siberia. Good-bye then, Petrograd, the beloved city!

On the way to the butcher's, her legs carried her toward the Neva, and she slowed down in front of the Summer Garden for the last time. She used to enjoy seeing places where nothing had changed in decades, but today it wasn't a happy feeling. It made her sad, melancholy. She walked through the lane where the snow under her feet crunched with the same sounds as before, and she remembered when the place had been peopled with those she knew and loved, when her own innocent happiness had bubbled and risen through the tree branches to reach the sky. Now those people were gone: Mama, Papa, Vadim, maybe Esther. Their ghosts filled the pathways, and suddenly nothing was the same anymore. Only the silence remained . . . and into it there again came the sounds and the whispers and the tiniest comfort that someone she loved was still alive.

Alexei.

Whether she would ever see him again did not seem important just then. What was immensely important was to believe that he was alive. And he *was* alive, or she would have heard about it by now. Bad news traveled fast.

What was she doing, thinking about Alexei at a time like this? But there it was, that hidden gladness, a small corner reserved for a stolen thought. Sergei had given up Esther for her and Katya, and here she was indulging in her fantasies. Thoroughly ashamed, she hurried on. At the corner, she paused to look back one last time.

"Good-bye, memories," she said softly, "good-bye. I wonder if it will be forever."

She turned and walked briskly toward the butcher shop.

PART II

Vladivostok, Far Eastern Russia

Chapter Eighteen

August 1920 was hot and humid, made more oppressive by the burgeoning population of Vladivostok, swollen six times its size by the influx of refugees. The once-elegant Svetlanskaya Street, with its shops and restaurants, had never seen such motley crowds or heard such a profusion of foreign tongues. Nevertheless, after eight months in Vladivostok, Nadya was accustomed to the sight of various military uniforms on crowded streets, of scurrying clerks in double-breasted coats rushing along aimlessly, of the mixture of European and Asian faces.

In spite of the city's turmoil, Nadya was glad that she and Sergei had stopped fleeing. What a different life it now was from their nomadic existence the last two years, when they had worked their way across Siberia, moving from one village to another. Befriended by partisans who fought the old regime with dedication, so different from the unruly angry mobs in Petrograd, Nadya and Sergei had stayed in forest camps, where Sergei treated the partisans' wounds and cared for their families. It had been a nightmarish life not so much because of the constant moves and privations as because of the slowly dwindling hope of returning to Petrograd. Each move stretched the distance from home and from Esther. Worse yet, they could not talk about it, for to mention it would be to strip the cover away from the core of their hope until there was nothing left to protect the truth they both wanted to hide: that it would now be a long time, if ever, before they found Esther or even learned what had happened to her.

Thank God Sergei was a doctor. The partisans and the suspicious bureaucrats in the hamlets who had need of his care never once asked him what his affiliations were or why he and Nadya were moving from place to place. It was enough for them to know that Dr. Efimov was there to take care of them, to bandage their festering wounds or lower their fevers. But brother and sister kept moving because of their conviction that if they fell into the hands of the Red Army, their luck would turn against them. Even this deep into Siberia, the specter of the Persiantsev name pursued them, and they were forced to hide their past.

Nadya had lost count of how many towns they had passed through. There was Perm before the Urals, and then Tomsk and Krasnoyarsk; and there was once the depth of the taiga north of Lake Baikal, where pines and cedars stood tall and tranquil. But even there, the civil war thrust its branding iron into the primeval forest, and Nadya and Sergei fled again, this time south to Chita and the White stronghold of Ataman Semenov which was supported by the Japanese. But Semenov Cossacks' reactionary tyranny frightened them, and they went to Khabarovsk, and finally to the edge of land—the port of Vladivostok.

The many moves had been hard on little Katya, and from the beginning, she was a fussy, colicky baby.

"Don't tell me infants don't understand what goes on around them," Nadya once said to Sergei after a particularly fretful night. "The child senses instinctively when the home life is disrupted."

She had regretted those words ever since, for Sergei doubled his efforts to pour love and attention upon his little charge, spoiling the child in the process. Across the vast steppes of Siberia and their eternal winter quiet, Sergei carried Katya in his arms, soothed her painful teething, showered her with kisses, and the child learned to cry for attention. Nadya did not scold Sergei for spoiling Katya. He was their only protector, and she encouraged his affection for the little girl. You couldn't spoil a child with an overabundance of love, she kept telling herself. How could she deprive him of the one outlet for his love when so much had been taken from him?

And so the months had melted away, and when at last they came to Vladivostok, they found a city still free of the Bolsheviks and the last haven for the refugees.

Although the American Expeditionary Forces headquartered in the city since July 1919 had been withdrawn the previous April, the other foreign troops remained. At first Nadya resented the Allied intervention in her country, but after the Armistice of November 1918, when the feuding factions of the civil war continued to fight, she had grudgingly come to appreciate the foreign presence under the terms of Allied protectorate. The Japanese troops especially were in evidence, and after listening to rumors that Sergei brought daily from the clinic, Nadya had to agree that were it not for the Japanese support of the Far Eastern Maritime Republic, the Bolsheviks would have been there long before.

It was dreadful to think that they were living on borrowed time. All around them the city seemed to crumble under the weight of the demoralized populace. On this warm morning, as Nadya was walking down Pushkinskaya Street toward the Kuperkin Clinic, where she worked as a nurse's aide, she could feel the tension in the air. She stepped off the curb and nearly collided with a Chinese coolie in baggy black pants and dirty white shirt, carrying two cans of water suspended from a long bamboo pole across his shoulders. In spite of his careful, mincing steps, some water spilled over, leaving a trail behind him. Like most other Siberian cities, Vladivostok depended largely on surface wells, and Nadya was sure that the water, delivered by just such filthy coolies, was largely responsible for the increase in typhoid fever raging in the city.

A young boy was peddling newspapers on the corner, the wrinkled copies of *Dalny Vostok* already shopworn and torn at the edges in the day's humidity. Nadya had long given up believing the newspapers. Total confusion pervaded the city, and no one knew from day to day who would be in charge the following morning. There was a succession of maritime governments, with fanatic monarchist groups advocating terrorist methods no less malignant than the ones they condemned in the Bolsheviks.

Vladivostok must have been a spectacular city in its peaceful days, thought Nadya, looking at tall, corniced windows of a bullet-pocked baroque mansion overlooking the bay. There were many such mansions in Vladivostok, and Nadya appreciated the elegance of the graceful city. Rising above the Bay of the Golden Horn, it was terraced against the hills covered with cedar, oak, linden, and alder trees. The golden onion domes of the cathedral glittered in the sun as Nadya walked past it on the corner of Sobornaya Street. So much beauty to enjoy! But now, in the heart of town, she saw emaciated opium addicts sleeping in doorways and street benches and was revolted by the feverish struggle of the unscrupulous to make fortunes through dealings with the Japanese during the political impermanency.

There was talk about a counterrevolution, about going back home after the monarchists had triumphed once again and the Bolsheviks had been overthrown. Nadya and Sergei no longer listened. They hoped only for the restoration of order, for some semblance of a democratic government, like the one Esther had dreamed about.

They had been lucky to find two rooms for rent in a mansion owned by wealthy merchants, the Rozmyatins, who had divided their house into several small flats. Fortunately for Nadya, Madame Rozmyatina, a heavyset short woman who had no children of her own, took to Katya right away and offered to care for her while Nadya worked at the clinic three days a week. Because of her affection and willingness to care for the child, Nadya swallowed her resentment of Madame Rozmyatina's hatred of Jews. Dismayed, Nadya realized that the woman typified a large number of monarchists in Vladivostok who had fanned their age-old anti-Semitic prejudices with the firm belief that Russia was now governed by Jews and that they were responsible for the Red Terror. She shuddered on hearing such virulent comments and desperately wanted to believe that Esther was safe somewhere.

Her brother worked hard at the clinic, and although she worked more out of a desire to be useful than necessity, Nadya was glad they were financially without need. She pitied former officials of the tsar's regime who were eking out a living by selling their belongings one by one and doing odd jobs that came their way.

Soon after their arrival in Vladivostok Nadya began to worry about the long hours Sergei was spending at the clinic. "Seryozha, you have to get away from daily pressures at work."

"I'm perfectly content to be busy at the clinic."

"Are you willing to devote all your time to the care of the sick? What about your research?"

Sergei shrugged and lifted Katya onto his lap. Shaking his knee steadily, he singsonged in her ear, "Over the smooth road we go, over the smooth road!"

Then he bounced the little girl higher by jerking his knee up. "Now over the bumps and the ruts we go!" Suddenly he spread his knees and, holding the child under her arms, let her drop to the floor. "Boom! Down we go!"

Katya squealed delightedly and cried, "More, please, more, Uncle Seryozha!"

All talk about research was deferred. Still, Nadya worried.

One cold, clear evening they went for a stroll along the busy Svetlanskaya Street, dotted with cafés and gambling places. On an impulse, they went into one of the cabarets. A game of lotto was in progress. They bought a card for a ruble and found a seat at a long table filled with several officers in faded uniforms.

The croupier pulled the numbers from a cylinder and called them out in a loud voice, simultaneously flashing them in red on an electric signboard above him. When one of the men at their table covered a row on his card, he cried out excitedly, *"Dovolno!* Enough!" and the wheel stopped. The croupier handed him the money, the cards were reshuffled, and a new game began.

Nadya watched with satisfaction how caught up in the game Sergei became. She had not seen him this relaxed in a long time, and she was pleased with herself for having encouraged him to go in.

But this morning deep nostalgia overtook Nadya. Home. Vadim. Her memory of him was a comforting one, no longer painful, only tinged with sadness; but the other memory—the passionate, undying image of Alexei—never dimmed, no matter how hard she wanted to suppress it, and finally she had given up trying to forget him. She had left Petrograd without finding out where he was, and she wondered if he was fleeing as they had been, bivouacking somewhere, or perhaps was out of the country entirely. Not once, through all these months, had she permitted herself to doubt his survival. She pictured him in uniform, remembering the hours they had spent together, his smile, his voice, the tender mischief in his eyes when he looked at her in quiet moments of their privacy. In bringing back these memories, in dwelling upon them, she felt the pain of such indulgence, felt the sting of self-inflicted torture. Yet she welcomed her fantasies, actually welcomed them! They sustained her, took her out of the drab existence into a dreamworld.

She began to write poems again, hiding her stanzas, realizing that her creativity was a personal catharsis she had no desire to share with the public. Sergei enjoyed his lotto, and she wed her mind to her poetry in the solitude of her nights. During the days, however, she worked hard, and today was no exception.

A few more steps, and she was inside the Kuperkin Clinic. Nina Yaraya, the chief nurse at the desk, was everything her last name implied—ardent and intense. Under her energetic supervision, discipline was maintained throughout the clinic. Tall, lean, and vocal, she defused the constant emergencies and chastised junior nurses and erring orderlies. Impressed, Nadya had come to appreciate her stable influence in a place where death, tears, and agony were as certain as the daily rising and setting of the sun.

She turned to Nadya with a list of duties in her hand. "Nadya! Glad you're early; there were several new *tifozniki* and *sypnyaki* brought in last night, and one is so sick his leg wound has reopened. Dr. Efimov has taken care of him, so get moving and pick up the dirty bandages."

Nadya knew what was expected of her: pick up wet bandages; collect dirty syringes; wash out half-filled glasses. She did not mind the first group Nina mentioned—the *tifozniki*—for she knew that typhoid fever was not directly contagious. It was the other, the *sypnyaki*, that she feared, for typhus was highly contagious, and she dreaded the scourge that could leave little Katya an orphan.

Quickly she put a white kerchief over her hair, tied a large apron around her waist, and entered the ward. Rows of narrow cots stood close together, and it was her duty to make sure the delirious patients did not reach for the wrong nightstand and drink from a contaminated glass. She picked up the dirty glasses and syringes and went to the kitchen to have them boiled and disinfected. Then she put on a mask and moved hurriedly through the typhus room, where feverish patients thrashed and moaned in delirium, their hands and chests covered with purplish rashes. The smell of kerosene was strong, but Nadya had grown accustomed to it, for the presence of the disinfectant was necessary to keep the lice away. Some of the sick, their respiratory systems affected by the disease, were gasping for air.

She had finished cleaning both wards and was passing Nina Yaraya's station when she remembered something.

"Nina, where is the wounded typhus patient? I didn't see any bandages."

Nina looked up from her desk. "Dr. Efimov ordered him into the operating room to clean up his wound."

Nadya gasped. "A typhus patient in the operating room!"

"It's all right, Nadya. He's a *tifoznik*. Dr. Lanov is operating on him right now; when they bring him back, check that he is well covered and won't fall out of bed. Dr. Efimov talked to him before we took him to surgery. I have a feeling he's someone he knows."

Must be one of the partisans we knew in Siberia, Nadya thought. So many had changed loyalties in the last few months, hiding from revenge, afraid for their lives!

"Where is Dr. Efimov?" she asked, interrupting her own thoughts.

Nina shrugged. "I don't know. He left after talking to the sick man and said he'd be back in an hour or so. He must have gone to the depot to check on our supplies. We're so short on medicines!"

Nadya went about her chores, waiting for the patient to be returned to his bed. It wasn't long before she saw two orderlies carry in the litter and lift the sick man onto his bed. "*Sidelka!*" the men called to Nadya. "He's all yours. Watch that he doesn't climb out of bed when he wakes up. Dr. Lanov said his leg has to be kept immobilized."

Nadya walked to the far end of the ward where the man was lying. *Sidelka*, she thought, smiling to herself. What a misnomer! How had they ever come up with the word "sitter" for the nurse's aide? She did everything in the hospital but sit!

She reached the patient's bed and stooped to tuck in the blanket. Then, straightening, she looked at the sleeping man.

Her heart lurched; her pulse pounded so fiercely that the room swayed before her eyes. Alexei! Alive, here, before her . . . the dear, beloved face. She stood over him trembling, her hands pressed tightly together, afraid to touch him, to lose control and throw her arms around his inert body.

Her mind raced. In this vast, confused, and bleeding land of theirs, fate had thrown them together again, had given her a second chance. He was ill, but she wouldn't let him die; she would nurse him back to health, watch over him carefully. She had seen sicker patients survive, and Alexei was young and strong. Yes, she would take good care of him.

Slowly she took the towel she was carrying and, leaning over him, wiped his damp forehead. A wild joy surged through her. "My Alexei!" she whispered. Shyly she touched his beautiful hair, still thick and black and wavy, and traced a new line across his forehead. Her fingers tingled so! She yearned to place her cheek against his but dared not here in the open ward.

She looked around. Some of the patients were in a fretful slumber, while others moaned with fever and pain. No one was watching her. She found a nearby chair—after all, she was called a sitter, wasn't she?—and sat by Alexei's bed. His breathing seemed regular, thank God, and he was not gasping for breath. Soon his color would return, and the fever go down. She would sit here and wait until he awakened.

How naïve she had been in Petrograd! He had begged her to stay with him, but because it hadn't been on her terms, she had run away. It all was changed now. The war had taken care of that. She was no longer a young, innocent girl, but a lonely widow with a child. He *had* loved her, and she was the one who had chosen to leave. She would make up for it now that she had found him.

Alexei's hands moved restlessly on the blanket. She leaned over and kissed his left hand. It felt hot, and she closed her eyes, savoring the contact.

Wonderful! *Oh, thank you, dear Lord, for giving him back to me.* Her eyes still closed, she pictured him well and smiling, surprised and delighted to see her again. The fantasy ran on: the tender words, his eager hands, the loving. Slowly she opened her eyes to look at him again, to straighten his covers. His right hand moved, turned, and there, on the ring finger, she saw a gold wedding band. Pink gold it was, plain and scratched from wear.

She caught her breath, stared, then let her gaze drift to the window above his bed. Someone had wiped clean a small patch of the dirty glass. Fogged with grime, it had not been touched in months, but that small patch gleamed above her, shining blue with the midday sky, a fuzzy edge of a stray cloud floating across.

Married. He was married. Foolish, foolish girl. What had she expected? She, too, had been married, hadn't she? It was four years since their last night together, when she had told him his terms were unacceptable, and she had never answered his letters after that. So it was understandable, logical; two people who say good-bye inevitably drift toward new relationships. But love was not logical, surely not *her* love. And now he was married. Another woman enjoyed his love, his warmth, his loving. Who was she? Someone from his own milieu, no doubt. Someone . . . acceptable. Jealousy choked her. Somewhere in Vladivostok, Countess Alexei Persiantsev was waiting for her husband's recovery. She would come to the clinic, ask for her husband. Nina Yaraya would call Nadya to take her to the sick man's bed. Never!

Some things were beyond endurance. Nadya rose abruptly, turned, and ran out of the ward. Nina Yaraya looked up. "Nadya! What's happened? You're ashen. Here, you'd better sit down."

Nina started toward her from behind her desk, but Nadya waved her back. "No! I'm going home. I'll be back tomorrow!"

She ran through the streets to her house, where she did not stop to explain her early return to Madame Rozmyatina. She swept a delighted Katya into her arms and hid in her room. There she hugged her daughter's warm body to her chest, rocked her from side to side, and sobbed.

Chapter Nineteen

Early that morning Sergei had gone to the clinic before Nadya awakened. Weary even before his work began, he nevertheless realized that the shortage of hours in his days was a blessing. It left him so tired at night he had no time to dwell on anything before he fell asleep. Yet sometimes, when he could not relax after a particularly stressful day, the worry returned, and he could not chase it away. He was a realist, and he knew that communication with Petrograd could properly be established only after the Bolsheviks had taken Vladivostok. That meant the Red Army in the city. It also meant that he and Nadya would have to flee again. Where to? Harbin, Manchuria would be the next step, for the city was built by the Russians at the turn of the century in the right-of-way area of the Chinese-Eastern Railway and would then become their Russian oasis. But that would be the last resort. While they were still in their country, they could cling to the illusion that somehow things would change and they could stay. As long as he believed that Esther was alive, he could hope that sometime in the future they would be reunited, and he would yet have a chance for personal happiness. Deep inside, he knew it would be a long time before that happened, but he could not give up hoping. In the meantime, his purpose in life was Nadya and his niece. What a joy Katya was to him, that little cherub, so innocent, so dependent upon him! At least he felt he was doing everything he could to fill the void Vadim had left.

But on those nights when he could not sleep in the safety of his Vladivostok room, he bitterly berated himself for not having waited longer to leave Petrograd.

Phantoms from the past pursued him, and he drove himself harder and harder at work, forcing his mind on the work of the day. Upon his arrival in Vladivostok, the first clinic he applied to accepted him instantly, for the patient load was great, and there was a critical shortage of qualified physicians. He was put to work immediately. The chief surgeon had briefed him: The wounded, who were brought in on the hospital trains, had first priority. They were casualties shipped directly from the outlying area where skirmishes with Red partisans and feuding factions of the civil war were daily occurrences. Their wounds were to be treated, and the injured were to be protected from the infectious diseases that were rampant in the city.

Sergei plunged into his work eagerly, seeing his opportunity to return to his first love—research into the treatment of infectious diseases. All too soon, however, he discovered that he could not spare the hours. The immediate care of the very ill demanded so much of his time that he had to be content with available medicines. He worked long and exhausting days, coping with the typhus epidemic that had been scything the population of Russia hand in hand with the revolution.

Today was no exception. Nina Yaraya had greeted him with the list of new arrivals, most of them stricken with typhoid fever and typhus, many already delirious.

"Dr. Efimov," she added, completing her report, "I'm particularly concerned about an officer on Ward Two-A. He has all the symptoms of the *tifoznik*—high fever, vomiting, diarrhea—and I have detected a few rose spots. He must have been ill for quite some time. But what worries me the most, Doctor, is that his recent leg wound has reopened. He will probably need surgery, so I hope you will take a look at him first. He's at the far end of the ward, on the right side, by the window."

Sergei nodded and, after looking in on a few seriously ill patients he had been treating, went directly to Ward 2-A.

The man's face was turned toward the wall, but in spite of the sickly pallor, the flawless profile was vaguely familiar: the dark brow, the finely shaped cheekbone, the crop of black, shiny hair. Recognition, slow and reluctant, crept over Sergei like a threatening cloud. His first impulse was to flee, but he knew it was a cowardly act unworthy of a professional. He coughed to cover his reaction.

The sick man had turned his face and was staring at him with a frown. Then a tentative smile spread on his flushed face, and the feverish eyes sparkled. "Are you—are you Sergei Efimov?" When Sergei nodded, he hurried on. "What incredible good luck! . . . So glad to see you!"

Bracing himself to conceal his true feelings, Sergei stood by the patient's cot, wincing inwardly at the man's obvious pleasure. He had to say something, to be at least civil, detached. "I see we meet again, Count Persiantsev."

The words sounded stiff, but Alexei did not seem to notice. He grabbed Sergei by the hand. "I can't believe it . . . so happy to see you . . ."

His hand felt hot and clammy, and the physician in Sergei took over. He took his wrist in his hand to feel the pulse and noticed a wedding band on his ring finger. The relief was so great that he wanted to laugh out loud. He could even afford to be generous to the count. The proud nobleman needed him now. The experience was very satisfying. He examined him briefly, then said, "We'll talk later, Count Alexei. We have to clean up your wound in the operating room, or we'll have a hard time bringing your fever down. I'll leave orders with the nurse and look in on you later in the day."

He called Nina Yaraya, gave her instructions, and then turned back to Alexei. "We have to know where to get in touch with your wife. Routine regulations."

Alexei moved restlessly in his bed. "Sergei, may we please talk privately?"

Reluctantly Sergei turned to Nina Yaraya and nodded toward the door. Nina looked at the two men curiously, then left.

Sergei stood by the bed, waiting. Count Alexei was married, and Nadya was safe; but his visceral hatred for him was too deep to overcome. As he looked at the feverish man, his resentment grew. The Persiantsevs' name destroyed his family—his father, Vadim, Esther. If not for the count's family, his beloved Esther would be with him now, not lost and suffering somewhere in Russia, and he would not have been deprived of his love. What right had Alexei had to survive, to appear in Vladivostok, to be safe from the Bolsheviks?

"My wife is dead, Sergei," Alexei whispered hoarsely. "I left her in Tomsk . . . she died giving birth to a stillborn."

The short-lived relief had vanished, and Sergei could not bring himself to say he was sorry.

Alexei went on. "It was someone my parents wanted me to marry. After they died . . . I felt obliged to marry her. . . ."

When Sergei remained silent, Alexei struggled on. "Sergei, I've always loved your sister! I yearn to see her again. . . . is she—is she with you?"

Sergei was not fooled. Alexei could have married Nadya long before his parents had died. *Does he take me for an imbecile?* he thought, his anger rising.

"How come you have suddenly forgotten that my sister is not an aristocrat?" Sergei asked maliciously. "There's no blue blood running through our veins, you know!"

Alexei moved on his cot restlessly. "I deserved that. But whatever you think, believe me, I have never loved anyone but your sister. War is a harsh teacher! I saw such misery at the front that it made me realize how tenuous our life is. I fled across Siberia, followed Kolchak to Irkutsk, then went on to Chita and Vladivostok. Now I want to see Nadya . . . to—to ask her to marry me. . . ."

Carefully Sergei folded his stethoscope, put it in one pocket of his white clinic coat, pulled a thermometer from the other, and placed it under Alexei's armpit.

"Many of us have been disillusioned, both by the tsar and by the

Bolsheviks," he finally said, trying to veer the conversation away from his sister.

Alexei became agitated. "Those who welcomed the Reds deserve everything they later suffered at their hands!"

Sergei clenched his fists. What right did this nobleman have to condemn those who had already paid the price for their cause? He wanted to tell him he had no right whatsoever to pass judgment, but instead, he said, "The nurse will come by in a few minutes to check your temperature again. Then you'll be prepared for surgery."

"Nadya—how is she?" Alexei's voice was shaking.

Sergei paused and looked Alexei in the eye. "Nadya was married to my friend. She's a widow now and has a three-year-old girl."

"What happened to her husband?"

Suddenly Sergei could not divulge that his father, Vadim, and Esther had been lost to them because of the Persiantsevs. Not because he wanted to spare Alexei that knowledge, but because, somehow, he would again feel connected to the Persiantsev family and to Alexei in particular. He could not bear his sympathy. With an effort, he finally said, "He was killed by the Bolsheviks."

Unsuspecting, Alexei smiled. "I shall adopt her little girl and love her as my own."

Hot rage blacked out Sergei's vision, choked him, pounded in his temples. Afraid of what he might say or do that he would regret later, he stalked out of the ward. At Nina's desk he scribbled orders on Alexei's chart and then turned to leave. "Nina, I'll be back in an hour. I need some fresh air."

Outside, he roamed the streets. Sweat poured down his temples, slipped under his shirt collar, tickled his collarbone. He felt a bitter taste in his mouth. Esther had been taken away from him, his personal happiness destroyed, but now his sister would be able to regain hers. His long-suppressed suspicions that Nadya loved Count Alexei were confirmed. God knows, she deserved happiness! He could not begrudge her that—what kind of brother would he be, denying her this joy? But somewhere in the back of his mind, a sad truth surfaced: As long as his life had a direction, a duty to protect and support Nadya and her child, his loss was sublimated by his responsibility toward his sister. Now even that purpose was threatened. He couldn't keep Alexei's presence at the clinic a secret from Nadya, and of course, he should not even contemplate such an unworthy move.

And little Katya! Alexei said he would adopt her, love her as his own daughter. Katya—Alexei's adopted child. Little Countess Persiantséva. That was the final indignity. Sergei hit his right fist into his left hand with such force he winced in pain. He struggled to control himself. He shouldn't hate Alexei so much. After all, Alexei, too, had lost his parents and grieved over them. Sergei was thoroughly confused.

He ambled along the sidewalk blindly, letting pedestrians bump into him and throw him curious and sometimes angry glances. He did not care. He went down to the bay, where ships and small boats were anchored near the shore, the water lapping gently against the dock. It smelled of seaweed, fish, and oil. He sat down on a wooden bench, staring at the sea gulls that sliced the air with their wings and dived into the water. Sergei watched as they rocked on the waves, then suddenly soared into the sky. Voices floated toward him—stevedores, sailors, coolies—their polyglot, disjointed phrases making no sense to him.

He slumped on the bench, looked down at the dusty cobble-stones at his feet. Silly to react this way. One worked and lived with a goal in mind, and if it was taken away, then another had to be found in its stead. Without it, life had no meaning. Maybe he had his priorities mixed. His goal, eternal, uncompromising, was to live for Esther, to find her—his beloved wife. True, Nadya was his responsibility; but now Alexei wanted to marry her, and Sergei would be free to direct his interests elsewhere. He could try to squeeze time for further study of infectious diseases, do some research perhaps, indulge himself in a pleasant game of lotto. Why not? And as soon as the civil war was over, he would start his search for Esther.

He went back to the clinic to finish his rounds. Nadya by now should have seen Alexei. At least he would be spared the chore of telling her about him and watching her reaction.

But at the clinic Nina Yaraya told him that Nadya had taken sick and went home.

Never a respite from worry . . . he rushed home.

One look at Nadya's tear-stained face and puffy eyes, and Sergei knew her illness was not physical.

"What happened, Nadya?" he asked, cupping her chin and searching her face.

"I—I saw Count Alexei."

Sergei was puzzled. "Have you spoken to him?"

Nadya shook her head. "I saw him after his surgery. He was still unconscious."

"I don't understand. Why are you so upset? I spoke to him earlier. He wants to see you."

Nadya's lips tightened. "Why? His wife wouldn't like that!"

So that was it! Sergei took his sister by the shoulders. "Nadya, Alexei's wife is dead."

Nadya stared at him, wide-eyed. Sergei shook her lightly. "Do you hear me? He is a widower!"

Nadya caught her breath. "He's free?"

Sergei nodded and watched as Nadya pressed her hand against her mouth and stood motionless. A wondrous metamorphosis was taking place on her face; surprise and slow comprehension had given way to a rising glow of shining radiance. It hurt to watch. It was shameful to resent it, to be jealous, but Sergei couldn't help himself. He turned away, afraid she would see the envy in his eyes.

Nadya faced her brother. Her eyes sparkled and danced. "Oh, Seryozha, I can hardly believe it! It's terrible of me, but I'm glad his wife is dead!" She clasped her hands in an obvious effort to control herself and walked over to the window. With her back to Sergei, she said quietly, "Seryozha, you must know that I love him."

When she turned to look at him, Sergei nodded, not trusting his voice. He did not want to spoil his sister's ingenuous, unabashed delight.

After a while she went on. "I don't know why you have resented the Persiantsevs all your life, but oh, Seryozha, I can't wait to see him again! Please try to like him a little. Please!"

Sergei patted her on the shoulder. "Calm down, Nadya. It will be a while before Count Alexei is up and around. You can see him, of course, and I promise to be civil. That's the least I can do."

It was the end of August. Nadya was enjoying the clear, sweet air from the sea and the shimmering, liquid turquoise splashing at the rocks, tracing lacy patterns on the sand. Alexei had rented a two-room cottage on the outskirts of town for a couple of days —Lord only knew how much he had to bribe the owners to move in with their relatives in town—but he only smiled at Nadya's question and said she would now have to spend the two days with him. But Nadya could not bring herself to do it. She could hardly explain her absence to Madame Rozmyatina, who would have to care for little Katya, and above all, she could not face Sergei if she stayed away all night. No. She would come and spend the days with Alexei, she told him, but at night, when Sergei returned from the clinic, she wanted to be home.

Their reunion had been shy, and while he recuperated, the joy and the anticipation of being alone together grew slowly, smoldering, waiting to be ignited. Although the leg wound left him with a slight limp, he regained his strength fully. Nothing, he told her, could keep him from marrying her now. He had sent to Chita for his wife's death certificate, and as soon as it came, they could be married in the church.

Nadya was ecstatic, overwhelmed by her sudden good fortune. During the day she could hardly keep from smiling, unable to conceal her happiness from Sergei. She felt guilty. They rarely mentioned Esther's name anymore, but her memory hung between them. Was it wrong to be happy when someone dear to her found her joy a sharp reminder of his own misery? For surely that was what Sergei must be feeling while she was savoring her love. But even if she denied herself, she couldn't make her brother happy. It would not bring Esther back. Life meted out happy moments in small doses and showered misery in abundance. Such a sacrifice would solve nothing.

The two days in the dacha were idyllic. The Vladivostok climate cooperated, and it was warm, pleasant, the evenings balmy, the air silky. The afternoon sun spilled glitter over her camisole thrown hurriedly over a chair by the window. The golden light showed her shoulders, kissed her neck. The fresh scent from the lapping sea waves filtered into their bedroom, the breeze gently caressing her thighs. Cradled in Alexei's arms, she talked, bridging the five years, wanting to hear all the details of his life.

"I collected all your letters at general delivery, read them at night, fought the temptation to see you again."

"Why didn't you answer my letters at least once?"

"With me, it was either all or nothing. As long as I did not try to communicate with you, I could hope. But I was afraid if I sat down to talk to you even on paper, my resistance would falter. And I was so hurt, Alexei . . . so hurt!"

He covered her mouth with his, moving his lips over hers with a whisper: "I know, my love. I know . . ."

"Would you have ever defied your parents and married me if I had come back to you in Petrograd?"

Alexei did not answer at once. He stared out the window, specks shining in his blue-gray eyes. "I don't know, Nadya. I honestly don't know. My parents kept pushing Marie into my life, and I was gone so much of the time. They exerted a formidable influence on me, and I was not as mature as I am now."

He turned, raised himself on one elbow, and looked down at Nadya. "Does that hurt you terribly to know?"

Nadya thought for a moment. "It does. But I'm more of a realist now. I understand. We're all victims of our environment at one time or another."

"One thing I can say without reservation. I've loved you always. I suffered dreadfully at the front when there were no letters from you. Not one single word! It's a good thing I never knew that you had married someone else. I would have gone crazy with jealousy."

"Aha! What's good for the goose is not good for the gander, is it? After all, you married, too!" She teased him lovingly.

"I married only as a duty to my parents after they had been

killed. Besides, I thought you were lost to me forever. But you —you married by choice! Did you love him?"

Nadya pulled his face closer, rubbed her cheek against his forehead. His eyelashes tickled her chin, sent a delicious shiver through her body.

She thought about his question. "Yes, I loved him," she said slowly. "But not the same way as I love you. He was a good and loyal friend. He knew about you and said he understood. You see, my love for you has never faltered. It is a part of me. It *is*. Forever."

"Then how could you keep from answering my letters? You're so strong!"

"I did consider writing you after Papa and Vadim died. After all, we both lost our parents on the same day. But then I thought nothing had changed between us, and I did not want to open old wounds. It hurt too much."

Alexei looked puzzled. "How do you know our parents died on the same day?"

It was Nadya's turn to be surprised. "Didn't Sergei tell you?"

Alexei shook his head, and gently Nadya told him. Tears glistened in his eyes as he listened to her account of how Sergei had found Count Pyotr and Countess Aline and how Anton Stepanovich and Vadim had been killed. And about Sergei and Esther.

"Oh, Nadyenka, my *golubka*, what terrible pain it must have been for you! Five wasted years . . . I begrudge them. I promise to make up to you for all the heartache I have caused!"

"Five years is a long time, Alexei, but then I think of Sergei and Esther. He may never find her. He left Petrograd because of me and Katya. I feel responsible. If he had stayed behind, he might have found her."

"It's destructive to regret the past. If Sergei had stayed behind to look for Esther, he himself could have been imprisoned. In taking you out of Petrograd, he may well have escaped a worse fate and quite possibly even death."

"Thank you, Alexei, for making me feel better about it!"

He pulled her up. "Let's go outside. It's so lovely on the beach."

The air was full of gentle murmurs: the rhythm of rolling waves; the rustling grass; the gentle wind's eternal song. They sat side by side on the sand, suffused in the summer languor, watching the clouds above them, the ever-changing shapes drifting slowly past. It was a secluded spot behind a rocky promontory that protected them from the commerce of the neighboring bay.

Nadya stirred. "I have to go soon, Alexei. I want to be home before Sergei gets back from the clinic."

Alexei circled her waist and led her back to the cottage. "Not just yet, darling," he whispered in her ear, tickling it with his lips. "Not just yet!"

Inside, the mellow shadows of the afternoon enveloped them. The scent of jasmine in the room, the velvet of his hands, the silky contact of their soft, soft skins—she lost herself again in all this softness. Their love could not be matched. She had loved Vadim, but not like this! She had no words to describe it even to herself. Her heart was cushioned, cradled in this joy. Surely this could happen only once in a lifetime. And to some, she was sure, it never happened at all. She thought: *We are one not only in body but in mind and soul as well.* It had always been thus with them: Two hearts did not exist. Their union was complete, their thoughts and feelings merged, their bodies joined in consummate attainment of their passion.

"Are you asleep, Nadyenka?" he whispered, his hand tracing sun patterns on her shoulder. She shook her head and smiled, stretching slowly to spread the love glow to all the far edges of her body. He propped up his head with one arm and looked down at her. "I want us to have a child. Katya is yours, and I'll love her, but I want one of our own. Can you understand that?"

Nadya nodded. Of course she understood. She, too, wanted to have his child. How could it be otherwise? Oh, Alexei, I love you, love you! She clung to him.

Alexei held her without a word, then whispered, "I'm so impatient to call you my own, Nadya. I wish we did not have to wait for the papers from Chita."

"But we *must* wait, and in the meantime, we're together. This time nothing can separate us!"

She did not mean her voice to rise, but the last words flew out with an intensity she did not expect. A slight tremor touched her body and was gone before she knew it. Alexei looked at her.

"Nothing *will*, my *golubka*. I promise you!"

Chapter Twenty

On October 23, 1920, word reached Vladivostok that the day before, Chita had fallen to the Bolsheviks and that Ataman Semenov had fled to China. Sergei brought home the news and told Nadya that he was no longer willing to wait for the Bolshevik onslaught on Vladivostok which would destroy their Far Eastern Maritime Republic, the DVR, as it was called.

"But Lenin agreed to leave this area in the hands of the DVR! It's not the same as the White government in Chita!" Nadya cried, stunned.

"That was before the Bolsheviks took Chita. At that time they didn't want to spread themselves too thin and agreed to tolerate the DVR. But now they are gaining strength, and with the Chita government out of the way it's only a matter of time before they wipe out the DVR and chase the Japanese forces out of the country. Nadya, I don't want to have to flee from Vladivostok on a moment's notice the way we did from Petrograd. I want to leave on our own, while there are still trains available to take us to Manchuria."

Nadya sat at the table, her hands folded in her lap. Calmly she raised her eyes and looked at her brother.

"Seryozha, I can't leave just yet—not until Alexei and I are married." She paused, swallowed hard, then said, "I'm carrying his child."

Sergei did not move. He stared at her until she flushed and averted her gaze. The window overlooking the busy Komarovskaya Street below was fogged from the outside cold. The lace curtains hung limply over it. They need to be washed and starched, she thought irrelevantly. Sergei rose and paced the floor.

"More reason to leave now, Nadya. Chita must be in a turmoil. Who knows how long it will be before Alexei gets those papers? We can't afford to wait until you're so heavy with child you won't be able to make the journey, and by then we don't know what the political situation will be."

Nadya went over to the window, pulled the curtains together, fluffed the embroidered pillow on the sofa, made it look worse, fluffed it again.

"I must go to Alexei, talk to him. There's no reason why he couldn't join us in Manchuria a little later, after he gets the papers."

Nadya hurried through the autumn dusk. The snow had not yet started, but the October chill with its damp wind from the sea discouraged pedestrians from idling on street corners. Coat collars up, hands in pockets, they dashed across the dusty cobblestones to reach the other side of the street and disappear into one of the doorways.

Nadya fretted. Why did Chita have to fall at the time when she was going to share her wonderful news with Alexei? She had suspected her pregnancy for a while now and should have told him earlier, but she wanted to be sure first. Now the happiness was going to be marred by her move to Manchuria, by yet another separation. It also meant another disappointment for Alexei: His belief that the monarchists still had a chance to uproot the Bolsheviks and his hope of wearing the White Army uniform again would now be all but destroyed.

When she reached his house and climbed the two flights of stairs to his room, Alexei scooped her into his arms at the door before she had a chance to look at him. He held her close against him, and she could feel his heart pounding.

She did not think the political news would affect him this much. She thought him more of a realist by now, one who would not be so shocked by this latest development. How glad she was that she could tell him her news, take his mind off their floundering country! Pulling back, she smiled. "Darling, I have something wonderful to tell you! That dream we had, remember? It has come true. We're going to have a child. Our own love child!"

She expected him to clasp her fiercely in his arms, to shower her face with kisses, to love her. Instead, he shut his eyes and took a deep breath. Nadya looked at him closely. His face was ashen, and there were dark circles under his eyes.

"My God, what happened? What's the matter, Alexei? Tell me —tell me quickly!"

His silence sent shivers through Nadya. He leaned over and reached for an envelope on the small table near the sofa. "Nadya, my beloved, this came this morning. Marie is alive! She was sick for a long time after childbirth, and somehow the message that she, too, had died got through to me. Her letter came from Chita, and she is now on her way to Vladivostok."

Alive. Countess Marie was alive. Nadya backed away from the letter he was passing to her. She couldn't read it. Not the personal, intimate words from his wife. My God, not again! This terrible *déjà vu* sensation of her happiness slipping through her fingers. It couldn't be happening to her twice. It couldn't! Surely not this time when there was a child to consider! She clasped her hands tightly together and pressed them against her chest.

"What are we going to do, Alexei? What are we going to do?"

Alexei walked over and took her hands. "Nadyenka, I haven't slept all night. When I read Marie's letter, I couldn't bear the thought of losing you again. I knew I would tell her the truth and ask for a divorce. But then I saw another letter postmarked in Chita. That one was from her doctor, who says that Marie is suffering from tuberculosis and that her natural resistance to the disease has been severely weakened by childbirth. He goes on to say that the only reason he allowed her to leave the hospital in Chita was that the advancing Bolsheviks were on their doorstep and Marie told him I would take care of her here."

Nadya felt her hands turn to ice. Something inside her broke, leaving a hollow, cold pain in a vacant spot. She listened and understood what he meant, and she also understood that her life was ending at that exact moment. Yet she could not give up this meekly.

"What about our baby? Who has the greater right, your sickly wife or our unborn child?"

He turned away and was silent for a long time. When he looked at her again, tears were glistening in his eyes.

"Marie has no one in the world left but me. I can't abandon her now, when she is so ill. She would perish. And then you and I would have that burden on our conscience."

Nadya wrenched her hands away from him and stepped back. "What about me? I'm carrying your child, remember?"

"You're strong, Nadya."

"I see. In this world it's the weak who are protected, and they are the victors. It doesn't pay to be strong, does it?" she said harshly, hearing the rasp in her voice.

"Don't, Nadya! Please try not to be bitter!"

"You dare say that?" Her voice rose in anger, and she began to shake. "I hate that woman! She has claimed you long after I won your heart! And you! I carry your child, and you're prepared to put a stigma on it because you have no courage to ask for a divorce!"

"I have the courage, Nadya. I do! But I cannot destroy a life, not when it is my responsibility to care for her."

"Your sense of honor is misplaced! What about your child?" Nadya screamed.

Alexei did not answer right away, and when he did, his voice shook. "Maybe it would be better if the child were never born."

Anger and shock blinded her, seeking escape, as she rushed at him, swung her arm, and slapped him across his face with all the passion of her pain. Then she ran out of the room, down the stairs, along the streets. She did not stop until she reached the secluded beach near the little dacha where they had spent those glorious days two months earlier.

There she stopped, gasping for breath, trembling. Twilight had suffused the sea, and in the reflections of the vanished sun the sky was luminous with a purplish hue, majestic in its brilliance. The waves lapped gently at her feet; a tiny crab scampered sideways to hide beneath the water. Nadya climbed a sea-washed rock on the jutting promontory, sat down on its cold surface, and, leaning on a boulder, wept uncontrollably.

When her tears were spent, she looked into the thickening shadows. Aware that it was time to leave, she remained motionless with grief. She had regained Alexei and had lost him. He was rejecting her again, this time forever, rejecting her for another woman, whom he did not even love. Love, then, was not the strongest emotion in life. Duty was. She threw her head back and looked up into the sky. With her arms high above her head, she shook her fists and cried, "Why are you doing this to me, God? Why me? What have I done to deserve so much pain? I'm only twenty-four years old, God. Do you hear? Only twenty-four! So many years to live yet. So many!"

Her cries pounded against the rocks, frightened a flock of sea gulls hidden behind a boulder. They rose, wings flapping frantically, and fanned out above her head, their piercing cries echoing hers.

They sobered her. Blaming God could not change things. And surely He was not up there in the sky, judging her in silence. Vadim's words came back: "In the final analysis you stand alone." Every time adversity came her way, she had to dig deeper and deeper to find strength within. She would find it again, of course. She had no alternative.

Sergei was right. They had to leave Vladivostok, leave Russia, for she had to think of Katya's safety. To stay now would be folly. Of one thing she was sure: Abortion was out of the question. Alexei said it would be better if the child weren't born, and that was the most hurtful thought of all. He was a man; he did not understand; he said it only to make it easier for her. But what he did not know was that she wanted desperately to retain a part of him to be with her for years to come. She would carry his seed under her heart, nourish it, and soon their child would grow, and he—she smiled spitefully—he would have nothing.

How she hated him at that moment! Yet she knew at the same

time that in this hate was an element of respect for his choice. The knowledge rankled her more than anything else because her conscience whispered that in this very action was the man she loved. Suddenly she thought: It could have been the other way around. Vadim could have survived, and then she would have had to do the same. It would have been impossible for her to reject Vadim, unimaginable to tell him that she wanted another man. Her happiness with Alexei, she knew now, would not, could not survive at the expense of someone else's heartbreak.

Marie, his wife, what was she like? Was she beautiful or plain? It really did not matter. She stood between her and Alexei, sickly and weak—and formidable.

Nadya couldn't bear the thought of allowing him to see and enjoy her child while he was married to another woman. Never! There was a limit to her endurance. But what if with time his memory of her became dim, less painful, and maybe even sweet to live with—this memory of youthful love and passion? The thought was intolerable. He must not forget her. No, she wanted to leave with him a vivid impression of herself, not one that could be transmuted into a fading memory, but one that would disturb him, plague him, rob him of the peace of healing time.

She had to see him once more.

The dampness from the wet rock on which she sat seeped through her skirt. She shivered. Time to go home. She rose and walked slowly along the beach, her arms crossed over her chest, her hands clasping her shoulders. At least she had Katya and the new child and one other human being who loved her—Sergei. A different kind of love, to be sure, but loyal beyond any doubt. He was, without reservation, totally on her side.

She looked around her. The sky had darkened, and the sea took on the color of pewter—grim and forbidding. The city clinging to the hills appeared precarious and hostile. They would leave, go to Harbin, Manchuria, establish themselves in that hospitable place. What had Sergei told her about Harbin? It had been built by the Russians, and the Chinese Eastern Railway was administered by the Russians. It would not be difficult to adjust, living in a bit of Russia outside its boundaries.

But first she must see Alexei one more time. One last time.

At home she went about her chores swiftly, moving around the rooms automatically, allowing her limbs to carry her wherever it was necessary, her hands undressing Katya, getting her ready for bed, answering her questions with a minimum of words.

Katya chatted on, mercifully not expecting any answers. Then, unexpectedly, she said, "Mama, why do you cry?"

Nadya hugged the little girl. She was growing up too fast; she had few children to play with. "I hurt myself, Katyusha," she said, "but I am better now." In a sense it was true. Nadya helped the little girl climb into her bed behind the wardrobe that separated her corner of the room from Nadya's and kissed her goodnight.

This evening Sergei was late coming home, and by the time he returned she had the simple dinner ready. He smiled briefly at the sight of his favorite cutlets, which she had rolled in bread crumbs and fried over a Primus burner, and the buttered macaroni that went with them.

He sat down, swallowed a couple of mouthfuls, and put his fork down. "Nadya, it's like a bad dream repeating itself. I told you this once before, and I'm saying it again: Start packing; we have to leave Vladivostok. I've been looking into the possibility of our settling in Harbin. You'll be surprised how good it sounds. I doubt we'll be able to tell we're not in Russia, for I hear that one sees few Chinese on the streets. They have their own section of town where they live, called Foudzyadyan, and even the *izvozchiki* are Russian muzhiks.

"I feel we must leave here as soon as possible. The monarchists are talking about overthrowing the DVR government and establishing White Army rule; they are dreamers!" Sergei shook his head. "I happened to overhear a rumor that the brothers Merkulov, the major manufacturers of matches here, are plotting a coup. If they succeed, it will only intensify the Bolshevik campaign for an immediate takeover of Vladivostok. They may tolerate the DVR awhile longer, but never the monarchists!"

When Nadya made no response, Sergei started to eat again. Then he glanced at her with a frown. "Why so quiet, Sestryonka?

Have you seen Alexei?" When she nodded, he asked, "Will he follow us to Manchuria?"

"Alexei's wife is alive. She's on her way from Chita to join him."

For a few minutes brother and sister sat in silence. The brass teakettle began to whistle. Nadya got up and poured tea for Sergei into a glass with a holder, then covered the kettle with a tea cozy which she had knitted in the winter evenings. A jar of black currant jam was already on the table, and she put a spoonful into Sergei's tea. Then she sat down again, folded her hands on the table, and looked at her brother.

"This time, Seryozha, I'm not going to argue with you. It's hard enough to leave our country, but at least we won't be fleeing like fugitives. Let's leave of our own free will, I hope, for a better, more secure life."

Nadya measured her words carefully, spacing them with each breath. She suspected that Sergei would be relieved at the news that Alexei could not marry her after all and braced herself for the sight of fleeting pleasure on his face. There was none. Sergei remained impassive. He took a gulp of hot tea, put the glass down with such force that the hot liquid spilled on his hand, and he swore. Then he looked at Nadya.

"I'm sorry for you, Sestryonka. Truly sorry. That man has brought you nothing but grief . . . good riddance!" he added with vehemence. "We've both lost the ones we love. You see, I'm fully aware that by our leaving Russia, my chances of ever seeing Esther again are remote. Maybe someday we all shall go to America and find her there. We can dream, can't we? One needs a dream to live through this revolution." He sighed, then reached over to squeeze Nadya's hand. "Nadyenka, be strong. For what it's worth, we have each other, and we have our Katya."

He studied Nadya's face for a few moments, then looked down at his hands. "You could make things a lot easier for yourself by considering abortion."

Seeing her shocked look, he changed the subject quickly. "I think leaving Vladivostok now would be a relief for you. There's another important reason for leaving: In another country, we can tell people that your new child's father was Vadim and that you lost him only recently. Katya is too young to remember, and no one else need ever know."

When Nadya said nothing, he went on. "Why add the pain of illegitimacy to the new baby? After all, the child will carry Vadim's name anyway!"

Nadya's lips began to quiver dangerously. When Sergei came around the table, she reached out to him, grasped his arms, and broke down. He led her to the sofa, hugged her, and rocked her in his arms as he had done when she was a little girl. This time the tears were healing.

The next day the most important thing on Nadya's mind was to see Alexei one more time and part amicably, without anger or bitterness. She was sorry, yet not sorry, she had slapped him. Dreadful it was to love and hate a man simultaneously. This time she was taking something away from him—their child—and she was determined not to tell him that they were leaving Vladivostok.

She dressed carefully, intending to leave a lasting impression on him and not at all sure how she was going to accomplish this. Several months earlier, at the elegant Kunst and Albers Store on the corner of Aleutskaya Street, she had bought a thin wool dress that flattered her waistline and was trimmed with ivory lace at the collar and cuffs. She surveyed herself in the mirror and was satisfied with the pale wheat color of her dress, which made her brown eyes sparkle and her skin glow. After she had dressed, she told Madame Rozmyatina she would not be back until late and left the house.

Pain and grief in Alexei's eyes quickly turned to surprise and then enormous relief as he greeted her at the door. She apologized for having slapped him the day before, but he silenced her gently by pressing his hand over her mouth. "Don't, Nadyenka. Let's not waste our time on painful matters. There is so much to talk to you about, but no matter what we say to each other, there will always be things left forgotten that will need to be said later."

He led her to a seat, pulled her down beside him. "I want you to listen to what I have to say. I can't bear the thought of never seeing you again. Surely when the baby is born, you will let me see the child. I beg you! You'll hear from me from wherever I'll be. I know Sergei will take good care of you, but I want to help. God, how he must hate me! I can only pray that someday I'll be able to make you happy again!"

He put his arm around Nadya, but she pulled away. "What are your plans for the future? Where will you go?"

"I did a lot of thinking during the night," Alexei said slowly. "I'll leave Vladivostok as soon as Marie is able to travel and go somewhere into the country to live with professional trappers and hunters and learn their business. I'm a good shot." He smiled ruefully, then added, "Instead of killing humans, I'll be hunting animals. Whatever training I have, I want to put to good use."

"But you're not used to such labor!"

"I'm not afraid of hard work." Alexei clenched his fists and pressed his lips into a thin line. "I'm not going to let the Bolsheviks break me. Perhaps I've been pampered in the past, but no matter what the accident of birth is, a man's spirit will not disintegrate if he is determined to adapt himself to circumstances."

He looked at Nadya and took her in his arms. "Oh, my love, my heart, I shall miss you always!"

Nadya was unmoved. The child was hers, and she was resolved not to let him see it or even know where she would be. In that she was implacable. But the thought that she was seeing him for the last time, his embrace, his warm breath on her cheek, his thudding heart could not help bringing a response in her own body, and with a long sigh she threw her head back and opened her lips to him.

But she had a purpose to accomplish, a bittersweet revenge to enact. She must not weaken now when he was at her mercy; she must love him and hurt him by leaving a vivid, undying memory of herself!

Never before had there been a time when she had struggled with such argument of love and hate. *Alexei, Alexei, will there ever be a day, a moment to love you once again with the simple purity of tenderness, without grief and overwhelming pain?*

She looked up at his darkened eyes and, placing the palms of her hands on his chest, began to slide them slowly, deliberately, down his body with a tickling, feathery touch, feeling him tense,

his muscles rigid with anticipation. She moved her hands then, up
from his thighs, to touch his face, and with her warm and
searching mouth she kissed his neck and felt his pulse beneath her
lips, each beat a monad of the whole, a rising rhythm to meet her
own in a perfect union of the two. She let her mind be drowned,
possessed by him.

What was she thinking? He was not her own—never again her
own man! Another woman would touch those eyes, claim his
hands and lips and breath. Oh, but she, Nadya, would hold his
mind, would trap his heart forever, and when his arms touched that
other woman, his thoughts would leap back to her and cry for—for
what? Her hands? Oh, no! Her mouth, her tongue, her hunger to
absorb, contain and hold him helpless, longing for her always.

And as she watched him reach that indescribable, excruciating
peak—the summit of his ecstasy—there came a cry from him so
rending, so full of understanding, she knew that in the passionate
collusion of her love and hate he was her prisoner for life.

"Nadya, Nadya!" he cried. "The gods are jealous of such a love,
and ours is doomed. . . . Oh, God, the past will follow me
forever!"

And so it shall, she thought, and felt an emptiness within, aware
with sudden clarity that in making him her captive, she inexorably
had chained herself to him as well.

She left him soon, afraid to change her mind and tell him of her
plan. Blindly she ran and ran into the dark and into emptiness.

Very little of the next few days could she remember. A fog of
blurred and dimmed activity, in which motion, thought, and words
swirled into a coil of vapor, floated around and around in her mind
and cushioned pain with numbness. Sergei made quick arrangements to transfer to the Russo-Asiatic Bank in Harbin all the assets
he had carefully husbanded during his months of work at the
clinic. He did not question Nadya's reasons for not telling
Madame Rozmyatina where they were going. They took a droshky
to the station, and as the carriage rode through the cobbled streets,
a sea of frightened, anxious faces swam past. Nadya hugged

Katya's bundled body to her chest and, incongruously, wanted to laugh.

"Seryozha," she said, "can it truly be that we are finally going to reach security and safety?"

PART III

Harbin, Manchuria

Chapter Twenty-one

In September 1931, the hot dust storms from the Gobi Desert that blew over Harbin each spring and early summer were only a memory, and autumn leaves floated to the sidewalks, nestling in grimy crevices of cobbled streets. Occasional gusts of wind filtering from Siberian steppes cooled the dry heat and chased the high clouds across the sky.

With the influx of Russian refugees during the 1917 Revolution, Harbin had now become a sprawling metropolis and a cultural center of its host nation. In uptown Novy Gorod schoolgirls in brown uniforms with black pinafores scurried to the Oksakovskaya School for Girls, and a few blocks away blue-uniformed children hurried to the YMCA Grammar School. Shortly thereafter their mothers appeared at the entrance of the Churin and Co. department store, a few blocks away, at the corner of the Bolshoi Prospekt and Novotorgovaya Street, to await its opening. The two-story gray-stone building occupied half a square block. With a Byzantine dome, ornate iron grille balcony above the main entrance, and fringed awnings over the ground-floor display windows, Churin's dominated a busy intersection of uptown commerce and was a favorite with fashionable shoppers.

Inside, the busiest department was a grocery section, where delicatessen counters boasted gourmet items. There were chocolates from France; Turkish halvah of sesame and honey in both chocolate and vanilla flavors; smoked eel; spiced sausage from Germany; and Nadya's favorite, Near Eastern prune sausage—a chewy, compact confection mixed with walnuts.

But it was beluga caviar from the Caspian Sea that she could never pass without buying at least a small can to take home. It gave her a certain sense of satisfaction to be able to indulge herself with an occasional treat without worrying about the expense.

She enjoyed shopping at Churin's—a pleasure enhanced by the deference and recognition shown her by store employees and, not least, by the admiring looks of male shoppers. At thirty-five she had bloomed into a beautiful woman. Her figure had filled out, but her graceful bearing made her appear more statuesque than heavy and taller than her five feet six.

Today, wearing a pale green wool suit with a narrow skirt that reached to mid-calf and a matching hat slanted over one brow, she shopped in the store for an hour before picking up the wrapped caviar and walking out into the cool morning.

The sidewalk teemed with people, many of whom were sitting on long benches where shrubbery protected them from the street. This was a favorite place among the young to see and be seen, and Nadya, chuckling to herself, compared them to the promenaders on the English Quay in St. Petersburg. She turned onto the Bolshoi Prospekt and headed toward Girinskaya Street and her home two blocks away. She nodded frequently to passersby who recognized her, for after eleven years in Harbin she was well known as the sister of a prominent physician in town and a talented poet in her own right.

It had not been easy at first. When they arrived in Harbin November 1920, they had been overwhelmed by the drastic difference between the frantic, peripatetic atmosphere of Vladivostok and the rhythmic pulse of this affluent metropolis. Yet it was truly a Russian city. It had the same broad boulevards, the same stone buildings with T-framed high windows, the same picket fences as in her homeland. It had streets with Russian names —Bulvarny Prospekt; Mostovaya Street. The tall wooden spire of the St. Nicholas Cathedral with its intricate fretwork dominated the city from the top of the hill where the Voksalny and Bolshoi prospekts met, with the blue and gold onion domes of the Russian Orthodox churches in the distance. Manchuria? Nadya could hardly believe it. The only reminder was the profusion of rickshaws and Chinese coolies with thin, dangling braids and cotton padded jackets drumming up business in pidgin Russian.

Little Katya, apprehensive about getting into this strange conveyance of what looked to her like a one-seated cradle with frilled white cushions, was persuaded to sit on her mother's lap and was soon squealing delightedly at being driven by a running, strange-looking *dyadya*. Nadya laughed. "Don't call him uncle, he's a rickshaw."

Within days of their arrival Sergei found a two-room flat which he rented from a family on Gogolevskaya Street, and although it was located on a busy thoroughfare between the Novy Gorod and Modyagow sections of town, Nadya didn't complain. Sergei began working at the Central Hospital, one of the largest in Harbin, and Nadya realized how infinitely more fortunate they were than many refugees whose professions were not in demand. Thank God Sergei was a doctor!

The following May a midwife delivered Nadya of a girl, whom she named Marina. She doted on the baby and was distressed that Katya's jealousy of her sister manifested itself in temper tantrums. Aware that Sergei favored Katya and was closely watching her own attitude toward the two girls, Nadya was determined to be a good mother to both. It was not easy to blot out memories, for Marina grew to become a miniature of her father with black hair and clear blue-gray eyes.

Sergei spent long hours at the hospital and was at long last able to devote part of his time to research. With cholera rampant in China, he directed his interest to the comma bacillus that caused Asiatic cholera and within two years became known as a leading researcher and a recognized authority in the field of infectious diseases.

Then, one day, unexpectedly a new worry surfaced. A prolonged nosebleed kept Sergei from going to the hospital, and Nadya, alarmed, insisted he get a checkup. Reluctantly Sergei complied, only to discover that he had high blood pressure. By then they had bought a two-story gray-stone house on Girinskaya Street, with several rooms sectioned off for his private practice. The house was large, and they were comfortably settled with a cook and a maid.

"Seryozha, you really have to watch your diet from now on," Nadya said to her brother. "I've instructed Dunya to use less salt in your food right away. You should lighten your work load and take some time off for recreation the way you did in Vladivostok."

Sergei shrugged. "I enjoy an occasional game of Mah-Jongg, so what else do I need? Besides, my research work is taking a lot of my time now, and to me it *is* recreation."

Nadya looked at her brother carefully. He seemed tense. Placing her hand gently over his, she said, "Seryozha, my dear! The guilt we carry is always with us . . . I know it! But we mustn't allow it to ruin our lives. Esther wouldn't want us to."

At the mention of his wife's name Sergei paled and, without replying, rose and left the room. Nadya winced. Their hopes were raised each time Sergei asked the Red Cross to trace Esther's whereabouts, but all inquiries had led to dead ends. Only once, shortly before Sergei's nosebleed, did someone from the Red Cross call, saying there was a letter for him. Buoyed by hopeful élan, Sergei rushed over, but it turned out to be a false lead. Devastated by disappointment, he went on a gambling spree, playing Mah-Jongg all night.

Worrying about her brother, Nadya sought an outlet for herself, for she realized that her concern over him was becoming an obsession. She turned to poetry again. To her delight, she discovered that many of her newly found friends were hungry for literature. Soon she was attending weekly meetings where young poets and writers gathered to read and criticize one another's work. It evolved into a stimulating, serious workshop, in which Nadya's talent was quickly recognized and encouraged.

In 1927 a prestigious literary magazine, *Rubezh*, was established, and after the first few issues had appeared, Nadya decided to show the editors her poems. She pulled out some of her favorite stanzas and went to see them.

The office of the fledgling publication was housed in one room of a private apartment. The editor was not in, and Nadya was asked to leave her manuscripts and return later. When she came back in a week, the editor's assistant, a friendly, plump woman in her forties, handed her a note with a smile.

"These editorial comments will tell you better than I can what we think of your work."

Nadya glanced at the slip of paper, and the words danced before her eyes: ". . . the poetess is talented, intelligent, with a feeling for beauty. Her work is mature with a wide range of skillfully handled themes. There is freshness and sincerity in her work, and her words build tension, line by line, toward a climax that ties in with the beginning. We hope she continues to write, for she will grow and take the place in literature which she deserves. . . ."

Nadya glowed with pleasure. The assistant nodded to a chair. "Sit down, please. Let's talk about your work."

When Nadya sat down, the woman continued. "I'd like to suggest a different theme from now on. I can well understand your youthful romanticism, but as refugees from our homeland we need something else. Dig deeper into the Russian soul. We've lost our country, and until and if we regain it, we need moral support. It's important for us to reassess our values, nourish our emotional needs.

"You have logic in your poetry. Redirect it from personal issues to the general public. Give us"—she paused, searching for the right word—"psychic energy to cope while we wait in limbo."

Nadya was impressed at the vehemence with which the woman spoke. "You're a visionary, aren't you?"

The woman shrugged. "I'd say I'm more of a pragmatist than most White Russians in Harbin. It's pointless, in my opinion, to wave our white, blue, and red flag and cry foul when we are impotent to do anything about it right now. But our intellectual and moral hunger, on the other hand, needs sustenance always. Who knows what the future will bring? In the meantime, we need introspection."

Nadya went home and did some thinking. She didn't want to write inflammatory rhetoric. The monarchists were not her cup of tea, and the socialists were lumped with the Bolsheviks; neither one appealed to her. Soon her poetry was published, but she knew the editor was right. At one of the poetry gatherings an older critic told her, "Every human being wants to belong to someone, and now we, the White Russians, belong to no one. Many of us write mediocre poetry as an escape from reality, but a major talent combined with discipline and training is rare. You have such a gift. Give us what we want the most: Tell us that we are no less the human beings we were before we lost our country. Especially we men need this reassurance. We're without a rudder, don't you know? Our dignity is smarting; we tend to feel inferior to even the lowest coolie because he has a country and a passport to protect him. In short, he belongs, and we do not."

Nadya listened carefully and turned to broader lyricism; it was easy. She had already done that in Vladivostok, and now she wrote:

> Our Russian soul!
> The strength of it lies
> in its power to survive adversity.
> It glows in the darkness
> like an immortal beacon . . .
> enduring.
> resilient,
> invincible. . . .

She had a new goal to pursue: She had a responsibility to her countrymen, to give them spiritual food. Her mind at last was taken off her unhappy memories, and the initial temptation to let Alexei know that he had a daughter had gradually waned. She was pleased she had not weakened. A clean break with the past was less painful now, and she forced her mind to dwell on her brother, who, she always reminded herself, had sacrificed so much for her.

Yet to force herself not to yearn for Alexei was impossible. At night, when her mind withdrew into itself, yielding to rest, her body took over, demanding her lover's passion. Restless, she thrashed under her covers, unable to control the longing, her body warm and lonely. She welcomed daylight, for her routine had fallen into a leisurely pattern. She had enough financial security to be free from the ever-present anxiety about money that had followed their journey across Siberia. Eleven years now—a good span of time to dim the memory. Today was what mattered.

Deep in thought, Nadya was crossing the median of the Bolshoi Prospekt, with its parked droshkies and dozing Russian *izvozchiki*, when she heard her name called. She turned. One of the young aspiring poets, Zina Lomova, a gaunt, disheveled schoolteacher, ran up to her.

"Nadya, may I walk with you?"

A little surprised that Zina was not at school, Nadya nodded.

"I have a day off and telephoned you, but you had already gone out," Zina began, then hesitated. "I was . . . I was wondering what you thought about all the rumors?"

"What rumors?"

"The Japanese want to occupy Manchuria!" Zina blurted out and, frightened, looked behind her.

"Why, Zina? Under what pretext would they do such a thing? I took those rumors as panicky gossip."

"Their excuse is to settle Manchurian strife between the nationalists and the communists, and to protect their nationals from so-called bandits."

"Bandits! An ambiguous word, to say the least!"

"I know, but if they refer to the *hunhuzi*, then it's a red herring for invasion because the *hunhuzi* have been here for a long time and are no threat to the country. Why, in the past the Chinese government even availed itself of *hunhuzi* to help clean out corruption among its employees."

Nadya looked at Zina curiously. "I didn't know that. I thought they were wild and unruly and far away from the cities, somewhere in the taiga, aren't they? I've heard of isolated kidnappings for ransom, but they are rare nowadays."

Zina shook her head. "The *hunhuzi* are more formidable than that, but then we take the good with the bad. However, that's not the point. Why all of a sudden is Japan concerned about protecting Manchuria from these outlaws?"

Nadya was silent for a while, digesting the news. Using the *hunhuzi* threat seemed incongruous indeed. These bandits had been part of Manchuria since the seventeenth century, when the loyalists of the fallen Ming dynasty hid in the taiga, and with time had become outlaws and bandits. To her knowledge, nothing had changed in recent months to give validity to the Japanese offensive.

"I really don't know what to make of it, Zina," Nadya said at length. "It could be that Japan isn't content with the Liaotang Peninsula and the port of Dairen they now occupy and wants more land. Let's hope it's only a rumor."

But it wasn't a rumor. Everyone in Harbin awoke that frosty morning of February 5, 1932, to scattered sounds of distant shots. No heavy artillery, not even a bomb. It was over quickly, and by midday the sidewalks in front of Churin's were packed with silent observers, watching truckload after truckload of soldiers roll up the hill from the Modyagow section of town. A few timid banzais from onlookers wedged into the roaring rhythm of truck engines; an occasional paper flag fluttered in the breeze, its red sun on the white background spotting the crowd like a glob of freshly spilled blood.

The soldiers' khaki uniforms and high-perched visored caps contrasted sharply with the gray uniforms of the Chinese Army. Although the soldiers' narrow eyes and saffron skins betrayed their Asian origin, the spectators, mostly White Russian refugees, knew that these did not belong to their host nation.

That morning, three blocks away on Girinskaya Street, in the gray-stone two-story house set well back from the street behind a slatted wooden fence, ten-year-old Marina snuggled in her bed, listening to the shots. Her mother had just told her there would be no school today. Whatever the reason, Marina was happy to stay in bed for a few extra minutes. Stretching, she looked at the double-paned window before her. It was frozen solid on the outside, and she loved to fantasize about the frost's intricate patterns, conjuring up fairyland cities and gardens out of the designs that crowded one upon the other in a collage of leaves and flowers. This morning the window sparkled in the sun with a rainbow of tints.

Tiny glass cups of alcohol buried in the mounds of cotton wool between the panes kept the inner glass from frosting; Marina wondered idly if the cups belonged to the set her mother kept in her wardrobe, together with a large cotton applicator and bottle of alcohol. These were used as suction cups on the chest when someone in the family had a cold.

At the foot of Marina's bed stood a cream-colored wardrobe. Across from it was her toy corner, crowded with a tiny cradle, dining and bedroom furniture, a metal bathtub and wash sink, and a tidily arranged collection of dolls and stuffed animals. A square table and two chairs stood by the window. It was here that she did her homework, memorizing Russia's major rivers, the country's longitudes and latitudes, and its ancient beginning when Varangian Prince Rurik had founded its first dynasty in 862.

But it was also here that Marina did her reading, yawning over *Robinson Crusoe* but immersing herself in the adventures of *Tom Saywer, The Call of the Wild*, and *Uncle Tom's Cabin*, or learning the morals of Krylov's fables and always crying over Charskaya's *Princess Dzhavakha*.

Right now her books were stacked in one corner, together with a notebook and a satchel, all ready to take to school. In the center of the table, neatly arranged in an oval loop, lay a gold chain with her baptismal cross inscribed "Save and Protect Marina."

This year her sister, Katya, had been given a separate room because she was fourteen years old and Uncle Sergei said she should have a room of her own. It was upstairs next to Uncle Sergei's spacious study and looked out over the nearby arboretum a block away to the right. The mansard roof was low, and the sill of Katya's dormer window was decorated with needlepoint pillows and an embroidered linen runner. By comparison, Marina's room was Spartan except for the paneled lace curtains on each side of the single tall window.

She envied her sister, who was fair and hazel-eyed and popular, in contrast with Marina's shiny black hair, gray eyes, and studious temperament. Vibrant and cheerful, Katya got away with almost anything because Uncle Sergei always found excuses for her, whereas Marina was not so lucky. Why, only yesterday, when she refused to eat her dessert—it was the hated lemon custard—she had had to sit on a chair in the middle of her room for an hour. She wished the floor could have opened and swallowed her, she was so embarrassed!

Yet her mother's pensive eyes filled with tenderness whenever she looked at Marina, and it made up for all the jealousy she felt toward her sister.

Tra-ta-ta—ra-ta-ta—

Were the shots coming closer?

Marina listened.

Her rambling thoughts came to an end when Vera, the seamstress, came into the room and leaned on the bed's metal railing.

"Time to get up, lazybones! Dunya will have breakfast ready for us in a short while."

Marina adored Vera, who came early in the morning, took her meals with the family, and stayed until after dinner. Only twenty years old, she was more like a sister to Marina and Katya than a family seamstress.

The daughter of an impoverished noblewoman, Vera was a skillful seamstress, and Marina's mother always managed to find work for her. Vera was tall and thin and quiet. Bent over the Singer sewing machine in one of the extra rooms upstairs, she pumped the elaborately grilled pedal most of the day and then doubled as companion to the two girls, helping them with homework. In the afternoons she took them for walks or accompanied them to her attic room, where her mother, dressed in widow's black, sat by the upright piano and gave them music lessons.

When Marina and Vera entered the dining room that morning, the family was already seated. This was unusual, for as a rule Uncle Sergei had his breakfast early and left the house before the girls were up. He was always in a hurry, and right now his clear gray eyes looked pointedly at Marina's mother, who was sipping a cup of coffee.

"Nadya, when this shooting is over, and I expect it will end shortly, we must go to Novotorgovaya Street and see what's happening. The girls are old enough to see history in the making."

Nadya shook her head. "Katya maybe, but not Marina. She's too young and impressionable. We don't know yet what will happen today."

Sergei raked his sandy hair off his high forehead. He still looked boyish in spite of his forty-six years.

"Nonsense, Nadya!" he said firmly. "It's time you stopped shielding Marina. Don't forget that we are refugees in Manchuria, and we don't know what tomorrow might bring. The sooner the girls face the real world, the better off they'll be."

An enigmatic smile touched Nadya's lips. "I'll let Marina go along if you promise to hold her by the hand all the time we're in the crowd."

Marina sprinkled sugar and cinnamon over her yogurt and ate it hurriedly. When she reached for the warm sesame seed encrusted bread, her eyes met Uncle Sergei's. Whenever he looked at her, he appeared not to see her. When she was old enough to understand, her mother had told her that her father had been killed in the revolution and that Uncle Sergei had saved her mother and Katya from the Bolsheviks and had brought them to Harbin, where Marina was born. Uncle Sergei took good care of them all, and she only wished he could have been her father.

She spread fresh liver pâté on her buttered bread. No matter how much she tried to compete with her sister, it was always Katya who got Uncle Sergei's attention. She bit into her bread and took a sip of hot cocoa, nearly scalding her tongue. Tears rose to her eyes, but she swallowed hard to keep from making a sound.

Dunya came in from the kitchen with a tray. Fat and short, she puffed at the round table. Reaching across to collect dishes, she knocked the tassels of the large silk lampshade that hung above the center of the table.

"Dunya, how many times do I have to tell you not to reach across the table?" Nadya chided.

"Yes, *barinya*." Dunya sighed, addressing Nadya by the respectful "mistress." "It's just that—" She shrugged and glided out of the room.

Sergei shook his head and smiled. "Give up, Nadya. You'll never teach her manners. Besides, her job is in the kitchen, and there she is unsurpassed. I forgive all to anyone who can cook pheasant in sour cream and roast snipe the way she does."

"I know, Seryozha. She's a cook, not a maid. Masha should be back in a few days, and Dunya can then stay in her domain."

Sergei turned to Katya, and his face softened. "Katyusha, I bet you're glad to skip school today, right?"

Marina felt a lump in her throat. Uncle Sergei spoke to Katya, not to her. Her mother had asked Uncle Sergei to hold Marina by the hand when they went out today. Perhaps she would then be able to speak to him, tell him about her good grades in school and the praise she had received from her piano teacher the day before.

The sisters attended the YMCA school at 47 Sadovaya Street, just two blocks from home. Marina was first in her class, while Katya barely made passing grades, daydreaming her way through the school hours.

That afternoon, during the three-block walk from their house, Marina held fast to Sergei's hand, chatting away about her lessons, telling him about her achievements. He listened, nodded, and Marina was happy that Katya and her mother were walking ahead because she could have Uncle Sergei to herself. Her sister turned around. "For heaven's sake, Marina, you're nothing but a braggart. Plug up!"

In spite of the biting air, Marina felt heat rise to her face. She wasn't bragging. She was telling the truth, and all she wanted was a little praise from her uncle. Was that so wrong?

"If your grades were as good as mine, you'd be telling Uncle Sergei about them. You're jealous, that's all."

"Stop bickering over such nonsense, girls," Nadya said. "Look at the rime on the tree branches. It looks like a Christmas tree."

The quarrel averted, Marina looked to where her mother was pointing. Barren autumn branches of yesterday were now coated with frost, white and brilliant in the sun, untouched by birds, too slippery for feathered things.

"You know, Sergei," Nadya went on with a sigh, "on a quiet day like this, when there are no Chinese around and I see only gray-stone houses and tall wooden fences, I have a feeling of *déjà vu*. It's uncanny how the buildings here remind me of home."

"That's not surprising, Nadya. When the Russian engineers for the Chinese Eastern Railroad patterned Harbin after our own cities, they did us a great favor. How could they have known that someday we would cling to Harbin as the last outpost of the country we lost?"

"Yes, and now even this haven is threatened," she said quietly, not wishing to alarm her daughter. "I'm afraid of this invasion, Seryozha. No good will come of it."

They reached the corner of Novotorgovaya Street and stopped near a privet hedge that separated the sidewalk from the snow-packed street. A contingent of Japanese troops rode through the streets, the din of heavy truck tires muffled by fresh snowfall of the previous night. A few scattered banzai greetings sounded thin and timorous, dissolving without an echo in the hushed crowd.

Dressed in beige muskrat coats with matching hats and muffs, Marina and Katya stood next to their mother, who was wrapped in a foalskin coat trimmed with silver fox. Their affluence was conspicuous in the crowd of other Russians and Chinese, most of whom were dressed in padded cloth coats.

With the corner entrance to Churin's directly behind them, Marina would have preferred to go inside and look around than be all but smothered in the dense crowd. Her attention was caught, however, by a soldier who held his rifle in front of him with both hands. He looked directly at her as the truck lumbered past, and suddenly his narrow eyes brightened.

Marina tugged at her mother's coat. "Mama, one of those soldiers with a rifle is looking at me. I know he is!"

Glancing at the truck, Nadya hesitated, then put her arm around Marina's shoulder. "I'm sure you've imagined it," she said, and drew her closer to her side.

A well-dressed man in a sealskin-trimmed coat moved toward them. He tipped his hat to Nadya, then turned to Sergei.

"Sergei Antonovich, fancy meeting you here! Just the man I want to see."

The two men shook hands, and Sergei introduced him to his

sister as Mr. Gorman. Then he looked at the man. "What can I do for you?"

Mr. Gorman smiled. "I'd like to call on you tomorrow. I've got a problem, I think."

Sergei thought for a moment. "I'm not sure of my schedule but I'll be glad to squeeze you in—about three o'clock?"

When the man moved away and was lost in the crowd, Nadya turned to Sergei. "Was that the owner of the Novaya pharmacy?"

"Yes. He's a patient of mine."

For a few minutes Sergei was pensive. Then he let go of Marina's hand. "Nadya, these trucks are coming from Modyagow. This means they entered the city from the direction of the airfield. Tomorrow I shall drive down there and take a look at what they have done."

Nadya shook her head. "There was fighting there. God only knows what you might see. Didn't you have enough of the war in Siberia? Don't go!"

But Sergei only shrugged and, taking Marina's hand, started for home.

The next day Katya came down with a cold and stayed home while Vera took Marina for a walk. They headed away from the center of town, past the old cemetery on the Bolshoi Prospekt and the Protestant church on the next corner on toward the distant new cemetery. Two blocks farther a procession of horse-drawn carts loaded with dead soldiers in gray uniforms labored past them. Bodies were piled high on top of one another, the legs and arms dangling over the sides like so many rag dolls thrown in a heap.

"This is something you shouldn't look at," Vera said, trying to cover Marina's eyes with her gloved hand. But Marina looked, and as she did, a sightless slanted eye glinted at her from the cart. The rest of the soldier's face was not there. Nausea rolled in her stomach, and she pressed her face against Vera's squirrel muff.

From then on, Marina never played with her dolls, and those that were soft to the touch with limp arms and legs she hid in the bottom drawer of her chiffonier.

Chapter Twenty-two

The small cottage cheese soufflés lay untouched on a china plate in front of Sergei. He brought the steaming glass of coffee in a silver holder to his lips and scalded them. He swore, put the glass down, shook his fingers to cool them. "God, why does the coffee take so long to cool?"

Nadya raised her head. "If you ate your soufflés first, the coffee would have time to cool. Why, you haven't touched them yet, and they're your favorites!"

"I'm not hungry this morning."

Nadya studied her brother reflectively. "Is anything wrong at the hospital, Seryozha? You haven't been yourself these last few days."

"No, nothing at the hospital."

"Are you upset about Mr. Gorman's kidnapping?"

Sergei jerked his head up. "What do you know about it?"

His sharp tone surprised Nadya. "Why, only what I've read in the newspaper, that the *hunhuzi* got him and are demanding an unreasonable ransom. Frankly I don't believe it for a minute. The *hunhuzi* operate in rural areas, and I doubt that they'd be so brazen as to challenge the Japanese gendarmerie." Nadya thought for a moment, then narrowed her eyes and looked at her brother. "Mr.

Gorman looked concerned that day we met him. Did he say anything to you when he came for his appointment?"

Sergei seemed unreasonably annoyed. "Of course not! It was strictly a medical visit."

"Is there something else that's bothering you, Seryozha? I hate to see you get so upset. It's bad for your blood pressure!"

"I guess I'm annoyed because some of our Russian zealots came to see me a few days ago all fired up to organize a counterrevolution in Russia. All these men talked about was the Japanese Expeditionary Forces in Siberia in 1920 and how they backed the White Army movement at that time. They live in the past, the fools!"

"But why come to you?"

Sergei glanced at his sister quickly and looked at his coffee. "They thought that since the Central Hospital has been taken over by the Japanese, I could approach the authorities on their behalf."

"Their fervor may be misguided, but surely without malice. I still don't see why it should annoy you this much."

Sergei pushed the chair back and rose abruptly. "I'm not annoyed anymore, I tell you! I have a lot on my mind this morning, that's all!"

Nadya watched him stalk out of the house. Why did this brother of hers think it a weakness to share his problems? Something else was troubling him, and he was determined to hide it. Very well. She wouldn't pry. Maybe he had had another disappointment in his search for Esther. There seemed little chance of his finding her now. Nadya sighed. Sergei was forty-six. Did he ever covet another woman? The only one he had ever loved was Esther, and he had had so little time to enjoy his love!

He was consumed by his work at the hospital, his outpatients at home, and his experimental studies of bacterial sensitivities to various drugs. What little time was left, he fussed over her and her children. Her emotional, solicitous brother.

She shifted in her seat. She knew he worried when an occasional suitor surfaced to court her. The truth of it was that she had no desire for another man, emotionally or even physically. The yearning, suppressed and dormant, was always for Alexei.

She was aware of gossip in town, wearied of her friends' questions about marriage. There were those who went so far as to say that Nadya's family life was *unnatural*. She fended off such remarks with a smile and a change of subject. Only once did she shrug her shoulders and drop a casual retort: "I don't need a husband. I'm more independent this way."

She was content to be serene, comfortable with her companion, her sibling who had loved and protected her for as long as she could remember, and he was loyal. No uncertainty, no fear of betrayal, total trust. Yes, she had everything an average woman coveted: material comforts, even luxury, family affection, unity, and, always her joy, her two girls.

There were things to attend to today: check the menu with Dunya, and with Masha off for the day, make a list for Dunya's shopping; try on the dress Vera was altering for her.

So the day went easily, lazily. In the afternoon the girls came home from school, and Katya went out to see a friend. Dunya had gone on an errand, Vera was upstairs, and Marina had just started her homework.

In the mellow afternoon light, Nadya reached for Vicky Baum's *Grand Hotel* and settled with a cup of tea.

It was a peaceful afternoon. Sparrows twittered outside the window. A dog barked in the distance. Must be Petrov's shepherd; he barked at each passerby routinely, the silly dog. Ivan Petrov was a good neighbor, but she would have to ask Sergei to speak to him about his dog. She smiled. It was so quiet that she could hear Marina's pen scratching laboriously in the next room. They were comfortable sounds.

She began to read and lost awareness of time.

When the pounding started on the front door, harsh, loud, Nadya knew instantly that it was not an ordinary visitor who had come to call.

There was little space under the bed between the creaking bedspring and Marina's upturned face. As the bed's rhythmic movement depressed the coil, it came within a centimeter of her head. She had to press her body flat against the floor to prevent her dress from catching in the wires. Her feet did not reach the end of the bed and were well hidden behind the bedspread's silk tassels. However, she was able to see the feet and ankles of those in the room.

The air under the bed was stuffy and smelled of dust. A few puffs settled on her face, and afraid she might sneeze, Marina worked her facial muscles to stop the tickle. Although her arms were trembling from tension, it did not occur to her to disobey her mother, who had said, "Don't move, don't make any sound, and don't come out until I tell you to."

Earlier, when someone pounded on the front door, her mother had looked through the side window but had not pulled the lace curtains aside as she did when Uncle Sergei was at home. Outside, it was a sunny April afternoon, bright and fresh from yesterday's rain, and no one could see through the curtained windows into the dark house.

Her mother swung away from the window and pulled Marina into the bedroom, ordering her to hide under the bed. "There are Japanese soldiers outside. I don't want them to see you," she whispered as Marina crawled under. Then her mother went to open the door. Moments later Marina heard men talking in the hall, loud and abrupt, but when she heard her mother's unruffled voice, her short laugh, she was not afraid.

She listened. Men's voices and the sound of booted feet came closer. Although she could not hear what was being said through the closed door, her mother's voice was reassuring. The door opened, and her mother said, "Take a look for yourselves. There's no one here. The girls are visiting friends and won't be back before my brother returns."

Marina caught her breath. Why did the men want to see her and her sister? They hadn't done anything wrong. She wished the men would leave the house so she could crawl out from under the bed. Her blue school uniform and black pinafore would be gray with dust, and she would have to take a bath before she could eat supper. It was a pity because her uniform was new, just finished by Vera, who had measured it carefully to fit Marina's rapid growth. There was dust in her mouth, too, and as she ran her tongue over her dry lips, the front door slammed and she heard her sister's voice.

"Mama, I'm home!"

"Katya, run to the neighbors—run!" Her mother's voice, queerly pitched, rang out as it had the time Uncle Sergei had scolded Marina for speaking out of turn.

The soldiers shuffled out of the room.

"Ma-a-ma!"

Katya's scream was shrill. There was a slapping sound, a gasp, a man's rasping laugh, a whimpering. Marina's palms tickled with sweat. She ran her hands down over the rough wool of her skirt to dry them, then lay still, taking shallow breaths, her arms at the sides of her body, waiting for her mother's voice. But she heard many voices and couldn't distinguish her mother's. Had the men slapped her? Or Katya? She did not want either of them to be hurt. If only Uncle Sergei would come home, he would chase the men away, and then she—all of them—would be safe. She lifted her head, but the sharp end of a bedspring caught on a strand of her hair; the pain brought tears to her eyes. After raising her hand carefully, she released the entangled strand, then lowered her head to the floor again. The bedroom door crashed against the wall. Boots came into view—men's boots. The men were dragging someone into the room. She recognized Katya's black patent leather shoes and white socks, then her mother's brown pumps close behind.

Boots were everywhere now. She counted nine pairs. Katya's kicking feet swung upward. A pair of boots followed, and the bedsprings began to creak. This was when the screaming started, high and piercing and terrible. Marina's head buzzed. Something dreadful was happening to her sister, but she couldn't see above the bedspread tassels to find out what it was.

A man grunted, accompanied by other men's jeering laughter, and the boots slipped down to the floor. Katya's shoes did not follow. Instead, another pair of boots replaced the first, and the creaking and the screams started all over again.

Through the noise of the bedsprings and Katya's screams, Marina heard her mother's voice. It was breathless and high-pitched as she asked the men over and over to follow her to the other end of the room and offered something Marina did not understand.

She counted the boots that climbed up onto the bed, and after she had counted six pairs, Katya stopped screaming and howled. The sound was worse than the screams. Her mother's pumps and a pair of boots went away to one side of the room, but the others stayed close to the bed, shuffling back and forth. Slowly Marina stuffed her fist into her mouth.

Above her, bedsprings continued to depress, then rise. Suddenly a boot came close enough to the bedspread tassels to push them in and touch Marina's forearm. So close to her face, it smelled of wax. It was cold and felt like an insect sting. She froze, afraid the man had felt her arm.

While she stared at the boots, they moved. One lifted off the floor but the other remained, still touching her arm. The silence was immediate and total. Katya's howls stopped. The creaking stopped. Time stopped. Seconds or minutes later, there was a scraping sound of metal against metal followed by a single thud above her. The noise began again, but now it was her mother who screamed. There was a scuffling, thumping sound from the other side of the room, but no more sounds from Katya. Marina's feet were numb, and her fingertips tingled; but she kept still and waited until all the boots had stamped out of the room, out of the house, and her mother's brown pumps came stumbling to the bed.

As her mother's knees came down slowly, slowly, and the weight of her body set the springs to creaking again, Marina heard her cry for the first time in her life.

It was then she disobeyed and came out from under the bed.

Two weeks. Two weeks of continuous nightmare. Nights were the only respite. Alone in her room, Nadya did not have to hide her anguish from Sergei and wept bitterly into her pillow, trying to stifle her cries. Sergei was devastated enough, and knowing his temper, she was afraid to tell him of her own submission to one of the Japanese soldiers. He couldn't have handled that. A woman sensed these things. There was nothing he could do against the whole occupational army. He could only hurt them all by trying. It wouldn't bring Katya back.

At night, lured into sleep by exhaustion, she relived the nightmare again and again, waking up, gasping and thrashing, to release the steely grip of the soldier's arms around her as she struggled at the other side of the room and saw the glint of a blade an instant before her Katya was stabbed.

Why had they killed her? Why?

She never dreamed of her own part in the horror. She could hardly remember the act. Her mind had been so completely detached from herself that while the soldier had used her, her body had mercifully numbed itself to reaction.

So there was no need to tell Sergei about it. Katya's death was enough to cope with without adding her own violation to his grief.

And what if Katya had lived? At fourteen, her life would have been damaged forever. Maybe it was kinder that she had died —oh, God, was that an awful thing to think! But that is what she *had* to think. Whatever the truth, she had to believe this. She was the one left to go on living, and there were still Marina and Sergei. Eleven years of peace were at an end. Complacent years, without fear. It could never be the same now.

She needed fresh air, sun, the comfort of street noise. So she went out to a sidewalk bench and sat down, letting her mind be soothed for the first time in two weeks by homey sounds around her, and unwanted memories came crowding back, unraveling her life before her.

She did not know how long she sat there or when she started thinking of her mother's diary. She had not thought about it in years. Perhaps this was the time for her to read it and perhaps find solace in her mother's words.

Nadya read late into the night. Harbin, the house on Girinskaya Street vanished, and she was back in St. Petersburg, on the Moika Canal. In her mother's delicate writing, her pain moved across the pages, unfolding the past. When Nadya came to the last entry, she started rereading from the beginning, flipping the pages, unable to believe Anna's confession, piecing together her story like patch-work.

> February 1885. Last night I was surely possessed by the devil. I love *Anton*. I've never loved anyone but my Anton. What happened to me last night? . . . I'm so ashamed. . . .

A few entries later, Anna's words rose in anguish from the pages:

> There's no longer any doubt what my sickness means. I carry the seed of the man I despise. This will be my punishment for life. I have to tell Anton, beg him to marry me right away. . . .
>
> The pain on Anton's face! I still see it . . . what I wouldn't give to have spared him my confession! I shall devote the rest of my life to making him happy. . . .
>
> August 1908. Yesterday Count Pyotr and Aline invited us to celebrate young Alexei's nineteenth birthday. "A family gathering," Aline called it, said Count Yevgeni was with them on one of his rare visits from Paris. His wife had died, Aline said, and he was in mourning, so there would be no big ball. Twenty-three years . . . I haven't seen him for twenty-three years. I didn't want to go, but Anton said we must, and I couldn't hurt him, couldn't tell him that I was terrified after all these years. . . .
>
> It was dreadful. I fought a fainting spell all evening, and couldn't look at Yevgeni. He ignored me completely. I should have been relieved, but instead, perversely, felt piqued. Only when our children were mentioned, and someone said we had a twenty-two-year-old son, did Yevgeni look at me directly. "What's his name?" he asked. Anton, I was sure, was watching me. I tried to remain calm, but I could feel my face grow hot as I said, "Sergei." Yevgeni smiled and said, "I'd like to meet him sometime." Anton then spoke up and said we also had a daughter, Nadya, but Yevgeni lost interest and turned away.

Nadya's hands shook as she lowered the diary and let it rest on her lap. Anton Stepanovich was not Sergei's father; Seryozha was Count Pyotr's nephew. This meant he was her half brother; this meant—dear God!—he and Alexei were first cousins, and Seryozha was a Persiantsev, too.

What bitter irony for her brother! She must never tell him; he must never know. He'd been hurt enough.

And then, Nadya came to the last entry.

I'm dying. Strange . . . only now has peace come to me at last. I feel I've paid my dues to God and Anton. I've dedicated my whole life to him, and what was there in it for me? Atonement? There was no time for anything else. One mistake . . . I go without regret. I'm glad Nadya is strong, resilient. She's in love now, I see it. I hope she takes from life the bits of happiness as they come her way; then the losses will be cushioned by sweet memories. That, perhaps, was the hardest for me—I have no sweet memories.

Nadya closed the diary. This, then, was what Anna meant on her deathbed when she said that she had refused to admit the existence of a strong emotion within her. She had forced herself to hate Count Yevgeni and spent the rest of her life in bitterness. With a deep sigh Nadya gave in to the cleansing tears, weeping silently, quietly, over her mother's words.

A few days later Vera came down the stairs, a tape measure around her neck, a thimble on her finger. "Nadezhda Antonovna, may I talk to you for a moment?"

Nadya raised her eyebrows. "But of course, Vera. Come into the dining room, and I'll ring for Masha to bring us tea."

Vera removed her thimble and sat down at the table. When the tea was poured, she fumbled nervously with her spoon. She had heard the whole ghastly thing from her sewing room upstairs. Heard and cowered behind a wardrobe and, after the men had left, vomited into a washbasin.

Now words did not come easily, and Nadya's silence wasn't

helping. Vera took a deep breath and looked straight into Nadya's clear, waiting eyes.

"I don't sleep well; I can't think about anything else except what has happened." Vera hesitated, then blurted out, "I keep hearing Katya's screams. Nadezhda Antonovna, it's driving me crazy, this guilt I feel for not helping you."

"Guilt is the ulcer of the soul, Vera. Don't do this to yourself."

"I blame myself for not coming down and—and distracting the men."

"My dear girl, from the moment those men came in, they kept asking for Katya. That was not a chance raid." Nadya looked away, her voice trailing off, her profile chiseled against the afternoon sun.

Vera was suddenly frightened. "Why would they want to hurt you?"

"I don't know. We may never know. But I'm convinced there was a reason behind it." Nadya looked at Vera with eyes shining with unspilled tears and then added, "Don't hold on to your feeling of guilt; let go of it. And now let's talk about tomorrow. Life has to go on, and I have some things that need to be sewn."

Nadya talked about little things, about yardage for draperies, Dunya's torn apron, Marina's school uniform, and as she talked, rivers of tears spilled over, rushing down her cheeks, falling over her folded arms, unchecked and ignored.

Chapter Twenty-three

In the next few weeks restless April gave way to May with its profusion of lilacs and violets. Chinese peddlers lined up buckets of flowers on the corner across from Churin's department store. Their fragrance cut through the dust that was forever rising behind taxicabs and horses' hooves.

To Marina, touching the dry sidewalk with a new pair of shoes unhampered by sound-muffling boots heralded approaching summer and, with it, a vacation trip to Tsitsikar or Imyanpo. This year it would be sad and lonely, for the memory of her sister's death lingered. She had never asked her mother why Katya died. It was enough to see her mother's silent grief. Besides, she had heard an argument between her and Uncle Sergei on that awful day, and she was afraid to bring it up. It happened after she had climbed from under the bed and found her mother weeping. She had had no time to look at Katya before her mother put her hand over her eyes and pulled her out of the room and into Marina's bedroom.

"Under no circumstances—do you hear?—no circumstances at all, are you to leave this room until I call you."

Marina had never heard her mother speak so harshly before. She began to cry partly because she was frightened and partly because she could not understand what she had done to anger her mother this much.

She sat in the room, shivering, and did not see Uncle Sergei come home and find Katya. She was afraid to disobey her mother a second time and stayed in her room; but her bedroom was next to her mother's, and when she heard their raised voices, she pressed her ear to the keyhole and listened. There were strange things Uncle Sergei said to her mother, and she did not understand all of them. But some of them she did.

"What happened, Nadya? What happened?" Uncle Sergei kept shouting over and over, and her mother cried.

"I saw soldiers through the window. They had that look on their faces—you know—so I hid Marina before I opened the door."

"And then—and then?"

"They kept asking for Katya. They knew her name! Why, Sergei, why? Why did they ask for her by name?"

"How the hell would I know? Why didn't you keep the door locked and telephone me?"

"Katya was not at home; she was due to come back any minute. God, Seryozha, I didn't want them to catch her on the street!"

"But they did catch her, didn't they?"

"She came home, and I shouted to her to run, but there was no time. No time!" A touch of hysteria crept into her mother's voice.

"So what did you do then? To save Katya, I mean?"

"I—I tried to divert the men, but it didn't help. Oh, God, help me!"

"I'll bet you tried—how hard, Nadya, how hard? You would have tried harder—wouldn't you?—if Marina's life had been at stake. Katya never meant as much to you as Marina. Admit it!"

Marina heard her mother gasp. Uncle Sergei was mean to her. Her mother had talked to those soldiers. Maybe if she opened the door and told Uncle Sergei that Mama had tried to help Katya, he wouldn't yell at her like that. But how could she do this without admitting her eavesdropping? And what did Uncle Sergei mean that Mama hadn't tried hard enough? Marina was confused. She listened some more.

". . . that's cruel, Sergei. It was a terrible experience! How could you possibly know . . . I've gone through hell. . . . I am her mother, and I saw the whole thing—I saw—" Her mother's voice broke, and she began to cry. Marina squeezed her fists so hard that her hands shook.

Suddenly Uncle Sergei's voice rose and shook. "Katya! Our Katya . . . precious Katya!"

"Seryozha! Please! Stop it!"

Ashamed to listen any longer, Marina slipped to the floor and rolled herself into a ball. The grown-ups quarreled, and it was terrifying not to understand all of it. After a while Uncle Sergei stomped out of the room and slammed the door. Her mother cried softly.

That night, as Marina lay awake, staring into the dark, watching red shadows from the flickering vigil light beneath the icon dart along the wall, she tried to guess what Uncle Sergei had meant. Her eyelids grew heavy and gritty, and she fell asleep before she could think of any answers.

After the funeral she returned to school, dreading the questions she would be asked, questions she could not answer. But there were none, and everyone pretended nothing had happened. For a while she felt isolated, as if her classmates were avoiding her intentionally. When she mentioned this to Vera, the young woman said that people did this sometimes when they didn't know what to say. Marina accepted the explanation and tried not to dwell on it.

Soon there were other things to think about, pleasant things. It was spring again. She could run out into the backyard of the circular complex of their houses and play with other children who lived in the neighborhood apartments. They congregated in the clean-swept center enclosure to play *lapta* or hopscotch.

One afternoon she had heard about a new boy who came to play from another neighborhood. His name was Michael Nikitin, and he was fifteen years old. The girls whispered about him. Today she saw him—a tall, lean boy playing idly with a ball, waiting for the *lapta* to begin. He had short, sandy hair and a funny freckled nose, like the shiny button on Dunya's apron. His light-colored eyes—hazel or green? Marina could not tell—were dancing, as if any minute he were going to laugh at some secret joke.

He reached his hand out to Marina and gave her a firm handshake, his large, warm palm covering her hand completely.

"My name is Michael Nikitin. What's yours?"

"Marina Razumova."

He nodded dismissal and turned to Lev Petrov, a scrawny ten-year-old boy who was standing near him with a bicycle. "I'll teach you how to ride. It's easy."

After a brief hesitation Marina sidled up to him. "I'd like to learn how to ride, too."

"You can't ride this bicycle. It's built for boys. See the bar in the middle?" Michael said, pointing to the bicycle. His voice was condescending, and Marina felt a blush rise to her face.

Several boys were lining up for a game of *lapta* on the narrow strip of the road behind a small fenced-in garden. Each team had its pitcher and catcher, and the run had two bases in a straight line. Marina had played the game many times and loved the challenge of competing with the boys. Although she could not hit the ball well, she had earned a reputation as one of the fastest runners. She was taking her place in the catcher's field when Michael ambled over.

"What do I see? This is a man's game. Girls are not supposed to play."

Marina raised her chin defiantly. "I've always played *lapta*, and what's more, I'm good at it. Ask the others!" But the boys looked embarrassed and said nothing.

Michael laughed and with a lazy motion pushed her out of the way. "I don't want to be responsible for you getting hurt. Go, little girl. Go play with your dolls!"

Afraid the other boys might see the tears filling her eyes, Marina turned on her heel and, holding her head high, stalked off. By the time she reached her front door she was running. Nasty boy. *Stuck-up, showoff nasty boy*, she thought, *I'll show him. I'll do something*, something *to get even!*

When she ran into the house, her mother looked up from the book she was reading—Nadya was always reading something —and asked, "What happened, Marinka?"

Marina burst into tears and buried her head in her mother's lap. "That—that new boy in the yard—Michael Nikitin—he's mean. He won't let me play *lapta* with the others."

Her mother rumpled her hair. "But you've always played with the boys. Didn't the others tell him?"

Marina shook her head. "They're all afraid of him because he is bigger than they are. And—and he pushed me!"

Her mother wanted to know how old the boy was, and when Marina told her, she nodded. "You did the right thing. There's nothing shameful in that. He's too old for you to fight, and besides, young ladies don't engage in fistfights."

Nadya closed her book firmly and set it aside. "Uncle Sergei is in the cellar, working with his microscope. Go to him, Marinka, and tell him what happened. He'll make you feel better."

"I don't want to go down there. Uncle Sergei doesn't like me."

Her mother looked startled. "What are you saying, Marinka? Uncle Sergei loves you!"

"No, he doesn't."

"What makes you say that?"

Marina pursed her lips stubbornly. "I just know, Mama!" Surely she couldn't tell her mother she'd overheard the argument between brother and sister the day Katya died.

Her mother looked at her closely, then smoothed her hair and said firmly, "Nonsense! Don't ever let Uncle Sergei hear that; it would hurt his feelings. Now do as I tell you. Go downstairs, and you'll see how wrong you are. Besides, don't you want to see the puppies?"

In the back of their yard Uncle Sergei kept a kennel of pedigreed Irish setters. He kept saying that one day he would try hunting, but he never did, spending his spare hours in the cellar with his slides and microscope instead. Sometimes he would bring one of the setters indoors with a new litter of puppies for the girls to play with. Marina loved the puppies but was afraid of the mother dog that watched her warily as she touched her young.

Maybe the puppies in the cellar needed cleaning. Marina wiped her tears and, without looking at her mother, turned toward the cellar door. She would give anything to have Uncle Sergei love her as he had Katya. He hadn't spoken to her or even looked at her since Katya died. Maybe if she stood quietly at his side and waited for him to say something to her first, he would not get angry with her for going down in the cellar.

She opened the door and took a cautious step on the steep stairs. Holding her breath for a moment, she listened. It was dark and quiet. The puppies were suckling. She heard them. She wanted to hold them. Carefully feeling each step with the soles of her shoes, she started to climb down.

In the cellar Marina felt the warm humidity hug her all over. The air was stuffy. It smelled rancid and dank, and as she stood there, uncertain of what to do next, the silence around her moved and rustled. She listened.

In the corner of the cellar she heard a clicking sound, a shuffling, a sigh. Aware that Uncle Sergei was busy behind a curtain that kept his microscope and slides isolated from the rest of the cellar, Marina stood still, afraid to move and make him angry. There was a click of the switch, and a faint glow appeared in the cellar. Dark shapes came into focus. The light cast an eerie gleam around the table where Uncle Sergei was working. He pushed the curtain back, and she saw his stooped figure bent over the miscroscope as he adjusted the scope, his hand bloodless in the dull light.

She turned toward the puppies. A strong, sour odor assailed her, but she ignored it and stooped to look at the babies. The mother was relaxed and didn't even raise her head to look at her. One of the more vigorous puppies was scampering around the pen, exploring its corners. Marina, unable to resist the urge to fondle the living toy, picked it up and rubbed her cheek against its silky, trembling body. Careful not to squeeze too hard, she stroked the tiny warm paws, kissing the soft back and moist, shiny nose.

"What happened out there in the yard? I heard you crying."

Uncle Sergei's voice startled Marina so much that she nearly dropped the puppy. She put it back in the pen, pushing one of its gluttonous siblings away and placing the puppy's muzzle against its mother's belly. Then she turned to look at her uncle.

"The new boy is nasty. He wouldn't let me play *lapta*."

"Everyone knows you can hold your own with the boys. Why didn't you assert yourself?"

"No one took my side. Maybe they don't want me to play with them anymore."

For a few seconds everything was quiet in the cellar, and then Uncle Sergei said, "Come over here, Marina. Would you like to look through the miscroscope?"

She ventured forward and leaned over his arm to look. Uncle Sergei moved back, and Marina watched in fascination the complex shape of the bacteria on the slide as Uncle Sergei explained it to her. Then he asked, "Did the new boy hurt you?"

"No. But he pushed me and told me to go away."

Uncle Sergei ruffled her hair. "Well, the best thing to do then is to ignore him for a while. He is taking advantage of you because you're smaller." He cupped her chin and smiled at her. "I'm glad you came down to see me. You shouldn't be playing with the bigger boys. There are plenty of girls your age in the yard. Why don't you bring one home to play sometime?"

Marina shrugged. "Most of them want to play with dolls, and I don't like dolls."

Uncle Sergei put his arm around her shoulders and gave her a squeeze. Marina didn't want to move. She felt secure, enveloped in his fragrance of shaving lotion and a strong smell of tobacco which wiped out the damp odors in the cellar. She lifted her head and put her arms around his neck. Slowly, slowly, Uncle Sergei pulled back, and she saw tears sparkle in his eyes. Marina squirmed uncomfortably. What was wrong with Uncle Sergei? Had she done something wrong? He pulled a handkerchief out of his pocket and wiped his nose. "That's all right, *dyetka*. Must be a sneeze coming up." His voice sounded strange.

She looked at him with wide-open eyes, and suddenly Uncle Sergei took her in his arms and pressed her head against his shoulder. "Oh, my dear, poor child! I do love you! I do!"

Surprised by his outburst, Marina pressed her face against his chest. She heard something that sounded like a choked sob. Uncle Sergei rocked her from side to side. "My little Marinka! You sweet child! Forgive an old fool!"

Marina was puzzled. What did he mean? But she did not want to ask. She just hugged him back.

A week later Marina brought her classmate Zoya Karelina home to play. Zoya was a small dark girl, full of mischief. The past week had been dull. Uncle Sergei had spent long hours seeing outpatients and afterward had gone to his study until suppertime. Today was no different. The waiting room was full of patients waiting to be seen, and in the living quarters Marina's mother had filled the largest room in the house—the dining room—with sewing patterns and sketches. She was going to school to learn tailoring "for future emergencies," as she had said when Uncle Sergei questioned her desire to study. Now, with Vera watching quietly, she spread the heavy oversize sketch book and designs all over the dining room table and, using pencil and compass, was drafting a new pattern.

Her mama was exceptional, not like other women who came to visit and talked about Mah-Jongg, which they played all day, and how Maria Ivanovna used too much paint on her face and doused herself with cheap cologne, or how Olga Petrovna lied to her husband to cover up her gambling losses. Mama was different. "A tragic woman," Marina had once overheard one of the women whisper about her mother. She was wrong. There was nothing tragic about Mama. She was smarter than the others, she could write poetry, and they were envious of her. That was all.

Marina knew better than to disturb her mother at work, and the girls tiptoed from the house to play outside.

After the girls had left the room, Vera leaned over Nadya's patterns. "I've never had a formal lesson in sewing. These look so complicated."

Nadya sighed. "I wish ready-made patterns existed; with each of us having to draft our own, the precision work is taxing. Pattern drafting is so mathematical I feel I'm back in school. But to know I could be self-supporting if I had to be gives me a sense of independence."

She paused and looked out the window. Yes, it was important to be self-supporting. Sergei was a good provider, but what if through circumstances beyond his control, he was unable to earn a living? Lord knows she had seen enough reversals of fortune in the revolution to be determined to avoid a similar fate. She wanted to learn a trade, she needed it for her own peace of mind. They were refugees enjoying prosperity under the wing of a generous host nation. But now, with the Japanese occupation, the future was uncertain; they were vulnerable.

Nadya became aware of a deep silence around her. Vera had slipped out quietly, the servants were readying tea in the kitchen, and she was alone in the dining room.

Vulnerable. That dreadful word. *My poor innocent Katya. Another spark gone out of my life. Dear Lord, don't let me think of Katya. I can't dwell on that loss, can't cope with it!* Grieving could not overcome death. She still had Marinka, a living part of the man she loved, would always love until the day she died. And she had Sergei, always Sergei. She pushed the sketches aside and sat down at the table.

She must not dwell on her fears of Armageddon. Sergei, so long alienated from Marina, was now showing signs of growing affection toward the child. Thus, her secretly nurtured wish was coming to pass. She shook her head. It was no wonder. No one could resist Marina for long. The child's large, trusting eyes won over even the most resistant. In that she was an image of her father.

A familiar pain seared Nadya. How unwise to think beyond yesterday. She could not touch those other yesterdays. They had been buried within her long ago.

She started sorting the papers and putting them in a large cardboard folder. Marinka and Zoya would soon be coming back from the yard, and she would ring for tea.

When the girls ran out into the courtyard, it was bathed in sunshine. The area was large and circular, with a small fenced-in garden in the center, surrounded by a cobblestoned driveway. Each house and the rows of apartments around the courtyard had a narrow stretch of fenced area with wooden benches and sparsely planted lilac and jasmine bushes. The ground was clean-swept and barren. The climate in Harbin was severe, with extremes of temperature, and tenants were too busy making a living to nurture and trim grass. Because the best cutting tool was a scythe, no city dweller wanted to spend what few leisure hours he had in labor befitting a farmer.

Most neighborly contacts and socializing were done in the inner courtyards, not all as large or neatly landscaped as the Razumovs'. The illusion that they were still in their motherland was carefully preserved in every architectural detail.

Content in their own suburb, the Chinese left the rest of the city in Russian hands, yet each side was aware of its interdependence.

All this peaceable coexistence had changed since the Japanese occupied Manchuria, imposing their censorship and rigid control on both sides of the city. On the surface, however, things appeared to go on as usual. Russian *izvozchiki* still sat in their droshkies, waiting for customers in the median of the Bolshoi Prospekt, strategically parked at a busy intersection of Novotorgovaya Street, where a row of small shops and Churin's did a brisk business. Russian taxicabs competed for trade, especially on longer distances, such as to the downtown Pristan section of town or to the Sungari shores with its busy commerce of junks and fishing boats.

May was still cool, though full of promise with its fragrant blossoms and sunny days. The frozen Sungari, having hugged the steep downtown shores throughout the winter, had melted and was flowing strongly downstream. Earlier, large blocks of ice had been carved out of the river by Chinese coolies and sold to homeowners for underground coolers, where food could now be safely stored during the hot months. Those who rushed the season drove down to the Sungari, where coolies in flat-bottomed boats taxied them across the river to their vacation cottages. In readiness for summer, they aired the houses, fumigated mattresses, and washed curtains to be rehung on cleaned windows. Since swimming in the Sungari was dangerous—its whirlpools and murky waters were ever-present hazards that claimed several victims each year —bathing was mostly confined to the Sunshine Lagoon with its placid waters or to floating wooden bathhouses where women could swim in enclosures and sunbathe privately in the nude on their wooden decks. The women felt secure in numbers, safe from the ever-present menace of the Japanese soldiers roaming the streets.

The Razumovs preferred to cross the Sungari in the winter. Coolies taxied their customers across the frozen river in large sleds, which they propelled by standing on a ledge behind the seat and stabbing the ice with a long spike. Nadya often chuckled at the enterprising Chinese, who had adapted the Russian word for "push" and called their sleds *tolkai-tolkai*.

There was an ice hill for the sled run at the hunting lodge across the river, and a warm dining room with steaming *pelmeni* and carafes of chilled vodka for the grown-ups. Marina loved tobogganing; she held her breath against the cold wind and hid her face behind the padded back of the driver or sprawled on top of her mother, who lay flat on a smaller sled and maneuvered it downhill. But that was all in winter, and now, close to vacation time, she waited eagerly for the train ride to one of the summer resorts along the western or eastern line of the railway. The family usually spent the summer months in one of the villages built and peopled by Russian farmers who had settled in Manchuria and carried on the business of living as though they had never left Russia. Sergei, who said he couldn't be away from his work too long, remained in Harbin and occasionally joined them for a weekend.

Although Marina counted the weeks till vacation, this year she was apprehensive. She missed her sister, and the emptiness that Katya's death had left in her life was particularly acute during the holidays. In the city her days were full, leaving little time for brooding. She studied diligently, went for walks with Vera, continued her piano lessons, and was beginning to chat haltingly in English and French, the result of her sessions with a Russian spinster who earned her living teaching languages. With so little time for play, it became a special treat when Marina was allowed to bring home a friend. Today, giggling and chasing each other around the center palisade, she and Zoya were acutely aware of being watched by a group of boys who stood idling in a corner of the yard.

"Marina, let's play hopscotch," Zoya said, tugging at Marina's sleeve. Marina looked for a place to play. The pathway along the fence was laid out in granite blocks, each slab consisting of small, neatly arranged squares. Counting off three large blocks, she picked up a sharp stone and drew hopscotch squares in the dirt alongside the sidewalk. The boys ambled over and watched them for a while. Then, grinning, they jumped off the granite slabs and dragged their feet over the outlined squares, erasing them. Before Marina could do anything, Michael rushed at the boys and with two swift punches sent them each staggering in opposite directions.

"Nothing better to do than pick on girls?" he said in a menacing baritone.

Taken by surprise, the boys grumbled. One of them said, "You're the one who shoved Marinka out of the *lapta* game the other day. How come you're taking her side now?"

"She doesn't belong in a man's game, and I told her so. This time it's the other way around. Now you're ruining their game."

The boy moved toward Michael with clenched fists but, sizing up his adversary's towering height, thought better of it and beat a retreat.

Marina took a timid step toward Michael. "Thank you, Misha."

A corner of his mouth twitched, then spread into a grin. He shook his head and a mop of curls bounced. "Not Misha. Michael. I'm called Michael." He stretched out his hand. "Friends?"

Marina felt no ground under her feet as she and Zoya ran home. She couldn't wait to tell everyone about Michael.

But at the house Vera was already gone, and Zoya left immediately when she heard there was a message for her to go home. While her mother was putting the books and folders away, Marina bubbled, telling her all about Michael.

Nadya smiled. "That's wonderful, *dyetka*. You must tell Uncle Sergei about it when he's through seeing patients."

A word triggered a memory. A pleasant memory. "Mamochka, Uncle Sergei called me *dyetka*, too, in the cellar."

Her mother looked up, and Marina saw that she was pleased.

Chapter Twenty-four

Summer was cool and windy. The sullen heavens spread sheets of water over the flatlands, engorging rivers and threatening plowed fields. Nature stormed as though Manchuria itself lashed out against its Japanese invaders with xenophobic spite, turning its harsh climate into an instrument of vengeance.

Gusting winds dumped heavy rain over the city of Harbin. It drummed on the roof like a frantic wanderer demanding entry and came in waves of thunderous sound—pounding, receding, and pounding again. At times Sergei looked up at the ceiling. Was the roof strong enough to withstand the onslaught? Didn't he see a damp spot in the corner?

Then the rain stopped, and the sun came out, steaming the roofs, and warming the sodden earth. But Sergei continued to brood. His agony over Katya's death was deep and lonely. He could not tell anyone that he felt responsible for the rape and murder of his sister's daughter. He could not share the horror of this knowledge with Nadya. He carried the pain alone. It was eating at him, driving him to the edge of sanity.

Katya's father had died so he could live, and he had been determined to protect his friend Vadim's child from any harm. Yet he not only had failed to shield her but had actually caused her death! Still, he hadn't known. And if he had, could he have acted against his principles and committed the crime asked of him? Yes! He would have had no alternative.

He could still hear Captain Yamada's fractured Russian that dismal March day five months ago, when he was summoned unexpectedly to the gendarmerie headquarters.

At first he was lulled into believing that the Japanese officer needed a favor from him. The courteous repeated bows, the hissing noise of sucked-in breath between sentences—all traditional signs of respect in Japan—led him to think that his services were being solicited.

Indeed they were, but not on any terms he had expected. Captain Yamada, a slender man with a short black mustache, began by asking him if the pharmacist Gorman was his friend.

"Yes, I know him quite well," Sergei replied, a vague uneasiness taking hold of him as he sat in the military offices of the occupational forces.

"The *hunhuzi* have kidnapped Gorman and are holding him for ransom. They ask for much money and that we assist in negotiations for his release. Pharmacist Gorman is stubborn, and he will not say how much money he has or where it is."

Captain Yamada paused, busying himself with refilling his pipe. "We want to help free the man." He looked directly at Sergei, his face enigmatic. "You are well known for your research and work on new drugs. Perhaps you can help us make Gorman talk. Otherwise, the *hunhuzi* will kill him."

"There are Japanese doctors working in Harbin. They can help you."

Captain Yamada shook his head. "We want to keep this confidential. Besides, you're his friend. He will trust you."

The cover was flimsy. It was inconceivable that the Japanese gendarmerie would be cooperating with the *hunhuzi* for altruistic reasons alone, and Sergei doubted that the *hunhuzi* were involved in the kidnapping at all. It sounded more and more like another extortion act by the Japanese. His suspicions were reinforced when a young Japanese officer walked in, and after bowing obsequiously to Yamada, talked to him rapidly in Japanese, throwing surreptitious glances at Sergei. The man's crafty eyes shifted, and he lowered his gaze, waiting respectfully for his superior to speak. Captain Yamada sucked in his breath again.

"My assistant tells me that Gorman is not going to live much longer under the *hunhuzi* interrogation. Tell me, isn't there a narcotic called truth serum that you could give Gorman to make him talk?"

Sergei's mouth went dry. "You want *me* to give a narcotic to Gorman?"

"We want no one else to know about this. After all, he's your friend," Yamada repeated with emphasis. "You want to save him, don't you? You will be taken to the hiding place by Lieutenant Matsui here"—Yamada nodded toward the younger officer—"who is in contact with the *hunhuzi*, and then brought back after you administer the narcotic."

"My medical license allows me to heal people, not to hurt them."

Sergei did not mean to sound sarcastic, but his voice shook, and the words escaped before he had time to weigh them.

Yamada's face remained impassive. "It would be tragic if you refused to cooperate, Dr. Efimov."

"I cannot be a party to this, Captain."

"But we have already taken you into our confidence and now must ensure your silence. It will be best for you, believe me, if you reconsider."

Sergei pursed his lips and breathed deeply. "I absolutely and categorically refuse to do such a thing!"

"Most unfortunate for all!"

Captain Yamada's voice rose slightly; but he remained polite, and Sergei went home angered, indignant, but not truly alarmed.

How could he have known then that the surface courtesy of Japanese often belied their true sentiments?

A few days later he was stopped on the street by Lieutenant

Matsui and forced into a car at gunpoint. Blindfolded, he was driven to the outskirts of town, where his blindfold was removed and he found himself standing before an isolated Chinese *fanza* with a thatched roof.

"You're wasting your time, Lieutenant. I have no drugs on me. Even if I had, I already told Captain Yamada I wouldn't use them on Gorman."

There was no reply, and he was pushed into a windowless room with only a wooden table and two chairs in the center. After adjusting his eyes to the dim light, he saw a man lying on a clump of hay in the corner. Lieutenant Matsui shoved him forward, and Sergei, barely retaining his balance, peered closer.

He recognized Gorman only by his wavy silver-streaked hair. The man was dead. Sergei stood over him, frozen in horror. Hardened as he had been to seeing mutilations during the war, he was nevertheless nauseated by what Gorman's captors had done to him.

When Sergei was taken back to Novy Gorod, Lieutenant Matsui spoke for the first time. "We want you to remember what your refusal to help did to your friend."

Sergei turned and looked at the Japanese. "I had nothing to do with this heinous crime."

"Then we shall have to impress upon you further that it is unwise to refuse cooperation."

He's threatening me, Sergei thought, *but I haven't done anything!* Yet a seed of doubt was planted. If Gorman had been kidnapped and killed, they could do the same to him. For several days afterward he made sure he did not walk alone at night and avoided deserted streets during the day.

How naïve he had been not to suspect that he was more valuable to them alive, that they would strike at him in the worst possible way to ensure his cooperation in the future!

Thus, when he came home that dreadful afternoon to find Katya bloodied and dead, he nearly blacked out from shock. Because he couldn't tell Nadya the truth, he blamed her irrationally for not protecting Katya, aware that there was nothing she could have done to save her daughter.

Burdened by his private hell, Sergei began to withdraw within himself. Everyone irritated him: Dunya, the cook; Masha, the maid, and even quiet Vera. He resented Nadya's search for an outlet for her sorrow, her continuing interest in poetry meetings, her sewing lessons. Yet at times he longed to place his hand on her shoulder, take her in his arms, and weep together. But after years of self-control it might be a sign of weakness, he thought. He couldn't do it. How acutely he yearned for Esther! And that yearning only magnified his agony.

He began to observe Marina. Alexei's child was a constant irritant. In moments of intense grief he had wished it were Marina, not Katya, who was dead. Shameful to think that! In the end he hadn't counted on the child's warmth, her ingenuous, trusting love, so, when she came down to the cellar that day and he realized she, too, had been hurt, his defenses had broken, and long-suppressed emotion had poured out.

What a fool he had been! That Alexei was her father wasn't the child's fault. There she was, trying to win his love all along, reaching out to be his little girl!

In the weeks that followed, Sergei spent all his free time with Marina, no longer eager to lose himself in a game of Mah-Jongg.

That spring and summer the family spent much time at home, for Nadya, sensing Sergei's need of their company, decided not to leave Harbin for their yearly vacation. In June they made excursions to the other side of the Sungari, where they rented a dacha for a few days at a time, but by the end of July the river was spilling over its banks, curtailing even these short trips.

By early August the dachas were submerged up to their rooftops, driving their owners to higher ground. Nadya and Sergei felt safe in Novy Gorod, which was on a higher plateau, and believed that they would not be involved in the flood.

Until Sunday, August 7, when they awoke in the morning and looked out the window.

Dozens of Chinese huddled on the sidewalk. Before Nadya and Sergei had time to comprehend the full impact of what they were seeing, Dunya rushed into the room.

"*Barinya, barinya,* they say the retaining wall in Foudzyadyan broke, and the whole of the Chinese quarter is flooded!"

Sergei put his arm around Nadya's shoulders. "I doubt I'll be able to get through to the hospital today. Since it's Sunday, I'll call in and check on my patients. We'd better stay close to the house."

The telephone rang, and he answered it. Nadya frowned as she watched him stiffen.

"Yes, Captain Yamada," Sergei said quietly, "I understand. Have the vaccine ready when I get there. Yes, of course. I shall ask my sister to help me."

Slowly he replaced the receiver on its hook and looked at Nadya. "It was a call from the Japanese gendarmerie. They're afraid of a cholera epidemic. Evidently the Chinese are pouring in from Foudzyadyan in all directions. I'll need your help because all medical personnel are out on emergencies. Better tell Dunya to keep Marina in the house. Give Vera a call, and have her come over to keep an eye on things." Sergei hesitated, then added, "Take your bludgeon stick with you, just in case. The poor in Foudzyadyan have lost what little they had, and the authorities are afraid of looting and kidnapping."

Nadya feared the lethal weapon that Sergei had given her several years before. With one swing of the arm, the heavy steel coils, topped by a weighted ball, ejected out of a short handle in tight springs that could crack a skull. Now, however, she took it because she knew that Foudzyadyan was not the only distressed area with probable looters on the rampage; Nakhalovka, one of the poorest sections of town, would also spawn crime.

The first day passed uneventfully. Provided with vaccine by Japanese authorities, Sergei stopped people on the street and inoculated them as Nadya issued immunization certificates.

By the next morning they were amazed to see what the enterprising Chinese had managed to do on the high bluff of Novy

Gorod that overlooked the flooded Foudzyadyan. On hurriedly set-up food stalls, skeins of garlic, celery, and dried mushrooms lay side by side with persimmons, split yellow watermelons, and pomelos imported from southern China. Carcasses of beef hung on large hooks above the counters. Next to them, baking *tyan-bin* —unleavened flat cakes made with millet flour—lined the edges above the ashes of an open urn, their delicate fragrance drifting toward Nadya and Sergei.

What callous merchants these people were, thought Nadya, looking at the abundance of produce for sale next to the destitute and the miserable flood refugees. Pitying them, she narrowly missed a huge *arba*. Its weighty thick wheels squeaking, the cart labored past her with a load of compressed yellow rings of soybean cake and bales of bullock and ramskins. The *arba* was pulled by four temperamental mules harnessed two abreast. The animals lifted their ears nervously at the surrounding noise, their bloodshot eyes rolling, kicking at any hapless pedestrian who strayed too close. Nadya skirted the cart as the Chinaman leading the mules snapped his long leather whip in the air.

A stream of rickshaws and wagons, loaded with the fleeing people, toiled up the hill. Thousands of the homeless were already huddling on the ground, while their sheep and pigs roamed unrestrained through the makeshift camp. Straw mats and patched bean sacks stretched between poles served as shelter.

"They seem to be more concerned about their sacks of flour than their families," Nadya remarked, watching half-naked, seemingly abandoned children cry.

Sergei shrugged. "To them it means survival. They're known to sell their little daughters for one sack of flour."

When they reached Nakhalovka, a different sight confronted them. Russian adolescents sat on the roofs of their houses, fishing in muddy waters. Several foundations around them had been washed out, and the houses had collapsed; but the youngsters seemed unconcerned with their plight. Their parents, on the other hand, were rowing along the flooded streets in makeshift boats fashioned from empty barrels or standing on rafts made of two doors nailed together, offering help to trapped neighbors.

Instructed to order residents to place disinfectant mats at each unflooded door, Nadya and Sergei covered as many blocks as they could before moving onto higher ground to escape the swirling Sungari waters.

Brother and sister worked late into the day. When night fell, the powerhouse was inundated, and downtown Pristan and Nakhalovka were plunged into darkness. Using torches, they headed toward home. For the last hour or two Captain Yamada had been following them with a guard, and Nadya, grateful for the protection, could not understand why Sergei seemed surly.

"We received word," Captain Yamada said when he first joined them, "that a large *hunhuzi* stronghold upriver has been flooded, and now, with the electricity out, we want to prevent as many looting incidents as possible."

"Seryozha," Nadya whispered to her brother at one point, "it's not wise to show your displeasure to the Japanese guard." When she saw Sergei clench his fist so hard his hands shook, she quickly changed the subject.

Her feet ached as they trudged up toward Novy Gorod, looking for an available *izvozchik* to take them home. When they found one, Yamada bade them good night and climbed into his droshky. Nadya relaxed and closed her eyes, anticipating a restful ride in the fresh air.

Without warning, and before the droshky had a chance to start moving, a rough hand clamped over Nadya's mouth from behind. Instinctively she wrenched her head sideways and screamed. Shadowy figures surrounded them, tugging at the sack of medical supplies she held on her lap. She let go of the sack and grabbed her purse to pull out the bludgeon stick. Slipping the leather strap over her wrist, she clasped the steel cylinder firmly and held the collapsed coils inside with her index finger. A torch flared behind her, and she watched in horror as Captain Yamada and his guard shot three of the Chinese attackers with deadly precision. The fourth bandit had jumped on Sergei from behind, bending his head backward and pulling him off the droshky seat.

Without thinking, Nadya raised her arm and with full force bludgeoned the bandit on the head. The snapping sound that followed, and the dull thud the attacker made when he fell, echoed in Nadya's stomach with instant, churning nausea.

"Well done, Madame Razumova!"

Shaking, Nadya turned toward the voice. Captain Yamada was looking at her with admiration, his narrow eyes reflecting the torch's unsteady flame. "You have great courage." There followed a sucked-in breath and deep, repeated bows.

Nadya nodded with as much composure as she could muster. Sergei jumped off the droshky and bowed stiffly to Yamada.

"We owe you our lives, Captain. Can I help you with these?" He nodded toward the bodies sprawled on the ground.

Nadya did not hear Yamada's reply and waited tensely until Sergei returned to his seat and nudged the cowering driver on. As the carriage began to move, she whispered, "Did I—did I kill the bandit?"

"I doubt it. He'll probably recover in jail. But if you did kill him, you did a service for the gendarmerie: one fewer criminal for them to track down."

With an effort, Nadya controlled her shaking. "Seryozha," she said, "you seemed barely civil to the officer. What's wrong?"

It was dark, and she could not see her brother's face, but his answer was slow in coming, and his voice strained. "He has not always been this helpful in the past."

Nadya did not pursue the subject. It was useless to probe into something Sergei seemed reluctant to talk about.

Foudzyadyan and Nakhalovka remained flooded until October. When at last the water receded from downtown Pristan, Sergei told Nadya that the streets were white with lime, which had been sprinkled over cobblestones to prevent a typhus epidemic. He looked drawn and thinner than usual, and Marina seemed the only one able to bring a smile to his face.

Still shaken by the bandit attack, Nadya had no desire to go downtown. For many weeks afterward she stayed close to home, venturing out to do her shopping only in Novy Gorod. Treachery, she thought, was everywhere. First, her daughter had been killed by the Japanese, and now the Chinese bandits had attacked her and Sergei. Loyalties shifted with expedience, and survivors were those on perpetual alert.

Vast areas of plowed fields had been flooded, crops ruined, and thousands left homeless. When the snow began to fall in early November, it covered the mud and devastation with a carpet of fresh, sparkling snowflakes. But the wounds underneath festered, and the anger smoldered.

The Russians and the Chinese, trained by centuries of patience, waited.

Chapter Twenty-five

The years between 1932 and 1940 slipped by, and the Japanese occupation forces continued to be firmly entrenched in Manchuria. On the surface, life pulsated with apparently unruffled precision in spite of rumors Nadya heard about arbitrary arrests, atrocities, and frame-ups that terrorized the population. An undercurrent of unrest was effectively throttled by stringent censorship, and in schools, factories, and courts, business went on as usual.

The Russians avoided contact with the Japanese as much as possible and went about their lives pretending their freedom had not been affected. What did it matter, they rationalized, if you heard of an isolated case of extortion, or rape, or even murder? The newspapers reported a growing rate of crime, dutifully listing the names of notorious bandits, mostly Russian and Chinese *hunhuzi*, and citing clues that often led to their apprehension. You strove to believe the convincing arguments of puppet police, but even if it were a clever setup by true perpetrators, what could you do about it? Nothing at all, for the military authorities had ordered the Russian papers, under threat of suspension, never to mention Japanese in connection with criminals. This was not official, mind you, but word was passed to say nothing if you knew what was good for you.

Thus, the druggist Gorman's kidnapping in 1932 went unsolved, in spite of the ransom his wife had paid for his release. He had simply disappeared, and Nadya heard nothing more about it, sensing that it was painful for Sergei to talk about his friend. A year later the kidnapping and murder of twenty-three-year-old Simon Kaspe drew international attention because the victim was a French citizen and son of a millionaire owner of the Hotel Moderne, the best in town. Protests by the French consul brought assurances from Japanese authorities that they were doing their utmost to find young Kaspe. Eventually they found him and delivered the corpse to his father, after the kidnappers had failed to collect the demanded ransom from him.

No, the best thing to do was to stay out of the way and not get involved. Besides, you couldn't trust your own friends, for chameleons existed even among the best of them. Subversive underground groups operated in the least expected places, and you never knew whether their loyalties belonged to the cause of the monarchists, the Bolsheviks, or Fascists, whether they were zealots who sought to report you to the Japanese and made friends with the Nazis in town. The Germans were not much in evidence, but they were Japanese allies and, as such, were to be feared and avoided.

"This divisiveness among the Russians here saddens me," Nadya once remarked to her brother as they were sitting in the parlor after Marina had gone to bed. "It has already cost us our country. On the other hand, if Hitler decides to overrun Russia, then perhaps our people will unite to defend Mother Russia."

Sergei looked at her reflectively. "Yet there are those who say our people in Russia will welcome Hitler as a liberator."

"That depends on how farsighted Hitler is. Does he know of our attachment to our motherland?"

Sergei shrugged and didn't answer.

"I have a feeling," Nadya went on, "the Russian people will rally to Stalin's side if Hitler humiliates our Russian soul."

"Whatever the outcome," Sergei said, "there's nothing we can do about it. You had better be careful about whom you express your views to, Nadya. The Japanese are staunchly behind Hitler, and it's best for us not to discuss politics with anyone. We've had our fling at activism with disastrous results. I want no part of it anymore."

Silence settled heavily between them, a familiar, palpable tension. Nadya studied him. Over the years his posture had become stooped and his head settled between his shoulders. Poor Seryozha! For twenty years now, since they had come to Harbin, Sergei had doggedly continued to write letters in search of Esther and waited for the same answers. Nadya suspected that it had become as much an integral part of his life as food and sleep. For her part, she settled into a comfortable coexistence with her love for Alexei. The hurt receded, but sweet memories lingered, and in that, Anna had been right. Without bitterness, those sweet memories were life-supporting, comforting.

Sergei broke the silence. "I'm glad you stay clear of politics in your poetry. I hope Marina doesn't get drawn into any of the local political groups. Some of their loyalties are shifty at best."

Over and over Nadya had warned Marina, who was eighteen, to stay away from such youth groups, the nihilists of the twentieth century, as she called them, even though many went no further than the heated debates held in some chilly cellar apartment.

She need not have worried. Marina had no stomach for these self-proclaimed political pundits, and the only meetings she ventured to attend were Nadya's literary evenings, where the most audacious voice was a reading by some impassioned young poet bewailing the loss of his homeland.

It was Michael, with his unruly mop of hair, her faithful shaggy St. Bernard, as Nadya had affectionately dubbed him, who had squired and encouraged Marina to participate in some of these poetry gatherings. Ever since she met him in the courtyard eight years ago, Marina had depended on Michael to be her pal, her broad-shouldered friend. Because she had never considered him a suitor, she leaned on him heavily after Vera had married a young Russian engineer and left their household.

Marina had grown into a willowy dark beauty. Her black hair was straight without a hint of curl—thick and stiff as a horse's tail, as Nadya had succinctly put it. Marina parted it in the middle, coiling the two thick tresses over her ears or around the crown of her head. The severe hairdo underscored the oval symmetry of her face, and only a slight suggestion of an uneven tilt to her eyes marred her nearly perfect features.

She wondered about being in love, but so far her greatest problem was how to fend off the string of suitors ringing her doorbell. She loved to dance and was in great demand at parties, at which her favorite partner was Michael.

Nadya worried about her daughter's disinterest in the young men who tried to court her. "You have to allow some of them to enter your life, Marina. Otherwise, you won't know how to deal with yourself when one comes along and touches your heart."

"Michael comes over often. We spend hours talking and walking and dancing together."

"That's not the same. He's only a pal to you. You're avoiding men in general. Why?"

Marina shrugged off these questions. She had spent her adolescent years suppressing the memory of Katya's rape, and it was only recently that she had begun to think about her suitors.

Her only deep love for a man was that for her uncle. As the years moved on, she recognized that Sergei had tried hard to make up to her for his early years of neglect by bringing presents, reading aloud to her, and encouraging her interest in literature and languages.

In June 1940, shortly after her nineteenth birthday, Marina was graduated from the YMCA high school with a gold medal. The same evening she announced her intention to get higher education. Influenced by her uncle, she wanted to be a nurse, but first she decided to perfect her languages. Although her French was excellent, her English was weak, and she wanted to study at the YMCA. With most of the girls in her class either looking for a job or dreaming of finding a suitable husband, she knew she'd have no trouble getting in.

She had already learned that sometimes in life a small thing tipped the scale in one's favor, and now she pointed out to Nadya and Sergei that the YMCA Institute of Liberal Arts was conveniently located a couple of blocks from their house. Thus, she would not have to walk a great distance to school.

Nadya laughed. "I know that, Marinka, but I'd be in favor of your attending the Institute even if it were downtown. Enjoy your summer because I suspect your studies this autumn will be intensive. I'm sorry that our vacation this year has to be postponed until August, but I have my heart set on spending it in Dzhalantun and there are no vacancies until August." Nadya chuckled. "Imagine, it's so popular that the railroad company has placed sleeping cars on the tracks to be used as a movable hotel!"

Marina did not mind. She spent many hours walking through the city gardens with her childhood friend Zoya Karelina or hours debating Dostoyevsky with Michael.

One afternoon on the way home she idled along the Bolshoi Prospekt, taking in every detail of the familiar scenery around her. She smiled inwardly as she passed the somber gray-stone houses and their fenced gardens with sparse trees, dry earth, and occasional privet bushes. Each home had its own type of fence to match the affluence of its owner. There were massive pillared fences with arched entrances, tall picket fences, whitewashed ones. Why this Russian preoccupation with fences? thought Marina. Was it a compulsion to draw private boundaries in a country where the land was limitless?

Suddenly she remembered that her mother had asked her to pick up some pastry and to stop at the pharmacy for Uncle Sergei's blood pressure medicine. She retraced her steps to Zazunov's bakery on Novotorgovaya Street to buy some of her favorite poppy seed sweet rolls. From there it would be a short walk across the street to the corner pharmacy near Churin's. That done, she would then take a detour home on the quieter Sadovaya Street. It would be pleasant to avoid the dusty thoroughfare of the Bolshoi Prospekt and enjoy the bonus of the arboretum fragrance wafting up from two blocks away.

Although Nadya had warned her frequently about walking alone on deserted streets, Marina thought her mother's fears were still distorted by Katya's tragic death.

The streets were teeming with people. Scurrying pedestrians hurried home with packages; teen-agers strolled arm in arm; the ever-present Japanese soldiers threaded their way through the crowds, vanishing and reappearing in the least expected places.

The fragrance inside Zazunov's bakery was dizzying, and Marina's stomach begged for the taste of rich Napoleon pastries. She bought three to share with her mother and Uncle Sergei and then selected several poppy seed buns. As she passed the money to the cashier, she could not resist glancing covetously over at the trays of rum-soaked cakes, wafer-layered chocolate Mikado tortes, latticed open-faced apricot tarts, whipped-cream-filled pastry cones, and the deep fried pastry twists called *khvorost* —crunchy, sprinkled with powdered sugar, and light enough to melt in the mouth. And the mint-flavored honey cakes, oh how she loved those! Better not look and be tempted beyond prudence. The remaining coins had to be saved for the pharmacy.

With a sigh she picked up her change, which she was putting in her purse when a man's voice behind her said in dreadfully broken Russian, *"Barishnya,* what cakes you recommend?"

Marina jumped at the nearness of the voice and turned to face a tall blond man looking at her with intense, unsmiling blue eyes. A giant of a man, he exuded an air of authority, or perhaps it only seemed so to Marina, who stared petrified at the foreigner who spoke to her with a German accent.

A German . . . a Japanese ally . . . flashed through her mind. A Nazi! She had never met a German before, and now she whirled around to the cashier, but the woman had busied herself placing trays of freshly baked breads on the shelves against the wall.

"You recommend?" repeated the man. Timidly Marina pointed to the tray of Napoleons and chocolate tortes.

"What name?" asked the man, nodding solemnly.

"This is a Napoleon, and that is a Mikado torte."

"Mikado?" asked the man, obviously amused by the Japanese name.

"Mikado," Marina confirmed. Scooping her package off the counter, she moved toward the door, but the man deftly blocked the way by stepping in front of her.

"You like Mikado?"

"Yes, very much," Marina responded emphatically.

"You help me, I buy you one." The man swept his arm in an imperious gesture toward the torte.

Marina shook her head. "No, thank you."

"Why?"

There was suspicion in the man's voice, and alarmed, Marina blurted the first thing that came to mind, "Chocolate is bad for me."

Then, carefully sidestepping the man, she hurried out and headed toward the pharmacy. In spite of the tremor in her legs, she walked briskly.

She felt good about the way she had handled herself. The last thing she wanted was to fraternize with a German national, be he a Nazi or not, for the Germans were Japanese allies, and she was afraid of them. Yet she could not be rude and perhaps invite a far greater danger to herself. No, she had done the right thing. She had been polite but formal, making it clear she did not encourage conversation with strangers. Had the man been Russian, she would have behaved the same. It did not occur to her to wonder until much later why the man had singled her out to ask for advice instead of the more obvious person behind the counter.

Across the Bolshoi Prospekt, she handed the prescription to a rotund gray-haired pharmacist and watched him shake his head.

"Your uncle's blood pressure does not improve, I see." He sighed and waved his hand, dismissing the subject. Then, squinting, he peered at Marina. "Are you all right yourself, my dear? You look pale today."

Marina feigned a bright smile. "I'm fine, thank you," she said. She realized her reply was not convincing, but these days it was dangerous to speak aloud in public places about one's fears of the Japanese or their German allies; the walls seemed to have ears.

The city-wide prejudice against all Japanese Occupational Forces was based on the misdeeds of the notorious few, and in this she was no exception. She thought of her encounter with the German. After all, there had been nothing wrong in his behavior, for what did she know about the customs of another nation? Maybe it was customary to repay a courtesy on the spot, and she had been unfair to jump to the conclusion that the man was brash.

Surely not all Germans were Nazis and collaborated with the Japanese!

After she had left the pharmacy, she turned right on Azhikheiskaya Street toward Sadovaya. The street noise abated instantly, and she welcomed the solitude she cherished.

"It isn't good for a young girl to be by herself too much," Nadya once said to her. "It's lonely out there in the world." But was loneliness a synonym for solitude? She didn't think so. She never felt lonely when she was alone; she enjoyed these short walks home when she could immerse herself in her thoughts without fear of interruption.

On quiet Sadovaya Street the city sounds were remote and lulling: a fading "whoa" of the *izvozchik* reining in his horse; the screeching brakes of the tramway dulled by distance; the sudden rustle of oak leaves; and on top of all that, the fragrance—the intoxicating fragrance of the multitude of flower beds in the arboretum. How foolish she had been never to have thought of taking this circuitous route home before. She decided to walk a block beyond her street.

She passed wooden slotted fences surrounding the many mansions along the street and indulged in her childhood game of guessing who the families inside might be. Were they rich, secure, happy? What furniture and prized possessions graced those rooms? Were they heirlooms from Russia or the flashy acquisitions of the nouveaux riches?

Deep in her fantasy, she was halfway to the corner of Tsitsikarskaya Street, where she would turn left to go back to the Bolshoi Prospekt, when she became aware of an echo to her footsteps. So unaccustomed was she to the quiet of the street that her own heels resounding loudly on the granite sidewalk surprised her. The echo magnified her step, heavy and strong.

Ahead, the street was broad and empty with no visible life except busy magpies plucking at the ground. They carked at her approach and, flapping their black and white wings, flew up into the trees, where they perched on the branches and watched her from their haven.

Now the silence was disrupted, and with it, the echo of

Marina's footsteps. Although she slowed her stride to watch the birds, the echo's rhythm remained the same. The clicking of a metal strip edging the heel of a boot. Click-click. Even, rhythmic, not at all compatible with her shorter, lighter gait. Perhaps a student going home. Which of these lovely houses was his? She resisted the temptation to turn around and see who it was. To display curiosity in such a way was not mannerly. Determined not to look behind her, Marina reached Tsitsikarskaya Street and headed toward the Bolshoi Prospekt one block away. The sound of the footsteps behind her receded, and she was enveloped once again in silence.

On her left was the former location of Oksakovskaya School for Girls, which had moved two years earlier to Tamozhennaya Street, and on her right lay an old cemetery protected by a four-foot-high fence with a graceful fretwork of latticed stone. Marina wanted to walk through the old cemetery. In this respect she was thoroughly Russian: It was not a place of gloom or depression; on the contrary, the quality of sadness there had its own intangible serenity, the monuments and epitaphs being a fusion of poetry and art. It was less the home of the dead than a memorial park where lilacs and jasmine bloomed and where a Russian soul could find peaceful refuge from the vicissitudes of daily life. But not today. She had already taken too much time to get home, and her mother would chide her for being late.

She neared the eight-foot-high pillared stone fence of the vacated Oksakovskaya School. Between the massive Doric columns of the fence she could see inside the yard. It was empty, and all was quiet around her. As she reached the arched gate, however, three Japanese soldiers appeared from behind one of the pillars and blocked the width of the sidewalk before her. "This riffraff," her mother once said in exasperation when she ran into one of the soldiers on the street, "they have an uncanny way of growing right out of the ground before you when you least expect them."

Marina stepped off the curb to avoid bumping into the soldiers. As she did so, one of them grabbed her arm. "Don't hurry. Come with us. We want to ask you something."

The soldier's voice was brusque, and his Russian garbled, but the menacing air was clear. They moved around her, cutting off her escape routes. One soldier pulled her toward the schoolyard. Another shoved her.

Marina fought, struggling to break free. *My God, Mama was right . . . she warned . . . this is unreal . . . half a block from the Bolshoi Prospekt!* Frantically she looked around, hoping someone would see her—a passing *izvozchik*, a pedestrian perhaps? Remembering her mother's instructions in self-defense, she brought her knee up into the nearest soldier's groin but missed it, and her knee glanced off his thigh. He twisted her arm, and she screamed.

A stinging slap seared her cheek, snapping her head sideways. She tried to scream again, but a hand clamped over her mouth, choking off her voice. She kicked and thrashed, aware that her only chance of escape was to delay being dragged through that gate. She had to stay out on the sidewalk. Surely someone would pass by and see the struggle.

But help came from the opposite direction.

"Chotto mate!"

The authoritative, angry voice worked instant magic. The soldiers released Marina and came to attention, staring at someone behind her.

"Doshita?"

"Nandemoarimasen. Shorui o shirabete irudakedesu."

"Heisha e kaere! Ore ga yaru!"

The soldiers whirled around and marched briskly toward the Bolshoi Prospekt.

Marina turned to look at her rescuer and found herself face-to-face with the blond German she had left earlier at Zazunov's bakery. He stooped to pick up her packages, which lay scattered on the ground. As he straightened, he placed a supporting hand under her elbow.

"Thank you," she whispered, fighting to contain unwelcome tears that threatened to spill over and reluctant to admit how grateful she was to see him.

He bowed to her abruptly. "Not to hate all Japanese from those three. They said they were checking your papers. I told them I take over."

He thrust his chin in the direction of the retreating soldiers. "Three bad men," he said. "They will be punished. You must understand."

"Yes, yes, I understand," mumbled Marina, wondering why the German spoke Japanese and why the soldiers had obeyed him. Reaction was setting in, and she was overly anxious to get away.

"You must understand," the man persisted doggedly, "I am friend of Japan. This incident is unusual."

She started to walk toward home, and this time she did not mind when the man kept pace with her. The heels of his boots clicked on the sidewalk with a metallic sound. She had heard it before. Timidly she gave him a sidelong glance. His profile was straight and refined, and his face lean. He did not look at her once as they walked the one block to her house, but at the gate he faced her solemnly and gave her another curt bow.

"My name is Rolf Weimer, with the German Consulate in Harbin."

"And my name is Marina Razumova," she heard herself say.

There was a glimmer of warmth in Weimer's blue eyes. Then the light went out, and he was sober again.

"Can you teach me Russian language?" he asked abruptly.

"No. I'm not a teacher; I'm a student."

How stupid to volunteer unsolicited information. What was the matter with her?

Weimer smiled for the first time. "You think, please. I want learn Russian better. Soon I ask once more. Maybe you think to say yes?"

He bowed again, turned quickly, and walked away.

Marina was shaken. If he were to come back and ask her again, she wouldn't know what to tell him.

Chapter Twenty-six

Marina told her mother about her encounter with the Japanese soldiers and Rolf Weimer. Nadya reached for her daughter impulsively, then, changing her mind, pressed her hands against her mouth and shook her head. Her eyes slowly filled with tears, and her voice shook as she said, "Thank God that German came to your rescue! Oh, God, when I think—" She gulped and swept Marina into her arms. "Oh, Marinka, my child, be careful . . . be careful!"

"Don't worry, Mama, I will. As for Mr. Weimer, I didn't encourage him about Russian lessons."

"Well, if he does come to call, we have to be courteous to him. We mustn't forget that he saved you from an assault by the soldiers."

A few days later Marina had gone to bed when the doorbell rang. She glanced at the alarm clock on her nightstand. It was nine o'clock. Sergei was out at a game of Mah-Jongg, and the servants were gone. Throwing on a terry-cloth robe, she looked out into the corridor. Nadya in her silk peach-colored robe was already standing at the door, talking to Rolf Weimer. Marina hid behind the door and listened.

"I come to have Russian lessons with Fräulein Razumova," he said.

Nadya's reply was muffled, and Marina strained to hear. "—very late. I'm sorry."

"This is only good time for me," Weimer said, stressing every word, but Nadya stood firm.

"But for us this is not a good time. Perhaps sometime during the day you can come back."

Marina failed to catch Weimer's words, but moments later Nadya closed the door and returned to her room.

The next morning she spoke to Marina. "We must be careful with the Germans," she said. "It's important to hide any fear we may have, but it doesn't mean we have to be overly friendly. Although I strongly disapprove of your giving him lessons, Uncle Sergei feels it may be dangerous to antagonize him. Maybe he won't return."

But Rolf Weimer did return, and hesitantly Marina agreed to give him lessons. At first he came in the mornings. He was a good student and learned so fast that in a short time he was able to use long, complex sentences. After a while he began to acquaint Marina with some of his heritage, showing her postcards of the Zugspitze, Germany's highest peak, and snapshots of Heidelberg, the seat of his country's oldest university, from which he had a degree in political science. Soon the one-hour lessons stretched into two.

One morning he did not come, and Marina, who had begun to enjoy these sessions, found herself fretting. He appeared that evening, however, with a bouquet of chrysanthemums and carnations and without explanation asked to take her through the arboretum while they studied his current lesson. Conscious of Nadya and Sergei's silent disapproval, embarrassed and at the same time defiant, Marina picked up her notebook and followed Rolf outside.

Since then it had become a nightly ritual. They had taken every pathway in the arboretum, walked among the linden trees and maples, studied each flower bed by moonlight. Gradually Rolf began to describe the beauty of his own country in glowing terms. Speaking haltingly, he rarely smiled, as if a smile might introduce between them an intimacy which, for now, neither was ready to admit. When she encouraged him to tell a story for practice, he stumbled over the words, searching his vocabulary with assiduous care.

He spoke freely of his youth. At thirty he was the youngest of five children, the only son of an army general and a descendant of a long line of ancestors who traditionally served in the military. When he was twenty, his mother had died. His four sisters had married and were living in various parts of Germany. His father, critical of his government's policies, had chosen to retire early.

By the time Rolf had come to telling Marina about his student years they were back at the door to her house. In the awkward silence that followed, Marina tried to select her words carefully.

"That was very good, Mr. Weimer, your Russian is improving. You made only two mistakes and small ones at that."

Then the handsome German looked at her with a long searching look and said, "My name is Rolf."

When she did not answer, he repeated, "Please call me Rolf."

Perturbed, Marina nodded, and whispering a barely audible good night, slipped into the sanctuary of the house.

Once in her room, she undressed hurriedly. But when she pulled the pins out of her hair letting the braids uncoil and fall down her back, she stopped to scrutinize herself in the mirror. That old-fashioned hairdo was ugly! How could she not have seen it before? She must do something about it. Cut it maybe, or get a permanent wave. She would look more modern, more up-to-date with curls about her face. She pushed a few dark strands forward, fluffed them, and held them cupped in her hands below her ears. A stranger looked back at her, a fresher, prettier stranger.

After turning the light out, Marina stayed awake a long time, thinking about Rolf. Suddenly he was no longer a puppet consular officer but a human being with feelings, convictions, family ties. A man of culture, a man with a proud, ancient heritage. Did he approve of his country's aggression? She had to find out.

At the next session, she ventured to broach the subject, and Rolf took a long time to answer. The stem of a slender tobacco plant broke in his fingers and he threw it away.

"Governments come and go, but the nation endures," he said at length, without looking at her. "I love my country too much to turn against it; so, I try to avoid using harsh measures in my work."

Rolf spoke rapidly, and it suddenly occurred to Marina that he was using far too large a vocabulary for someone who had spoken so haltingly only a short time ago. She stopped, and without thinking, touched his arm.

"Your vocabulary is staggering! Where have you learned those words?"

For the first time Rolf looked embarrassed. He fell silent and for a while seemed at a loss for words. Then, spreading his arms, he smiled disarmingly. "You caught me! Very well, I confess. I fell into my own trap by telling you about something so close to my heart."

His Russian had become flawless, unaccented. "I was brought up by a Russian governess who taught me to read and write. Thanks to her, I grew up bilingual."

He continued to smile, and the smile disturbed her far more than the relevation of how completely she had been duped.

"Why then?" she asked softly, and immediately felt foolish for seeking an obvious answer.

Rolf smiled. "That was the only way I could think of approaching you. You see, I'd been following you for a long time before I spoke to you at the bakery."

His smile faded. He took a step forward, placed his hands on her arms, and firmly but slowly drew her to him. Marina did not resist. How could she? This was inevitable. Weeks of unspoken tension grew inexorably to a climax in this feared-for, this yearned-for moment. Held in his arms, she felt her heart thump wildly as he pressed her against him and kept her thus without moving, without touching her face.

She was drowning in his eyes, in the dark, mysterious look that subjugated her. His embrace tightened; then his lips brushed over her mouth, withdrew, touched once more and held. Softly, gently, the pressure mounted until her lips gave way.

She had never dreamed it could be like this: the breathlessness, the strange, delicious current coursing through her body to all the centers of her being. Rolf. The stranger. The beloved alien.

He released her. "Marina," he said, holding her hands. Then, after turning abruptly toward a flower bed, he cut a few blossoms with a pocketknife. Solemnly he faced her again and handed her a bouquet of peonies and roses. Marina looked at them.

They all were red.

"Marina, how could you have fallen in love with a German? I thought I had warned you!"

Nadya was sitting in her room facing Marina across a small coffee table.

"He's a German subject," Nadya went on. *"Hitler's* subject. No leader in the modern world has persecuted the Jews as Hitler is beginning to do."

She's saying this because of Esther, Marina thought. Uncle Sergei's ever-suffering wife. They'd made a saint out of her, and now there was no logic in her mother's argument.

"Mama," Marina said patiently, "you can't condemn the whole nation for the actions of one man."

"All Germans who live in China now are suspect because they collaborate with the Japanese, and Weimer impresses me as a fiercely nationalistic man who wouldn't marry a Russian refugee."

Marina felt the sting of rising tears. "He hasn't said he loved me, Mama. He gave me red roses, that's all!"

Nadya drummed the arm of her chair with her fingers. "That's practically a declaration of love. But should he propose, are you prepared to enter an alien culture and live among people whose customs and language you don't understand? What if they don't accept you?"

Cornered, Marina struck back. "Aren't you imagining things, Mama? You talk about alien culture, but what you're really objecting to is that Rolf is German. At least I'd be able to give my child a passport and a country he could call his own!"

A slow flush rose to Nadya's face as she looked at her daughter for a few moments in silence. Then she reached across the table and took Marina's hand in both of hers. "Marinka," she said in a strangled voice, "I want only the best for you. A country and a passport for your child are not going to bring you personal happiness. Call it a mother's instinct, but I can't see you being happy with Rolf. We women tend to see only the good, the noble in the men we love; we place them on a pedestal, and if they topple, we hurt. Take your time, and be careful!"

Nadya pulled Marina into her arms and held her close. Something in her mother's embrace began to suffocate Marina. She freed herself and walked to the door. "Where's Uncle Sergei, Mama? It's time for dinner."

In August Sergei encouraged his sister to take Marina to Dzhalantun as planned. Concerned about the blossoming romance between his niece and Rolf, he hoped that a vacation away from the German would cool Marina's infatuation and give her time to think things through.

Located on the western line of the railway in the valley of the river Yalu, Dzhalantun was one of the most beautiful and fashionable resorts in Manchuria. Surrounded by parks, sports grounds, and an open-air stand for symphony orchestra and theater performances, it was Marina's favorite resort, where she had spent many summers as a child, and ordinarily she would have loved going there again. But the lacy gazebos, the garlands of colored lights strung along the river, and the nightly romantic music—all contributed to her yearning for Rolf. Soon Nadya realized that the separation had only intensified her daughter's love for the handsome German.

When they returned to Harbin, autumn was already in the air. The summer heat had abated, leaving the city to gather its resources for the harsh season of winter. Shortly before starting her studies, Marina announced that Rolf had proposed and she had accepted. Nadya reacted cautiously.

"My warning to you still stands, Marinka, and I'm not at all sure of the reaction you will get among our own friends in the city." She paused, looked at her daughter significantly, and although she had not finished her thought, Marina understood. She was marrying a Japanese ally and would carry the stigma of having married for personal gain. Well, so what? She would keep her head high and rise above it. It might be that those who gossiped the most were just plain envious.

Contrary to Nadya's fears, Marina's engagement announcement in the newspaper brought phone calls from friends and acquaintances with congratulations and good wishes. She had worried that she'd be ostracized for marrying a German, but the opposite proved true.

"It shows you how fickle some people are," Nadya commented. "The Germans and the Japanese are in power, and now everyone wants to be friends with us."

Marina fretted about her uncle's reaction to Rolf, whom Sergei had managed to avoid most of the time. She adored her uncle, and she desperately sought his approval. But every time she extolled Rolf's character Sergei either left the room or changed the subject. She wasn't sure whose objections were stronger, her mother's or Sergei's, and she had begun to resent Esther's invisible influence.

"You can't forget Esther, can you, Mama?" she said to her mother in exasperation shortly before the wedding. "Don't blame every German for the persecution of the Jews! Have you forgotten that if Esther suffered at all, it was at the hands of our own Russians, not the Germans?"

Her logic went unchallenged. Marina sensed that the trauma was so deep it was useless to stress her argument.

Soon after his proposal Rolf said he had to go to Shanghai for a few days on consular business. When he returned, he remained formal and polite with Nadya and Sergei, seemingly unaware of the cold, though courteous, reception he received at her home. More than ever Marina was determined to prove that her choice of a husband was a good one.

A few days before the wedding she was walking home from having visited Zoya, who was to be one of her bridesmaids. In love, fantasizing about her forthcoming wedding, she was oblivious of her surroundings and didn't see her mother until she was upon her.

"Are you smiling at some private joke? Let me in on it!"

Marina looked at her mother. Nadya looked festive in her beautifully tailored beige suit purchased in the salon department of

Churin's downtown store. Marina recognized her mother's dress outfit and wondered where she was going.

"Madame Volkova is having an afternoon tea," Nadya explained, seeing her daughter's raised brows. "I thought I'd get some exercise and walk to Tsentralnaya Street. Marina, she included you in her invitation, so why don't you come with me?"

A notorious busybody, Madame Volkova was called Gossip Maria behind her back. Marina could not think of anything drearier than joining her mother at such a tea. She declined firmly.

Nadya chuckled and took Marina's arm. "Well, then at least keep me company for a few blocks."

"Mamochka, why in the world are you going to tea at Madame Volkova's? You've never liked her."

"We can't always do what we want, Marina. Mr. Volkov is one of Sergei's patients, and we don't want to hurt her feelings."

"Very well, I'll walk with you as far as the English Tennis Club, but it's a good five or six blocks to Tsentralnaya Street from here. Are you sure you can walk that far in those high heels?" Marina pointed at her mother's camel-colored snakeskin pumps.

"You know I never buy anything that isn't comfortable. These are Swiss Ballys. I find them the most comfortable of all."

"I thought you liked the Czech Batas the best for your feet?" Marina teased, well aware of her mother's extravagance in shoes.

Nadya laughed. "You're the smart one, aren't you? You know as well as I do that Ballys have more elegance than Batas, and why shouldn't I splurge when I feel like it?"

At the busy thoroughfare of Novotorgovaya Street, Marina took her mother by the arm. The noise around them was deafening: Taxis blew their horns incessantly, and tramways, making a sharp turn from Gogolevskaya Street, screeched on their tracks.

"Marinka," Nadya said suddenly, "doesn't Michael often play tennis at the English club?"

Marina nodded. "Yes, he does. I might drop in and see if he's there today."

"He's a bright young man. He chose a profession not common among the Russians here. Engineers abound in Harbin, but accountants are relatively few. How smart he was to affiliate himself with an American firm and get in with the foreigners!"

"I've never denied that he's intelligent. He's not only good with figures, but he knows literature well. That's why I enjoy talking to him so much."

"He's a fine young man, Marina, with a good future, and in case you're not aware of it, very much in love with you."

Marina stopped and looked at her mother. "Mama! You're still fighting the idea of my marrying a German!"

"Well, you've hit me not in the brow but straight in the eye, as the saying goes. I do admit that I wish it were Michael instead of Rolf. You're my daughter, and I worry. You had so many young men interested in you, but you gave none of them a chance, not even Michael."

"But I'm in love with Rolf, remember?"

"Well, I hope you don't regret it later."

Marina sighed in exasperation. "My wedding is only a few days away, and you're telling me this? I assure you I can take care of myself. Our marriage will be on equal terms. This is one of the reasons why I want to get higher education and become a nurse. I don't want to depend on Rolf to support me entirely."

"You already have an equal relationship with Michael," Nadya said quietly. "He's been patient enough not to push his love on you. Why haven't you considered him first?"

Marina hedged. "I never thought of him in terms of marriage. Besides, you know very well that there has to be a physical attraction, too, and I can't imagine me and Michael . . ." She fumbled for words and then blurted out, "Mama, for heaven's sake, let's end this conversation! I love Rolf! How many times must I say this to convince you? I don't want to think of Michael as anything other than a good friend."

They crossed the large square around St. Nicholas Cathedral and were near the opposite side by the English Club when suddenly Nadya gasped and stumbled over the curb.

Grabbing her mother's arm, Marina chuckled. "Aha! Those Ballys are not that comfortable, after all!"

Her smile faded when she looked at her mother's face. It was ashen, and she was staring ahead in shock. Frightened, Marina bent over her mother and put her arm around her waist.

"Mamochka, what's the matter? Are you sick?"

Nadya continued to stare, and Marina looked up.

A tall man was limping slowly toward them. Dressed in a well-fitted brown suit, he leaned heavily on a cane. His dark hair was touched with gray and neatly combed, but it was his eyes that intrigued Marina. Elongated under a generous sweep of arched brows, they looked out with the assurance of a man accustomed to command, a man obviously undaunted by his physical handicap.

There was something vaguely familiar about his features, yet Marina knew she had never met him before. Who was he? As she wondered, the man stopped and peered at them. A look of stunned recognition swept over his face and then faded quickly. There was no doubt whatever that Nadya knew the man and that he had recognized her. She recovered enough to grab Marina by the arm and pull her toward Tsentralnaya Street, away from him.

"Marinka, please! Come with me to the door. Stay with me!"

Marina had never seen her mother this flustered before. Who was this man to have affected her this way? They hurried the two blocks to Volkov's house, and at the gate Nadya stopped to catch her breath. Marina took her mother by the shoulders. "Mamochka, who is that man? I've never seen you so upset. Who is he?" When Nadya remained silent, Marina shook her. "Answer me!"

Nadya stared at her daughter with tear-filled eyes. At last, blinking, she stammered, "Marinka, I can't . . . not now! . . . I have to go into that house! Oh, God, help me . . . I don't know if I can. . . . Go home, but don't say anything to Uncle Sergei. . . . Do you hear?"

"Why don't you come home with me and Michael? You can telephone Madame Volkova and make some excuse. You're in no shape to endure social chatter right now."

"No! . . . You don't understand . . . I need time before I go home . . . I can't let Sergei see me this way. . . . He'd ask questions, and I don't—" Nadya turned and rushed through the gate, forcing Marina to back off to keep from being seen by Madame Volkova. After her mother had entered the house, Marina stood for a few moments thinking. Then she headed back toward the tennis club.

Chapter Twenty-seven

At the corner of the Bolshoi Prospekt Marina turned left. Deep in thought, she did not see the man until she was almost upon him, for he stood leaning on his cane in the middle of the sidewalk. Struck by his pallor and the same frozen look she had seen on her mother's face, she slowed down and paused, studying the man curiously. For a few moments they looked at each other. Then the man bowed stiffly. "Forgive me, mademoiselle, but the lady walking with you—was that by any chance Madame Razumova?"

"Yes, it was," Marina replied after a moment's hesitation.

The man's eyes came alive, and with keen interest he searched her face. "Then—then you are Katya Razumova?"

At the mention of her sister's name Marina flinched. Katya's death announcement in the paper had been framed in a larger than usual black-rimmed block. But that had been more than eight years ago. The man must be fairly new in Harbin, or he would have known about her sister's death. Her mother must have known him in Siberia, where Katya was born. Had he been her father's friend? That seemed unlikely. She knew that her father had been a socialist, and this man looked every inch a nobleman.

Aloud she said, "No, I'm Katya's sister, Marina. And you, monsieur?"

The man's face suffused with color. With a trembling hand he reached toward Marina's arm, faltered, withdrew.

"Who are you?" Marina's voice had an edge to it.

The man shook his head. "I beg your pardon, mademoiselle. Your mother will tell you my name. Please tell her—tell her I beg to speak to her. I'll wait at this corner every afternoon next week." He hesitated a moment, then asked, "How is your uncle Sergei?"

Marina was becoming unnerved by this strange man who appeared to know her family, yet refused to identify himself. What right did he have to speak to her, question her on the street? She shouldn't have stopped to talk to a stranger, especially one who had frightened her mother, and she couldn't understand why she was still standing there, answering his questions.

Reluctantly she murmured, "He's fine, thank you."

A new light shone in the man's eyes—a secret flicker that flared brightly and died down before Marina had time to recognize it fully. He bowed again. "Forgive me for addressing you like this on the street, mademoiselle, but circumstances made me forget my manners."

Glad to end this strange conversation, Marina nodded and hurried on.

At the club Michael had already finished his game and she was surprised to find how relieved she was to find him there. Tanned, vigorous, and full of good humor, he was a reassuring sight.

"Well, well, where have you materialized from?"

His curly hair forever tousled, his lopsided grin, his ready wit were all that she needed to recover.

"From a fairyland. I waved my magic wand, and here I am, come to recruit my faithful subject to walk me home."

Michael swept her a courtly bow. "Your obedient servant, Your Highness, is ready to escort you to the end of the earth. Well, almost ready; this servant has to collect his tennis shoes and racket if Her Highness doesn't mind such mundane details."

Marina laughed and waved her hand. "Come on, silly, hurry up!"

In a few minutes he came back with a redheaded man in tennis shorts, a wet T-shirt, and a towel around his neck.

"Marina, may I present my friend, Wayne Morrison," Michael said in English. "He gave me stiff competition today."

The man smiled. "How do you do, miss. Don't you believe Michael; it was sheer luck that I beat him today. He serves a mean ball."

The man spoke with an American accent, and Marina had difficulty understanding him. Why was the ball mean? she thought, but recovered quickly and smiled politely.

"It was nice to meet you, Mr. Morrison."

"My pleasure, miss."

Morrison turned to Michael and placed a hand on his shoulder. "Think it over, and let me hear from you in a few days, okay?"

Michael nodded and ushered Marina outside.

"Who's this Morrison?" Marina asked.

"He's an American lawyer with whom I occasionally play tennis."

At the cathedral square Marina found herself hurrying as if pursued by a ghost.

"What's the rush? I thought I was supposed to walk you home, not run. You're racing as if someone had brushed you with turpentine and you were burning up."

Marina enjoyed bantering with her friend, and appreciated the light touch with which he handled even the grimmest of subjects. The verbal liberties she allow him discouraged any venture into the shaky grounds of courtship; in this kind of fraternal language there was no room for subtleties, and that was the way she liked it.

"What happened today, Marinka? That frown doesn't belong on your face. Kindly erase it!"

"I wasn't aware I was frowning. It's just that I hate mysteries of any kind."

It never occurred to Marina to keep secrets from Michael, for he had always been the one with whom she had shared all her thoughts and worries—well, almost all. Her courtship with Rolf she had kept to herself. Michael changed the subject every time she had brought up Rolf's name in the past, and she suspected that he, too, disapproved of him. Or was he jealous? She wondered now that her mother had brought up that possibility. No matter!

Right now, without hesitation, she told him about the strange encounter with the lame man.

"There's something disturbing about him, Michael. Mama asked me not to say anything to Uncle Sergei, and while that in itself is peculiar, I'm puzzled by something else. I know I've never seen him before, yet he looks familiar."

Michael gave her a sidelong glance. "I see no mystery here. I bet your mother will tell you that he was a family friend and you knew him when you were a toddler."

Marina shook her head dubiously. "Why then keep it a secret from Uncle Sergei, and why such a shocked reaction from Mama?" They were nearing her house, and at the gate Marina stopped. "Whoever he turns out to be, remember that Mama has asked me not to say anything to Uncle Sergei. Come in, let's have some tea."

Michael shook his head. "Thanks, Marinka, but not today. I have to go home and do some serious thinking."

"Well, now that's a switch. I thought we did all our deep thinking together."

"Not this time. I'm on the brink of a major change in my life."

Marina's eyes widened. "A major change? Stop talking in riddles."

"Give me a chance, I'll explain. Wayne Morrison, the fellow you've just met, is leaving Harbin to join another firm in Shanghai, and today he asked if I'd be interested in an accounting job with that firm."

Marina's mouth dropped open, and she stared at him.

Michael blinked. "Well, quit looking at me as though there were maps on my face," he said peevishly.

"I see no maps but some foggy messages. Are you telling me you're leaving Harbin?"

"I haven't had a chance to make up my mind yet. What do you think of it?"

"You hit me on the head with a bolt and then ask for my opinion?"

Michael grinned maliciously. "Didn't know you cared."

Unaccountably Marina became irritated. "Of course I care!

We're friends, aren't we? I'd think you'd want to share such colossal news right away. After all, moving to Shanghai is like going abroad. I can't imagine your walking all this distance and not saying a word about it."

She was overreacting, and she knew it. He hadn't accepted the offer yet, and she was jumping to conclusions. A nasty day. What was it her mother often said? "When one problem arrives, open the gate wide for another."

"What's the matter, are you worried there won't be anyone to fight with over Dostoyevsky? Or walk you home from school? After all, you're making a big change in your life yourself!"

"Since when have you started to needle?"

He gave her a crooked smile. "I didn't mean to, Marinka. Let's not start a fight!"

"Are you seriously considering this offer?"

"Yes, I am. This kind of opportunity doesn't come to us Russian fellows too often. I'd be a fool not to think about it seriously. It's a big step, however, and I want to talk to my parents before I give Wayne my answer."

"And what about me?" Marina demanded.

"Well, I've told you, haven't I? Think it over, and let's argue about it in a couple of days. In the meantime, don't try to figure out who that lame man is. He may turn out to be Count Dracula. And speaking of Dracula, are you really serious about marrying that Nazi Viking of yours?"

Marina controlled her temper with difficulty. "I don't appreciate your insults to my fiancé, Michael."

"Sorry! He may not be a Viking, but he's a Nazi for sure!"

With a flippant wave, Michael sauntered off, whistling the popular "On the Hills of Manchuria."

Marina stood riveted to the sidewalk and watched his receding figure, fighting an impulse to run after him and tell him— She checked herself. Tell him what? She pursed her lips, confused. What she needed was to clear her head.

She looked around. It was quiet here. The light was brilliant, sharpening the outline of their house in the setting sun. A block away pedestrians hurried across the road. As the flitting images shifted and moved, the man with the cane appeared among them. Her imagination was playing tricks on her; she had to get hold of herself.

Angry and frightened, she shut her eyes tight, then opened them and peered into the crowd.

The man was gone.

Nadya could hardly remember how she managed to get through the rest of the afternoon. As the women sat around the tea table talking, she listened to their chitchat with a fixed smile and watched the grandfather clock in the corner tick off minutes with unhurried precision.

Madame Volkova, a diminutive woman with the face of a Pekinese, fluttered around her guests. She looked at Nadya curiously. "You're so quiet today, Nadezhda Antonovna. Is anything wrong?"

"I always listen more than I talk, Maria Stepanovna," Nadya replied evenly. The look of anticipation faded from Madame Volkova's face, and she busied herself with the silver samovar. At any other time Nadya would have chuckled inwardly for having disappointed her hostess by not providing her with a choice bit of gossip, but today she was in no mood for humor. When at last she could make her excuses and leave, it was after six o'clock.

Once outside, she hailed a passing *izvozchik* and sank back into the cushioned seat. The clip-clop of hooves on cobblestones, usually a pleasant cadence, was now jarring to her ears, like a loud retort, a host of hammering insistent orders: *Run, Nadya, escape from the past, don't let it hurt you again!*

As the droshky rode past the familiar landmarks, Nadya studied them with meticulous attention—a kind of visual exercise akin to the tidying ritual she followed whenever she wanted to avoid tackling a particularly difficult piece of work.

Beyond Tsitsikarskaya Street, on the left, towering above the street, was the tall Catholic cathedral; on the right, the low gray-stone fence enclosed the old cemetery with the Pokrovskaya church at its far end. Beyond, across Mukdenskaya, a whole block was taken by the Protestant church with its tall wooden fence stretching around the corner on Telinskaya Street.

On the other side of the avenue and directly opposite the Protestant compound, as if in mockery of the three exhibits of Christian divisiveness, sprawled a mental sanitarium. In the past Nadya had pitied its inmates who had failed to cope with life. She had lost faith in a selective God who punished legions and favored few, for time and again she had had to find strength from the power within herself. She needed to convince herself that the past had ceased to affect her and that she could face the present.

What was it that Vadim had said shortly before they were married? Something about the past's having an uncanny way of surfacing at the least propitious moment. Well, that past had caught up with her once in Vladivostok. It had taken years to overcome the pain and to convince herself that the choice she had made was the right one.

Now she was not so sure. She had been more shaken by today's encounter than she was willing to admit, stunned, in fact, by the flesh-and-blood figure of the man she thought she'd never see again. For more than twenty years she had believed Alexei was dead to her. Now he had appeared once again to haunt her, and the devil of it was that this time she couldn't run away. No matter what, she mustn't upset her brother. His high blood pressure was a continuous worry, and Alexei's reappearance would be a shock to him. It was a subtle twist of irony—wasn't it?—she thought wryly, that now her primary concern was for her brother, not for the man who had caused her many sleepless nights.

She felt light-headed; then, slowly, her mood shifted. Whatever her complex reactions were to having seen Alexei again—older, tired-looking, but somehow still the same—receded before an enormous, overwhelming delight at the physical sight of him. She was embarrassed to give in to the shameful pleasure. But the thoughts, like busy ants, were tugging at her.

Alexei . . . her love . . . why had he come to Harbin? Was Marie, his wife, still with him? If she met him again—and she had a feeling she would—she'd speak to him, find out everything about his life during the past twenty years. But first things first.

*Don't panic, Nadya. Marina has to learn the truth—well, not all
of it—and not now with the wedding only a few days off, but
sometime later.* And there was Sergei. . . . He'd have to be told,
too, but she must choose her words carefully.

Marina had decided to be married in the Pokrovskaya church
over Nadya's objections. Her mother thought it was a bad omen to
choose a cemetery church.

Marina dismissed her with a shrug. "Mama, I've weathered
your opposition, and I'll manage this one, too. I love the old
cemetery, and I've never considered it gloomy."

When the day of the wedding arrived, the church was packed
with the invited and the curious, and Marina was pleased by the
public support. Dressed in an ivory satin gown with a four-foot
train, a broad peaked cummerbund cinching her waist, her black
hair set off with a *kokoshnik* embroidered with seed pearls, Marina
was a beautiful bride. Her only disappointment was that Michael
had declined to be one of the ushers and didn't come to the
wedding at all, claiming to have a bad cold. She thought his
excuse was flimsy, and her irritation was aggravated by her
mother's sad smile which Marina interpreted to mean "I told you
so."

True to the tradition of the bride's parents' absenting themselves
from the church ceremony, Nadya and Sergei waited downtown at
the Fantasia restaurant, where the reception was to take place. As
Marina climbed the steps and crossed the threshold of the
Pokrovskaya church on the arm of one of the ushers, a colleague
of Rolf's who had been asked to replace Michael, the choir burst
forth in a jubilant hymn.

How beautiful it all was and how sad that her mother and Uncle
Sergei steadfastly adhered to the old custom! Rolf, erect and
handsome in his tuxedo, met her at the door and led her to the
center of the church, where a corpulent priest in a white chasuble
was waiting for them at the *analoy*, a stand with an icon placed in
the center of the church where the wedding ceremony was to be
conducted.

During the wedding several ushers took turns holding the church crowns over the couple's heads, and they managed not to step on the bride's long train as the priest led the procession three times around the *analoy*.

After the ceremony Marina nodded and smiled at the well-wishers as she and Rolf walked through the crowd toward the exit. Just as they reached it, Marina stopped, and a barely audible gasp escaped her. Standing near the door was the man with the cane.

Her eyes locked with his, and she was astonished to see tears rolling down his handsome face despite his glowing smile. As her hand touched his arm, he impulsively raised it to his lips. Then, recovering, he said something to Rolf in German. The groom looked at him in surprise, but before he could answer, the man backed away and disappeared into the crowd.

Inside the automobile Rolf asked, "Who was that man at the church door?"

"I don't know. What did he say to you?"

"He told me to take good care of you, of all things! He must be a well-educated man. He spoke flawless German." Rolf looked at Marina intently. "Are you sure you don't know him?"

Marina shook her head. "I saw him once a few days ago when Mother and I were going to a friend's house. She became very upset when she saw him, but she wouldn't tell me who he is; she said it was a long story, and she'd tell me sometime later." Marina thought for a moment, then added quietly, "I've been wondering about him ever since."

Rolf chuckled and, taking her chin in his hand, made her look at him. "You really don't suspect?" When Marina's eyes opened wide, he added, "There's such a resemblance between you that I'd venture a guess the man is at least your uncle. . . ."

Marina was stunned. So that is why she thought the man looked familiar—she resembled him! But she knew Uncle Sergei was her mother's only brother. Could this be her father's brother, another Razumov? Her mother never talked much about her father, except to say he was killed during the revolution and it was painful for her to speak about him. She'd ask her again.

For now, though, her excitement overshadowed any thoughts of a mystery in her mother's life. After the reception at the Fantasia they were to spend their wedding night at the elegant three-story Hotel Moderne, and then Rolf was taking her on a honeymoon to the southern resort of Hoshigaura, a suburb of Dairen.

"Well, Frau Weimer, why so pensive?"

Rolf's voice was teasing, but her new German name startled her. She must not let this interfere with her happiness. The world was changing, and she could not cling to the past—the Russia that no longer existed and that she did not even know. Although she loved her heritage, she did not feel the same powerful attachment to the motherland her mother and uncle felt. From now on she would have to try to balance her loyalties between husband and family.

After the reception at the Fantasia, where she and Rolf were toasted and serenaded by a Gypsy orchestra, he whisked her away to the Hotel Moderne.

Counseled by Nadya, who had instructed her in the mysteries of the conjugal bed, Marina thought she knew what to expect, but *now*, in the immense hotel suite, she was totally unprepared for Rolf's lovemaking.

It was an onslaught without warning. He crushed her to him without a word, devoured her mouth, overwhelmed her with the hurricane force of his passion. What had happened to the man who had given her a gentle, lingering kiss in the arboretum and who had courted her with such restraint? This was a new Rolf, an aggressive, demanding man, taking his due with speed and assertiveness. His caresses were invasive, pedestrian, designed to explore rather than to stimulate, and Marina, frightened by his haste, drew rigid beside him. Her skin burned from his impatient hands squeezing her flesh, pushing . . . hurting. Disappointed, breathless, she submitted to him meekly, crying out in pain in the final assault. When it was over, he patted her roughly on the shoulder and said, "I know it hurt the first time, but it will get better as time passes. *Gute Nacht, Liebchen!*" He gave her a kiss on the forehead, rolled over, and was soon asleep.

Marina lay without moving for a long time, staring into the darkness. The moon suffused the room with a pale blue light. A gentle breeze played with the lace curtains, their elongated patterns cavorting on the wall in mute derision of her young dreams.

She wrapped her naked arms around the pillow and closed her eyes, begging for sleep to come. A tear slipped out of the corner of her eye, tickling her temple, wetting her hair. There were hurdles yet to weather; she must not think of them tonight.

But sleep eluded her. The midnight silence in the room seemed to be filled with sounds of Gypsy music, bits of phrases, a kaleidoscope of unfinished thoughts crowding upon her to whisper doubts in her ear. Silly to let this eerie moonlight upset her so! She was independent, determined, wasn't she?

Her Rolf. Her blond, distinguished foreigner—she was in love with him. As for tonight, a man does not always understand these things. . . . in the morning, everything would look brighter.

Thus she lay, her mind drifting toward dawn with hope and hidden apprehension.

Chapter Twenty-eight

Marina was gone, and without her young and vibrant presence the house seemed empty. When Sergei began to follow Nadya around, something he had never done before, she understood that he could not face being alone and needed the reassurance of her continuing presence and affection. They sat on the divan in the living room —brother and sister bonded to each other by their loneliness more firmly than ever before—and talked of events in Europe, the growing aggression of Japan, the occupation now spreading to French Indochina. Sergei mentioned rumors of a new research laboratory being built by the Japanese a few miles from Harbin. It was shrouded in great secrecy, and he wondered why.

"After all," he said matter-of-factly, "a recent issue of the *Lancet* reports a new agent, called penicillin, as a promising weapon against infections."

Poor Seryozha, Nadya thought looking at him sadly, every opportunity to broaden his research work had been thwarted in spite of his good name.

They talked some more about their house and the food for the winter to be stored in their cooler, about repairing a leaking roof. Then Nadya said good night.

In her room she undressed hurriedly and slipped under the covers, pursued by one relentless thought she could not share with her brother. Every afternoon this week Alexei must have waited for her on the corner, as Marina told her he would. Tomorrow would be the last day. What then? Could she live without seeing him again, without knowing what happened to him during the last twenty years?

How childish, how immature to deceive herself, to pretend she was strong enough to stay away, while all along she knew she would not be able to let the week go by without seeing him. What games people play with themselves! Tomorrow she would be there, talk to him, touch him, ask him how he lived and if the years had been as difficult for him as for her.

She saw him first. He was waiting on the corner, looking in the opposite direction. Her legs trembled, her heart threatened to leap away, as she walked toward him. He had changed remarkably little in twenty years: a deeper line at the corner of his mouth, a sharper jaw, silver in his hair. The change had mellowed the handsome face.

A few more steps, and then he saw her. A joy so clear, so jubilant radiated from him that it left no doubt of what he was feeling. He grasped her hands and looked at her without a word —so long, so deeply she felt her skin tingle, as if the love in his eyes had bridged the years between them and touched her face.

"My own, my precious Nadya!" he said softly. His voice. The years rolled back, and once again they were standing beneath the linden trees in the beauty of the Summer Garden.

"Alexei, my dear!" was all Nadya managed to whisper, and there they stood, clasping hands, weeping unashamedly.

"You look beautiful! Still beautiful!" he said in wonder. "How did I survive all these years without you?"

"And I thought I could resist coming here today," Nadya said, looking into his face, unable to hold back a bubbling laugh.

Alexei smiled and took her arm. "Darling, where can we talk undisturbed?"

Nadya thought quickly. "We're only a few blocks from the lovely Zhelsob Club garden. In the summer there is much outdoor activity; but it is empty now, and we should have the whole place to ourselves."

By the side of a flower bed full of asters and marigolds, they found a lacy gazebo and sat on a bench.

"Nadyenka," she heard him say, "I love you! Love you as strongly as ever!"

Nadya's eyes filled with tears, blurred his face. "Why are you telling me this after all these years?" she cried out in anguish, surprised at the effect of his confession. "Why are you torturing me again?"

Alexei took her hands in his. "Forgive me, my love! I should have told you right away! Marie is dead, and I'm a free man again . . . she died six months ago. I came to Harbin to look for you . . . didn't know how to approach you!"

Nadya closed her eyes. In Vladivostok, too, she had heard that his wife had died and he was free.

"Are you sure?" she asked before she could think, and when he seemed startled, she realized how foolish her question seemed.

He looked at her for a moment in surprise, then nodded. "I understand. Yes, she died of pneumonia, and I buried her in Pogranichnaya. But, darling, tell me about yourself, about our daughter. I want to know everything about you and Marina from the day she was born to yesterday."

Nadya withheld nothing until she came to Katya's death. Then the words got in her way. Alexei listened, shocked. "But why Katya? Why her?"

Nadya spread her hands helplessly. "I don't know. . . . Sergei was devastated, and I often wondered if somehow he had angered the Japanese. He has a temper. But I could never ask him, and perhaps it's just as well I don't know!"

She shook her head, trying to chase away the terrible memories, then looked at him. "What did you do in Pogranichnaya? How have you lived these twenty years?"

"I don't know how I survived after losing you. At first, while I cared for Marie, I hoped to hear from you, to learn about our child, to see you again. Then, when I discovered that you left Vladivostok, I guessed your purpose and was heartbroken.

"Marie was ill for a long time, but finally we fled Vladivostok, days before the Bolsheviks took over, crossed the border, and settled in the nearest town, wanting to be as close to Russia as possible. Childish, wasn't it? It took me several years to fully accept the truth that I had lost you once again and that Russia was lost to us both."

"What did you do then?" Nadya repeated.

"I became a professional hunter, as I told you I would." He told her how he had made friends with the Manchurians, both Chinese and Russian, and had lived in villages deep in the taiga of the Girin province. It was slow learning. The velvet antlers of a young deer brought the greatest profit, for the Chinese used them for medicinal purposes, claiming they strengthened the bone marrow, nourished the blood, improved hearing, and performed other esoteric cures. In June, when the deer were in velvet, he and his Chinese colleagues collected the antlers. Later in the season they hunted for fur. They trapped sable, kolinsky, and squirrel, spread strichnine capsules in the underbrush for the fox, and hunted the leopard with dogs and rifles. The king of the taiga, the magnificent Manchurian tiger, was an extremely dangerous animal to hunt, requiring skill and dexterity, and Alexei, aware of his lameness, never went after it.

"Are you still hunting?" Nadya asked.

"Not anymore. I've done well over the years and am trading exclusively in fur now."

"Are you planning to move to Harbin?"

"No. I love the taiga." He turned to face her and took her hands in his. "Now, will you marry me, Nadya, and come with me?"

When Nadya remained silent, he leaned forward. "You must still love me. You wouldn't be here now if you didn't. What is it, darling? Marina, our beautiful daughter?" Alexei's eyes clouded. "I seem to miss out on every glory in a man's life. Are you worried about her marrying a German?"

Nadya nodded. Alexei put his hand over hers. "She may be much safer with a passport, Nadyenka, and a country to protect her rights. As for that German husband of hers, he's very much in love with her; I was in the church and watched the wedding." Alexei gave her an apologetic smile. "I know, I know . . . I shouldn't have been there. But some things are beyond a man's willpower! She was beautiful!" he concluded, chuckling.

They rose and started for home. As they neared St. Nicholas Cathedral, Alexei stopped. "Nadyenka," he said, "let's go to the Grand Hotel where I'm staying; we can sit over a cup of coffee at the café and talk some more."

Once inside the hotel he led her up to his room, and she did not protest. If she had any will of her own before. it was gone now. His room was small but cozy, the walls covered with tapestries and Chinese silk hangings. They sat on the sofa and held hands.

"Tell me more about yourself," Alexei begged. "What have you done all these years? What about your poetry? Do you write?"

Nadya told him about her literary work and quoted some of her latest efforts.

"This is the one thing I miss in the taiga," Alexei said after she had finished, "the good literature. We don't get much in our wilderness, and I've never seen *Rubezh*. Sergei must be very proud of you," Alexei said, bringing up the man who had stood silently between them all afternoon.

"He has always approved of my writing, but he's immersed in science and doesn't share my interest," Nadya said, quickly changing the subject.

They talked awhile longer, reminiscing about their youth, and soon, inexorably, the mood changed. The present receded, leading them back through the pages of their memories. She longed for his first embrace, yet dared not touch him first. The happiness of their having found each other after all those years, the knowledge that at long last they were free to marry overwhelmed her. When he took her in his arms, she burst into tears, weeping against his chest, repeating over and over, "I thought I'd never see you again. Till the end of my days I thought I'd never see you again. . . ."

He held her gently, stroking her hair. "And I wondered where you had gone and whether we had a son or a daughter. I thought about our child growing up, asking about me. In the early days I still hoped you would get in touch with me, let me know where you were. But as the years went on, I finally realized what you were doing and why, and while it hurt, I understood."

He threaded his fingers through her hair now, pulled her head back, kissed her on the mouth with a thirsty kiss: delicious, intoxicating. Their dormant love awakened with a power fortified by twenty years of longing.

To feel him tremble at her touch, to let his hands caress her skin into exquisite tension, to give him full, submissive love again—no greater happiness could she imagine, could ask for after years of silent resignation.

The joy of rediscovering his body, of recognizing his special ways of loving—so long forgotten, yet never lost—removed all her restraint. Wildly she gave herself to him and took from him what she desired without modesty, without reservation.

Disarmed he was, and thrilled, and with a woman's intuition, she let him see her sensuality in its astonishing catharsis perhaps for the first time ever. He lost control then and, with a wild and primitive intent, pressed her tightly against him, a silent lover now, whose hands and mouth and body love could speak in better rhythm and deeper understanding than any word.

She roped her arms and legs around him and pulled his lips into her mouth, at once to taste and to contain him. This time their union was a melding of two bodies into one human being—a perfect, sated human being. Oh, but to hold this moment forever in eternity! Then, at length, there came the languorous descent into a bliss, almost as great as the explosive passion that preceded it.

The sun had disappeared behind the roof, and the room darkened. At last Alexei stirred.

"Nadyenka, my beloved, what happiness for me! The lost years haven't diminished our ardor; they have broadened our love. And now I can't wait to take you into the taiga, not yet touched by man and still free of war and strife. I'll show you its beauty, its primeval splendor, its birds, its rustling leaves! It has a language all its own. We shall be happy there!" His voice rose, caught in his own enthusiasm.

Nadya closed her eyes, trying to imagine what he was describing. What an idyllic life it would be for them! She, Nadya, would be Countess Persiantseva at last—so little meaning in it now, yet all the more important to her! Alexei, her great elusive love, sometimes within her grasp, yet always lost, would now be surely hers!

"—and we won't be so far away from Marina and her Rolf, and Sergei," Alexei went on, "that we can't see them often. My darling, I can't believe that I have found you, that you're mine at last!"

His hand caressed her brow and cheekbone, brushed back a tangled curl from her moist forehead. Leaning over, he kissed her eyelids. Nadya moved. The spoken words had chased the fantasy away, brought back a multitude of doubts.

"Alexei, I have to go now. Will you be here tomorrow?"

Alexei frowned. "You look at me so strangely. What is it, darling?"

"Nothing! I'm late." She freed herself from him, dressed with shaking hands, and did not understand what had spoiled the mood. What was it he had just said? Something about Marina and Rolf and Sergei. Especially about Sergei.

She must hurry home. It was late. Seryozha would be waiting for her at the house. She would talk to him, explain about her love for Alexei. Oh, God, Alexei was his cousin! What a secret to keep from both of them! This time Sergei must surely understand that after twenty years she deserved another chance at happiness.

At home Sergei was waiting for her in the dining room, a cold piece of meat untouched in front of him. He looked up and said, "I've been waiting for you all these hours. Sit down! There's something I have to tell you."

He looked flushed, distraught.

"What is it, Seryozha?"

"I lost a large amount of money in a Mah-Jongg game last night," he blurted out. "I didn't come home until the early-morning hours. I must have been crazy, but I kept on playing—I guess I was hoping to regain my losses." His mouth twisted. "A classic excuse, isn't it?"

"In the beginning I thought it was recreation for you, Seryozha," Nadya said sadly. "Now it seems to have become an addiction. Why?"

"I've been under a lot of stress lately, so I'm asking for your understanding and a little tolerance, not preaching."

Nadya ignored his petulance. "How much did you lose?"

He rose and began to pace the floor. "I'm not going to tell you. You'll have to be careful with extras for the next few months. That's all I'm going to say."

His voice was strained, irritable, and Nadya said nothing.

That night she could not sleep. Propping her head with her arms, she stared into darkness. She guessed what was bothering Sergei. She felt it, too. Everything in the house reminded them of Marina: the empty chair at the table, the furniture in her room, the untouched bed. But then all parents, real or adoptive, must go through this traumatic time; why should it be different with her and Sergei? Only more intense perhaps. Surely there couldn't be anything else pressuring Seryozha. Surely. They'd weather this together. . . .

Together! What had she been thinking of earlier? What a charming fantasy she had had with Alexei! How could she even think of leaving Sergei at this time? He had lost so much already —Esther and Katya, his best friend's child—had learned to love another child, and now she, too, had left his home.

Suddenly this new development, this growing passion for gambling, had surfaced in Sergei's character. She hadn't realized till now that it was great enough to make him lose his common sense, and she sensed that at the Mah-Jongg table reality disappeared for him. Their roles were changing, and Sergei was becoming her responsibility.

She could not leave him now. She would have to wait, and Alexei would have to be patient. If not marriage right away, then crumbs of happiness would have to do. In a sense, she would be better off than she had been the past twenty years.

It would not be easy to tell Alexei that once again fate had interfered, but then he should know all about duty and responsibility. She turned restlessly in bed. It was dark in her room. Only the vigil light in its red container flickered in the corner with a crimson glow.

Having made her decision about what she was going to do, she gradually found peace within herself. *At some unknown time*, she promised herself, *in this imperfect world, I'll have my happiness, I swear*!

Chapter Twenty-nine

Marina's honeymoon was almost over. They spent two weeks in Hoshigaura, collecting seashells on the beach, taking leisurely walks alongside the manicured flower beds, drinking tea at the elegant Yamato Hotel in neighboring Dairen with Japanese officials whose deference to Rolf both flattered and surprised her. It was a new world, and a heady one at that.

Dairen, a Manchurian port built by the Russians and lost in the Russo-Japanese War of 1905, had been leased to Japan for ninety-nine years. Long in the hands of the Japanese, it was a bit of Japan in Manchuria; but if Rolf wanted to take her there, he must have had his reasons, and Marina was not going to question him.

"He must feel at home in a Japanese environment," Nadya remarked when she heard about it. "He could have chosen any one of our Russian resorts along both the western and eastern branches of the railroad. I'm afraid Rolf will try to convert you into a German Frau Weimer; you must not forget that you are also Marina Razumova." Marina had ignored her mother's remark, and now she was thoroughly enjoying the beautiful city. Its cleanliness impressed her. Streets were paved, clean-swept, and broad; flower beds, weeded; lawns, edged. Japanese women, graceful in narrow kimonos and colorful obis, shuffled pigeon-toed in their getas, carrying children on their backs. In the shiny tramcars, men rose with smiles to give their seats to the children.

Marina could not reconcile these friendly, peaceful people with the arrogant men she had encountered in Harbin, and her conflicting reactions to the Japanese made her uncomfortable. These were the people who had raped and killed her sister and had instilled fear in the Harbin population, but in their own city the atmosphere was permeated with serenity and beauty.

When she asked Rolf about it, he shrugged. "In times of war soldiers act differently in occupied countries from the way they behave at home," he said, and before she could pursue the subject, he turned to other matters.

During the days Rolf was attentive and considerate, but the nights continued to be a treadmill of unfulfilled expectations. The physical contact no longer hurt; but she was disappointed in Rolf's one-sided passion, his obvious disinterest in her feelings, and she was distressed by her own inability to match his quick arousal. Unwilling to delve into it deeper, she kept telling herself not to expect too much too soon.

Right now she had other things on her mind: their new house on the Bulvarny Prospekt in Harbin, which she would have to furnish, and her new status as Madame Weimer. Yes, it would have to be "Madame," she decided, rather than "Frau," for it would sound less radical to the ears of her Russian friends.

She was still disturbed by her mother's reaction to the lame stranger and by his presence at her wedding. A vague suspicion hovered over her, and she grappled with the conflict of both wanting and fearing her mother's confession. She remembered Michael's flippant reaction to her encounter with the man. Maybe he was right, and she was giving free rein to her imagination. She would get in touch with Michael and introduce him to Rolf in spite of Michael's feeble excuses in the past when she had tried to have the two men meet. They would like each other, she was sure.

But when they returned to Harbin, Nadya told her that Michael had left for his new job in Shanghai and would not be back.

"That was a fast decision," Marina said. "What about his parents? Are they going with him?"

"No, they're staying here. Michael's American friend has already rented an apartment for him in Shanghai, and it looks as if Michael has a fine career ahead."

"I'm glad. But I do think he could have left a letter to say good-bye to me. Not very polite of him, to say the least!"

Nadya did not say anything, and Marina was annoyed. She looked directly at her mother. "Now, Mama, you promised to tell me about the lame man. Who is he?"

Calmly, slowly, Nadya told her. Stunned, Marina listened in silence until her mother had finished. Then she rose and began to pace the floor.

"So! I'm illegitimate! My sister was the real Razumova, and I was not! Thank God no one knows about it. No wonder Uncle Seryozha loved Katya more than me! I can hardly blame him. She was his friend's daughter, and I was a bastard child of the man who had wronged his sister. He must hate him!" Marina said harshly.

Nadya averted her eyes. "They never had an opportunity to become friends," she said quietly. "Sergei resented him long before you were born."

"And you, Mama! How you must have suffered all these years because of this man who is my natural father. He has caused you so much heartache!"

"He's the love of my life, Marina, and I have forgiven him, yet now, ironically, I have done to him what he did to me a long time ago."

"Tit for tat, eh? What poetic justice!" she said angrily.

"Not at all. I didn't intend it to be a revenge. It's just that right now Sergei needs me more than Alexei." Nadya looked at her daughter. "Your father has delayed his departure for the taiga until you returned from your honeymoon. He's been waiting at his hotel. I'd like you to see him."

"Oh, please, don't ask me to do that! After twenty years he suddenly wants to see me! Where has he been all this time? It's Uncle Seryozha who has been a true father to me—not this stranger."

"Don't be bitter, Marina. Whether he chose or was forced to stay away is in the point of view."

"I don't care! I refuse to see him!"

"Why are you so angry, so uncompromising, Marina? I'm the one who was hurt the most, yet I don't hold it against him."

"That's exactly why, Mama. It insults my pride to think that you've allowed this man to put you repeatedly in second place. I would never permit this to happen to me."

"That's false pride, Marina. Should I have refused to see him and thus denied myself those moments of happiness that I've had, and will have in the future?"

Marina looked at her mother intensely. "Strange, isn't it, Mama, that you're willing to swallow your pride and forgive him everything, yet at the same time you can't get over your own prejudice against Rolf. The old cliché—do as I tell you and not as I do, right?"

"It's an entirely different thing," Nadya protested.

"Oh, is it? Think about it. You objected to my marrying Rolf because you are prejudiced against him, yet you yourself suffered from Alexei's prejudice, which denied you your happiness."

"Your father was a victim of his environment, but my objection to Rolf is his choice of political career."

"And what is that supposed to mean? Your prejudice against all Germans is grossly unfair and narrow-minded!"

"Let's not argue, Marina. All I'm asking is that you forgive your father as I have."

Marina wheeled. "You love him and I don't!"

"I'm asking this of you as a special favor to me. You, too, love a man now. Surely you must realize how much this means to me. Go see him!"

Marina hedged. "Give me a little time, Mama. All this is too sudden. What does Uncle Seryozha think about it?"

Nadya made a strange, strangled noise. "He doesn't know Alexei is in town. Now that I've decided to stay with Seryozha for the time being, I don't want him to feel that he's responsible for my decision. Why add to his burden?"

Marina thought for a moment. "I agree with you," she said

slowly. "That's the first intelligent decision I've heard you make today, Mama."

With a quick intake of breath, Nadya frowned. "I don't deserve this, Marina." Her voice shook. "Where did you learn to be so self-righteous?"

In a second Marina was beside her mother, kneeling and clasping her hand between hers. "I'm sorry, Mamochka. I didn't mean to hurt you. Lord knows, you've been hurt enough, and perhaps that's why I'm so angry." She paused, kissed her mother's hand, and looked up. "So where do we go from here?"

"We begin by forgiving. Go see your father!"

They stood in his room, facing each other, father and daughter, silent and embarrassed, she near the door, her hand on the knob, ready to escape, and he holding on to a high-backed chair to steady himself, unable to take his eyes off his child.

Only as a favor to her mother had she come to see him, and moody and resentful, she looked at him with reluctance and antipathy. A cloudy sky thrust a wan shaft of light into the room, shrouding Alexei in a sickly pallor. Braced for self-justifications and awkward displays of affection, Marina stared at her father with hostile eyes, but as she looked, it came to her that he had made no attempt to touch her or even to speak. Was he overcome, or was he waiting for her to make the first move? If so, what did you say to a man who was supposed to be your father and whom you were meeting for the first time at the age of nineteen? "Hello, there! Pleased to meet you, Father. Where have you been all my life?"

The thought was so incongruous that unexpectedly Marina smiled. Alexei's brows went up for a moment, and then he, too, smiled and spread his hands in a helpless gesture.

"We don't know what to say to each other! Awkward, isn't it?"

Marina nodded. Suddenly her anger and hostility vanished like a punctured balloon. Alexei grabbed another chair, pulled it away from the table, then, changing his mind, pushed it back and motioned for her to sit on a small love seat. As she did so, he sat on a chair facing her.

"Did I upset you in the church? I didn't mean to, but I wanted to be at your wedding so badly!"

"I wondered who you were. . . . Rolf saw a resemblance between us, but I still did not guess."

"Are you happy with him? He seemed so much in love with you! He's a good-looking man, and you make a handsome couple."

All at once Marina found it difficult to speak. "Thank you," she whispered. "He's a fine man, and I love him very much."

Alexei looked at her searchingly. "Your mother is worried about your marriage, but I told her that in my opinion, you made a wise choice."

Marina could not believe her ears. Her aristocratic, prejudiced father, who had caused so much heartache for her mother, was approving of her marriage to a German!

Alexei offered her a glass of cognac. She took a sip and choked on the fiery liquid, grateful for his gentle pat on her back. She looked at him and smiled. "When are you going back into the taiga?" she asked, taking another sip of the cognac with greater care. This time it went down without mishap.

"Tomorrow morning. As it is, I've been gone longer than I expected."

"Next time you come to Harbin, I'd like you to meet Rolf. I know you'll like him."

"I'm sure I will. Your mother has given me your new address, and I'll write you before I come. She doesn't want Sergei to know that we've met again, and I respect her wishes."

Embarrassed, Marina looked down at her hands. "I'm truly sorry it has turned out for you like this, but Uncle Seryozha needs her right now."

Alexei nodded. "I'd be the last person in the world not to understand her motivation. But it could have been worse. I'm grateful for having found your mother at all!"

They talked awhile longer, and then Marina rose. "I have to leave now. Rolf will be home soon."

She offered him her hand. "Good-bye . . . Papa."

The last word slipped out unexpectedly. Slowly color rose to her face, and she looked at him timidly. So much gratitude poured from his eyes it took her breath away. In the next instant she was in his arms and hugging him.

"Marinka, my own lovely child! Thank you, thank you, dear heart, for not rejecting me!"

When he finally let her go, her face was wet with tears. She picked up her purse, fumbled for her handkerchief, then headed for the door.

"We have a lot to catch up on, Papa. Hurry back!"

Chapter Thirty

"Dr. Efimov, your reputation as a researcher is going to be of use to us once again," Captain Yamada said when he called Sergei into his office a few days after Marina's wedding.

As Sergei tried to protest, Yamada raised his hand to silence him. "I know, I know! But hear me out, please. I can assure you that the tragic incident of long ago is not going to be repeated as long as I'm in charge here. We need your help." He pointed to a chair. "Sit down, please, and I shall explain."

Sergei lowered himself wearily into a leather armchair, wondering what was expected of him now and marveling at how polished Yamada's Russian had become over the years of occupation.

Yamada joined his fingertips and leaned back in his swivel chair. "Our country is constantly working on new developments in weaponry," he began slowly, "and we're now experimenting with something called bacteriological warfare."

Sergei's mouth went dry. When he nodded, Yamada went on. "We recently built a new laboratory a few miles outside Harbin." He blinked and looked at a point somewhere above Sergei's head. "It's a top secret project, but we believe you can be trusted. That's why we want you to work for us at the laboratory."

Sergei remained silent, and Yamada coughed politely. "Right now we're adding a new wing to the complex. Lieutenant Matsui is in charge there, and he tells me it's to be completed shortly. We want you to start work when it's ready, and in the meantime, please make arrangements to reduce your patient load."

At the mention of Lieutenant Matsui's name Sergei's heart began to race. "What about my private practice? How can I explain my absence from the Central Hospital?"

"You can still have your practice in your home after hours; as for the hospital, you can simply say that you're now occupied full time in research."

Sergei left Yamada's office with an overwhelming sense of foreboding. The mere thought of bacteriological warfare and what it implied revolted him, and anything connected with Matsui's name was bound to be bad. He knew he would be involved in experiments that would be contrary to his principles.

To take his mind off the ominous future, he turned toward Foudzyadyan and a gambling den he frequented, hoping to forget himself in a game of Mah-Jongg.

Many hours later, after counting his money, he was appalled at how much he had lost. He wanted to get home as quickly as possible and take a bath to wash out the dense smoke of the den that permeated his clothes. Once home, he scrubbed his skin red, as if in the raw contact of his luffa he would rid himself of Yamada's tenacious web.

He waited for Nadya impatiently, and when at last she came home, he told her about his gambling loss, but he kept his visit to Yamada secret.

A couple of weeks later a car with a Japanese soldier at the wheel appeared at the entrance to the hospital. Sergei was driven to a heavily guarded compound in the vicinity of the Pingfang Station, outside Harbin. There Sergei was met by Lieutenant Matsui and taken inside a building with barred doors and dark corridors. At the sight of the hated enemy and the silent, dank prison, Sergei's heart sank.

There was nothing deferential in Matsui's manner as he waved Sergei to a seat across from his large desk. He was a short man who stood barely above Sergei's shoulder, yet there was something arrogant about his stance as he came around the desk and sat down in a large chair, talking in surprisingly fluent Russian, shuffling the folders on his desk, and never once meeting Sergei's eyes.

"I'm glad to see you in a better frame of mind than the last time we met, and I'm sure we can work together now," he said. "You will be working in our laboratory. You won't have to check on our infected prisoners because we have our own physician to treat them. Come, I'll show you around our laboratory."

Matsui rose, then hesitated. "Before we start, I want to warn you that this is a highly classified project, and even Captain Yamada has only a general idea of the nature of our work here. It will be healthier for you and your family if you keep all you see here to yourself."

As casually as he could Sergei asked, "Has Captain Yamada been to see your establishment here?"

"He knows the purpose of this complex, but he has his own work in the city. *I'm in charge here!*"

Sergei guessed that Captain Yamada probably knew very little of the true nature of the place. He also knew that he could not tell Yamada of what he would learn without risking Matsui's wrath. He had been its recipient once and could not dare test it again.

Matsui handed him a surgical mask. "Put it on. We have to pass through a contaminated prison block. From now on, you can enter from the other end of the compound and go directly to the laboratory without going through these barracks."

In the corridor Sergei heard moans and the rasping breathing of fevered lungs, but Matsui did not pause to let him look through the small openings in the doors.

"What types of bacteria are you testing?" Sergei asked.

"You'll meet our doctor in the laboratory, and he'll explain in detail what we have been using. I only know a few. We're well equipped for testing plague, typhus, typhoid, cholera, and dysentery."

Sergei kept his voice even. "What types of prisoners are you using in your experiments?"

Matsui shot him a quick glance. "What difference does it make?"

Without looking at him, Sergei shrugged. "It makes quite a bit of difference, especially in the ethnic backgrounds as far as physical and emotional stamina is concerned."

"Interesting. This must be looked into. Our logs are of various backgrounds and nationalities."

"Logs?"

"Our code name for prisoners. There are over four hundred here right now. All are criminals, of course. We have Chinese murderers and the *hunhuzi* bandits who defy our authority. Others are ideological criminals—mostly spies and those caught in subversive Communist activities. The Russians are, for the most part, Soviet criminals fleeing their own authorities and arrested while crossing the border."

"You must have a large turnover. How often do you need new prisoners?"

"Not as often as you might think," Matsui said flatly. "We have a good physician who cares for them, and those who recover are used for other experiments. He lets us know in advance when recovery is no longer possible and a log must be replaced. But we have no shortage of prisoners. As a matter of fact, those who make good recoveries are often sent to our other research center near Changchun for further experiments under battlefield conditions. Those, of course, are more . . . strenuous. We don't get *them* back."

Sergei pressed his elbows into his body to maintain a surface calm. His countrymen—fleeing the Bolsheviks—trapped into this. He could never face them. Yet never before had he been more aware that his own safety and that of Nadya and Marina depended on his self-control and his ability to convince Matsui that he was docile enough to go along with what was expected of him.

The laboratory was large and airy, in total contrast with the dark, stuffy prison block. Several shiny microscopes stood on long tables with petri dishes and test tubes about them. White-gowned technicians were working over their projects, and none paused to look at the visitors.

Matsui pointed to an empty stool at the end of the room. "You can have that one. It's near the window and will give you plenty of light. Now come back with me to the office."

Sergei's mind raced. Somehow he had to bluff his way out of Matsui's office without making him suspicious of his real sentiments. Matsui interrupted his thoughts. "We want you to start work immediately."

Sergei thought fast. "I was planning to take my yearly two-week vacation now."

Matsui gave him a hooded reptilian look. "The summer is over; why so late in the season?"

"My niece was married recently, and I postponed going away until now."

"Very well. I shall expect you to report here two weeks from today."

The twelve-mile ride back to Harbin gave him time to think. The circumstances of Katya's death came flashing back with all their horror. He couldn't live through anything like that again. How much could one human being stand? He would do anything to safeguard the lives of his family. Anything! When the alternative was death, integrity be damned! But how long could he survive before breaking under the psychological pressure of using his medical knowledge to kill, not to cure, and of seeing innocent prisoners—and he had no doubt that most were—die in agony before his eyes? It took a special kind of wartime logic to anesthetize the conscience, and that he did not have.

He had escaped danger many times before. His country's civil war had taught him the truth of the words he had heard back in Petrograd, from Yakov Oblevich, who said that it took courage to play the coward. Time and again he had had to summon that unique courage. But there was a limit to what he could face! He felt trapped.

Swallowing his pride, he leaned forward, tapped the driver on the shoulder, and gave him Rolf Weimer's address.

October 24. A loaded Packard pulled away from the two-story stone house, heading toward the Vokzalny Prospekt and the railroad station. Before it disappeared around the corner, the people inside the automobile stirred. Rolf, in front with the driver, watched the sparse traffic, but the three people in the back seat turned to look through the rear window. They caught a last glimpse of a lonely figure standing outside their gate, waving a white handkerchief: loyal Vera.

Taken into their confidence at the last minute, she wept copiously and asked between sobs, "When are you coming back, Nadezhda Antonovna?"

Nadya shrugged and, spreading her hands in a helpless gesture, answered with a Russian proverb: "It's as vague as writing on water with a pitchfork, Vera."

Poor Vera! They had become her family, and although she was married, she would still miss them acutely. She promised to pack their belongings and send them on to Shanghai after a reasonable number of weeks. In the car with them now were only a few suitcases such as one would take for a two-week vacation. (Since that's what Sergei had told Matsui, Rolf had said, the appearances had to be kept).

We misjudged Rolf, Nadya thought. He had come to their rescue without hesitation and planned the whole escape with typical German attention to detail. Yes, Rolf had surprised her. When Sergei told her about his trip to the laboratory, she panicked, but then, when he described his visit to Rolf and how helpful he had been, a wave of relief swept over her, and she forgot for a moment the immensity of what they were about to lose.

Rolf had agreed to help them go to Shanghai but insisted they all, including Marina and himself, leave together. Otherwise, he said, Marina would become an easy target, and although she was now married to a German citizen, he was sure the Japanese gendarmerie would find a way to keep her hostage on a trumped-up charge. Besides, he told Sergei, he would welcome a move to an international city like Shanghai. On his recent trip there, he added, he had been offered a post at the German Consulate, and now he would accept the position.

It was so convenient and comforting that Nadya and Sergei did not stop to ponder how strange a coincidence it really was. All they could think of was that this would justify Sergei's desire to spend his vacation in Shanghai, where his niece was going to settle. Once out of Matsui's jurisdiction, Sergei would be safely out of danger, they thought.

Nadya settled back in her seat and sighed. It was heartbreaking that they could take only a few suitcases with them, but they knew that the Japanese gendarmerie was not easily fooled. Still, Nadya knew there would be talk by their well-meaning friends about their taking such a peculiar vacation outside the boundaries of Manchuria, all the way to distant Shanghai, a foreign city where Russians were in the minority and the climate austere.

Well, we women are adaptable, she thought. It was rumored that there were close to thirty thousand Russians in Shanghai, a fraction of Harbin's population to be sure, but enough, nonetheless, for them to make new contacts and for her to seek out poets and organize new evening workshops. It would be exciting to broaden her horizons. She had to hold on to that thought. What good would it do to dwell on the past twenty years in Harbin, the home she had learned to love, and the little Russia she was leaving behind? She must not forget that it had not always been good or happy. Her Katya had died in that house, and time would never erase that memory.

The packing was difficult and painful, for they had to decide what pittance they could take with them and pretend it was for only two weeks when in fact it was forever. Forever! Nadya shunned the thought.

She and Marina talked about Alexei and agreed to keep their secret from Sergei for the time being. Although the idea of yet another separation hurt Nadya deeply, she tried not to show it to her daughter.

And poor Seryozha! It was difficult for him to leave his comfortable life, his established practice, and his distinguished reputation, so sedulously cultivated over the years. He would be fifty-five next month. How many men start anew at that age? Thank God that at least Marina was happy to move. And Michael was in Shanghai. They had sent him a telegram telling him about their arrival, and he would surely help them meet other Russians in the city. He was a fragile link with Harbin, a good friend who had known them before. It was important to have been known by someone before . . .

Nadya shifted in her seat, squeezed Sergei's hand, and closed her eyes. No tears this time. She had things to look forward to: personal, secret joys. Her separation from Alexei would not be irrevocable this time. How different had been her flight from Vladivostok when she thought she would never see him again! This war couldn't last forever; the borders were open, and Alexei was now free. Sooner or later they would meet; of that she was sure, and at the age of forty-four, she still had many years of happiness to look forward to.

Shortly before they left, Nadya had asked Vera to wait for a month and then write to Alexei and tell him that she would write when she could safely do so. Vera asked no questions and took down the address. As soon as they were settled in Shanghai and Sergei was adjusted to their new environment, she would be able to think of her own future.

The car pulled up to the railway station. Without thinking, Nadya looked back. At the top of Vokzalny Prospekt, the wooden spire of St. Nicholas Cathedral appeared through the clouds, and the triple-domed belfry on the left loomed dark under the overcast skies. She turned quickly and entered the station.

Inside, she paused. In an alcove to her left, was a large icon of St. Nicholas the Miracle Worker, the candle stand before it filled with flickering candles. Here, at the Chinese Railway Station, he was revered by Russians, respected by Chinese . . . She was leaving something tangibly her own, a comforting reminder of her heritage.

Pursued by memories, she walked out on the platform, grateful that no one spoke.

PART IV

Shanghai, China

Chapter Thirty-one

Shanghai, the fourth largest port in the world, Mecca for opportunists, a European's paradise. Nadya had read all about it and expected the city to look entirely European; but nothing seemed quite as she imagined it, and she tried to analyze the difference.

In 1842 the Treaty of Nanking ended the Opium War with England and gave the British extraterritorial rights within the city to form their own municipal council and police force and the option to enforce British law. These privileges were later extended to the United States and to other European countries that claimed jurisdiction over the piece of land which became known as the International Settlement—a unique European enclave in China. The French signed a separate treaty which gave them authority to govern their own area in the French Concession, adjacent to the International Settlement.

In a city of more than six million people, 120,000 were Europeans, and only 25,000 or so of these were Russians. Did Nadya foolishly think that such a minority could reproduce Harbin?

Shanghai was hailed as a truly international city, yet their docking ship was greeted by a Chinese crowd. Perhaps farther up the river, near the famous waterfront street, the Bund, she would see a more familiar Western scene.

It had been a long tiring journey, full of anxieties and fears of the unknown. After the train had delivered them to Dairen, they boarded the *Hachi-Maru* and sailed for Shanghai. Tense, silent, they counted the days and hours until the ship left the sea and started up the Yangtze River. From there the fifty-odd miles seemed interminable to Nadya, and when at last the ship turned into the river's tributary, the Whangpoo, she clutched the cold metal of the railing and stared ahead. In the distance the cloudy skies met the turbid river, and she half expected to see some yellow dragon rise from the muddy water and threaten her future with a warning, like an arcane oracle of ancient times.

Looking around her in dismay, Nadya thought: No more Russia, real or even imaginary. Everything familiar was gone. Now, irrevocably, they were in a foreign world, surrounded by Japanese warships. Crowding around the larger boats were brown junks with patched sails, some of their prows decorated with garish painted eyes like some monster from an exotic medieval tale. Swarming with people, straw mat-covered sampans bobbed crazily around small steamers, vying for space near the shore.

"Hey-ho! Hey-ho!" Stooped under poles slung across their shoulders and weighted down with baskets full of produce, the coolies singsonged their warning onshore as they maneuvered with rhythmic steps among throngs of milling pedestrians.

Although one of the officials from the German Consulate met them at the dock with a waiting automobile, it was the familiar lopsided grin on Michael's face that Nadya saw first. She ran down the gangplank and hugged the young man. Michael's grin broadened.

"Well, Nadezhda Antonovana, fancy meeting you here! I see our Shanghai wet weather hasn't dampened your spirits. Welcome to the Chinese Casbah!"

Then he looked over her head, and Nadya knew that he saw Marina. She released him, and he sauntered toward Marina with outstretched hand. Nadya watched, unable to repress an indulgent smile, seeing in Michael a small handful of Harbin's essence.

"Hello, Marinka! Haven't seen you since before your wedding. You look beautiful and quite grown-up!" Michael tilted his head to one side and gave her an exaggerated once-over from head to foot. Marina flushed.

"Still a joker, I see. Good of you to meet us, Michael. Come meet my husband."

Rolf, his face impassive, shook hands with Michael.

"I've rented an apartment for Dr. Efimov in the French Concession, and I might as well take them there," Michael said.

Rolf nodded. "It was thoughtful of you, Mr. Nikitin. The German Consulate has found an apartment for Mrs. Weimer and me on the corner of Avenue Haig and Route de Say-Zoong."

Michael smiled. "That's unexpected good luck. It's less than three blocks from where Dr. Efimov will be on the Route Lorton."

Rolf turned to hail a coolie for the suitcases.

Nadya went through the next half hour in a daze, only half registering what went on around her: Sergei's warmth in greeting Michael and his American friend Wayne Morrison, who had come with him; Rolf's efficiency in herding them toward the car, as he issued orders in his precise, calm voice. She could have kissed Michael when he informed Rolf that he would take her and Sergei in Wayne Morrison's Fiat to avoid everyone's crowding into one car.

For the first time since they had left Harbin, Nadya was able to relax, for she was always tense in Rolf's presence, never quite sure of what he was thinking or if his unwavering courtesy to her was truly sincere.

As they drove through the crowded streets, she listened to Michael's descriptions. When they left the Hongkew sector and its twenty-story skyscraper, the Broadway Mansions, they started to cross the iron-trussed Garden Bridge spanning Soochow Creek, the narrow fork of the Whangpoo. In spite of the closed windows, she could smell the refuse which floated between dozens of sampans and barges. Chinese youngsters ran around the decks, urinating over the edge into the odiferous canal through their split pants. Piles of fish lay uncovered on straw mats, and steaming caldrons sent billowing clouds of vapor into the air as old women stirred their food and screamed high-pitched invectives at the errant children.

When the Fiat rolled down from the Garden Bridge and touched the edge of the Bund, a miracle took place. The junks and sampans disappeared on the right side of the street, and a compound with manicured lawns, its gates guarded by turbaned Sikhs, stretched out before Nadya.

As if reading her thoughts, Michael grinned and pointed to himself. "Listen to the best tour guide in Shanghai! We're now at the beginning of the most famous street in the Orient, the Shanghai Bund, and you're looking at the British Consulate. The tall buildings ahead are the trading houses—Jardine Matheson, Butterfield and Swire, Sassoon—and the banks—the Hongkong and Shanghai, the Yokohama Specie, the Central Bank of China. The building on your right, ladies and gentlemen, with its pyramid-shaped tower, is the magnificent Cathay Hotel, built only a few years ago. It's on the corner of Nanking Road, the main street of the International Settlement. Wayne tells me the hotel's suites boast marble baths with silver faucets." Michael looked at Nadya and winked mischievously. "Of course, it's too rich for us poor Russians, and I have to take Wayne's word for it."

The last sentence was said without rancor, and Nadya, fascinated by the beautiful buildings before her, ignored the remark. She had never seen anything like these tall, imposing structures hugging one another along the treelined sidewalk. The concrete giants seemed to dominate the Bund with their stately opulence, dwarfing the scurrying crowds across the street to an army of ants.

As Sergei questioned Michael about various offices, Nadya thought of a Russian saying that could well be applied to her now: "Her eyes were running apart." Indeed, she was taking in unbelievable scenes before her—Europe on her right, rural China on her left. In the center of the wide boulevard was a row of parked automobilies, and on the sidewalk bordering the river, a throng of street vendors and hawkers was selling slippers, pens, and kitchen utensils as well as food steaming in open urns. Beyond them, jetties sprouted like bamboo shoots in the water, their bobbing, moored junks and sampans filled with produce waiting to be unloaded.

Wayne Morrison drove his Fiat slowly, maneuvering among

bicycles, wheelbarrows, pedicabs, rickshaws, and tramcars. As the car left the Bund, Michael pointed to a building on the corner. "This is the famous Shanghai Club, the snootiest in the city." He glanced quickly at Wayne, then went on. "It's supposed to have the longest bar in the world and is patronized by the British and the American elite."

Nadya looked at the back of Wayne's head. "Your friend does not understand Russian. Please apologize for us, and tell him that our departure from Harbin was rather unexpected, and we had no time to learn English."

Michael nodded. "I gathered as much from your telegram. I won't press for details, but I can surmise."

The farther they drove, the greater became the illusion of a European city. Chinese vendors hawking their goods had given way to paved streets and treelined boulevards. The French Concession with its stately houses hidden deep behind bamboo fences sprawled serenely around them. Soon the broad Avenue Edouard VII became the Avenue Foch, and as the car crawled along the crowded streets, she read the names: Avenue du Roi Albert, Route Ratard, and, finally, Route Lorton. The car slowed at a narrow entry into a cobbled passage of two-story yellow stucco apartment buildings, each with a separate outside entrance, and stopped at Number 16. Two steps to the front door, and they were inside. Immediately to the left were the stairs to the second floor, and straight ahead was a dark corridor which led to a living-dining room combination. To the right was a small kitchen, and under the stairs, a slanted dark closet.

The upstairs had one large bedroom and a cubbyhole with a small bed, a desk, and one chair. A short hall led to the bathroom.

The apartment was gloomy with walnut furniture slipcovered in faded floral chintz. A single window looked out on a sandy courtyard, and beyond, to the back entrance of a tall apartment house. Greeting them with obsequious smiles was an amah with shiny yellow forehead, and black hair pulled back in a knot.

"I hired her for you to save you immediate housekeeping worry," Michael said. "Besides, she'll know where to shop for food."

The four of them sat down at the table, and Nadya stared at the Chinese servant nodding and smiling as she served them tea. With Michael doing the interpreting, Sergei asked Wayne about hospitals and the possibility of setting up private practice.

Though Nadya tried to recall phrases that Vadim had taught her in Petrograd, she could not understand Wayne, for his English had an American accent, and his r's were more guttural than she had ever heard before. Even after Michael had translated the conversation, the substance seemed to elude her.

All at once the room appeared to close in on her. The voices softened, receded, and the faces blurred. The air became stuffy, and the glum, pedestrian furniture, the crowded room, the American stranger, and the ingratiating amah's face—all marched in tandem, growing, growing, voices humming, ringing in her ears. Suddenly, without warning—any warning at all—she folded her arms on the table, slumped over, and broke down crying.

"I'm sorry! Oh, I'm sorry! I don't know what has happened to me!"

The adjustment to the new enviroment was far more difficult for Nadya than ever before, and the discovery that they were in the heart of a Russian oasis in Shanghai did nothing to sustain the feeling of Little Russia. There were other Russians living in their row of apartments; but there were just as many Chinese families, and every time she went out on the street, she saw more Chinese than Europeans. It didn't help to see the Cyrillic alphabet on shopkeepers' billboards on the main Avenue Joffre, for it was shared with English letters and Chinese characters. True, two blocks away from her apartment, the onion-domed Orthodox cathedral faced Lorton from Route Paul Henry, and a privately owned Russian library was only a block farther. But the illusion was ruined by an unpaved broad alley that stretched behind the cathedral connecting Paul Henry with Joffre. There dirty Chinese urchins and emaciated beggars rummaged through putrid garbage, picking out scraps of food and fighting off stray dogs.

Between their apartment and the cathedral, many Russians lived in narrow boardinghouses, sharing one bathroom with three or four families, creating their own minuscule worlds behind closed doors. Odors of fried onions and boiled cabbage escaped from the communal kitchens to permeate the dark corridors that led to their private sanctuaries, where they slept, entertained, fantasized, grieved, and, sometimes, committed suicide.

The tiny corner grocery, owned by a middle-aged Russian couple, was a meeting place during the winter to chase away the damp chill with a shot of vodka and to discuss rumors in hushed tones in case the invisible but ever-present Japanese authorities were listening.

In spite of the cosmopolitan metropolis, Nadya was developing claustrophobia. The stuffy boarding houses, the small apartments, the narrow alleys—where were the large homes, the picket fences, the spacious gardens of Harbin? Michael chuckled when she asked him.

"There are magnificent mansions in Shanghai," he said, "but they're hidden behind bamboo fences and belong to wealthy foreigners or Chinese millionaires. The more affluent Russians live in modern apartments, but since most of us are poor, perhaps it's best that these plush homes are hidden from our view!"

"Where do you live, Michael?" Nadya asked.

The young man shrugged apologetically. "I'm one of the luckier ones. Wayne got me a job with an American firm, and I have a roomy apartment just off Bubbling Well Road in the International Settlement. But there aren't many Russians living there, and I feel more at home in the French Concession." Michael tapped his temple and grinned. "It's all up here, don't you know?"

Nadya did not find it amusing. She spent her days looking for a roomier and brighter apartment, telling Sergei they needed to move immediately in order to set up his private practice before their money ran out. Although she had accepted Sergei's explanation that Rolf had influential connections among the Japanese authorities and had been able to arrange a secret transfer of all their assets to a Shanghai bank, she worried about the devaluation of Chinese money that seemed to be taking place almost every day. To complicate matters, Nadya discovered that to move into an apartment, the new occupant had to pay key money to the former tenant for the privilege of renting his vacated flat. Because of the instability of official currency, the money exchanged in this clandestine transaction was always U.S. dollars.

Winter was setting in, damp, windy, slushy. No white snow here; only mud, icy rain, and the crawling, pervasive cold. It didn't take long to find a lovely, spacious flat in the Astrid Apartments at 309 Rue Cardinal Mercier, on the corner of Route Vallon, where several Russian doctors had offices in their homes. Sergei was pleased with Nadya's find and, after paying three thousand U.S. dollars in key money, quickly set about outfitting his examining room and picking out expensive furniture for the waiting alcove at the entrance, assuring Nadya that they were spending money wisely. She agreed. In both Vladivostok and Harbin Sergei's practice had flourished, and it was important to get it started again. She tried not to think about all their possessions left behind in Harbin and consoled herself with the thought that sooner or later Vera would be able to ship their furniture to them.

Brother and sister leaned on each other, closer than ever before. Marina moved in different circles now—somehow alien to them —in a world of Nazi arrogance. There seemed little doubt of it, although they didn't talk openly about the people Marina met or what Rolf did in his office at the German Consulate. There would be time to talk later, but right now Nadya busied herself with getting settled in their large, sunny third-floor apartment. It held so much light that she stood in the middle of the waiting alcove surrounded by bay windows, clasping her hands to her chest and inhaling the sun-warmed air with relish.

A few days earlier Sergei had put an ad in the Russian-language newspaper, the Shanghai *Zarya*, announcing the opening of his practice. His waiting room was flooded with Russian patients almost immediately. He realized he would need to extend his laboratory facilities and inquired among other doctors in his building.

"There seems to be no shortage of laboratories in Shanghai," he said to Nadya one evening. "I found out that in the last two years thousands of German and Austrian Jews have fled to Shanghai from Hitler's persecution. Many of them are highly educated and are doing well in their professions. Some have opened their own laboratories, but others are penniless. The wealthier Jews, however, have set up kitchens and lodgings for them, and you will never see a Jew begging in the streets, something we could learn from them. I saw a Russian heroin addict begging on Avenue Joffre in front of a delicatessen today."

Sergei paused, then added, "Too bad the Soviet Jews can't follow the suit of their German brothers and leave their country."

Brother and sister looked at each other. The silence deepened, the unspoken words heavy with familiar pain. Nadya had been too busy and preoccupied with the tumultuous events of her own life to think of Esther. Now Esther's ghost hovered between them. Slowly Nadya placed her hand over Sergei's, as she had so many times in the past. "Who knows, Seryozha. She may have escaped and be safe somewhere in America. After all, that was her ultimate dream!"

He sighed. "I don't like Shanghai. I shall never feel safe here. When this war is over, we should seriously consider immigrating to America."

Nadya nodded and said nothing. They had to hold on to a dream. What was life without a dream? Hers was of a different kind, but she couldn't share it with Sergei, at least not yet. She had already written to Alexei, sure that the Japanese in Shanghai were too busy with the problems of their puppet government controlling the communications system and battling partisan groups in the city to bother with personal vendettas. Harbin was far away, and besides, Rolf had assured them that they were safe. Somehow Nadya sensed there was a lot more to it than he was admitting, but this time she didn't want to know more and hoped only that Marina was happy. Somewhere deep inside, her maternal instinct fretted. After three months in Shanghai there was a subtle change in Marina that disturbed Nadya. Her daughter was taking nursing courses, studying hard, and whenever she smiled, her clear gray eyes remained serious.

She would have to talk to her, ask questions. What were

mothers for but to listen and offer whatever support they could? It wouldn't do to repeat her own mother's error of silent empathy. She must ask Marina about Rolf and whether he was treating her well.

Chapter Thirty-two

Rolf dismissed the chauffeured consular car five blocks short of his destination. He waited until the car was lost in the traffic before starting to cross to the French Concession side of Avenue Foch where Yates Road became Route des Soeurs. Then he hesitated. The temptation to stroll along the block of elegant Chinese gift stores on *Yatsess* Road, as the Russians pronounced it, was too great, and he turned back. He looked at his wristwatch; it was only two o'clock. There was plenty of time. Although the September afternoon was still humid, the dreadful summer heat had diminished, and he was comfortable in his custom-tailored linen suit. He walked into the first shop where a smiling young Chinese clerk greeted him in pidgin English.

"Good afternoon, mastah. What you wanchi this time?"

A white silk satin jacket with heavily embroidered dragons in gold thread caught Rolf's eye, and the clerk took it down from the rack.

"Very good work, mastah. Special price for you today!"

Rolf enjoyed bargaining with the shopkeepers for embroidered linens, a piece of jade, or some unusual piece of cloisonné, and today was no exception. He went through the motions of offering a counterprice and walking out the door before the clerk stopped him for a further test of wits. When they finally settled on a mutually agreeable sum, he left the shop with a neatly wrapped package containing the satin jacket and a pair of matching slippers.

He walked the length of Route des Soeurs to Avenue Joffre, avoiding the noisier shortcut through Avenue Foch. He wanted a little time to think.

Life had treated him well, and in the past he had no complaints. It had been ten years since he had left his ancestral castle near Koblenz to join the Nazi party in 1931. He had risen fast through the ranks, learning early to be flexible and to justify his superiors' orders. There came a time, however, when it became progressively more difficult for him to rationalize the existence of the dreaded Gestapo.

Rolf loosened his tie. The humidity seeped through his clothes so that they stuck to his skin. He recalled his conversations with Marina when, early in their acquaintance, he had defended his patriotism. What he hadn't told her was that he had finally asked to be sent overseas, away from his country's alarming motto, *Deutschland über Alles*. He worried about Germany's aggression and how it would end; the worry had followed him, of course, but he had more freedom in his foreign assignment.

To protect his covert activities as a collaborator with Japanese authorities in ferreting out enemy agents, he was given a seemingly minor post at the consulate in Harbin, and after the Japanese had overrun Shanghai in 1937, he made frequent trips to that city to report to his superiors. Thus, when he and Marina moved, he was no stranger to Shanghai, and he greatly welcomed the change from the provincial Harbin to this cosmopolitan, exciting metropolis.

Marina. He sighed. He had always thought that when he decided to marry, he would choose a German girl, but he had been charmed by Marina's dark, fresh-faced beauty and her lithe, graceful figure when he first saw her on the streets of Harbin. Then her clear, innocent eyes and her aloofness that day in the Zazunov bakery intrigued him.

After she had questioned his political philosophy early in his courtship, he should have realized that she'd continue to ask difficult questions, but he had been smitten by her youthful zest and her ingenuous candor. Then, too, she had an air of self-assurance giving her a sense of presence that completely captivated him. In spite of his opinion that Russians were inferior, he was disarmed by Marina's sincerity. He thought that by marrying her, he would acquire both a dedicated, obedient housewife and a beautiful woman who would be an asset to him in the elite German circles.

What a mistake he had made! She was becoming an embarrassment to him, for she was learning German and beginning to ask his Nazi colleagues some awkward questions.

At first Marina seemed curious about his work, but when he became evasive, she did not pursue the subject. After a while he noticed that she had become avidly involved in her nursing school, and he encouraged her interest in a career of her own. To distract her further from his affairs, he also supported her seeking out Russian friends among the nursing students. Initially he had considered it a stroke of good luck that she had an outside interest and seemed less aware of the long hours he was keeping at the office. Her own absences from home, however, had become more frequent, and perversely he began to resent them.

In their intimate life she was passive and submissive in bed. He curled his lips. One had to seek the *grande passion* elsewhere.

He was nearing Avenue Dubail and the large complex of the Béarn Apartments, the lower level of which was now occupied by the Japanese authorities. This suited his purposes very well indeed, as no one would dare enter the building out of idle curiosity.

He climbed the stairs to the third floor and rang a bell. The woman who let him in smiled warmly. "You're half an hour late. I started to worry."

Rolf handed her the package. "This is why I'm late, Xenia. I thought this would look good on you."

He watched her as she eagerly unwrapped the package. She was tall and voluptuous, with her red hair that fell to her shoulders in broad, feathery waves. The sun, filtering through the lace curtains, glittered like copper in her luxurious strands. Xenia put on the beautifully embroidered jacket, threw off her shoes, stepped into the matching slippers, and pirouetted around him, her green eyes sparkling mischief.

"What will it be? Dinner first or . . . me?"

Rolf smiled. "It isn't good for one's health to make love on a full stomach."

Xenia threw her head back and laughed. Her hair bounced gently in studied disarray. Every motion was carefully practiced to show her to the best advantage. *A real pro,* thought Rolf, slipping his arm around her waist and leading her toward the living room sofa.

"May I have a glass of Campari first?" he asked, sitting down, repeating a ritual which was familiar to them both. Xenia poured him a glass of the amber aperitif, and as he sipped it, he watched her sinuous movements.

Xenia sat in a deep chair opposite him, her long mandarin dress slit to her thigh, exposing her well-shaped legs clad in flesh-colored silk stockings. His glance followed her outstretched arm which reached to the table behind her and picked up a snapshot of them both. Rolf winced. "Do you have to keep that picture here? It was taken so long ago!"

Xenia smiled. "I love this picture, Rolf. It's so like you! The strong, blond, blue-eyed Rolf I know! I look at it when you are not here. Can you blame me? Now tell me what you've been doing these last few days? I hear you've been inundated with your wife's family activities. I'm amused. Do any of them realize what role you played in their escape from Harbin?"

"They're not aware of my work in ferreting out enemy agents. All they know is that I had connections in the right places and thus was able to get them out of Harbin."

Xenia shook her head. "How naïve some of my compatriots are! We tend to believe what we want, don't we? Have you been in touch with Yamada since your arrival?"

"Yes, of course. He's not without honor and quite accommodating. He was infuriated by Matsui's arrogance and what he was doing behind his back. You see, Yamada follows orders from above, but Matsui interprets them to satisfy his"—Rolf hesitated and shrugged—"his sadistic streak. I think this was one of the reasons why Yamada made it so easy for us to leave. A matter of honor for him. I hope Yamada is transferred to Shanghai. He deserves better than that dreary Russian city."

"Careful! You're speaking of my birthplace!" Xenia said coyly. "It does have great intellectual and artistic talent."

Rolf shrugged. "Why did your parents come to Shanghai then? Weren't they happy in Harbin?"

Xenia shifted in her seat and recrossed her long legs. Rolf watched, amused by her maneuver.

"Mama thought I'd have better opportunities here in the field I was interested in—interpretive dancing. You know the rest."

Rolf's glance slid down her legs. "Yes, it's a shame that you had to give up your studies to support your parents. On the other hand, I'm not sure you would have earned as good a living on the stage as you do now, using your talents—in other capacities. The competition in Shanghai is fierce."

A slow flush crawled along Xenia's neck, rose to her cheeks, moistened her eyes with unspilled tears. Rolf was enjoying himself immensely. He loved seeing those large green eyes glisten with tears; they glittered then like chrysolites and made her look helpless and vulnerable, arousing in him a yearning for her expert lovemaking. And expert it was! There was no question in his mind as to how she had become a popular and sought-after dancing girl in the elegant Del Monte nightclub.

When he first met her at the German club in Shanghai, she was escorted by a Japanese officer, who told Rolf later that she was an informer for the Kempetai, the Japanese military secret police. Although Rolf had no direct dealings with the Kempetai and reported to his superior at the German Consulate, he sought Xenia out under the pretext of double-checking some of the findings of his own network of agents. Her sexual allure was potent, and before long, Rolf set her up in the Béarn Apartments, where they could have complete privacy on his frequent trips from Harbin.

She accepted his marriage to Marina without comment, and if she had ever had any aspirations to marry him, he had not been aware of them. Only once had she hinted at the possibility that she was pregnant, but when he shrugged and said that it was too bad she couldn't tell who the father was, Xenia never mentioned it again. His financial support allowed her to live alone and take care of her parents' rent in their boardinghouse on the Route Vallon.

He reached for her now. After slipping easily from her chair and kneeling beside him, she began to unbutton his clothes. Rolf relaxed under the delicious search of her nimble, experienced hands. Her gestures were calculated to arouse, every caress slow and teasing. By now she held few surprises for him, but the very anticipation of her next move was an excitement in itself.

She led him to her bedroom, where he impatiently discarded his clothes, but she took time to unbutton her frogged collar with deliberate languor, slipping out of each garment with the grace of a trained dancer. He watched hungrily, his body tingling and starting to tremble as it touched her tanned smooth skin.

Then, with his eyes closed and his muscles tensed to an unbearable pitch, he lay rigid, surrendering to the voluptuous caresses of this beautiful woman, inflamed by the insistence of her warm, silky mouth and the pursuit of her searching tongue, aware all the while of her ultimate goal.

Oh, the luxury of it! He didn't have to cover his masculinity, for he was aroused by her desire to watch him—whether real or pretended he did not care. And then, as she waited for him to achieve the ultimate in ecstasy before her, the very awareness that she was watching his climax drove him to the final, shuddering thrill.

He lay with his eyes closed, enjoying the sensation of floating on the down comforter which he liked to place under him. As he gathered his strength, directing his energy into a new rise of desire, he pulled her down beside him, and began to caress her glowing, unblemished skin. It wouldn't occur to him to use his hands or mouth specifically to please her. On the contrary, she was there to please *him*, and he would never consider doing to her what she had so often done to him.

And now he was the active partner in this, their second coupling today, and he took her with a slow, gratifying rhythm, feeling his passion rise on a predictable, pleasurable wave, then sliding down to spill over into the magnificent specimen of womanhood beneath him.

Sated, relaxed, he finally rose and dressed. What singular good fortune to have captured this sensuous woman for his own private enjoyment! He had successfully managed to keep his distance from Xenia's emotional arsenal by making it clear to her that their relationship was a thing apart from their personal lives.

"I'm ravenous now," he said. "Do you have any of my favorite *vatrushki* today?"

Without a word, Xenia served him the fluffy pastry with cottage cheese filling and a glass of tea.

"Do you have anything to report?" Rolf asked, looking at her over the steaming tea, feeling a thrill of possession toward the beautiful woman before him.

"Not much, except that your wife's uncle is a devotee of Mah-Jongg."

Rolf waited, knowing from past experience that there was more to come.

"He seems to frequent our friend C. Lee's den in Nantao."

"And how did you come by that bit of priceless information? Do you frequent Mr. Lee's den, too?"

Xenia bit her lip. "You know better than that, Rolf. C. Lee is a loyal servant of the Kempetai, and my source there passed the information on to me. I'm told that Dr. Efimov's stakes are getting higher. Whether this is due to the profits from his growing medical practice—after all, he's been in Shanghai almost a year—or his growing addiction to gambling remains to be seen."

Later, riding the ten blocks to Route de Say-Zoong on the Avenue Joffre tramcar, Rolf was annoyed. Damn those relatives of Marina! Of all the gambling dens in Nantao to pick! C. Lee was a valuable agent of the Kempetai, and a ruthless one, and it would be better if Sergei had no association with C. Lee whatsoever. The devil of it was he couldn't speak to him about it without revealing the source of his information.

He walked the four blocks from the tramcar to Avenue Haig, enjoying the first cool breezes of the September evening. At home he emptied the mailbox and looked through the mail. Marina was still at the hospital, working late that day. *Let the child amuse herself, just so she doesn't cry*, he thought, echoing one of Nadya's Russian proverbs. Yet her late hours irked him. A name on an envelope caught his attention. It was addressed to Marina in a sprawling masculine handwriting, and it was from Pogranichnaya.

Marina's father.

Unaccountably Rolf was irritated. *Does Count Persiantsev want to come to Shanghai, too?* he wondered. He should have married an orphan. In the living room he poured himself a glass of Campari from a crystal decanter that stood on the carved lacquered sideboard and settled into an armchair.

Somehow his carefully planned life was now being complicated by developments he hadn't counted on. Marina's clear-eyed look and fresh-faced beauty had begun to pall, and her straightforward ways had become an irritant. As soon as the war ended, he would leave China. He'd made enough money now to refurbish his home and settle in Koblenz again. As for Marina, she was nothing more than a possession to him now, like the crystal glass in his hand.

He sipped his Campari, feeling its warmth slip down his throat. Then he leaned back in his chair and twirled the stem of his glass, daydreaming of the future.

Chapter Thirty-three

The summer humidity lingered throughout the autumn months of 1941, slipping into the chill of penetrating, moist winds of winter. December 8 dawned murky and grim. Dark, heavy mist hung over the rooftops, wrapping the city in a gray fog. Fragmented news filtered to the populace that day, announcing that the Imperial Japanese Air Force had been victorious at Pearl Harbor—and where was Pearl Harbor? What was it? the people asked one another—and that Japan was now at war with both the United States and Great Britain.

Early in the day shots were heard in the distance, and rumor had it that a British gunboat had opened fire on the Japanese cruiser moored on the Whangpoo and the behemoth cruiser had promptly sunk the feisty offender. But residents in the French Concession of the city were not too concerned. After all, the Japanese occupation of Shanghai had allowed this oasis to continue under the French jurisdiction, and surely this new development would not affect them.

Heated debates over the dining tables of Shanghai's Russians lasted far into the night. America and Britain had entered the war. What would this do to the White Russians' future? Some thought the war would end quickly, and the Japanese would be driven off the mainland of China, restoring prewar prosperity; others saw a global Armageddon. Rumors abounded, and no one knew anything for sure.

Allied nationals were soon easily recognized by the telltale armbands identifying them as Americans or British citizens. If the Japanese authorities intended to humiliate them, the result was quite the opposite. The Russians eyed the armbands with envy, for the Allies were now clearly distinguishable from the stateless Russians on Avenue Joffre. Although enemies of the Japanese, they were the privileged ones who belonged to a country, the fortunate ones with passports, and the distinction between "them" and "us" had never been more apparent than now.

At 309 Rue Cardinal Mercier, in the apartment of Dr. Sergei Efimov, the momentous news caused immediate concern, for Nadya's first thought was of Michael and his job with the American firm. If his friend and sponsor Wayne Morrison were to be interned and the firm closed, what would Michael do for a living? His parents were now dead, and Nadya had become as attached to the lighthearted young man as if he were her son.

Her life had not been affected by the latest political developments. She continued to correspond with the faithful Vera, who had shipped their furniture in due time. After keeping her favorite pieces, Nadya ended up selling most of it at a reduced price, for their apartment was full, and so was Marina's. One of the things she kept, though, was the oak rolltop desk where she worked on her poems. She had gained recognition in Shanghai; her poems were published in the Shanghai *Zarya* newspaper and the literary journal *Thought and Art*, and they continued to appear in Harbin's *Rubezh*. She had become a valued member of the literary circle that met weekly. She urged Marina to join, but her daughter came only occasionally, sometimes accompanied by the ever-faithful Michael. Watching the two young people, Nadya wondered sadly if Marina was aware of how deeply Michael loved her or of how warmly she responded to him whenever he spoke to her.

As for herself, Nadya concealed her longing for the man whose letters she picked up at Marina's apartment and read and reread in the privacy of her bedroom. Why did she feel it was still necessary to keep her secret from Sergei, now that she was in Shanghai and

Alexei somewhere in the Manchurian taiga? Perhaps she was reluctant to face her brother and tell him that her love was as strong as ever and that she nurtured the hope for a life of her own. As long as there was no immediate pressure to tell Sergei, Nadya demurred.

Alexei wrote impassioned, tender letters, full of plans for their reunion, telling her of his loneliness and his hope of moving to Shanghai. "After all," he wrote, "I'm still strong and healthy, and there is no reason why I couldn't join a furrier business in Shanghai." But Nadya was afraid to encourage him to take the chance of starting afresh in Shanghai. Now, with the Allies fighting against Japan, the war would not last long, and then they would return to Harbin.

But as the weeks and months slipped away, the war intensified, and in 1943 the French were forced to return the concession to the Chinese government. That, in turn, meant the Japanese were now in control of the whole city. They made their presence felt quickly. Antiaircraft guns appeared on the roof of the Astrid apartment house along with other strategically chosen sites in town, and the nightly curfew was strictly enforced.

Then Sergei began to worry Nadya. There was a listlessness about him that she could not understand, a loss of vigor perhaps. He no longer continued his research and had reduced the hours of his medical practice. More and more he frequented the gambling dens in Nantao. Nadya fretted.

"Seryozha, this pastime of yours can become an addiction. What happened to your research?"

Sergei sighed. "I've lost interest, Nadya. I'm content with hospital rounds and my outpatients. We're making enough money to survive and pay the rent. What more could we want?"

Nadya hesitated a long moment and then asked, "Have you had any word from the Red Cross?"

Sergei shook his head. "I don't want to talk about it ever again. I'm tired of reaching for an unrealistic dream only to have it dashed time and again." He paused, then went on. "Esther is gone. You know, it's strange, but I'm resigned to my loss now. It's easier this way."

But Nadya did not believe him. On more than one occasion she had caught him reaching for the packet of neatly stacked letters he received from the Red Cross, only to close the drawer of his desk quickly when he heard her coming into the room. Now she would not give up.

"Seryozha, what about the ghetto for the German Jews that the Japanese have just established in the Hongkew district? Since all those Jews are now required to live in one area, maybe we could ask around. Some of them may know something—"

"It would be another dead end," Sergei said harshly. "What could German Jews, most of whom don't even speak Russian, know about a Jew living under Stalin? I tell you again"—his voice rose sharply—"from now on, please don't mention Esther's name in my presence. As far as I'm concerned, she's dead." His voice wavered. Then he went on. "I'll always love her, but I'm more comfortable now with her memory."

As Nadya studied him with compassion, he added, "For twenty-five years I've written letters to the Red Cross trying to find her, always with the same results. That does something to a human psyche. It's time we gave up and accepted the truth that she is lost to us forever."

Nadya wasn't so sure. She was an optimist who never lost hope for a better future no matter how grim the present, even when she had to dig deep within her to sustain that hope. Alarmed, she saw hopelessness and increasing signs of depression in Sergei. He looked drawn and he tired easily.

"Do you feel well, Seryozha? You look thinner to me."

"I seem to have contracted a mild case of sprue."

Nadya looked up sharply. "Isn't that the same as dysentery?"

"It has similar symptoms, but I'm sure I'll be able to control it in short order."

"You need more rest; why don't you lighten your patient load some more?"

"I don't want to reduce our budget any further. Besides, I don't feel the need as yet."

"I disagree. You could use a few more hours of rest each day. As for the budget, I'd welcome the chance to use the trade I learned in Harbin. Remember? I've always enjoyed sewing, and it would be fun to try my hand at it now."

And so it was that Nadya insisted on Sergei's limiting his outpatient hours while she took in orders for alterations, with the idea of creating her own designs later. For the first time she was doing something for remuneration, and it gave her a sense of accomplishment and confidence in herself. Poetry was good for the soul and the intellect, and she would continue to write; but it was no way to earn a living.

Her satisfaction was marred, though, by a growing tension and nervousness that she had noticed of late in Marina. After finishing nursing courses, Marina had started her training at the Russian Hospital on Route Monseigneur Maresca. Sergei had said to Nadya once how much he admired the hospital's director for maintaining the clinic's high standards. How gratifying that her daughter had trained under such expert supervision. It was too bad Marina had plunged into it with such single-minded zeal. Nadya thought that Rolf was a good provider, so she saw in Marina's dedication to her work an escape from a deep-seated disappointment in her life. More often now she found Marina absent from her five-room apartment on Avenue Haig, caring for the sick at the hospital and doing volunteer work in Nantao, the Chinese sector of town, where sanitation was poor and crime rampant.

She could not understand Rolf's lackadaisical attitude toward Marina's activities, for it seemed contrary to his otherwise demanding character. However, he did not seem to be home very much, spending long hours at his consular office. Thank God that Michael frequently accompanied Marina to Nantao!

There never seemed to be the right moment for Nadya to ask Marina about her concerns. In the spring of 1943 she noticed a dullness in Marina's eyes, a look of resignation that she thought was new, and she decided it was time to have a talk with her daughter.

One day in May she walked out of her apartment and headed toward Avenue Haig. She had been sitting behind her Singer sewing machine all morning, and it felt good to stretch her legs and walk in the spring air. She gauged her time for midafternoon, when Rolf would still be at the office and Marina home from the hospital. Outside the Astrid Apartments a line of people was queued up for two blocks, waiting for sugar. Shopping had become more difficult, for shortages in food were increasing and prices rising; she was glad she had stood in line for her supplies of butter and flour the previous week, leaving the housecleaning chores to the old amah.

Inured to the sight of Chinese beggars with their deformities and fly-infested ulcers deliberately exposed to arouse pity from passing pedestrians, she slowly walked the one block to Avenue Joffre.

There, all Europeans took on anonymity once again. The armbands had disappeared when the Japanese interned the Allied nationals in the Pootung district on the other side of the Whangpoo. Thus, Wayne Morrison was in a camp that was no more than an unheated godown, and Michael had lost his job. Nadya smiled. Enterprising young man, that one! Without hesitation, he had moved from his comfortable apartment to a rented room in a boardinghouse, taken a crash refresher course in his dormant French, and, before long, been hired as an accountant at the prestigious pharmaceutical firm Olivier-Chine, located near the Bund. With his customary verve he commuted the four miles every morning on his bicycle.

At the corner of Rue du Roi Albert and Avenue Joffre, Nadya stopped to pick up some pomelos for Sergei at the outdoor fruit stand. She walked along the avenue, ignoring a shortcut through Route Paul Henry and Lorton to avoid any reminder of the dingy neighborhood they had lived in when they first arrived.

The weather was balmy. The street was full of people, both European and Chinese. Although the Japanese were not seen in this part of town, their influence was felt everywhere: in the fast pace of the scurrying pedestrians, the long lines for staples, the deserted streets at night. The Nazis were far more evident in restaurants, theaters, private clubs. Although they took no active part in governing the city, their arrogance and aloofness set them apart from other Europeans.

Nadya paused by a coffee store, enjoying the fragrance emanating from the open door. As she looked in the window, the air-raid siren sounded in the distance. She had come to hate the whining sound that sent people hiding for cover, for although the Allies tried to avoid bombing the foreign sectors, there were isolated incidents of injury from the antiaircraft guns. As she hastened her step, she looked up to see the planes streak across the sky, glittering silver in the sun. Instead of fearing their deadly mission, she wanted to lift her arms and bridge the space between her and those distant steel birds that promised freedom from the Japanese yoke.

But moments later, as she reached the apartment block near the corner of Route de Say-Zoong, a window shattered in the third story, and when she looked up, she froze. The shards of glass fell down around her, seemingly in slow motion. She threw herself against the building, her face scraping the wall's rough stucco. The pain was sharp and instant. She pulled a handkerchief out of her purse and dabbed at the side of her cheek, and as she did so, one of the shards tore through her brown sweater and cut her wrist. Blood soaked through the wool, and for the first time in many years Nadya panicked. She didn't want to injure her hands; she needed them to handle her sewing, now that she was acquiring a wide clientele. She pressed her handkerchief over her wrist and ran the rest of the way.

After Marina had finished bandaging Nadya's wrist and told her it was only a superficial wound, Nadya was able to relax over a cup of spice tea, admitting to her daughter for the first time how important her work had become to her. They talked for a few minutes about the shortages of food, the nuisance of curfew, the frequent air raids, and then Marina surveyed her mother warily.

"Mama, it's unusual for you to come at this time of the day. I don't mean to be rude, but I have to call on a sick family in Nantao, and Michael is coming over to walk with me. Is there something in particular you wish to discuss?"

When Nadya hesitated, Marina added, "Is there something I can do for you?"

The slight coolness in her daughter's voice was unmistakable. That daughter of hers certainly did not share confidences, did she? Nadya put her spoon down and looked squarely into Marina's eyes, only to see a guarded look that discouraged open communication.

"You leave me no choice but to be blunt," Nadya said, resolving to forge ahead. "You've changed in the past three years, Marinka. You're tense, distant, and you work too hard. What's wrong?"

When Marina did not answer right away, Nadya pressed. "You're hiding something from me! I'm not only your mother, but, I hope, also your friend. I'm here to ask if I can help you in any way or at least to listen."

"Your generation, Mamochka, tends to be a bit melodramatic. There's nothing wrong in my life. What could it possibly be?" Marina said, her nervous fingers displaying the unease her voice masked.

Saddened by the defiance in her daughter's voice, Nadya leaned over and touched her hand. "Please, Marinka, talk to me!"

Marina pursed her lips and shook her head firmly. "You're looking for trouble where there is none. I have a husband who provides me with every possible luxury in spite of war and food shortages; we have a full social life, and I have the work I love. What more could I want?"

"Seems to me you've omitted one important ingredient: love. How are things between you and Rolf?"

"There's absolutely nothing wrong between us!" Marina's response was quick and emphatic. "Rolf loves me and I love him. Frankly I resent your probing into my private life. I'm no longer a youngster who needs guidance. I've just turned twenty-two, remember? I can take care of myself." Marina spoke fast, her voice rising, irritable.

"There's no need to be upset, dear," Nadya said quietly. "I wanted only to be of help."

"I appreciate your concern," Marina said, her voice softening, "but there's nothing to discuss. Truly! It's just that I'm in a hurry to make my call before the blackout."

Nadya rose. "Please be careful when you make your calls. If you get caught in the blackout . . . who knows who roams the streets at night?" Nadya kissed her daughter on the cheek. "Thanks for bandaging my hand."

"I'm glad it was nothing more serious," Marina said with a smile.

Nadya nodded, then said, "As for my being here today, remember one thing: No matter what, I love you!"

"I know, I know! You've never gotten over the fact that I married Rolf instead of Michael. Please let's not bring up the subject again."

"I'm glad Michael is coming over," Nadya said. "I'd hate to think of you alone in Nantao." Her last words were muffled by a loud ringing of the doorbell. When Marina opened the door, Michael filled the foyer with his broad smile.

"Just the person I want to see," he said, kissing Nadya's hand. "I called your apartment, but Dr. Efimov said you were on your way here."

Michael took both her hands and looked into her eyes. "Nadezhda Antonovna, I have some news for you! I've been playing host to someone you know. Count Persiantsev came to Shanghai two weeks ago."

Nadya caught her breath and leaned against the wall to steady herself. Michael motioned to Marina to get a chair. When Nadya sat down, he continued. "We first met in Harbin while Marina was on her honeymoon and have been corresponding ever since. When he arrived, he didn't want either of you to know he was in town until he found a job. He's now employed by the Siberian fur store on Bubbling Well Road, and yesterday, after he moved into his own apartment on Avenue Foch, he wanted me to tell you that he was in Shanghai."

Michael dug into his pocket and brought out a piece of paper. "Here's his address and telephone number."

Nadya took the crumpled paper with shaking hands and stared at it. God, what a surprise! It was so sudden. She had to get used to the idea that he was in Shanghai, that he loved her enough to give up his lucrative business in Manchuria to be near her, that he would hold her in his arms again. . . . A flush rose to her face, enveloped her whole body. Alexei! Here, waiting for her . . . She couldn't wait to see him. What would he say? What would *she* say? Thoughts somersaulted in her head, made her giddy.

Out on the street, she said good-bye to the two young people and stood on Rue de Say-Zoong, watching them disappear around the corner of Rue Ratard. Still dazed by the wonderful news, she listened to Michael's receding voice and Marina's soft laughter. What wouldn't she have given to have seen her daughter married to Michael! She wanted a loving and tender man for her only daughter instead of that cold and distant German. And Michael would have given her a great and gentle love. Why couldn't Marina see that? Well, it was not the time to dwell on it. Right now she wanted to savor the happiness that her own love was waiting for her around the corner. But first she had to go home and face Sergei and pretend nothing had happened.

Hiding, always hiding her secret from Sergei. How long was she going to protect him? Enough was enough. She must tell him about Alexei, about her love that had lived undaunted all these years. It was time Sergei accepted it.

Resolutely she turned and took the tramcar home.

Chapter Thirty-four

Halfway down Rue Ratard, Michael stopped. "This is silly, Marinka. There's such a long way to go. Let's splurge and take a pedicab. The faster we go through the Chinese slums, the better. I've seen enough frozen bodies stripped naked by scavengers this winter to want to avoid the area."

Marina shuddered. "It's spring, Michael, you won't see them now."

"Just the same, I ride my bicycle to work through that district. It's hardly a place for a walk."

Michael turned and hailed a pedicab. As they climbed in, Marina sighed. "Still stubborn as ever. What happens when you can't have your way?"

Michael put his arm around her shoulders and gave her a friendly pat. "I've got to have a few faults, don't I? If I were a saint, I wouldn't have any friends left. Imagine, being friends with a saint—how intimidating!"

Marina chuckled. "You're incorrigible. You always manage to make me laugh. Thanks, Michael."

The last two words came out with a slight tremolo, and she coughed to cover it up; but Michael must have heard it, for he dipped his head sideways to look into her face. "Hey! What's going on? Snap out of it!"

Marina ignored the remark. "Tell me about my father," she said pensively. "How is he?"

"He's a remarkable man, a fine man," Michael replied. "I've had a chance to get to know him these past two weeks; I insisted on his staying with me. I felt it would be difficult for him to be all alone in a strange and foreign city. He is thoughtful and dignified —that's what he is. There wasn't a word of complaint from him for having given up his business in Manchuria. After all, it's quite a step for a man of his age to take. He looks great, though, and is full of optimism."

Michael gave Marina a sidelong glance. "Your mother is a lucky lady to have such love. Let's hope they'll soon be together."

"I hope so, too. I've never been able to understand why Uncle Sergei dislikes him so much. I look forward to getting to know him, and I think it's a mistake that mother is so overprotective of my uncle. She should have told him by now that my father is alive and in China."

"It's not up to you to decide, Marinka. Let her do it in her own good time."

Marina didn't answer. Michael was right. It wasn't up to her to interfere in her parents' love affair. She had other things to think about. After three years of her marriage she could not conjure up her husband in the role of an affectionate man. Their relationship had settled into a routine of mandatory consular parties, superficial conversations increasingly grim as German war news worsened, and, in the privacy of their home, a schedule of mechanical coupling, predictable in his grunting satisfaction and her frustration. She felt used and ignored. She tried to convince herself that it was the turning tide of world events that affected Rolf, and when the war was over, he would soften, and they could bridge the distance that was growing between them. Maybe. At this point she wasn't sure of the quality of her own love for her husband. She would make all her decisions after the war. . . .

When she was with Rolf, she wore a courteous mask before his German friends, who clicked their heels, kissed her hand, and deftly excluded her from their personal world. She thought she had successfully hidden her disappointment in her marriage, and it was annoying to learn that her mother had guessed the truth. What made all mothers assume they had an obligation to guide their children forever? Marina shifted in her seat.

"Are you still with me, Marinka?"

Michael's voice startled her. "Just daydreaming, I guess. We're almost there."

They were entering the narrow alleys of Nantao, with their red and green billboards covered by lacquered hieroglyphics, and passing the parading prostitutes clad in tight cheongsams with slits high up their thighs, their cheeks garishly painted in red circles.

Around the corner a mixture of pungent odors assailed them: fish frying in soybean oil over charcoal in five-gallon kerosene cans; salted mustard greens steaming with noodles; and, above all, rancid garlic that seemed to permeate the very cobblestones beneath them.

Marina directed the pedicab driver toward a row of closely built tile-roofed dwellings. He stopped in front of a doorway covered with a blue cloth. As Marina stepped out of the cab, a young woman pushed the cloth aside and emptied a laundry bucket on the ground. Immediately the air steamed up with the smell of raw yellow soap. Marina jumped aside to avoid the hot sudsy water, and the woman giggled and apologized in a high-pitched voice. Marina understood a few words of the Shanghai dialect and waved aside the woman's apologies.

Inside, the hardened earth floor was littered with empty buckets and stacked laundry, and in the middle stood a square cherrywood table covered with terry-cloth towels. An old woman was ironing shirts with a heavy iron, its red coals glowing through the side vents. She looked up at Marina and nodded toward the far corner of the room. There, on a wooden pallet covered with a straw mattress, lay a young girl, her bandaged leg raised on a quilted wadding.

Marina unwrapped the bandage, examined the inflamed ulcer on the girl's ankle, and indicated to the woman that she needed a clean towel. The woman nodded, picked up a tin cup on the table and, after filling her mouth with water, sprayed the wrinkled towel before her. The moisture sizzled under the hot iron. When the towel was pressed, she handed it to Marina, who only sighed, aware that her admonition would have been beyond the woman's understanding.

Michael stood at the door waiting, and when she finished cleaning and bandaging the wound, he hailed another pedicab and took her home.

Michael had fallen into the habit of escorting Marina on her nursing calls whenever he had a day off. Early in June 1944 they were returning from two hours of visits in Nantao. Although Marina was weary, she loved nursing and worked with dedication, spending more and more time with her patients. Now, at the end of the day, she was glad Michael was with her. It was cozy in the narrow pedicab, close to him. Her leg was pressed against his strong, muscular body, and she felt its warmth. She couldn't help comparing this closeness to Michael with the feeling of distance between her and Rolf. Only the day before, when she mentioned to him that she would be going to Nantao the next afternoon, Rolf had looked at her over his newspaper with unseeing eyes, shrugged, and said coldly, "I wish you stayed home more often, *Liebchen.*"

Marina was irked by his patronizing tone of voice. Even a negative reaction with a spark of anger would have been more welcome than this total disinterest in her work.

A few blocks out of Nantao, Michael leaned forward and tapped the pedaling coolie's back. "Yu-Yuen Road," he instructed.

Marina looked at him. "I'm going home, Michael; why Yu-Yuen Road?"

"Because I'm taking you for a breath of fresh air in Jessfield Park, to clear your head a little," he said without looking at her. "You need to see some beauty right now."

"What makes you think I don't get to see beauty around me?"

Michael threw her a quick glance. "I didn't say that. I only said that at this very moment you need to be in Jessfield Park. Mimosas are blooming, and the giant magnolias may not be all gone."

Touched by Michael's sensitivity, Marina said nothing. The stubborn, seemingly flippant Michael, she thought, knew exactly what she needed at that moment. Oh, well, why not enjoy the rest of the afternoon, away from the hustle and bustle of a city where tensions were palpable in the atmosphere?

In the park the air was filled with the lingering fragrance of giant magnolia blossoms that still clustered precariously on a few tree branches defying the lateness of season. The afternoon light shimmered through the delicate mimosa trees, and near a small pond children knelt on clean-swept ground and pushed their toy sailboats over the rippling water. A semitropical grove of tall trees and lianas hugged a Grecian gazebo peopled with marble statues. Michael led Marina toward a secluded meadow where lush greenery surrounded them on all sides and the roof of late-afternoon sky bathed them in its pale crystal light.

They walked slowly. "It's a long way from home, isn't it?" Michael said pensively.

"We can walk back; it's not that far," Marina said, a little surprised by his remark.

"I didn't mean your apartment. I meant Harbin." His voice was quiet.

Marina glanced at him curiously. "Do you miss it?"

He shrugged. "I'd be a liar to deny it. Now that Morrison is interned and I work among French strangers, I feel more isolated than ever. Our Russian associates are okay, but somehow I miss the whole environment of Harbin."

"Tell me about Wayne. When did you see him last?"

Michael shuddered slightly. "He's in Pootung. Wives who are not citizens are allowed to visit only once a year, but since Wayne has no family here, I'm the only one who is permitted to see him. We stand facing each other in an open compound with a Japanese guard close enough to hear every word we say. Wayne has lost a lot of weight but otherwise seems to hold up quite well, although I have noticed that his chin quivers when he speaks."

Marina was silent for a few minutes, then asked, "Do you think we shall ever have our own country again?"

"Our country is managing to survive," Michael replied, then added with uncharacteristic bitterness, "unfortunately. Those Bolsheviks in Moscow would be delighted to have us all return to Mother Russia, so that they could bury us in the coal mines of

Siberia. No, I aim to wait out this war right here in Shanghai and then try my luck in getting to America. Our hope is there, in a free and generous country. Every American I met while I worked with Wayne was friendly and outgoing. They're more like us than any other people I know."

They were nearing the opposite end of the meadow, where a thickness of palm fronds created a dark arch above. Abruptly two Japanese soldiers appeared from that darkness, walking briskly toward them. Marina felt Michael's hand tighten on her arm. The men in their khaki uniforms and narrow caps went past without looking at them.

"Stupid to get ourselves in such a secluded spot," Michael grumbled, hurrying her along. "Let's not stretch our luck."

Guiding her forward, he turned left and walked out into the open. The mood of serenity was broken, and the lovely magnolia trees lost their appeal as they walked through the perfumed grove without pausing.

Marina shuddered. Even here there was no escape from the grim reminder of who ran the city these days. They rode the pedicab back in silence. Unable to control a slight tremor, Marina pressed her shoulder against Michael's. It felt good, and she wished the ride lasted longer. Before long, Michael seemed to regain his good humor.

"It's too bad, Marinka, that you're married now. Remember how we used to dance every week at the Zhelsob? There's a good orchestra tonight at the ROS. You're the best tango partner I ever had. I miss twirling you around."

Marina flushed. Michael was well aware that she adored dancing and that the tango was her favorite. There was nothing she'd like better than to go to the Russian Social Club, ROS for short, where they could pretend they were back in Harbin's Zhelsob.

"Are you going there tonight?" she asked now, secretly hoping he would say no, but Michael nodded.

"It's just too bad I haven't found a partner as good as you."

Marina was afraid to answer and not quite sure what she was

afraid of. A subtle change was taking place in her relationship with Michael, and she was flustered.

Maybe she was expecting too much from life. After all, she was well-to-do, had a lovely apartment and a foreign husband with a country to protect them, and was the envy of many Russian women. Her family was near her, and now that her father was in Shanghai, she should count her blessings and not flirt with fate.

They spoke little on the way to Avenue Haig and parted quickly at the door to her apartment. She unlocked the front door, turned on the light in the hallway, and stood still. Alone in an island of light, she was surrounded by the gaping mouths of doorways leading into dark rooms—the bedroom on the left, the dining and living rooms on the right. Funny, how the silence acquired a hollow quality without a human presence.

In the living room she found a curt note. "Don't wait up for me tonight, Marina," it said in Rolf's careful, geometric scroll. "I have a late conference at the consulate and will be gone most of the night."

Strange. Marina sat with the note in her lap for a few moments, her mind wandering, skirting conscious thought. Dusk had darkened the furniture in the living room, where she sat with her hands limp, Rolf's note fallen on the carpet at her feet. Her gaze drifted from object to object. The red-lacquered Buddha she had picked up on Yates Road grinned at her from the sideboard. *Why, there's something obscene about his glistening fat belly,* she thought idly; *I have to move him to another spot.* She had never liked him in the first place and had bought him in a weak moment because it was a bargain, and she could never resist a bargain. She rose and walked slowly into the hall on her way to the bedroom. The black telephone hung on the wall, and as she passed it, she suddenly turned, picked up the receiver, and dialed Rolf's office.

It rang a long time before a crisp male voice answered. In her halting German, Marina asked for Rolf. There was a pause, and then the man said, "He's in a meeting, *gnädige Frau.*"

Marina thanked him and hung up. She felt ashamed. Rolf had never given her reason to suspect him of lying, and it was unseemly of her to have checked on him now. He was married to his work, and she was penalized to spend her evenings alone. This year especially she had noticed Rolf's increasing tension as the war news filtered down through heavy censorship. It had become obvious that the tide of war was turning against the Axis countries. In Europe, Mussolini had been forced to resign a year ago, and now the Allied troops had taken Rome. The Soviets had relieved Leningrad of its siege in January, and closer to home; in the Pacific, the Allies had landed in the Marshalls in February and in New Guinea in April.

Marina stood indecisively in the dark hallway. The tall ceiling and empty walls began to crowd her. She wanted lights, people, laughter, and somehow she knew that even if Rolf were aware of her desires, it would have made no difference in her life. After turning on a lamp, she went to the phone and dialed again. "Michael? Rolf is at a meeting in the consulate and will be gone most of the night. If you're still planning to go to ROS, I'll go with you."

Mercifully he made no flip remark, and if he was surprised, he gave no sign of it.

Hurriedly she slipped on her favorite party dress—a burgundy crepe with a flared skirt and black belt—put on high-heeled black patent leather shoes, and combed her hair into a cluster of dark curls. Soon after they arrived in Shanghai, she had tired of her severe hairdo and had cut her long tresses. She remembered her first permanent in a Russian beauty parlor in an alley off the Avenue Joffre, where the owner wrapped her hair in curlers and then snapped the snaking wires of the permanent wave machine onto her head. The weight had given her a headache that lasted into the next day. A voluntary torture machine, she had called it then, but later she was pleased with the fluffy effect of her curls that fell below her ears in casual disarray.

Once on the ROS dance floor, Marina expected to enjoy herself. After all, she reasoned earlier, what would be so different there from the many evenings she had spent in Harbin, dancing with her old friend—a marvelous and innovative partner? That was why she loved a tango, for there were steps one could invent without losing the sensuous rhythm.

Sensuous. A discomforting warmth flooded her. She was treading on precarious ground. She was now a married woman, and what was she doing in a public place in the arms of another man? Did she foolishly think that because Michael was an old friend, nothing had changed? Better not dwell on this dangerous thought. But try as she might, it wouldn't go away. Everything seemed different from those nights in Harbin. She thought she caught curious glances directed her way and was afraid someone might ask why Rolf wasn't there.

Surrounded by laughter, Russian conversation, a full orchestra, and the vigorous, rich tones of an accordion, Marina was shaken. Michael tried to keep up a light conversation, but his attempts fell flat. After listening to a lively jazz number which they sat out drinking pinot noir, they watched the accordionist move forward. A few moments later the first strains of the doleful French tango "J'attendrai" reached out to hold Marina spellbound. Michael led her onto the dance floor. They had danced the tango many times before, but she had forgotten the absorbing pleasure of the languid, flowing dance, as Michael guided her into a pattern of intricate steps. Her forehead against his cheek, his warm breath against her ear, their bodies close, they swayed to the graceful rhythm. The words—"*J'attendrai . . . toujours . . . mon amour . . .*" the lyric hymn to a patient love, forever waiting —suddenly became significant. Her mother's words, "Michael is in love with you," sounded in her ear again, and Marina, disturbed, confused, abruptly pulled away.

Michael stopped in the middle of the floor and, still holding her arms, searched her face for several moments. Marina felt her face burn under his scrutiny, fearful of his questions, but Michael only squeezed her hands, kissed one of them, and led her back to the table.

"What do you say we walk home, Marinka?" he said, looking at his watch. "It's so smoky here that I'll probably have to shake my suit out the window to get rid of the smell. And your hair"—he reached toward her and with a grin flicked a curl from her ear—"is probably so filled with it now that your husband might wonder if you had started smoking."

He never referred to Rolf by name; it was always "your husband," and even then he rarely mentioned him. They had started toward the exit when a smiling husky man walked toward them from the other side of the dance floor.

"Michael! Leaving so early?"

Michael's hand tightened on Marina's arm. "That's a classmate of mine from high school days. He's a waiter now at the Renaissance restaurant," he said quietly before the man approached.

As the man slapped Michael on the shoulder and grinned, Marina smelled alcohol on his breath.

"Aren't you going to introduce me to the beautiful girl?" he said, nodding in Marina's direction.

"Madame Weimer, may I present Igor Boltov, a former classmate of mine," Michael said with uncharacteristic formality.

Boltov raised his brows in surprise. "Any relation to *Rolf* Weimer?"

Before Marina could recover from her surprise, Michael asked, "How do you know Rolf Weimer?"

Boltov guffawed. "How do I know him? He's my biggest tipper at the Renaissance!" He winked. "Especially when he's with the gorgeous Xenia! I should know! It's always the same: Campari for him and Château Latour for her."

The man swayed a little, then peered again at Marina. "Are you related?"

Before Marina could answer, Michael pulled her by the arm and propelled her quickly toward the exit, waving to Boltov over his shoulder. "See you soon, Igor!"

Outside, the air was still cool and the summer humidity had not yet set in. "Well, Your Highness," quipped Michael, trying to fall back into the banter of Harbin days, "what is your pleasure —pedicab, rickshaw, or two faithful feet?"

Marina's lips quivered so badly she had to press them tightly together and dared not answer.

Michael turned and hailed a pedicab. After an uncomfortable silence he spoke. "The stupid fool was drunk, Marinka. There must be another explanation."

In spite of his casual voice, Michael's words sounded totally unconvincing, and Marina shook her head. "Michael! Please!"

The ride to Avenue Haig seemed interminable, and when they finally reached her apartment, she couldn't bring herself to look him in the face. She whispered a barely audible good night and started to leave, but he held her hands and tried to pull her toward him.

Distraught, on the verge of tears, Marina resisted. Tension, subtle, intangible, was growing between them, and wrenching her hands away, she fled.

In the apartment she turned on the light in the living room and went directly to the sideboard, where she picked up the crystal decanter, opened the top, and sniffed the amber liquid.

Campari. She knew, of course, what it was, but instinctively, irrationally, she went through the motions of making sure. Boltov knew Rolf. There was no mistake. Rolf and Campari were synonymous, but her pride wouldn't let her admit it to Michael.

Slowly she replaced the decanter on the sideboard, then turned to look around the room as if seeing it for the first time. It was very quiet in the apartment, but Marina's eardrums began to vibrate from the throbbing pulse that pounded in her head. She felt a suffocating tightness around her throat as if an invisible presence had wrapped its tentacles around her neck and were choking her.

The shame of it! Michael had witnessed her humiliation, had tried to be charitable, and that, perhaps, was the greatest hurt of all. She tried to sort out her feelings. Funny, she felt no jealousy, no deep pain at Rolf's infidelity, only a smarting pride. Her mother had warned her against him, for different reasons, to be sure, but with a mother's instinct she had known. Uncle Sergei had had the same feeling. She couldn't go to them now for comfort. Some things were too difficult to confess. She was alone with her pride. Alone in this gloomy large apartment, facing the long, long hours of silence in the night. Oh, God, she couldn't stand being alone . . . couldn't stand it! If only there were someone who could hold her close, maybe rock her like a child and let her cry out her shame. Someone to whom she wouldn't have to tell anything, someone who already knew . . .

Michael. *He* knew. . . . He had tried to console her, and she, in her shame, read something into his kindness that made her run. How foolish to have rejected his helping hand! Her foolish pride! She was distraught, confused.

She had to get out of this empty oppressive apartment. Michael's boardinghouse was only three blocks away on Route Grouchy. With a shaking hand she turned out the light and ran out.

The look of surprise on Michael's face was brief as he opened the door, and then at once he was smiling his usual engaging smile and ushering her in.

His room was cozy and cheerful and hopelessly messy. Pictures of his parents and school friends were crowded on a chest of drawers, and mixed among them were snapshots of her taken in Harbin. Two or three books lay opened facedown on the carved camphor chest in front of a wide divan. The dining table in the center of the room was covered with magazines and newspapers, some of which had spilled over on the floor. Michael made no effort to pick them up.

"Survey my bachelor abode, Your Highness," he said, "and judge me not too harshly."

He was obviously comfortable in this disorder, and Marina was surprised to find herself pleased with this change from Rolf's compulsive tidiness.

Shoving the magazines to one side, Michael pulled out a chair. "Here's your throne, Princess. What may I offer you? A glass of tea, cognac, or black currant juice that my kind landlady gave me yesterday? I'll even spice it up with a touch of brandy!"

"The juice, please. You know how I love black currant."

As Michael handed her a glass of currant juice with brandy, he touched her hand and said softly, "Marinka, do you want to talk about it?"

She shook her head vehemently and felt her eyes grow hot with tears. Michael drew a chair near her, sat down, and sipped his own glass of brandy.

They talked about this and that: the tide of the war, the nuisance of blackouts, the nightly curfews, the increasing intensity of

Allied air raids, and the shortage of coal. After a while Michael said, "After the war is over, your future will be secure, Marinka." He gave her a lopsided smile. "You'll be going to Germany, and you'll have a country to protect you, no matter what the outcome. It's for us stateless Russians that the future will hold a big question mark."

He said "us . . . Russians . . ." He made a clear distinction between her and the rest of her family and friends. She had never thought much beyond the immediate future, beyond the tomorrows and the following weeks. She had never dwelt on the possibility of having to go with Rolf to Germany and living among people who were alien to her. The meaning of Michael's words sank in painfully. She looked at her friend, the room so still that she could hear the silence humming in her ears.

A dam was opening somewhere inside her, rising slowly, flooding, and drowning her mind. A stinging pain spread behind her eyes, and Michael's face began to blur. She struggled to contain her tears; but it was too late, and they spilled over her cheeks. The quiver in her lips was impossible to control, and shamed by the breakdown, she dropped her head onto her arms and let the crying out, choking down the sobs as best she could.

A hand slipped through her hair and ruffled it, then eased the weeping by stroking away the tension in the nape of her neck. It felt so good, so soothing. She gulped back the tears and gasped for air in great sighs, not yet ready to raise her head and face Michael, but another hand slipped under her chin and slowly pulled her resisting face upward.

She stopped crying. Michael was standing above her, and now he pulled her up. She rose obediently and they stood looking at each other for a long time, tension mounting, the warmth of his breath close to her cheek, the unexpected yearning for his touch tingling her skin. Still, he did not move, only looked down at her, his green eyes clouding, deep affection caressing her face until she thought she would cry out and say some silly, incredible thing and be ashamed of it forever.

Slowly, slowly, he cradled her face and held it between his hands but made no attempt to pull her close. She stared at him, her eyes widening, catching her breath as if she were seeing him for the first time: the sun-speckled eyes, the firm outline of his generous mouth.

"Oh, my God," she whispered, "what's happening?"

She closed her eyes, the eyelids flickering, afraid his face would disappear and she'd wake up to find it all a feverish dream. Her heart pounded so fast in her chest; so fast! His hand moved through her hair, and he began to pull her slowly toward him. His mouth brushed hers with a feathery touch and then again and again with soft, lambent caresses until she parted her lips to receive his first lingering kiss. It lasted a blissful eternity but, like the radiance of a revelation, became a fleeting spark. So gentle was his touch, so delicate the contact it was as if he feared to bruise her—already bruised and aching.

She circled his neck with her arms and clung to him fiercely. It was then that hesitantly, cautiously, his arms wrapped around her, and like the floating motes in languid motion, they settled on the sofa. Suspended in time, in silent absorption of this stolen magic, they shed their clothes, reaching out in wondrous discovery of each other: his muscular shoulders, her delicate arms; his broad chest, her silken mounds. They moved imperceptibly toward each other, locked in the depths of their eyes, closer to bridging the gulf of the past, aware of the majesty of the moment.

Shimmering, undulating colors blurred and suffused in space through Marina's closed eyelids as she absorbed Michael's worshiping love. Surely he worshiped her, cradled and loved her with a tenderness nurtured by years of wordless adoration. His patient intent in their union was solely to please her, to reach for the dormant, delicate source of her being and coax that bud into flower.

Awakened at length, she cried out with a surprised but delicious thrill, robbing him at last of his singular control and sending him into a fugue of ecstasy to raise her with him to the ultimate heights of what she thought was surely a glimpse of unreachable heaven. Floating softness . . . that's what it was; softness in his arms, tender pressure of his muscle, the warm friction of his skin.

She didn't want to part from him or wade through her

distressing thoughts right now. The warmth of Michael's love, his sensitivity, his tenderness had overwhelmed her, and she clung to him, wanting to prolong this time they had stolen from life. She dreaded words, those instruments of thought that would convey the truth she wasn't ready to accept.

Michael stirred and leaned over her, but she panicked and placed her hand over his mouth. "Please, don't say anything . . . oh, please!"

But Michael removed her hand and held it. "Marinka, I must. I *need* to tell you that I love you. Do you understand? *I love you!* I can't let you think that I took advantage of you tonight. I've loved you ever since I can remember and always will. I want you to know this."

Marina tried to speak, but this time it was Michael who placed his hand over her mouth. The familiar crooked smile spread over his face. "Oh, no, you don't! I've said my piece, and you don't have to say a thing. Now stay put and go to sleep. You're not going home at this late hour, you silly goose! Besides, curfew is in effect, and I wouldn't want you to be caught. I'll see you home early in the morning."

Oh, God, what had she done to herself and to Michael? It was *she* who had taken advantage of him. She had no right to wound this man who understood, who had loved her always and had never asked for anything in return.

She was lonely, vulnerable. Yes, vulnerable. After what had happened at ROS tonight, she had needed comfort, affection, tenderness. The warmth of his room, the brandy, his gentleness —it had been too much to resist, and she had lost her head.

Chapter Thirty-five

Nadya kept busy all her waking hours. With Alexei in the city, the weariness she had begun to feel before his arrival disappeared, and the awareness that his love for her was so strong that he had sacrificed everything to be near her made her feel young and vibrant again. She finally told her brother about Alexei. After his initial outburst of anger and adamant refusal to see him, Sergei made no more comments whatsoever, and she took his silence for a tacit acceptance of something that was now beyond his control.

Conscious of her grooming, Nadya glanced in the mirror more frequently, making sure her short, smoothly waved hair was in place over her forehead and the clipped neckline that made her look years younger was always trim. Yes, she was still beautiful, she thought without undue modesty, and the glow of love added a sparkle to her eyes and a spring to her walk. At night she wrote poetry that came to life with renewed freshness and passion.

> . . . I love you. My confession
> soars to reach your tender glance
> and capture it forever. . . .

Her critics raised their brows. "*Une affaire de coeur*, Nadya?" one teased, and she blushed like a young girl, remembering her first visit to Alexei's apartment on the Avenue Foch. How surprised she had been by her reaction to the sight of him! The yearning of her body had taken second place to the visual delight of recognizing every line of that beloved face: the firm and rounded jaw, the dark and sweeping brow, the passion language of the eye. How had she lived without them? How had she managed?

"Oh, Alexei, my dear, my own love," she whispered over and over, content to hold him close and have the comfort of his presence. And all this time she had thought she could survive without him! The lonely years—they were over now, over forever, and yes, she had paid her debt to her brother. Soon Sergei would recover, and she and Alexei would then have a clear path to their future happiness. Naïve? Perhaps. She did not care to analyze her rambling thoughts.

And oh, the loving! To be encompassed in his arms again, to touch, to feel, to press her face against his chest and listen to the joyous drumming of his heart! In the aftermath of hungry loving, she lay content against the hollow of his shoulder, her mind adrift, her fingers buried in the thickness of his graying hair. Alexei moved.

"Nadyenka, what now?"

Nadya shifted uncomfortably and said, "We have to wait awhile, darling. Sergei is ill, and I'm worried about him."

Alexei nodded, pushed a stray curl off her forehead, and kissed her moist brow. "I'll wait forever," he whispered, "and in the meantime, I look forward to getting to know my lovely daughter."

Nadya was thrilled. What a delight to hear Marina describe her reunion with Alexei! It had been joyous, not at all like their first awkward meeting in Harbin. Her father had glowed with happiness, Marina said, and told her that he was not going to press Nadya into marriage right away. He understood that Sergei was ill and needed his sister. "Besides," he said to his daughter, "it wouldn't be right for me to make her move from her lovely apartment into this small flat."

"You know," Marina said to Nadya, "he told me that only young people can be happy in a hut. He thinks his two-room flat is a hut! The old aristocrat is still chafing underneath. But he's lovable, Mama, and I'm crazy about him. He said he's waiting for new horizons to open up for you. Can't imagine what horizons he's talking about, but I agree that you should wait awhile."

Nadya nodded, studying her daughter reflectively. Marina's cheerful tone of voice seemed strained, her speech a little too fast. She looked drawn, nervous. *There's something wrong, and she's hiding it from me,* Nadya thought sadly. *Somehow I must draw her out, make her talk.* An idea came to her. Maybe Marina would talk more easily to her father, confide in him what she was reluctant to tell her mother. Nadya sighed at her own thoughts. She'd talk to Alexei, see what he could do to help his daughter.

Times were difficult for everyone. Shanghai strained against the tightening of Japanese control. City limits were narrowed, and no one was allowed to venture beyond the newly established boundaries. Nadya had heard rumors of increased assaults and rapes in the streets at night, and she strictly adhered to the curfew when she visited Alexei. When the roaring military trucks sped through the silent avenues in the dark toward the outskirts of the city, fear spread through her. The trucks were carefully covered to hide their cargoes from the eyes of the curious, but word went around that they carried machine guns and ammunition for fortifications built around the city in preparation for enemy attacks.

The Allies were surely winning the war, and Nadya learned to read the papers twice: once for what they said and the second time for what they implied. The Japanese reported their battles in the Pacific, no longer calling them victorious but courageous and omitting the outcome.

Soon, very soon, the war would end. She did not want to think too carefully about the future, what difference it would make in Sergei's health, if any, or what would happen to Marina and Rolf. There were more immediate concerns. Food lines were more frequent now, there was a shortage of dairy products, and the milk was diluted with water. Petty theft was on the increase, and even the empty milk bottles had to be left in a locked box for the deliveryman to pick up.

Weeks stretched into months. By the autumn of 1944 Allied planes were bombing Shanghai almost daily, and Nadya stayed indoors as much as possible. She went out, however, to study designer salon displays in the gallery of expensive shops on Rue Cardinal Mercier that stretched between Avenue Joffre and Rue Bourgeat. It faced the exclusive block-long French club, Cercle Sportif, and boasted a wealthy clientele.

After memorizing the designs, she hurried home to sketch and show them to her Russian customers. Nadya reveled in the pleased look on the women's faces at the sight of an elegant copy of the original, and as orders multiplied, she labeled her designs "Nadine" and stopped doing alterations.

On a damp day in November 1944 Nadya set out with samples of her designs to call on a new customer to whom she had been recommended by a friend. The address was 3 Béarn Apartments, on Avenue Joffre. It was a long walk, but Nadya was well protected from the wind in her muskrat coat, which Alexei had got her for half price from the Siberian furrier where he worked.

All she knew about her prospective customer was that she was young, beautiful, and redheaded. It was not unusual for Nadya to be recommended to strangers, and she enjoyed their delighted reaction to her sketches. Unobtrusively she would size up the customer's age, figure, and coloring and then suggest the fabric and shade of the dress in question.

The door to the apartment was opened by a tall, lithe redhead, who invited her in with casual politeness. Dressed in a loose kimono, the young woman stepped back and let Nadya come into a spacious foyer that led to a large living room tastefully furnished with blond oak furniture.

The young woman stretched out her hand to Nadya. "I know you only as Nadine. I am Xenia Polyvina."

"I'm sorry," Nadya said, moving toward the living room, "I thought you knew my name. I'm Nadezhda Antonovna Razumova."

With a sharp intake of breath the woman bit her lip and quickly stepped forward to block Nadya's way. Puzzled by this strange reaction, Nadya paused when Xenia took her arm and pulled her the other way. "Not here! Let's go to the dining room, where we can use the big table for your sketches."

What is wrong? Nadya thought, and was about to turn away from the living room door when her eye was caught by a large photograph on a side table. It stood slightly apart from a collection of Chinese snuff bottles and carved soapstone vases. She blinked and looked again. No mistake. It was a snapshot of Rolf and Xenia taken in a restaurant, smiling, arms around each other.

Following her gaze, Xenia cleared her throat. "Rolf is a good friend," she said a little too flippantly. "We've known each other for a long time."

Nadya turned and looked at her carefully, taking in her heavy makeup, meticulous manicure, expensive kimono. *So that's Marina's problem! My God, how long has this been going on?*

The two women looked at each other, and their eyes locked. Xenia's face flushed; her eyes shifted and took on a veiled look.

"As I said, we've known each other for a long time. He knows my parents, and he helped me with my dancing career." She spoke a little too fast, too breathlessly.

Nadya's throat tightened. She raised her hand and shook her head. "Please!" she said, forcing the words out. "Please don't!"

Xenia shrugged. "As you wish!"

Nadya clutched her sketches to her chest. "God, how could he —I mean—why?" She leaned against the wall, her legs suddenly weak.

"Rolf knew me long before he married your daughter!" Xenia said, her voice defiant now.

"Yes!" Nadya heard herself say, "but he is *married* now, and you—you are—" She stopped, groping for words.

Xenia's eyes narrowed. "I am *what*?" she demanded, taking a step forward.

"Well, I don't know what you are, but whatever there is between you, I can't believe that Rolf—"

A patch of red was spreading on Xenia's neck. "And just how much do you know about your precious son-in-law?"

Appalled, Nadya controlled her voice with difficulty. "I know that my son-in-law is a good husband and an honorable man, and it is women like you—who—who—"

"Honorable?" Xenia threw her head back with a mirthless laugh. "Ha! You don't know him at all!"

"Let me be the judge of that!"

Eyes flashing, Xenia raised her voice. "You don't know him, I tell you! He's no better than I!"

"What do you mean?"

"Just what I said! He's an informer!" she blurted out, then, with a gasp, clamped her lips shut.

Nadya was aghast. "You're disgraceful," she said, her voice shaking, "and—and I don't believe you!"

Xenia propped her waist with her fists and sneered. "And what would you say if I told you that Rolf has led a double life not only in private but in the consulate as well?"

"I'd say that your slander is despicable, and I won't stay here and listen to it any longer!"

But Xenia blocked her way and, twisting her mouth, spit out the words with relish: "Slander? You're accusing me of slander? Have you ever stopped to wonder how he managed to get you out of Harbin so easily?"

Nadya gasped, her mind stunned. "How do you know about that?"

"Never mind how I know about that. But for your information, your very proper son-in-law is an undercover agent who collaborates with the Kempetai."

Nadya looked at Xenia in shock. The woman's eyes glared at her. *A veritable Megaera*, she thought, listening, yet not hearing the spiteful words. Her mind went back in time: comfortable train ride from Harbin, luxurious accommodations in Dairen while they waited for their ship, Rolf's arrangements during the journey, Japanese courtesy throughout. It *was* too easy.

Agent. Rolf is a Nazi agent working with the dreaded Kempetai. Could that be really true? The room tilted. The air became stifling, and she had to get out of the apartment. She fought to hide her tremor. Don't stoop to ask any more questions; don't say anything to this nasty woman. Silence blunts the verbal daggers; let them boomerang upon their source. Hurry out!

Outside, she leaned against a shopwindow and gulped vast breaths of air.

Marinka. Her beautiful, willful Marinka. Did she know about this other woman? Was she aware of Rolf's involvement with stool pigeons who denounced their friends to gain favors with the authorities? An agonizing thought crossed Nadya's feverish mind. After the war Rolf would be taking Marina to a bombed-out country, possibly torn by internal strife, filled with tragedy. Could she, Nadya, sit back and watch passively as an unfaithful Nazi agent took her daughter to faraway Germany? In spite of the afternoon sun, a chill settled in her bones.

Nadya stopped her aimless wandering and looked around. It was quiet here. But quiet streets harbored hidden horrors that lurked around corners, spreading menace through the air. She had seen enough of it in Petrograd. She didn't want to see this happen to her only living child. She had already lost one daughter, and she'd do anything—*anything*—to protect the other one from harm.

She walked slowly, arguing with herself, digging again for the strength within, searching for an answer and not finding one. After a while she stopped, opened her purse, pulled out a mirror to straighten her hair and rouge her lips, then turned around decisively and headed toward Alexei's flat.

In the loving sanctuary of his modest flat, Nadya told her story to Alexei. She spoke breathlessly, relating every detail of her visit to Xenia's apartment, repeating the conversation word for word. Alexei listened intently without interrupting, and her outpouring had its beneficial effect. Nadya relaxed and, looking pleadingly into Alexei's face, asked, "What are we going to do, Alexei? Shouldn't we do *something*?" When Alexei, obviously overcome with the ugly news, nodded, she grabbed his hands impatiently and cried, "Tell me, tell me!"

Alexei rose, freed his hands from hers, and started to pace the floor. As he passed a mirrored wardrobe, he hit it with his fist so hard the veneer doors rattled.

"The bastard!" he swore through clenched teeth. "How wrong I was about that man! I thought Marina was making a good marriage because she would have a passport and a country to protect her and because he seemed so in love with her at the wedding!" He stopped in front of Nadya and looked at her, his face pale and somber.

"Nadyenka, Marina has to be told. We would be doing her a great wrong by protecting her."

Nadya squirmed in her seat. "I've noticed a change in her for quite some time now. She may already know. Why embarrass her by telling her that *we* know?"

"That's the chance we have to take. She doesn't have to know about Rolf's infidelity, but she *must* be told about his undercover work."

"I can't tell her that, Alexei! I've tried to talk to her before, but she has built a wall between us. She doesn't want to open up to me. She won't listen!"

Alexei sat down beside Nadya on the sofa. "Darling, I didn't say that *you* have to tell her. I am her father, and we have a good relationship. It is my place to talk to her."

"And when you tell her, what good will it do? What can she do about it?"

Alexei looked at Nadya for a long moment, then said, "She can divorce him. The sooner she is free of him, the better."

"But she may still love him!" Nadya cried. "What then?"

"In that case, it is still up to her to make a choice. She is a grown woman and has to decide her own future. All we can do is tell her."

Nadya wrung her hands. "She'll be hurt! So hurt!"

Alexei grabbed her hands. "Listen to me! She'll be hurt far worse in the long run if we *don't* tell her."

As Nadya nodded miserably, Alexei walked out into the boardinghouse hallway where the communal telephone hung on the wall and dialed his daughter's number.

Chapter Thirty-six

The months since that painful incident on the ROS dance floor were difficult for Marina. After the initial shock of discovery that Rolf was having an affair, she realized that she wasn't hurt nearly as much as she had expected. It confirmed what she had tried to deny all along: that since her marriage her budding love for Rolf had never come to flower. After a few days of soul-searching she had to face the truth that she no longer loved her husband. What was there to do?

She thought of divorce. Notoriety, gossip were minor compared to her fear of Rolf's reaction, for to ask him for a divorce would be to wound his ego. She didn't dare antagonize him. As long as she was married to him, she had security, for she had his and his country's protection. She must not forget that Japan exerted power in Shanghai, and Germany was its strong ally. It would be foolish to turn Rolf into a powerful enemy.

Then, too, there was the question of financial arrangement. If he refused to pay her rent, she couldn't keep the apartment on her nursing salary and would have to move. But where? She couldn't afford to pay key money even for a smaller one. A rented room in a boardinghouse was a possibility, but sharing a bathroom and kitchen with three or four other families was more than she could cope with at that moment. Nadya and Sergei would take her in; but with only two bedrooms, her mother would have to share her room with her, and she hated to crowd them.

No, while the war lasted, she would wait it out. She was reasonably sure that Germany would be defeated, and then there would be no cause for fear. After she had secured her freedom, she and her family might be able to get out of China and go to America, as Uncle Sergei had dreamed of all these years.

As for now, she could not confront Rolf with her knowledge. Instinctively she knew it would gain her nothing and would only strain their relationship to a breaking point. Now she was grateful for his frequent long absences from home and his diminishing physical demands on her. He hadn't even questioned her why she stayed out that one night, taking it for granted that she spent it nursing at the hospital.

Strange that as a result of that emotional night it was Michael, not Rolf, she thought about. A conflict raged within her, and she was unable to resolve it. On one hand, she was mortified that in a moment of weakness she had *used* Michael's love in such a selfish way, but on the other hand, the memory of that sweetness flooded her with warmth and physical yearning every time she thought of the hours spent in his arms. The only thing to do, she decided, was to avoid being alone with him as much as possible. They met at poetry meetings, in her mother's home, and although Michael never tried to force another rendezvous, she no longer felt at ease in his presence. How much easier it would have been, she thought, if she had been in love with Michael! As it was, she no longer dared reach out to him for comfort, afraid that in another vulnerable moment she'd succumb to his loving again.

On this chilly November afternoon she was sitting with a book on her lap, trying to read and unable to concentrate after a difficult day at the hospital. Rolf was still at the consulate, and she was wondering what to fix for dinner when the telephone rang.

Delighted to hear her father's voice, she was pleased when he asked if he could come over. Only much later did she realize that his somber voice should have alerted her to the gravity of his visit.

As gently as he could, Alexei told Marina about Rolf's

undercover work, which, he said, explained why they were able to leave Harbin so easily.

Stunned, disbelieving, Marina stared at her father. Oh, God, what was he saying? She couldn't believe it. Grasping her father's arms, she shook him. "Papa! Papa! It can't be, it can't!"

Suddenly she stopped. "How do you know, Papa? Who told you? Who?"

She searched her father's face, but he avoided her eyes and looked somewhere above her head. "Your mother was showing her designs to someone . . . it came out. . . ."

Marina's heart began to hammer painfully. Now it was she who couldn't look at him. Over on the sideboard the crystal decanter stood on a silver tray. Without thinking, she walked to it, flicked a crumb from the crocheted runner, moved the decanter with the Campari aside, put it back in its original place.

Although she had trouble getting the words out, she forced herself to ask, "Was her name Xenia, Papa?" And when he didn't say anything, she turned and looked at him.

He didn't have to answer. The pain and the pity in his face confirmed what she already suspected.

"How long have you known this, Marinka?" he asked softly.

"Five months," she whispered, averting her eyes. "But I didn't know about his work!" she cried. "Oh, God, I didn't know about *that!*"

She looked at her father and began to tremble. "Papa! I can't live with a man like that! I can't!"

Alexei took her in his arms and pressed her head against his shoulder. For a few minutes Marina wept. Then she pulled away. "Five months ago I wanted to ask for a divorce," she said tearfully, "but was afraid. Now I can't go on like this, pretending I know nothing. He'll suspect." Marina rubbed her hands together nervously. "What shall I do, Papa?"

"You don't have to tell him what you know, Marinka. Give him a chance to take the initiative. Make him believe that you're offering him a way out of an unfortunate mistake."

Yes. Her father was right. She must swallow her pride and not accuse Rolf of anything. Somehow she knew that he would not hold her to her vows and be relieved to have his freedom.

Shadows lengthened in the room: dark, long fingers on the wall behind the rubber philodendron, creeping like a giant centipede. She shivered. Rolf was due home in another hour, and she must be ready for him.

She dreaded facing him, repulsed by the thought of what he represented and of how she lived with him in ignorance all this time. But when he came home, she found it wasn't nearly as difficult as she had anticipated.

They ate dinner in silence, Rolf's mind miles away, his face unsmiling, distant. He made it easier for her to bring up the difference in their interests and the seeming lack of communication that contributed to their growing estrangement. He listened without interrupting, and when she asked what he wanted to do about it, he was quick to suggest divorce.

With a detachment and formality that sent shivers down her spine, Rolf said, "I am glad we can discuss this like civilized people and part without unpleasantness. I detest emotional outbursts. You need not worry about the settlement, for I shall provide for you adequately."

And so he did. The divorce was amicable, and Marina was left without financial worries. They parted like strangers, without emotion or surplus words, and she felt like a bird freed from a dark and confining cage. She could not see herself alone in their large apartment, which held no sweet memories for her, and insisted that Rolf stay in it. It wasn't easy to find another apartment, however, and Nadya came to her rescue.

"Why don't you move in with us?" she said to her. "My room is large, and I'll enjoy your company. Besides, you'd be such a help to me in caring for Uncle Sergei."

When Marina hesitated, wondering if her mother was doing it to please her, Nadya added softly, "You'd be doing me a big favor, Marinka. If it doesn't work out for you, you can always move."

Marina hugged her mother and swallowed her tears. "Thank

you, Mamochka, and thank you for not insisting that I talk. You see, I couldn't admit my mistake then, even to myself."

She couldn't wait to leave the now gloomy place where happiness had eluded her. What a difference to be in her family's apartment! Large windows and lots of them; the sun pouring in, filling every room with a warm glow; the light oak floor shining in reflection; and on cloudy days, the light—silver, not pewter.

Suddenly she couldn't get enough of Russian words, of Sunday church services, of her Russian friends and their evening get-togethers to argue philosophy and literature over endless cups of tea. Only now did she realize how alienated she had become from her Russian friends because of her marriage to a German.

Glad to be needed at the Russian Hospital on the Route Maresca, she worked an eight-hour daytime shift and then helped her uncle at home with the outpatients. She worried about him, for he was careless about his diet and ignored his chronic sprue. Her love for him was deep, but now she extended that love to her father. How easy it was to understand her mother's love for him, and how hard to see Uncle Sergei's unbending antagonism! In an effort to bring the two men together, she once asked her mother to invite Alexei to their apartment, but Nadya demurred. Marina didn't insist, sensing a more serious reason than that appearing on the surface.

In contrast, she was enormously impressed by her father's kind words about Sergei.

"How can I feel anything but gratitude toward your uncle, Marina, when he sacrificed so much for your mother?" Alexei smiled shyly and spread his hands. "Nadya is mine at last—before God, if not yet before man. I can now afford the luxury of humility."

"Yes, I know. I noticed that you have even dropped your title. Why, Papa? Aren't you proud of it?"

"I am, my dear, but when I first came to Shanghai, I found that almost every family I met made it a point to tell me that they had a prince or a count in their midst, or at least a member of landed gentry. They quoted names I never heard of. The other day a woman came into our Siberian fur store and told me she was a graduate of *Smolensky* Institute in St. Petersburg. When I tactfully asked her if she meant the *Smolny* Institute for young girls of noble birth, she shrugged and changed the subject." So you see, my dear child, I gain nothing by introducing myself as *Count* Persiansev!"

They laughed together, and watching him, Marina thought how young and handsome he still looked and wondered how lóng it would be before he and her mother were united and if Nadya was as happy as she appeared to be.

For Nadya it was indeed a time of renewed hope. Alexei was doing well in his work and had already received two raises. Although busy with her sewing, she managed to visit him often, grateful that Marina was home to look after Sergei.

Relieved to have her daughter free of Rolf and back in the family fold, she nurtured a long-buried idea: Given time, Marina might see her destiny at the doorstep. Loyal, cheerful Michael began to frequent their apartment, never demanding, always bringing a choice bit of fruit or flowers. That Marina seemed uneasy in his presence and avoided being left alone with him was surely understandable for a while, and Michael's sensitivity in not asking Marina out did not escape her mother. All in due time, Nadya concluded, all in due time. Michael had waited so long he must know that time was on his side. Thank God Sergei liked him and enjoyed his company.

Sergei. Nadya worried about him. His weight loss, blood pressure, and despondency were mounting, and of all these, his growing depression disturbed her the most. Even gambling no longer attracted him as much as before, and more and more he took to his bed. By the spring of 1945 the sprue had become so acute that he was no longer able to eat a full meal. Even the war news failed to cheer or inspire him. When General Douglas MacArthur invaded the Philippines and took Manila in February, and Iwo Jima was occupied in March, the unconcealed excitement among the Russians waiting for the imminent Allied victory affected Sergei adversely.

"Be careful what you say, Nadya, and to whom. In their death throes the Japanese may strike at us at the least expected moment.

Who knows what they have up their sleeves? Don't show your delight."

As if in answer to his warning, the Japanese intensified their random persecution after the early May bulletins had brought news of Hitler's death and Germany's defeat. For the slightest infraction of imposed rules or an overheard careless remark, individuals were arrested, beaten, or tortured, and some disappeared without a trace. The Bridge House, Kempetai headquarters in the Hongkew district, took on an even more sinister aura. Tension pulsated in Shanghai. The Allies were closing in, their grip tightening—a strangling noose for the Japanese, but a welcome embrace for the Russians. On the streets, in the shops, at the theaters, people smiled and whispered and waited.

In preparing for Easter that spring, Nadya and Marina worked together, making the *paskha* cheese cake. Marina labored willingly in putting the cottage cheese through a fine sieve. She watched her mother mix it with sour cream and sugar and crushed vanilla bean, then pour the mixture into a pyramid-shaped wooden form lined with cheesecloth. She helped Nadya knead the dough for the *kulich*, pound cake heavy with butter and eggs and yeast, and was sad that Sergei would not be able to eat the traditional rich delicacies this year. When the time came to attend the Easter midnight mass, mother and daughter left the ailing Sergei at home and went to the cathedral on Route Paul Henry with Michael and Alexei.

Throughout the magnificent service with dozens of flickering candles, bejeweled icons, the fragrance of incense, and operatic voices in the choir loft, Marina's tension grew in anticipation of the first proclamation of *"Khristos Voskrese"* ("Christ has risen") from the priest. With hundreds of voices responding joyfully, *"Voistinu Voskrese"* ("Indeed has risen"), the custom called for friends to exchange a triple kiss on each cheek.

When Michael bent over her to whisper, *"Khristos Voskrese,"* she could barely respond, hoping that the flame in her cheeks was not visible. Shameful it was to succumb to her yearnings, to allow the memory of one night to pursue her! She could not take advantage of him again. She must avoid Michael more, discourage his frequent visits to her family.

Chapter Thirty-seven

Spring ended early in June that year, and the debilitating heat crawled from the Whangpoo. On a particularly long day Sergei's last patient left at six o'clock, and he went to his bedroom to rest before dinner. Nadya had gone to the kitchen, and when the bell rang, it was Marina who opened the door.

A gaunt dark-haired woman stood on the other side, nervously kneading the strap of her purse.

"Is . . . Dr. Efimov at home?" she asked, peering at Marina intently.

Marina was annoyed. Why did these patients wait until they were so sick that they had to show up after hours? Uncle Sergei must have just dozed off in his room.

"I'm sorry," she said, "but visiting hours are over."

The woman shook her head. "I'm not—I mean—I'm not a patient. I came to see Dr. Efimov on a personal matter."

Marina sized the woman up. That she was very poor was obvious. An outmoded few-sizes-too-large gray dress of limp cotton fabric slumped off her shoulders and hung to her ankles. Around her forehead and temples her black hair had faded to silver, and although it was pulled back into a small knot, a few wisps escaped and dangled over her ears. The dark agates of her eyes shone with feverish and searching brilliance from a colorless face, but traces of a former beauty were unmistakably there.

Marina stepped aside and motioned the woman into the waiting room. "Please sit down. I'll see if Dr. Efimov is available."

Sergei was talking to Nadya in the kitchen when Marina announced the visitor.

Brother and sister exchanged glances and went to the waiting alcove, while Marina paused in the doorway behind them. Frowning and peering, Sergei approached the stranger slowly, but Nadya gasped and pressed both hands to her neck, staring at the woman, who by now was shaking visibly in an obvious effort to say something, yet unable to utter a word. The black eyes opened wide, and tears poured down her cheeks. Sergei stood rooted to the floor, blinking, mouthing a name Marina could not hear and shaking his head in disbelief. It was Nadya who broke the silence.

With a piercing cry of "Esther! Esther!" she threw her arms around the frail woman and swung her from side to side in tight embrace.

Sergei moved forward, seemingly in a trance, a shaky smile on his face, a half sob, half laugh coming from his lips. "Esther? My God, my Esther! I can't believe it!"

Carefully, tenderly, as if he were afraid to break her, Sergei took Esther's arm, pulled her away from Nadya, and held her in front of him, searching her face with his eyes, touching it with trembling hands.

After a moment the woman spoke. "Seryozha! Nadya! A miracle . . . after twenty-seven years—a miracle! I found you. . . . With all the Russians scattered throughout the world like feathers in the wind, I found you! God, oh, God, at last!"

Marina watched. What joy sparkled in the room as the three people hugged and kissed and laughed! She had never before seen such a look on her uncle's face, and with a shock she realized that Michael had looked at her the same way that night in his room. . . . Heat rose to her face, and quickly she stepped forward.

"Aunt Esther, I'm your niece, Marina!"

The laughter and the chatter died down, and Esther blinked. "Marina . . . Marina?"

A perplexed look spread over her face, and as she was about to say something, Nadya interrupted. "This is my daughter, Marina. She was born in Harbin."

When Esther looked at Nadya with a question in her eyes, Marina answered for her mother. "My sister, Katya, died in Harbin."

With her arm around Esther's shoulders Nadya led her toward the dining room. "We'll talk about it later. Right now we have so much to catch up on! You must be hungry. It's dinnertime."

But Esther wanted to hear all about Nadya and Sergei and her nieces. Her hunger for details of their lives was insatiable, and when they had finally told her everything, her own story poured out in bits and pieces over the food that Nadya and Marina served and that she barely touched.

The years rolled back as Esther talked, and Nadya listened with growing dismay at the appalling tragedy of her sister-in-law's life.

After a year in prison Esther had been released for lack of evidence. With the help of the faithful Yakov Oblevich, who told her how he had encouraged Nadya and Sergei to leave Petrograd, she managed to leave Russia and go to Germany. She wanted to search for them in Siberia but bowed to Yakov's reasoning that her best chance of survival was to leave the country immediately.

For the next twenty-two years, without a profession she could do only menial work in various small towns in Germany, moving from place to place and pleading continually with the International Red Cross to find her family. When Hitler's persecution of Jews intensified, she fled again, this time to France, where she boarded a cargo ship bound for China, following the route taken by thousands of other German Jews seeking the land of opportunity. She arrived in Shanghai in 1941, emaciated and weakened by years of malnutrition.

In the beginning a Jewish relief organization helped her find room and work in a Japanese restaurant, where she washed dishes in a steaming kitchen all day. After the Japanese had rounded up the German Jews in 1943 and forced them to live in a ghetto in the Hongkew district in poorly heated, crowded conditions, her health worsened. Then, two weeks ago, she lost her job. Desperate, she finally went to the Russian Emigrants' Committee and asked for help.

The news that Esther had been in Shanghai the last four years stunned Nadya.

"Why did you wait this long before going to the Emigrants' Committee?" she asked.

Sadly, without rancor, Esther looked at her. "My memories of Russia were too painful," she replied in a flat voice. "After all those years I thought I'd lost you forever and avoided any contact with the Russians in Shanghai—afraid to be reminded of what happened to me before I left Petrograd."

When no one said anything, Esther looked around the table. "I didn't want to speak Russian. I changed my name to Engel and didn't even read your Russian newspaper. Don't you see?"

She paused, looked down at her hands, then finished her story. At the Emigrants' Committee, where identification cards were issued in lieu of passports to all Russian refugees, she explained that her real name was Efimova. The clerk glanced at her curiously and asked if she was related to Dr. Sergei Efimov.

"I nearly fainted from shock," Esther said, shaking her head in wonder. "I couldn't believe it after all these years. I thought I was dreaming, and the clerk had to ask me several times before I could answer."

Nadya looked at Sergei. Her brother sat quietly, his eyes riveted to Esther's face, following her every word, every gesture, as if he were afraid to look away and then wake up and discover it was all a taunting dream.

Horrified by Esther's story, Nadya thought: *My God, I'm responsible for what happened to her. If not for me and Katya, Sergei would have stayed in Petrograd, would have waited and been reunited with Esther in a year.* They were lucky to have a happy ending within their reach. It was up to her now to nurse her brother and Esther back to health, to let them have their long-delayed happiness.

She turned to her brother. "Seryozha, Esther must be exhausted after such an emotional day. Take her to your room and make her comfortable. Marina and I will clean up here."

In the privacy of his bedroom Sergei held Esther in his arms gently, afraid to crush her in his embrace, still unable to believe that they had been reunited. The suffering, the aging had taken its toll; but in his love he saw her only as she had been, and every deep furrow in her face was an intruder on this memory. With a trembling hand he traced each wrinkle, so painful, yet so precious to his eye.

Tears streaming down her cheeks, she kissed his eyes and brows and nose and lips and then said, "Seryozha, through all the years one thought sustained me: You were somewhere out there in the world, loving me as I loved you. Now, suddenly, I am embarrassed. How long will it take us to get reacquainted?"

Sergei smiled, pulled her tenderly to him, and whispered, "How about two minutes?"

She nestled against him, and they talked about their lives, laughing and crying at the miracle of their union.

Then came the sweet loving, gentle and shy and burdened by sorrow of wasted years. Later they slept in each other's arms, cradled and comforted by their bodies' warmth.

The next morning the physician in Sergei took over. He examined Esther and wanted to run some tests.

"Our Marina is a nurse," he said, "and we'll get you on your feet in no time. You'll move in with us immediately. I'll have Marina and her young friend, Michael, collect your things at the ghetto and bring them here. I won't let you go back there again."

When all the results of laboratory tests were in, the diagnosis appalled Sergei. "Nadya," he said to her privately, his voice shaking, "Esther has an advanced case of beriberi."

Frightened by the exotic name, Nadya asked, "What is it?"

"It's a vitamin B_1 deficiency, and hers is complicated by myocarditis, an inflammation of the heart muscle. She has all the classic symptoms: leg edema, cramps in her calves at night, shortness of breath. She needs more care right now than we can give her at home. I'll see if the Russian Hospital has room."

"Won't proper nourishment at home do it? Home care and love usually work miracles."

"I'm afraid not, Nadya. She is too sick. But until we can find a bed for her in the hospital, you can start feeding her liver and pork. Kidneys are good, too, and from what I remember, she used to love *rassolnik* soup. Put in an extra portion of kidneys when you give it to her."

"Marina and I will do all we can to help you, Seryozha, you know that!"

But Sergei frowned. "I'm sorry to bring this up, but there will be a lot of extra expenses. We'll need to tighten our budget."

Nadya patted him on the shoulder. "I have more sewing orders than I can handle. We'll have enough money."

Two weeks later, however, Nadya was dismayed to find Sergei's hurriedly scrawled note on her dressing table telling her that he had gone to relax over a game of Mah-Jongg. Nadya wasn't fooled. She was sure that he was hoping to win a quick sum of money for Esther's care. How foolish to take such chances!

Esther was now in the hospital, and Marina spent most of her time nursing her. She had the best of care, and there was enough money to pay the bills. True, they had none left for luxuries, but nobody complained.

Nadya felt sorry only for her daughter. Michael did not have much money, but he came over often and cheered the family with his unfailing good humor. . . . Was Marina ever going to wake up and see the treasure at her feet?

As for herself, she thanked God for Alexei. He was understanding and supportive, and although he occasionally wanted to take her to the opera or a concert at the Lyceum Theater and she declined, he did not press, glad to have her give him what spare time she had.

Nadya sighed. Her sister-in-law's health was not yet improving, but at least she was holding her own. There was always hope.

Looking at Sergei's note in her hand, she was furious with her brother. How much money was he going to lose tonight? she thought. No one had ever come out ahead in gambling. They were saving every kopeck, and he was wasting it!

Sometime in the middle of the night she awakened, aware of a strong smell of tobacco, and knew immediately that Sergei had come home permeated with the thick smoke from the Nantao den, always the same unmistakable, nauseating odor. Without looking at the clock, she pulled the blanket over her head and tried to go back to sleep.

The next day a Chinese messenger brought a letter for Sergei. As he was reading it, Nadya watched him out of the corner of her eye. Of late, his pallor had taken on a sickly shade, but now his face turned raspberry, a vein bulged on the right temple, and his eyelid began to twitch. Nadya rushed to his side and knelt by the chair. His lips were tight, and his chest heaved in deep and wheezing breaths.

"Seryozha, my dear, what is it? Remember your blood pressure . . . you can't get this excited!"

"Leave me alone!" His voice was raspy and forced, and he suddenly shoved Nadya aside with such force that she grabbed the arm of the chair to keep her balance. Sergei tore the letter in half, threw it into a wastebasket, and started for the front door.

With the agility born of desperation Nadya ran past him and blocked the door before him.

"I won't let you leave the house in this state!" she cried. "Calm down first!"

Sergei grabbed her wrist and tried to pull her away.

"Let me go, I tell you!" he shouted, wrestling with her arm, but Nadya, terrified by the sight of his engorged face, threw her arms around his neck and pressed his face against her cheek.

"Seryozha, come to your senses! I don't want you to have a stroke somewhere on the street! Please wait a few minutes!"

Rigid at first, Sergei began to relax after a few moments, and Nadya continued to hold him. He finally said, "I'm better now. Thank you, Nadya, and . . . forgive me!"

After he had left, Nadya pulled the crumpled note from the wastebasket and put the torn pieces together. It said:

Your IOU is valid for twenty-four hours. This is a reminder that according to our rules, the money must be paid in cash by tonight. Since you are an old client, however, we extend the deadline until tomorrow evening.

C. Lee

Nadya stared at the signature: C. Lee. He must be the owner of the gambling den Sergei frequented. How well did he know him, and what kind of man was he?

Her fingers were cold and stiff as she tore the paper in shreds and threw them back into the wastebasket.

Chapter Thirty-eight

For several days afterward Nadya watched her brother surreptitiously for signs of anxiety, but Sergei seemed to have regained his composure and hadn't said a word about the incident. Where had he gone that day after he had read the note?

Nadya wondered if he had gone to make some kind of bargain with C. Lee to postpone the payment or if he had tried to borrow the money elsewhere. She concluded that either solution was unsatisfactory when she pondered the consequences. One did not make an easy bargain with a gambling den owner, and borrowing money to pay the debt was substituting one problem for another. She wanted to ask Sergei how much money he had lost that night, but how? Any indirect approach to the question of gambling made him abruptly change the subject. She didn't dare question him outright for fear of causing another outburst that might play havoc with his blood pressure. If he had only shared his problem with her, she could work longer hours sewing to help pay his debt.

There was another concern right now. After a week in the hospital Esther developed double pneumonia. That day Sergei came home early and told Nadya to cancel the outpatient appointments for the rest of the day. He lowered himself slowly onto a dining room chair and, placing his arms on the table, propped up his forehead with one hand. Nadya placed a glass of tea before him and sat down across the table. In a moment Sergei's other hand closed into a fist and began to shake. He slammed it against the dining table with such force that a crystal bowl with raspberry jam crashed to the floor, breaking in half. He looked down at the fragment smeared with jam and then up at Nadya.

"Say it! Why don't you say it?" he shouted. "A bad omen! You all say it's a bad omen to break something—damn you superstitious women!"

"I've never been superstitious, and you know it, Seryozha," Nadya said quietly, leaving the broken bowl on the floor for the moment. "No great damage has been done; we can easily replace the bowl."

Sergei's eyes roamed wildly around the room. "Penicillin! That's what Esther needs—penicillin! That drug can cure pneumonia, and we can't get it. Can you imagine? Can't get it! Damn, damn, damn! Without it, Esther doesn't stand a chance in her weakened condition. Only a miracle could save her, and I've run out of miracles."

With his fist still clenched, Sergei drummed the table. "The Allies have it! They must be only weeks away from us, but not soon enough for my Esther. We're beaten! No money can buy even a small vial of penicillin here."

Sergei raised his head and looked at Nadya. Such agony poured out of his bloodshot eyes that her heart turned over with pity.

"What kind of God is it," he cried, "who plays games with us?"

"Don't blaspheme, Seryozha."

"Who are you to tell me not to blaspheme? You don't believe in the Almighty either."

"I believe there is a power greater than we are," she said quietly.

"What of it? Can that power get us penicillin for Esther? I ask you, can it? The travesty on happy endings! For twenty-seven years I knocked on every Red Cross threshold, begged them to look for her, finally gave up, accepted my loss, tried to live with it. And what happens? She appears to overwhelm me with happiness —the kind of happiness I dared not hope for. Now——" He choked, then added, "A yo-yo! That God of yours plays yo-yo with humans. . . ."

He slumped over the table, and his shoulders shook with dry sobs. Nadya pulled her chair next to his and stroked his hair silently. There was nothing to say.

A day went by; two days, then three and four. Like a flickering candle flame, Esther began to withdraw from life. On Saturday, July 21, Marina telephoned home and told Nadya that she was staying overnight at the hospital to nurse Esther. "It's the weekend, Mama, and the nursing staff is reduced. I'll feel better if I stay over."

The night was fretful. Marina did not dare leave Esther's bedside even to sleep on a cot outside her room; having placed a wooden armchair at the foot of the bed, she propped herself up with pillows and dozed. Esther's breathing was rasping and shallow. Through the humid July night she thrashed with chills and fever.

By morning Esther's restlessness had subsided. The early light paled the electric light bulb in the ceiling and filled the hospital room with brilliant hues of dawn. After wiping Esther's face gently with a damp cloth, Marina settled back into her chair and noticed that Esther's breathing had become less rasping and more even. A cool hand reached out and tugged at Marina's arm. After pulling her chair closer, Marina took Esther's hand between her own to warm it. Fragile it was and seemingly translucent. Esther's dark eyes shone brightly as she searched Marina's face.

"Marina . . . what a beautiful name Nadya gave you . . . Marina . . . listen to me . . . I want to be cremated, do you hear?"

Shocked, Marina tried to say something, but Esther silenced her with an intense, steady look. "Don't try to lie to me. I know I'm dying. So listen! I want no funeral . . . no dug-up earth or incantations, no pilgrimages, no flowers on the grave. I don't believe in it; it puts an onus on the living. Who lies beneath those tombstones anyway? A shell—a skeleton to haunt the loved ones . . . no!"

Esther paused, seized suddenly by a paroxysm of coughing. Marina raised her pillow and lifted her shoulders to ease the spell.

When it was over, Esther lay back and sighed. "Thank you, child. . . . Promise you'll tell Sergei."

Shaken by her labored speech, Marina asked, "Wouldn't you like Uncle Sergei to come over now?"

Esther shook her head. "No, I want to be remembered as a living, breathing wife. . . . Through the years my search for Sergei and Nadya kept me alive, and now I am at peace. . . . Strange, I have no argument with fate. It robbed me of my future . . . so be it. There is no bitterness left in me . . . I found my loved ones, and maybe—maybe such happiness cannot survive in an uncertain future." She smiled, and her gaze wandered off to the window, her eyes reflecting sunlight.

"It is a river—life of ours . . ." Her voice drifted and Marina thought: she is hallucinating—I should call the doctor—but instead, she listened.

". . . it brings its tired waters to the sea . . . that river, child —I have reached my sea. You tell Sergei, I love him . . ."

Her voice faded and soon she drifted off into sleep. Still holding her hand and watching that beautiful, serene face, Marina dared not leave her. A few minutes more, and her eyelids fluttered, her body gave a little shudder, and then the essence that had been Esther was gone.

Esther had been right. It was better this way, Marina thought, without Sergei and Nadya. It wouldn't have been peaceful with them present. Marina felt unaccountably cold. It was the first death of a family member she had ever witnessed. When her sister, Katya, died, she didn't *see* her die. She thought that being a trained nurse had prepared her for the death of a loved one. *Hadn't she?* Not so! She was shaken. It was up to her now to take charge of the necessary nursing duties to the dead, then to go home and tell Sergei his wife was gone.

Nadya feared Sergei's reaction to Esther's death, but there was no violent outburst from her brother. It was as if had spent himself in trying to save her, and with the finality of death there was no energy in him for anger and despair. He shut himself in his room, and for several days Nadya stayed home, afraid to leave him. He barely touched the food she brought him and refused to talk.

When Anna died, he had behaved the same, Nadya thought. Years rolled back to revive the memory of her mother's death, vivid and frightening, for it had been her first experience with death. *We grieve in our own ways,* she thought, taking the dishes into the kitchen. They had lost so many loved ones: Papa, Vadim, Katya. Who knew the secrets of another's soul?

When at last Sergei emerged from his room, it was impossible to reach him. Nadya, suffocating in the atmosphere of silent grief, urged Marina to go to the movies and, needing solace herself, ran to Alexei.

Knowing that after the movies Marina would be home with Sergei, Nadya lost awareness of time, and Alexei, humbly pleased that she had come to him for comfort, did not remind her of the midnight curfew. He read her thoughts, anticipated them, and when in her distress, she could not find the words, he voiced them. Uncanny! His gentle fingers touched her face and smoothed her forehead, where he pressed his palm to pour his warmth into her veins.

There was no room for passion on this grieving night. There was a time—a brief ecstatic moment—when Esther's return had brought a stunning thrill of joy into their lives; that spark was now gone. Never once did Alexei betray his disappointment and long-suppressed frustration that again their marriage would have to be postponed.

"Alexei, will this war ever end? What more can happen now?" Nadya knew there was no ready answer, yet she had to hear his reassurance.

"Nadyenka, of course the war will end. It's almost over now. But we won't go back to Harbin. It's too close to Russia for comfort. Who knows what the Soviets will do after the Japanese are driven out of Manchuria? They've had their eye on it for a long time. No, I think we should consider going to America."

"America! Sergei talks about America. He said that they have penicillin. Do you suppose it would help cure his sprue?"

"I don't know, Nadyenka, but if the Americans have penicillin, they might also have other drugs that could help him."

Nadya rested her head against his shoulder. "Everyone dreams of America. I remember when we were in Petrograd, Esther was the first to mention going there long before we ever thought of leaving our homeland."

"Yes, darling, it's the land of promise. It is sad—isn't it?—that our people failed to achieve through a bloody revolution what was achieved by Americans a long time ago. We paid a high price for our dream of democracy."

Nadya raised her head and looked into Alexei's eyes. "Let's hope that country will accept us."

"I'm sure it will," he said. "We may have to wait a while for the immigration visas, but in the meantime, we shall be together. As soon as Sergei accepts Esther's death, Nadya, you must tell him that we intend to marry. Sooner or later you have to stop protecting him. Make him understand our love."

Nadya squirmed out of his arms. "I know, I know! But this is hardly the time to do it! We must still wait a little longer." She paced the floor in anguish. "Oh, Alexei, why is life so complicated?"

Alexei only spread his hands and shook his head. "I've never had anything but respect and admiration for your brother, Nadya. Why is he so unforgiving, so rigid and unbending?"

Her arms around him, Nadya thought: *What would you think, my dear, if I told you that Sergei is your first cousin?* But betraying her mother's secret was unthinkable. Aloud she said, "Let's not talk about it now. I promise to tell him soon."

"I'm a patient man, Nadyenka; but you and I deserve our happiness, and we can't wait forever." He smiled at her and pointed to the clock on the table. "The clock ticks off the hours, days, and months. How long yet must we wait?"

Nadya nodded. The situation was becoming intolerable, and she knew she must do something about it soon. Alexei was right. This time she must be firm. How much more of her life should she sacrifice for her brother?

There was a flower stand on the corner of Avenue Foch and Rue Cardinal Mercier, where Nadya bought a bouquet of pink carnations to take home. Marina had already gone to the hospital, and Sergei was sitting in the waiting room alcove. When he looked up, Nadya caught her breath, stopped in the middle of the hall, and dropped the flowers on a nearby chair. Her heart thrashed inside her chest.

"Where have you been all night?" he thundered. "Have you no thought of my grief to worry me like this?"

"I'm grieving, too! I went to see Alexei."

"That's disgraceful! You stay out all night when there is mourning in your house! You're no better than a trollop!"

Stung, Nadya cried, "How dare you speak to me like this? When Esther became so ill, I never thought of myself! It was all for you and Esther and Marinka . . . I'm only human, and—and—" Nadya groped for words, and then blurted, "I love him!"

God, what was happening to her? Sergei had become too demanding, too jealous, and it was all her own fault. She had spoiled him, protected him. No more!

Slowly Sergei rose from his chair and took a step toward her. His face turned red. "I still say it's disgraceful that you couldn't restrain yourself from going to that man so soon after my tragedy. Shame on you!"

"What makes you think it isn't my tragedy as well? Did it ever occur to you that I too need comforting? Tenderness?"

"Nonsense! I know what is deep inside your head. Now that you have him back, you can't wait to marry him!"

Sergei's voice rose, and he was screaming—actually screaming at her! "Admit it! All your life you wanted to be Countess Persiantseva!"

Sergei's words pounded against her ears, became a roar. What was he saying? It was too much. For all her years of love and sacrifice for him, now this! Impossible man! Tears stinging her eyes, she shook her fist at him. "And you—you're so sanctimonious! Who gave you the right to sit in judgment? For a bastard son of Count Persiantsev, you shouldn't behave so righteously!"

Who had screamed those words? Oh, God! Anna's secret! Too late she pressed both hands to her mouth. With a piteous cry she reached out to her brother. "Seryozha, Seryozha! What are we doing to each other?"

But Sergei backed away from her, shaking his head in mute denial, his eyes bulging, shocked. Suddenly he was upon her, shaking her shoulders.

"What did you say?" he shouted. "What did you say, I ask you, Nadezhda?"

It was impossible to lie, so she told him. When he sat down, stunned, she went to her bedroom, opened the camphor chest she kept near her bed, and brought out their mother's diary. He looked at it, hesitated, then waved it aside. "I can't! I won't read it. I believe you. It has to be true. To tell such a lie would be monstrous." He covered his face with his hands, then looked up. "So many things come together now, so much is clear . . . Count Yevgeni Persiantsev! That pompous rake was my father! . . . Our saintly mother, Anna, and Count Yevgeni!"

Suddenly Sergei threw his head back and began to laugh with dreadful, hiccuping sounds. Terrible were those sounds, torn from the guts of a broken man. Nadya went to him and put her arms around his shoulders. He slumped against her, gulped, and broke into racking sobs.

After a while Nadya sensed that he needed to be alone and turned to go into the kitchen. As she reached the door, the telephone rang shrilly. She picked up the receiver and clutched it compulsively when she heard the voice on the other end of the line. Rolf's self-assured baritone was asking for Sergei.

"He's not able to come to the phone right now, Rolf. May I give him a message?"

There was only a slight hesitation, and then Rolf said, "Yes. Please tell him that I'll be leaving soon for Argentina, and I need to settle some financial business with him immediately."

Slowly Nadya replaced the receiver. So that's where Sergei had got the money to pay C. Lee for his gambling loss! Now Rolf wanted the money back. Where did he think Sergei would get it?

Rolf was leaving for Argentina. Why Argentina? Even as she

asked herself the question, the answer came. The palms of her hands tickled with sudden moisture. Rolf was fleeing. With the Allies on Shanghai's doorstep, he must be afraid of exposure as an undercover agent. Is this why he chose not to return to a defeated Germany? She almost laughed with relief. If Marina were still married to Rolf, he would have taken her to that faraway country.

Marina was safe! The thought overwhelmed her with such happiness and relief that she almost forgot to give Sergei the message.

"Who was it?" Sergei asked.

She'd have given anything not to tell him, but she dared not. He simply nodded and slumped back into his chair. He waved her away.

"Leave me!" he said quietly, so quietly that Nadya backed away.

Without a word she picked up the scattered flowers and left the room.

Chapter Thirty-nine

The air stood still. The afternoon sun was obscured by heavy clouds, and an early twilight hung over Shanghai. A dry leaf struggled on the ground and suddenly rolled, picked up by the first gust of hot summer wind. In the next instant the silence was cut by the snap of a broken twig. Now the wind whistled through the branches of a tree, slamming shut a squeaky bamboo gate across Route Vallon. Huge drops of rain lazily hit the sidewalk, followed by a flash of lightning and thunder. The smell of wet dust filled the air.

Sergei reached the building before the downpour began and shuffled from the elevator toward the apartment. It had been too much of a day, and he felt old and tired. His energy was sapped, and this morning's scene with Nadya haunted him. The argument he could take, but the shock of the shattering discovery was a blow. What was there left?

He tried the door. It was locked. With a shaking hand he fumbled for the keys in his pocket and opened the door. The ball of his foot stung and burned. After lowering himself into a soft armchair in his bedroom, he took off his shoe and sock and examined the inflamed area. With the weight he had lost in recent months, his shoes were loose, and the ten blocks he walked today had aggravated the sore foot. He should have taken a pedicab or a tramcar, but he had been too weary to bargain with the coolie and too exhausted to struggle against the pushing crowd on the tramcar. A leisurely walk would help clear his mind, he had thought, but instead, it had tired him.

He opened the wardrobe, took out the washbasin, limped to the bathroom, grateful no one was home to see him. After filling the basin with cold water, he returned to the bedroom and immersed his foot. Leaning back in the chair, he shaded his eyes with the palm of his hand.

Chase away the shame. What a mess he had made of his life! The gambling! The addictive urge that plagued him—it *was* really an addiction. That's what they called it in psychology books, didn't they? Cold, impartial words. Those who wrote those books —did they know what torment went into that kind of weakness?

The humiliation, the degradation of the spirit—he had swallowed his pride and gone to Rolf, begging for a loan. True, Rolf, had behaved as a gentleman, even though he was no longer a member of their family, given him the money, and stopped him in mid-sentence from trying to justify his request.

"Pay me back when you can," he had said then, but who could have predicted the sudden turn of events, his decision to leave China?

To think that all had been in vain was almost too much to dwell on. *Esther, my Esther!* he thought. *I would have done anything —do you hear, my dear?—anything for you if you had only lived! Those few days of bliss that we had together before you went to the hospital—those days were not real . . . couldn't have been real!*

Everything in his life was too late now. His interest in research had burned itself out; his body, weakened by sprue, had plunged him into depression; and perhaps the worst thought of all was that he was still alive and had to live without hope. "Exist" was probably a better word.

The foot stopped throbbing. He dried it and let it rest on a stool. Today's trip to Rolf's office to plead for a postponement of his payment was a wasted effort, for he was told that Rolf would not be back until the following day. Why hadn't he telephoned first? He wasn't reasoning well these days. Everything seemed to come upon him all at once. What could he say to Nadya now? How could he look her in the face? There was nowhere to hide, nowhere to escape from this terrible, shocking revelation that he was Persiantsev's bastard son . . . The hated name was his by birthright!

Sergei cringed in his chair, suddenly remembering the day his father—he shouldn't call him his father anymore—had taken him to the Blue Palace for the first time. How old had he been then? Nine? Ten? He couldn't remember. But what he had never forgotten was his father's scolding him in front of Count Pyotr and that proud little aristocrat Alexei. Had Anton Stepanovich known that Sergei was not his son?

He put on his sock and shoe and stretched out on the bed, thinking. His lifelong hatred of aristocracy, his resentment against the Persiantsev family in particular, had been a sham, and the greatest, the most bitter irony of all was the realization that Count Alexei was his first cousin—his blood relative.

The thought of Alexei sent his pulse pounding painfully in his temples. Nadya was going to marry the man he had hated since he was nine years old. The thought was intolerable. The old hatred was still so strong that it choked him. That incident of a child's shame had grown, festered within him over the years, and he had centered it on the other child—on young Count Alexei—an innocent witness to his humiliation, whom he used as the focal point of his resentment against all aristocrats. He laughed out loud. What a farce! A lifetime of self-delusion that he hated all aristocrats, not the individual.

The hell we live through is here on earth, he thought wearily. Esther had endured it, but his was not yet over. Years of loneliness stretched ahead. He rose from the bed, started pacing the room. How was he going to overcome facing Alexei without resentment? He'd lived with the animosity for so long that it had grown with him, had become a part of him.

The front door opened and closed. He heard Nadya's footsteps outside his door. Had Alexei come here with her? How was he going to watch the two together, see his sister's love for Alexei, catch their loving glances? The throbbing in his temples intensified, deafened him, filled his ears with whispers, mocking laughter. His heart began to race faster and faster, then lost its rhythm. He grabbed the doorknob, pulled the door open, and saw his sister standing on the other side, her face frightened, swimming through a watery blur as a sudden convulsion seized him and spun him around. He slumped into Nadya's outstretched arms and tried to say something, but only a gurgling sound escaped, his tongue no longer obedient.

"Aaaaah!" came the sound from his throat. He struggled in a dimming light and, struggling, suddenly understood, and having understood, no longer fought the paralyzing force that overwhelmed him. With eyes wide open, he stared at Nadya, wanting to say something eternally memorable and realizing that he couldn't. So he closed his eyes and gave in for the last time, to the comfort of her love.

They sat around the dining table—Nadya, Marina, Alexei, not knowing what to say to one another. In the heavy silence their teaspoons made clinking sounds against their cups.

Marina's eyes were red from crying. "Mama, say something, for heaven's sake! You're so quiet. It's not good for you. Why don't you cry?"

Nadya, who was sitting with her eyes shaded by one hand, looked up. "I hurt too much. It's too deep for tears," she said in a flat voice, and then glanced across the table. Because she was used to seeing Sergei in that spot, it pained her to see Alexei instead. An uneasiness filled her stomach—a squeezing, dull ache. It was Sergei's chair. Alexei was sitting in Sergei's favorite chair! Dead twenty-four hours, and someone else was already occupying his place. It was indecent to have Alexei in the apartment so soon, disloyal to her brother's memory. She had to do something about it. Why was Alexei so insensitive not to have seen it himself? Shaking, she rose from the table.

"We all grieve in our own way. Mine is private. Alexei, I have to ask you to leave me alone for a while. Please!"

She tried not to see the hurt in his eyes when he came around the table, kissed her hand, and moved toward the door. There he paused.

"Don't shut me out, Nadya. Don't suppress your grief. Release it!"

Nadya's lips trembled. "Only for a while, Alexei. Only for a short while!"

Left alone, the two women stared at each other.

"Mama, how could you?" Marina said, her voice shaking. "How could you do this to him? Sometimes I wonder!"

"You're too young to understand. Someday you will. I need a little time, that's all. Why don't you go see Michael? You should have told him yesterday."

"I've already called twice and left messages. I don't understand why he's not here by now. I don't want to leave you alone."

"I'm capable of taking care of myself. You needn't stay with me."

"But I want to," Marina said stubbornly, and Nadya did not insist.

The funeral was the following day. The two women stood by the open grave site in Lukawei Cemetery, listening to the priest's prayers, watching him swing his censer over the lowered coffin. Soon, she knew, the priest would throw a clump of earth over the coffin and expect her and Marina to do the same. *I can't do it*, she thought. *I can't bear to hear the dull thud over the lid*. Panic threatened to overcome her, and she fought it, angry with herself. The sound—the dull sound—that was aeons ago in St. Petersburg over Mama's coffin and, later, Katya's. She mustn't let it bother her again now. She bent over, picked up a handful of the earth, shut her eyes, and threw it into the grave. The thud thundered in her ears—a loud, obscene sound. *Stay in your grave, Sergei*, it said. *There should be a lot of earth to separate the dead from the living!* A mist clouded her eyes, obscured the scene. She blinked quickly, fighting for control, then, straightening, looked up.

She was surrounded by Russian Orthodox crosses, black and gray and white marble tombstones with busts and graceful sculptures. An epitaph on a nearby grave caught her eye. It read: "I loved you. Love you now. Will love you eternally." She would have to order a tombstone for Sergei. What could she say on it? Words would not come. She was weary, and the afternoon sun beat down mercilessly through the humid air. Someone was walking up the sandy path. She squinted.

Slowly, leaning on his cane, Alexei was coming toward her. At a discreet distance he stopped and waited for the service to be over.

Nadya looked at him, unable to tear her gaze from his face. *Oh, God, Alexei,* her mind screamed, *I need you! We have come a long way, you and I!* Tears clouded her eyes as she kept looking at him. The dashing young officer she had fallen in love with was no longer there. Neither was the proud aristocrat. What she saw was a familiar and changed man who had loved her all his life and in the end had sacrificed much for her. She looked at him with a sudden flood of warmth, her heart quickening not with the youthful love of long ago but with the tempered love of maturity. He must have been terribly hurt when she had excluded him from her grief, had asked him to leave the apartment. Yet here he was, understanding, waiting for her to reach out to him once again. Yes, they both had grown through suffering, both had paid their debts to life, and now nothing seemed to stand in their way. Nadya wiped her tears.

The priest was intoning the service: "Eternal memory to your servant. . . ." She sighed deeply. *Rest in peace, Seryozha. No more suffering for you. We women must adapt ourselves to life's arrangements the best way we can. . . .* Those familiar words that flowed through her mind made her gasp, for they were her mother's deathbed words. It was not too late for her to adapt.

The ceremony was over. Nadya took Marina's arm and started toward Alexei.

Seeing her parents walk out of the cemetery arm in arm, Marina thought of Michael. Why hadn't he come to the funeral or responded to her messages? It was not like him. In spite of the heat of the August afternoon, Marina shook her shoulders to get rid of a sudden chill. It was so out of character for him not to have come immediately that something extraordinary must have happened. Why hadn't she thought of it before?

The walk back to the apartment seemed interminable, and after she had served tea to her parents, she ran out and hailed a rickshaw. As the coolie trotted along the familiar street, Marina's fear grew. What could possibly have happened to Michael? Though she thought of a dozen reasons, none seemed valid enough to have kept him away. At his boardinghouse she took two steps at a time to his second-floor room and knocked loudly at the door. There was no answer, and as she turned to leave, she spotted two pieces of paper stuck under the mat. Scrawled in an unfamiliar hand, they were her two telephone messages. Michael hadn't been home for two days. She ran downstairs and knocked at the landlady's door. When a gray-haired buxom woman opened the door, Marina held up the messages in her hand.

"I see Michael hasn't been home in two days. Do you know where he is?"

The landlady looked at the messages. "I wasn't the one who answered your calls, or I would have told you then what happened." The woman's eyes narrowed and seemed to size up Marina before going on.

"What happened?" Marina pressed. Her anxiety must have been apparent, for the landlady looked out into the corridor, then motioned Marina inside her room and closed the door behind her

"Is Michael a close friend of yours?" she asked, nervously twisting a strand of her hair.

Marina nodded. "He's a childhood friend. He—he's closer than a brother to me," she stammered.

"Well, I don't know what he had done—you would know more about it—but three days ago, late at night, two Japanese men from the gendarmerie came and took him away."

"My God! Why? Did Michael say anything before they took him away?"

The landlady pressed her lips together and avoided Marina's gaze. "I didn't hear anything. All I know is that they went to his room and were there only a few minutes before they came down again and took him away."

Marina could not remember later if she thanked the landlady for the information or even if she had said good-bye. Michael taken away by the Kempetai men! Easygoing, outspoken Michael must have committed some indiscretion, some small thing, enough to provoke the Japanese. That's all the gendarmerie needed to unleash its vengeance on yet another hapless victim. Where was he now? Where was he?

She ran out onto the street. Sitting immobile in a rickshaw was impossible. She had to move, to run to—to where?

At the corner of the Avenue Joffre she looked at her watch. It was four o'clock. Offices were still open everywhere. There was only one person to whom she could run for help, only one, and she knew, without hesitation, that there was no other way and that she would do it.

Rolf was the only person she knew who had connections with the Kempetai. It was a twist of irony perhaps, but his undercover work could be her only hope of rescuing Michael from the clutches of the Kempetai.

Chapter Forty

After she had been ushered into Rolf's office by a somber German secretary, Marina stood in the middle of the room, embarrassed and at a loss for words.

"Marina! What's wrong?" Rolf's voice, though controlled, was solicitous as he came toward her, maneuvering around cartons of files and boxes of office papers stacked on the floor.

"Everything is wrong!" she blurted out, and suddenly felt her knees begin to buckle.

Lowering herself into a leather armchair, she told him that Sergei had died and watched Rolf's lips press together into a thin line. "I am truly sorry to hear that," he said with an edge to his voice that didn't match his words.

Marina struggled to rein in her galloping thoughts: *He hasn't changed much . . . stiffer perhaps . . . circles under his eyes . . . his hands are shaking . . . this is the first time we've met since the divorce. . . .*

She told him about Michael, and he listened politely, asked brief, pointed questions, and then lapsed into silence. After what seemed like an endless time, he cleared his throat and looked at her. He blinked, and his face suddenly softened.

"There's one possibility. I don't know if you remember Captain

Yamada, who helped us leave Harbin. He was recently transferred to Shanghai. Let me call him and see what I can do." He smiled ruefully. "Since Germany is no longer at war, my influence with the Kempetai has diminished considerably."

"Please, Rolf! You have no idea how concerned I am for Michael's safety. I can't imagine why he was arrested. He has never been involved in any political activity."

Her voice broke, and Rolf looked at her sharply. "Why, you're in love with him!"

"I've known him since I was eleven years old," Marina struggled to explain. "We grew up together! I don't want anything to happen to him, Rolf. Can you understand that?"

He shrugged. "I'm leaving for Argentina in a few days, but I'll do what I can. I suggest you stay by the telephone for the next few hours. May I call a pedicab for you?"

Marina thanked him and let him escort her outside. Sitting in the pedicab on the way home, she had time to think. Rolf was leaving for Argentina, and she hadn't even wished him well. Her anxiety for Michael had blocked out all other thoughts. Rolf had assumed she was in love with Michael, and she realized that she had neither confirmed nor denied his observation. Why hadn't she? Michael had been part of her life so long that she couldn't sort out her feelings. The memory of that night in his apartment flashed before her mind's eye. Then she agonized. What were the Kempetai men doing to him at that very moment while she was remembering the hours of love?

It was dusk when she got home. Alexei and Nadya listened to what had happened, and then the three of them sat, waiting. Marina was grateful that her parents were not trying to divert her from the overwhelming anxiety. It would have been intolerable to channel her mind elsewhere. Consumed by worry, she watched the clock on the wall, its pendulum swinging back and forth . . . back and forth. So slow . . . maddeningly slow! Its gentle ticking grew to a clapping sound in the room, its quarter-hour chimes like hammers in her ears.

Three days in the hands of the Kempetai. He must be in the Bridge House. Terrible things went on inside that building. No one had ever come out of there unscathed. Where were the Americans, how far away? She wrung her hands and started to pace the floor. Three days of twenty-four hours each. An eternity!

She pleaded with God: *Please, please, don't let anything happen to Michael! Don't let this be too late!*

Nadya went to the kitchen and busied herself with the dishes. Alexei tried to read the paper. The clock ticked on. Seven o'clock. Eight. Then nine.

The telephone rang at a quarter to ten, and Marina rushed at it so fast she dropped the receiver. She picked it up and with a shaking hand pressed it against her ear.

"Hello, hello?"

Rolf's voice sounded muffled and faraway, as if he were holding his hand over the mouthpiece. "I'm bringing the package over to your apartment now," he said.

"The package! The package?" Marina repeated, not comprehending.

"Yes, the package." Rolf enunciated carefully the three words. "I'm in a hurry and won't be able to come in. Please wait for me downstairs. I should be there in about twenty minutes."

"Michael? What about Michael?" Marina screamed into the phone, but Rolf had already hung up. When she repeated the conversation to Alexei, he put his arm around her trembling shoulders.

"I'm glad he hung up before you asked. Don't you understand? He was giving you a coded message. Obviously someone was listening, or else he was afraid that the phone was tapped. Michael must be the package he was talking about. Let's go downstairs and wait."

They stood in the dark, father and daughter, lurking at the hallway door, sensing that they should not be seen by patrolling sentries watching for careless slivers of light in the blackouts and suspicious of anything unusual. Noises reached them from the street. A slow thudding sound of patrolman's boots; hurried clicking of someone's high-heeled shoes; the deafening roar of a passing truck.

A small dog barked frantically somewhere in the distance and then all was quiet.

Then she heard tires rolling slowly over the asphalt. So slight was the sound she thought her imagination was playing tricks with her hearing. But it grew louder and closer, and then a vehicle rolled to a stop just short of the entrance where she stood. A car door was opened and shut quietly. A few whispers, and then she heard the slow, shuffling gait of someone approaching the door. She moved to meet those sounds, but Alexei grabbed her arm so tightly it hurt. She froze not so much because he held her but because she did not recognize the gait. Someone was dragging one foot in a slow, limping step, and Michael's walk had a spring to it. No, it wasn't Michael; it must be someone else. She held her breath.

He appeared at the entrance and stood holding on to the molding. At first she did not recognize him. Then it was Michael's familiar brown and beige shirt that made her gasp and rush toward him. In the dim light she could not see his face; but his body was stooped, and he clutched his side.

Outside, gears shifted, and the car drove rapidly away. Alexei and Marina supported Michael up the stairs, and it wasn't until they were inside their well-lit apartment that she really looked at his face. With a gasp she cried out his name over and over and then, kneeling in front of him, wrapped her arms around his knees and leaned her cheek against his thigh.

Nadya and Alexei helped him into a chair. His eyes, black and blue, were almost swollen shut, and his lips were cracked and puffed. When Marina tried to put her arms around him, he grimaced and a fresh drop of blood formed on the lower lip.

"Better not touch me, Princess. I think I have a couple of broken ribs on the left side. Hurts to breathe."

Marina clasped her hands, then spread them to reach his face but dared not touch him; pulling back, she looked at him and could not tear her eyes away. Slowly she lowered her head, picked up his hand, and kissed it reverently once, twice, three times, then pressed it to her tear-dampened cheek.

Anger welled inside her, and she turned upon herself. A blind, stubborn fool! *It took a near tragedy, a beating to make you see, to admit you love him, and have loved him these many years!* The words pounded in her head, made her giddy with happiness. *I love him, I have always loved him! That lovely, beautiful night in his room . . . how could I not have realized it then? Oh, Michael, Michael, I love you, I love you!*

Shy laughter made a small, timid sound, spilled out, and Michael looked down at her in surprise. "Do I look so funny to you, Princess?"

She gulped, swallowed her tears, and shook her head. Suddenly embarrassed, she saw that both Alexei and Nadya had left the room.

"I love you, Michael. *My* Michael, I love you! Do you hear me? *I love you!* How have you put up with me all these years? I'm so stupid, so blind. I love you, I adore you, I want to scream it from all the rooftops in Shanghai."

Nadya rushed in. "Have you lost your mind, Marinka? The windows are open. It's summer, remember? Someone may hear you outside."

"Oh, Mama, I love him, I love him!"

"It's a fine time to discover that! Michael is hurt, he needs care, and you're cavorting like a two-year-old. Come to your senses. Let's get him to bed."

Michael stretched his mouth sideways in a crooked smile. "That's good medicine for me, Nadezhda Antonovna. My princess has finally wised up!"

As quickly as the happiness had overwhelmed her, now Marina burst into tears. "Oh, Michael, forgive me! What have they done to you? Where does it hurt the most?"

"Don't worry. I look worse than I feel. One or two cracked ribs and a couple of black eyes. Nothing that time won't heal." Then he grew serious. "Rolf told me that Captain Yamada had no authority to release me but did it anyway on the condition that I stay hidden and not leave your apartment for a while."

It was the first time Michael had referred to Rolf by name, and the thought registered in Marina's mind without pleasure.

As Nadya placed a cold washcloth over his eyes, she asked, "What happened, Michael? Why did they arrest you?"

"Wayne Morrison tried to escape from camp, but they caught him. He wouldn't tell them his accomplice's name, and since I was the only one who visited him, they assumed it was I. A case of mistaken identity, but once they had me, right or wrong, they worked me over. I'm sure they took it out on me because they were mad at their mistake. They're frantic out there at the Bridge House, burning papers, covering up everything that they don't want the Allies to see. I saw cartons of stuff packed in a hall; they're obviously in a great hurry to clear out. The city should be free of them in a matter of days."

Marina rose, but Michael held her hand. "Hey, where do you think you're going, Princess?" When she told him that she wanted to fetch some bandages to immobilize his chest, he shook his head.

"I'm afraid to let you out of my sight. Maybe I only dreamed I heard you say those lovely three words. Do you think, Your Highness, you could condescend to repeat them again just one more time for good measure?"

Marina knelt by his side. "I love you, Michael. I'm only sorry —so terribly sorry—that you had to be hurt so viciously before I woke up. I love you, *love you!*"

"All right, Michael." Nadya laughed. "I'm your witness, and now let her go get the bandages, so we can start making you comfortable."

For the next three days Michael stayed in their apartment, gathering strength and never once complaining about his ordeal. He was making a remarkable recovery. The strapped chest helped relieve his pain, and only a slight discoloration remained around his eyes. With the help of ice, the swollen muscle in his thigh subsided, and he was eager for the news.

On August 15, 1945, Emperor Hirohito made a formal radio broadcast announcing the end of the war. There was jubilation everywhere. Hundreds of thousands of people roamed the streets, shouting, waving Allied flags, carrying long hidden posters of Chiang Kai-shek, Franklin Roosevelt and Winston Churchill.

"But President Roosevelt died in April," Nadya mused the next day when Alexei came home from work.

"I guess people still associate the victory with him rather than with his successor," he said. "Anyway, the mobs are going wild. Steamers on the Whangpoo are blowing their whistles; temple gongs and church bells are ringing throughout the city. Stores are closed, and the vendors are dancing in circles with passersby. Chiang Kai-shek's Nationalist forces are due to take over the city, and the Allies are reportedly close by. The American marines are expected to be entering Shanghai soon."

"Did you get caught up in the spirit of rejoicing?" Nadya asked.

Alexei shook his head. "Not yet, Nadya, not yet. The Japanese sentries are still guarding the key posts, and there are rumors of mobs on the rampage, looting shops on Nanking Road. As long as the occupation forces are not yet in Shanghai, it is better for us to stay off the streets."

So they did. United at last, happy and full of anticipation of the promising days ahead, they stayed home and made plans. Then, on August 23, a friend telephoned excitedly to tell them that the American marines had entered the city and were marching up from Nantao along the Avenue Joffre. Alexei was at work, but Nadya, Marina, and Michael rushed out into the street.

What a sight greeted them! The sidewalks were mobbed with happy, laughing people, young girls held bouquets of flowers, and as the first ranks of marines approached them, the street became carpeted with blossoms.

Nadya's eyes blurred with tears while she watched the pandemonium around her. Most of all, she was happy to see Marina and

Michael standing there with arms around each other. Now, at last, her wish had come true. As she stood watching the young couple, she heard her name called. She looked around.

Hurrying toward her was Alexei. *Oh, my dearest!* she thought, reaching out to him with a smile. *At long last we are together! Through tears and laughter, tragedy and happiness, our love has endured.*

As he moved to stand beside her and their daughter, Nadya watched the smiling American marines march by. Suddenly she was determined to realize Sergei and Esther's cherished dream of going to America.